She's seen her share of devils in this Angel town

'Lullaby', Shawn Mullins (US folk-rock singer)

Several years ago, I read a comment in a magazine article which said that glamour has the power to re-arrange people's emotions. That comment stayed with me as I began this book.

More recently, I read another apposite saying (though, again, I cannot recollect where/who), essentially stating that in today's world, we live in a youth-obsessed, beauty-obsessed culture which is no more evident than in the film industry.

Both sayings are equally compelling and no-where more true than in southern California.

◆

Phoebe Hamilton has worked in advertising, publishing, public relations and marketing communications for some 25 years – primarily within the international luxury hotels and travel/tourism arenas in both England and America – before turning her hand to fiction.

Her hotel marcomms roles have afforded her the chance to meet, and work with, many high profile people and celebrities in the UK and USA.

Phoebe was born in Kenya, East Africa, and grew up on the south coast of England. Having spent her professional life in London, she now lives in West Sussex.

www.phoebehamilton.co.uk

Acknowledgements

While many people have helped me on the 'journey' of writing this book, there are a few specific people I should like to thank, for without them I would neither have started, nor finished, this journey:

Special thanks go to my dearest friends Bob and Julie Gilbert for their unfailing encouragement and continued suppport; also to screenwriter David Rothmiller and filmmaker LD Thompson for their unwavering belief that I could, and should, write this story, and for their ongoing motivation.

I'd also like to thank Producer Joel Douglas and über-publicist Catherine Olim of PMK for their kindness and generosity of spirit both during, and after, the tumultuous rollercoaster that was the film festival. I would also like to express my eternal thanks to Darryl Macdonald for his amazing leap of faith in believing I'd be able to ride the 'tsunami'.

I am very grateful to American folk-rock singer-songwriter Shawn Mullins for his kind permission to quote lyrics from his wonderful hit song 'Lullaby', and to his manager Russell Carter for facilitating this request.

And finally – but most importantly – I owe an enormous debt of gratitude to Deborah Hardy-Godley for her "crazy idea" which enabled me to have the experience of a lifetime and meet some truly amazing people.

The Blood Carpet

ISBN-13: 978-1981708024

This is a work of fiction. Names, characters, businesses, events and incidents are either the products of the author's imagination or used in a fictitious manner. Any resemblance to actual persons, living or dead, or actual events is purely coincidental.

Book design by The Art of Communication www.book-design.co.uk
First printed in 2018

The BLOOD Carpet

Phoebe Hamilton

CHAPTER ONE

'No more celebrity wallpaper. Vanessa is on overload. We are maxed out of rooms and going over budget,' Duncan Northcote, the film festival's Executive Director, wrote in a furious response to Chairman Ed Harrison's email which had come in to the two of us just minutes earlier advising that he had added Lana Lazmann to the 'wallpaper' roster. Ed, used to Duncan's outbursts, was sanguine and his response circumspect.

'As of this moment, we are booking no more celebrities. However, if Robert Redford or his friends from Sundance call, we shall accommodate them.'

I smiled as I read his email, for I knew that Robert Redford was not due to attend, though the Hollywood A-List stars coming in for the festival's Awards Gala were of equal stellar status. But I also knew that if Mr. Redford did decide to check out the competition, Ed would expect multiple rabbits to be pulled immediately out of the hat.

It was the week of opening. The festival would start in three days and we were not ready. We were all, by now, existing solely on Danish pastries, cookies and coffee purely to keep the adrenaline going, and not one of us had been getting out of the office until midnight or one a.m. each night for the past week – the fifteen-hour days that Duncan alluded to during his interview with the local newspaper reporter yesterday. Little did I know that, from now on, it would be twenty-hour days.

'La La Land' had awoken from its festive slumber; everyone in the entertainment industry was now back at work after the Christmas and New Year holiday, and the tsunami I feared I would encounter was already making its way towards us. From seven-thirty that morning, my on-screen e-message alert constantly flashed to denote another missive: the Hollywood studios and LA publicists were revving from nought – sixty m.p.h in a nano-second.

One of my gazillion emails stopped me in my tracks. It was a response from a studio stating that one of the stars being honoured at the Awards Gala, one of Hollywood's most revered actors and directors, would do neither the red carpet, the reception nor the Green Room. He would arrive at the rear of the venue – we had to agree the rather unglamorous loading dock as the rendezvous point – and simply be escorted to the area backstage to await his call on stage. He would receive his award, make his speech and then leave the proceedings via the loading dock. He would do neither media interviews, nor photographs and this was all non-negotiable. The email asked for extra security on the night, suggesting that we engage the services of the Los Angeles Police Department and, possibly, the FBI.

I read, re-read and then again re-read the email in utter astonishment before taking it to Duncan, who erupted in mocking laughter as he read it.

'Oh dear God, the crap we have to put up with. Well, darlin', I suggest you get onto the FBI.'

Assuming he was joking, I returned to my desk and continued scanning the subject headlines of the tidal wave of emails, secretly wishing I could just highlight the lot and hit delete. But I could not blame the senders; the Awards Gala was considered a barometer of Oscar success and was way too big a deal to get it wrong.

I had entered a world where reality and fantasy were already colliding in titanic proportions.

It had all seemed such a good idea when Diana Harmsworth called out of the blue one evening in early November. Diana had been my client when I was handling the European PR division of the 'I Love New York' public relations campaign; we had worked closely together, remaining good friends to this day.

'Hey Vanessa, it's been a while since we spoke and I have no idea what you're up to, but I've got a crazy idea for you.' (This, at least, turned out to be true!) 'I'm working at the film festival here as Head of Marketing and they need someone to look after all the celebrities attending the festival, set up and run the hospitality suite, organise all the goody bags, liaise with their PR agency in LA and generally look after all the filmmakers. I've told the Executive Director about you and he's interested in talking to you. What are you doing now work-wise? Could you come out to California? You'd need to be out here for a couple of months, and then you could stay on with me for some vacation. We could hang out at Newport Beach and sail over to Catalina Island.'

Was I hearing this right? It sounded too good to be true. *Of course* I could just drop everything and go to California for the winter, run a festival hospitality suite, mingle with some A-List stars. Who would give up an opportunity like that? Emailing my résume to Diana that evening, I stated I would love to give it a shot if Duncan felt my background was relevant and useful. The next evening Duncan rang from LA – where he was in a meeting with two studio executives, trying to pin down a star's appearance at the opening of the festival – and, after a succinct conversation, casually said, 'When can you get out here and start?'

Taken aback that it appeared as simple as that, I asked him if he wanted me to fly out for an interview, or even to just think about it for twenty-four hours and, if he still felt I would be suitable for the role, to call me the next evening.

Going to work the next day, I prayed that he would call that evening and again offer me the position. That evening, as I nervously paced the sitting room of my cottage, the phone rang at about ten o'clock. This time Duncan was not alone.

'So, Vanessa, I have with me our Financial Director Romy and Christian, who is Head of Programming. They've both read your impressive résumé and we all agree you have the background experience to be able to do this job, even though you've never worked at a film festival before. We'd like you on board. Are you still interested?'

Before I could answer, Christian came on the speakerphone.

'Hi Vanessa, I'm Christian. We like the fact that you have some showbiz experience in your marcomms career and that you've handled celebs in London and worked with the paparazzi there, so I think you'll be perfect. I only have one question though and that is, what do you look like?'

This is where it all falls down, I thought, for I am not the stereotypical, blonde, blue-eyed, chest-sculpted California beach babe that they were probably hoping for.

Taking a deep breath, I ventured, 'Well, I guess I am somewhere between Angelica Huston and Cher.'

There was a pause. Damn, I thought, I've fallen at the

first hurdle.

'Oh, you are perfect!' trilled Christian. 'All our film-maker guests will love you!'

Duncan came back on. 'OK, Vanessa, are you on board? And if so, when can you get out here?'

Without having time to think about what was happening, I quickly shot back my answer. 'Yes, I'd love the opportunity and I'll fly out on 30th November to start on 1st December, if that suits you.'

'We'd ideally like you out a bit earlier, but I appreciate the 30th is only three weeks away, so we can live with December 1 as the start date. We're looking forward to having you out here.'

It was as simple as that. I was off to California.

The lights of the rush-hour traffic snaked along Santa Monica Boulevard as I made my way up to Route 405 and then onto the Ventura Freeway. The early evening air, still warm at six o'clock, enveloped me in its wonderfully soporific aroma – a heady mix of Eucalyptus, Jasmine and Bougainvillea – and it felt good to have a warm breeze blowing through my hair.

Picking up the rental car at Los Angeles Airport, I had instantly felt at home, even though it had been twelve years since I had last been in LA, and it seemed perfectly natural to hop into the 'wrong' front seat and glide her out onto the 'wrong side' of the road.

The guy at the rental office was so amazed that an English girl, having just had an eleven-plus-hour flight from London, was now calmly going to negotiate the LA Freeway traffic that he up-graded my compact car to a convertible. I selected a red Mustang and christened her Sally.

Mustang Sally and I joined the gridlock that is normal LA traffic; my eyes started to feel heavy, though this was no time to fall asleep as I had a good three-hour drive ahead of me. Moving over onto the 405, the gridlocked five lanes continued for some fifteen miles until the commuters started turning off towards their homes and the congestion eased. I pressed on ahead, slapping my face every few minutes to keep awake while I tried to keep pace with the urban warriors speeding homewards, now roaring merrily along at seventy miles per hour and switching lanes every two seconds to get that inch further forward.

After what seemed an eternity, I pulled off the highway and gulped the fresh mountain air. It was five-thirty a.m. in the morning UK time, though only nine-thirty p.m. Pacific Standard time, but it felt so good breathing the crisp late evening air that I forgot my exhaustion. Finding a motel, I called Diana to let her know I was on the outskirts of the city.

'Hey Vanessa,' she screamed exuberantly down the phone. 'You are almost here! Just carry on down the highway, exit at Washington Street and I'll meet you at the junction of Washington and Main. Can't wait to see you.'

'Yes, likewise,' I yelled back, to the consternation of the receptionist who was more than happy to give me the directions in order to get me out of the lobby.

Thirty minutes later, Diana and I were hugging each other at the appointed rendezvous.

'Oh my God, you are so thin,' she screamed, hugging me again. 'My anorexic friend from England!'

This was hardly true, for while slim I was not a Size Zero - the only size that matters in LA.

Diana looked different from when I had last seen her in the mid-nineties; she now sported a mass of long blonde curly hair, a fuller face and a more athletic build.

'Diana, you look fantastic, look how long your hair is now. I hardly recognized you.'

I followed her back to her house at the foot of the mountains and set within an enclave of similar houses, replete with standard California swimming pool and surrounded by golf courses. We talked non-stop over supper, consisting mostly of margaritas augmented by a little pasta, and I fell into bed, utterly exhausted but feeling very upbeat.

An exciting new adventure was about to begin, but I had absolutely no idea just what was lying in store for me.

The next morning Diana rang Duncan Northcote to say that I was too jet-lagged to start work today (strictly not true) and instead spent most of the day driving me around the city so that I could get my bearings. These translated into the best restaurants, bars and nail spa, though I was soon to discover that I would not be visiting any of these 'bearings' until the film festival was over, as it would consume my life for the next seven weeks. Diana decreed that today was the day we would have off and, as it turned out, it was about the *only* day off – apart from forty-eight hours at Christmas – that I would have for the next seven weeks.

Our first port of call was Happiness Nails, an oasis of tranquility run by a lovely Vietnamese lady called Lin. Introducing me to Lin as her 'anorexic friend from England,' Diana said nonchalantly, 'can you do her nails and her feet. Oh, and can you look at her teeth?'

Lin looked bemused; I did not. 'Diana, I am not a horse.'

'Oh, for heaven's sake, you English all think it is alright to walk around with ivory-yellow teeth. You're in

California now and teeth here are white!'

I had forgotten that Californian women were groomed to within an inch of their life and with that admonishment, promptly found myself lying on a vibrating chair-bed, attended upon by two of Lin's girls, one massaging my feet and giving me a pedicure, the other massaging my neck, arms and hands and giving me a long overdue manicure. As for the teeth, Lin agreed with me that my teeth were OK, *even* by Californian standards.

After lunch at The Yard House, a sublimely smart-casual restaurant known for its classic rock music and the world's largest selection of draught beers, we went to the film festival's offices so I could meet Duncan Northcote and his small coterie of eclectic staff. I was the first of the core staff volunteers to arrive – all film festivals rely on the largess of volunteers who work their butts off for what amounted to pocket money but get the opportunity to see the stars at close hand and enjoy the movies for free. I was to be in charge of all the A-List celebrities attending the festival, as well as some two-hundred film-makers from all over the world. No small task, as it turned out.

We found Duncan outside at the rear entrance to the offices puffing heavily on a cigarette while deep in conversation with Christian and Ingrid, the Head of Special Events. Duncan was good-looking, about five feet ten inches tall, with a honed physique found on most fifty-ish Californian men. His dark hair greyed distinctively at the temples and on his neat, trimmed beard, and his piercing blue eyes bore straight through everyone. In short, he had the classic film star look; the downside, as I soon discovered, was his mercurial personality and volcanic temper.

We chatted briefly, for I could sense that Duncan was somewhat distracted, even though we were five weeks out from the festival starting, and I assured him that I would be there early the next morning to start work. Saying he was delighted I had agreed to come over and do the job, he kissed me goodbye, apologized for being "somewhere else"and said he would be less hassled in the morning when he had sorted out a niggling problem with one of the major studios.

'Is he gay?' I asked Diana.

'Of course. Most of the entertainment industry is gay,' she replied airily. 'Most of the guys in LA are gay and practically all of them here are gay, as you will soon find out.'

'Oh God, how am I going to meet anyone?'

Diana laughed. 'You think you are going to have time to meet anyone? You have no idea what you are heading into with this festival, do you?'

CHAPTER TWO

Turning onto the mountain-lined Freeway, I tried to work out whether I was excited or just bloody scared. It was all so surreal; three weeks ago I was Head of Marketing for some land agents in England. Now I was in California, in brilliant sunshine in December, with a glamorous, but daunting, new role. Diana had a breakfast meeting with the printers to discuss the Awards Gala programme, so I decided to find my own way in; remembering her instructions, I took the Buena Drive North exit, made a right onto Chino Canyon, right again onto Main Street and eventually found myself at the film festival's offices.

Walking into the offices, I sought out Duncan's formidable assistant Anna. We had spoken on the phone a couple of times when Duncan and I were discussing the position and I knew I would like her; she was the glue keeping the seismic cracks together. Anna greeted me in typical American fashion – with a huge hug.

'Welcome Vanessa. We are so glad you are here. Please let me know if there is anything at all I can do to help you. I'll just let Duncan know you're here.'

Waiting in Reception, I looked at the different logos and myriad promotional items that the office produced every year to highlight the festivals. This year's logo, in its vivid primary colours, was a Size Zero starlet walking the red carpet from her stretch limo, surrounded by palm trees and mountains under a starry night, replete with large monolith in the background billing the film festival and its date. It would soon adorn the posters, banners – which would later be tethered on the palm trees at the airport, along the boulevards and around the main tourist attractions – and programme guide covers, not to mention on the ubiquitous mugs and T-shirts. As we later came to see the logo *everywhere* in the town, it became as intrinsic to the festival as the movies and the stars.

Duncan appeared a few minutes later. 'Do you like the logo?' he asked. 'I'm asking you from a marketing perspective, even though that's your friend Diana's job.'

'I do. I think it encapsulates perfectly the emotion and drive of the festival.'

Pleased that I had affirmed his recommendation to the Board to run with it, he led me through the key-coded door into the main bank of offices and suites. My desk, and those of my four staff, were located on the right-hand side of the offices, away from the constant deliveries of film cans, the other departments – Business Development, Hotel Partnerships, Marketing and Accounts – and the main traffic of visitors who would come in to purchase movie tickets once they went on sale.

I was flanked by Duncan's and Anna's office suite and Special Events; to the side was the Programming Department, the core of which comprised Head of Programming Christian Thomas, whom I had 'met' over the phone in England, Hannah Upton, his Programme Manager, Alexis Davidson, Print Traffic Manager, Alan Tighe, Film Administrator, Curtis Bryant, Programming Assistant and Bud, who as Transporter, kept the whole logistical show moving.

The bank of desks that would be home to Guest Services, the blanket name for my department, were neatly arranged in lines; I selected the desk at the end, next to Special Events so that I would be in the loop as to what receptions and venues were being arranged for the movie after-show parties. The desks, all on a raised level, were euphemistically known as the 'Hollywood Hills' (the Programmers would trill 'Hello Hollywood Hills' every time they walked past us), while the Programming Department, set on a slightly lower level, was sometimes disparagingly called 'the Valley' – after the San Fernando Valley in LA and on what is often referred to as the 'wrong' side of Mulholland Drive.

Duncan, Anna, Christian, Hannah and I sat down in the boardroom for a quick briefing to identify my main priorities – I soon learned that everything, but *everything*, was a priority – and how I wanted to apportion my staff to the various roles within the Guest Services Department: flights, hotels, limos, cars, airport transfers, the hospitality suite, food and beverage sponsorship and presents for the goody bags. As only one other member of my team, who would be doing flights, was here, I saw that everything was going to fall directly into my lap.

I decided hotels were to be the first priority; we would be using some twenty-two hotels throughout the city to accommodate all the filmmakers, studio executives, publicists, celebrity wallpaper (more of which later) and other assorted guests. The A-List celebrities – the majority of whom were being honoured at a glitzy Black Tie Awards Gala dinner on the first weekend of the festival – were all to stay in individual villas at the deluxe Four Seasons hotel. The roll-call of celebs attending the festival was indeed impressive: Olivia Lautner, Liam Taylor, Lawrence

Eppstein, Barbro Innes, Cody Quinn, Tommy Kane, Kevin Upstone, Taylor Quentin, Ed Tyler and Daniel Eversleigh, among others. I could see this was not going to be a picnic in the park.

I suggested that I should first go and see all the hotels and meet the General Manager of the host hotel to go over our requirements for the hospitality suite. Duncan and Christian agreed; later in the day, I would start on the equally unenviable task of phoning around the upmarket grocery stores and restaurants to enlist their support of the festival through the donation of food and beverage for the hospitality suite. No walk in the park either, given that I needed to feed two-hundred invited industry guests for ten days, with breakfast, beverages throughout the day, appetizers and drinks during the cocktail period, plus a buffet supper before they went off to their various receptions and parties.

I set off on my hotel tour. After what seemed the thousandth handshake, I ended up at the host hotel, The Wyndham, for a meeting with the General Manager. He seemed rather bemused that I, as the festival's Guest Services Director, would want (indeed *need*) to inspect the room designated for the hospitality suite and to have the names of staff members who would have responsibility for various elements of the suite, such as telephones, audio-visual, Banqueting and Housekeeping.

At The Four Seasons earlier, I had had a superb meeting with the General Manager, a delightful guy called Charles Rutherford who deployed a wicked sense of fun. After the walk-through of all the main hotel bedrooms, suites and fabulous private villas – set at the far end of the grounds with their own butlers, and which would be home to the A-List stars – he sat me down in the main bar and insisted

I tried the signature cocktail they were planning to serve the stars when they checked-in. As this was research, I told myself, I could hardly refuse, thus Charles and I bonded over a wonderfully lethal cocktail (if one drank two or more) and I had a new best friend. A lunch meeting was hastily arranged for early the following week to officially run through which villas and rooms the stars would be allocated; in reality, it was just to have some fun and, at this point, I had no idea how much I would need.

The first of my four assistants was at the office when I returned. He was a funny little chap and looked more like a goblin than a business executive. He had travelled down from Oregon and had worked at the Seattle film festival several times. His name was Mike and he was designated to handle all the flights, both domestic and international. With some two-hundred guests flying in from around the world, and flight requests constantly changing, he would have his work cut out for him, as he soon found out.

I did not particularly take to him and had an uneasy feeling, but he had been hired, he was here, and we needed to hit the deck. Flights were obviously central to the whole function of Guest Services. I called him Mike 1 (though he would soon be known as The Goblin), as there was another staffer on my roster also called Mike and their last names both began with the same letter.

I sat down with Mike 1 and briefed him, suggesting he might like to go and see the hotels the next day to get a feel for them; I said that as we would no doubt be juggling like crazy once we got nearer to the festival, he needed to know what the hotels were like so that he could – with or without me – allocate a guest an appropriate level of hotel.

He, on the other hand, did not think this was necessary for him to do. I begged to differ and after a few long minutes, sullenly deferred to my authority, saying he would do so the next day. Afterwards, I took my instinct straight to Duncan.

'Just a heads up, but I'm not at all sure about this one. Might become trouble.' (We were later to learn just how true this would be).

'Yeah, got the same gut feeling when he arrived,' Duncan said, in a somewhat measured tone. 'You're all outside my office, so I'll probably hear what's going on, but keep me in the loop anyway.' Diana, having been at the printers all day, had now arrived with the programme guide's editor, layout and design manager, and the sponsoring newspaper's creative director. There had been several glitches to sort out: missing logos from sponsoring organisations, endless debate over pagination, the usual squabble over the running order of the stars being honoured at the Awards Gala dinner and the sponsors' credits, as well as the eternal battle of editorial and print deadlines. She looked exhausted; marching straight into Duncan's office to brief him on the day's events, she breezily pre-empted it, 'So, how's my friend been on her first day?'

'Oh, she's already making her mark,' chuckled Duncan. 'I don't think she'll take any sh** from anyone!'

Butting in, Anna raised a crucial point. 'Ah, but she hasn't yet met, or been briefed about Kane. That will be the litmus test if there ever was one.'

'Who's Kane?' I asked, nonchalantly.

'Ah, Kane,' said Anna, Duncan and Christian in unison, as if on cue. 'This briefing needs to be done over a bucket of margaritas!

'Oh thank God,' added Diana. 'I am dying for a drink. Medicinal of course.'

We repaired to Midnight Rescue for me to be tutored

about my nemesis. Over the course of several bowls – glasses the size of small fishbowls – of margaritas, I learnt all about Kane. He was a scion of a Hollywood legend who had long been considered Hollywood 'royalty' and, therefore, he and his siblings were fêted as such. While tragedy had struck the family with the loss of one child, and success had taken another brother to international stardom, Kane was, nonetheless, a successful producer in his own right – the family name naturally opened many doors – but he shunned the spotlight of Tinseltown, preferring a more private life in the city where his parents, and many of their contemporaries, had had weekend retreats during their Hollywood heydays. He was, allegedly, rude to absolutely *everybody*, believing that people would shrink in awe just at the mention of his name. He never asked for things to be done, merely demanded that they be, and variously shouted at people or just ignored them in contempt. Terrific, I thought, this will be fun.

'Hey, you've forgotten I am English and we don't fawn over people in the way you guys do over here,' I said, wondering if I should have retracted this sentence as I uttered it. 'I don't think I'll have a problem with Kane. After all, for the purposes of the festival, he probably needs us more than we need him. I shall just be professional, do what is needed for his father's visit and that will be that. But I am not taking any crap from him.'

There was a stunned silence.

'Umm, Oh-k-a-y,' ventured Duncan, again in a measured tone. 'But you have to remember that his father is our top honouree this year and Kane is his wing-man for the visit, so there can't be any, how shall I say it politely, cluster-f***'s, if you know what I mean.'

We continued on to Flemings for a quick supper,

spotting Darryl Cainer, a hot actor who had had massive success in the Eighties in a major hit TV series about the LA legal profession (no doubt the idea for the later, and equally successful, Ally McBeal series), eating a burger at the bar. Shortly after, several other well-known faces dropped in: a powerful Hollywood TV producer, a senior talent agent from CAA (Creative Artists Agency), a film director who had won a Golden Globe a year earlier, and a senior Vice President of another top talent agent, United Talent Agency. This was obviously the place to be for spotting people and picking up industry gossip and innuendo.

Following Diana back along the Freeway to her house, I reflected on the day; it had not been as bad as I thought it might be.

But I still had no idea of the tsunami that was to come.

CHAPTER THREE

How civilized to start a December morning this way I mused, as Diana and I breakfasted by the pool on coffee, scrambled eggs and toasted Rye. Our intake of Vitamins E and D completed, I drove to the office, stopping en route at the printers to pick up the first proof covers of the programme guide for Duncan, as Diana would not be in the office until the late afternoon.

Arriving at the office, Anna arm-locked me and quickly steered me to the conference room. 'Hey, heads up, Kane is here in Duncan's office,' she said conspiratorially. 'Just wanted to prepare you. Come and make some coffee in the kitchen, that way you can hear what's being said.'

She walked swiftly back to her desk to keep her own audio brief and I dutifully did as I was told. I could hear Kane kicking off over some minor mishap, demanding that this was done and that was done, and then I heard Duncan utter the words I was dreading.

'Our new Guest Services Manager has just arrived. She's from England and seems pretty savvy. She'll do a great job for you Kane, but you might just have met your match with her. In the twenty-four hours I've known her, I can't see her taking any prisoners.'

Quickly pouring the coffee into the oversized mugs that

would soon be the only source of sustenance during the long days ahead, I rushed back to my desk and turned on the computer. Oh My God. There were already over seventy-five emails for me and this was only my first day. Just as I was pouring over the messages – most of which were from studio publicists wanting confirmation of dates and timings of screenings, receptions and key events – Duncan, with Kane following, bounded up the steps to the 'Hollywood Hills' desks and perched on the edge of mine.

'Vanessa, this is Kane Eppstein. He is overseeing his father's visit, so he'll be your point-man for everything to do with Lawrence – hotel, cars, limos on Gala night, driver, etc. As you know, the Eppsteins have lived in the area for many years, so there'll be certain things that Lawrence and Kane will specifically need and want. I'll leave you two to get to know each other.'

With his exit strategy completed, he winked at me as he bounded down the 'Hollywood Hills' steps. My alleged nemesis proved true to the words uttered to me only twelve hours earlier. He was strident and certainly had no time for pleasantries.

'For starters,' he growled, not even having said hello, 'my father is not staying at The Four Seasons. He wants to be at the Spa Resort and you will, of course, get the best suite. Now in terms of cars and drivers…'

It may have been latent jet lag or just a bruising of my English sensibilities, but I was not going to be spoken to like this, by him or anyone else.

'*Good Morning* Mr Eppstein,' I butted in, firing the first broadside to let him know I knew all about him. 'You'll have to forgive me, but from where I come, we usually start with the basic courtesies. So, it's nice to meet you and I've heard a lot about you. I'm sure we are going to get along just great and I shall naturally do everything I can to make your father's visit seamless and enjoyable, but I will *not* be spoken to in the manner in which you just started.'

Taken aback that anyone had the temerity to lock horns with him, he was floored for a few seconds. The battle of wills had just begun.

'Look, lady, I'm assuming you *do* know who my father is? You are here to do a job and there are a million gals like you out there that can do it. If you don't do what I tell you to do, then I can always have Duncan remove you.'

Realizing he was probably lacking in the irony department, I decided to mock him, but with a smidgeon of charm.

'Oh that *won't* be necessary Mr. Eppstein,' I said coolly. 'I am here to ensure your father's, and the other major stars' needs are met and to ensure they have a perfect time at the festival. But I do not work for you, so please don't treat me like a junior intern. Now, shall we get on with what we need to do?'

Again flummoxed by the fact that someone had dared to stand up to him, he shot me a withering look and growled, even louder, 'My father *will* stay at the Spa Resort and these are his dates. He wants a dedicated driver, he will not share one. He wants to have Erik Hughes. He hates stretch limos, so don't bother with one for the Awards ceremony. Get a Mercedes S-Class Sedan instead. OK, got that?'

Teeth firmly clenched, I nodded as he got up and walked off, without so much as a thank you or goodbye. Dear Lord, are they all going to be like this, I wondered? Anna came rushing over, having heard it all from her and Duncan's office suite.

'Hey Vanessa, you were awesome! No one in this office has ever spoken to him like that, everyone's too scared of him. I can't believe you did that. Well done you.'

'Thanks, but is Duncan mad?' I asked, assuming that he, too, would have heard it all.

'No, don't worry, he's been on the phone to Paramount, having a, how shall we say it, frank discussion with one of the more difficult studio execs in town about the logistics of getting their talent to the festival. He'll be passing this one over to you later today. And anyway, he'd have been tickled to have heard you with Kane. He likes gutsy women who can stand up for themselves which, I might add, is needed in heaps in this job.'

I needed something uplifting to sort out before the next hassle, which looked as if it was to be the Paramount Studios executive, so I accompanied Ingrid, the Special Events Manager, on my first location *recce* for a reception that Starbucks wanted to co-host with the festival shortly after it began. We set off for the old part of town and to a Hollywood legend's former home, an art-deco classic house with a swimming pool shaped like a grand piano. We were met by Peter from the rental company – the house is available for parties at a cool $1,700 per evening – and he gave us an in-depth tour of the property.

The reception was to be early evening, from six o'clock to eight-thirty p.m., outside by the pool, but with the entrance hall and sitting room also available. We planned on having the bar by the pool, with the dressed trestle tables under the enchanting pergola, which had been designed to cast shadows resembling black piano keys in the pool. The aspect was wonderful – palm trees, interspersed with Jacaranda, Tamarisk and Citrus trees, swayed gently in the soft breeze, mountains with a blue and purple hue, grass so green it shimmered and water in the pool so clear that it dazzled like a carpet of diamonds.

One could imagine the Rat Pack of the day all enjoying their supremely decadent lifestyle there – the master bathroom still sporting the cracked basin where the owner allegedly hit his new lover after a particularly exuberant drinking session. Ingrid and I declared this the perfect venue.

'We'll take it,' she said to Peter. 'There'll be about two hundred guests and we'll use our own caterers, so no need for you to worry. The only issue is security. Can you provide that or do you want us to arrange it? Send the contract to the office and I'll have it signed and authorized for you by return.'

One venue sorted, onto the next; this time for a late evening party for an LA-based entertainment industry magazine wanting to host an after-show party for a particular movie – on the assumption that the lead star was going to be in town for the festival and would, hopefully, be at the party. We looked at several venues along Canyon Drive, finally settling on The Upper Deck for its enormous balcony area, replete with fire-pit, which augmented the cavernous bar and dining area. Formalities completed, we drove off to source another location, this time for a more formal dinner; after scouting some five or six venues, we agreed on Bouchon – one of the city's most expensive and glamourous restaurants, and with an unsurpassed reputation.

Returning to the office around four o'clock, I had no option but to tackle Duncan's problematical executive from Paramount. There were six voice-mails and three emails from her, each one increasingly agitated and insistent that I get back to her *immediately* – or was that to be *before* immediately? – to discuss arrangements for their talent's participation at the Awards Gala. This is what I learned to love about LA – that *everyone* is just so damned important. Except, of course, that they are not and are only mere mortals like the rest of us. Rather than embarrassing her by revealing her name, I'll simply refer to her as "Miss Demented", for that was what she was. Calling her, I was rewarded with the full force of her stress down the receiver.

'Hey chill,' I said breezily, still woefully unaware that soon enough I would sound as demented as her. 'What's the problem?'

'I need to know the exact hotel Tommy Kane will be staying at, when he needs to be there, what car he'll have – a limo presumably?, who will be driving him, who is his handler, what time does he goes up on stage to receive his award, how long his acceptance speech is expected to be and who will be writing it – your office or our publicists? Oh, and we want full editorial control over speeches and any other publicity pitch material.'

Oh Good God, we were still five weeks out from the festival starting. Why was she so wrung-out?

'I'm sorry, but at this stage all I can tell you is the hotel,' I replied. 'The rest will be sorted within the next week or two. As regards the Awards Gala itself, the show producer won't have timings or speech lengths ready for at least another three weeks, but I'll keep you fully briefed.'

I did not dare say that I had been told that, in prior years, the show producer often changed the script and timings up to twenty-four hours beforehand. Not being fully conversant with the protocol over awards ceremonies and speeches, I ventured that, to save a lot of time and aggravation, it might be better if their publicists wrote the acceptance speech if we provided them with an outline of the format of the Awards Gala and the other honourees. She was still in stress-stratosphere for some reason, kicking off on another tangent about hotels for other studio executives coming in, would limos be picking them up in Hollywood?, what cars would they have while in town?, which receptions would they all be going to? And so on.

'I'm sorry, but I only got here yesterday. I'm picking up the reigns as quickly as I can, but you'll appreciate there is a hell of a lot to sort out. I'll get back to you as soon as things fall into place,' I said firmly.

By now she was yelling down the phone, demanding to have this information immediately and it simply could not wait. I told her it would have to, saying that I had to go as a call was coming in from Brazil about a director whom we had asked to attend. She kicked off again that I was 'cutting her short' and threatened to report me to Duncan.

'Feel free to do so,' I said, knowing this would be a red rag to a bull. There was, of course, no call coming in from South America, but I went straight to Duncan and told him about the conversation. He was up to his proverbial eyebrows in emails and caught up in a dispute between two Board members which did not look as if it would soon be resolved. He was incredibly non-plussed, saying those kind of conversations took place every day in the run-up to a festival and that I was not to take any notice of it. However, he would put in a call to her boss at Paramount, just to ensure that lines of communication were fully open and that Miss Demented did not overstep the mark again. Then he came out with a classic.

'This is nothing Vanessa, the studio execs are not the problem in this industry. You want to know what is? You wait until you start dealing with the publicists. They are rude, arrogant, a total nightmare.'

Having been one myself, I could not quite believe this.

'They can't be that bad,' I sighed. 'They need people on

their side, surely?'

'Oh, just you wait and see. They're like scud missiles.'

Although there were three exceptions – Raine Daysen, Cate Phellim (Olivia Lautner's) and Stephanie Yorke (Liam Taylor's) – as we got closer to the festival I was to see just how right he was. It was time for Diana and I to leave for the day and once again repair to Midnight Rescue for another medicinal bowl of margarita.

'Hi, could I please speak to the manager. I'm head of Guest Services at the film festival offices and I'm calling to see if you would like to be a sponsoring partner for the Guest & Industry Suite?'

This call was made over and over again during the course of the next two weeks to myriad upscale provisions stores in the city and neighbouring districts. 'Hi, could I speak to …' The most thankless part of the job and one which nobody else in the office was prepared to do. As most of the companies – many of which were independent grocers or small restaurants – had supported the festival during the prior few years, it would be hard to get them interested in my call. Time to revert to my marketing communications background and introduce a bit of spin into the conversation.

'We have some stellar names coming to the festival this time, such as Olivia Lautner, Liam Taylor, Tommy Kane, Lawrence Eppstein, Barbro Innes, Kevin Upstone, Taylor Quentin and Ed Tyler, to name but a few, and they will naturally be at the Guest & Industry Suite mingling with the film directors and studio heads, so it's a great opportunity to showcase your new foods range or menu.'

I felt awful saying this, as I fully knew that the A-List

stars would not be anywhere near the hospitality suite while they were in town. Far too *déclassé!* But, for some reason, they all took the bait and I managed to reel them in one by one, punching the air each time one verbally consented. It did, however, take the best part of three weeks to get agreements from around eighteen companies and for the proverbial dotted lines to be signed; it then took another two weeks to sort out the logistics of how we would get the food to the suite every day.

Would they deliver? (usually "no"), could we pick up? ("yes, but only at certain times") and so it went on. Looking back over the previous years' logs, I noticed that my predecessors had really only concentrated on basics like bagels for breakfast and tortillas for supper. I had decided, in a fit of madness no doubt, that the suite would *cater*, in its truest sense, for all our guests – and that meant proper meals and an array of beverages and drinks. The suite was, after all, to be a showcase for the festival and somewhere for the industry guests to relax and do business in a conducive and ambient environment.

Under my watch, there would be no scraggy snacks and soda. It would be more like dining at the Hard Rock Cafe than a fast-food burger chain. I knew I was being too ambitious; Diana thought I had gone completely mad.

'You're trying to do far too much here and there's a ton of stuff still to get done before the fest starts. I know you want it to be perfect, but I can guarantee it'll probably end up being more Hell's Kitchen than River Cottage!'

She was right, of course, but by the end of it all, I had managed to secure eighteen food suppliers and over $45,000-worth of complimentary food and drinks for our guests – including a new Asian-fusion restaurant that had received rave reviews since it opened and was booked weeks in advance – and who had, after much cajoling, been persuaded to deliver a full-blown supper menu for five nights out of the ten-day festival period. Our guests had better bloody well be pleased, I thought.

I had now to repeat a similar exercise for the goody bags, those ubiquitous freebies that are expected at awards ceremonies and, as such, has now spawned its own gifting industry – suites in hotels, particularly in LA during the 'awards season' from mid January, starting with the Film Critics Awards and the Golden Globes, through to late February with the Oscars, are set aside just for the selection of 'swag bags'. These days, the stars, and, dare I say it, even the Z-List ones, all expect a goody bag, and a good one at that.

Needing a break from my begging bowl, I joined the Mercedes-Benz meeting in LA the next day with festival Chairman, Ed Harrison, Board Managing Director Harry Neumann, Duncan and Christian.

I had not yet met Ed, but had heard a lot about him – that he was solipsistic, but enigmatic. He had been Head of Daytime Programming at NBC in Los Angeles and knew absolutely everyone, both there and in New York. Unbeknown to me, Duncan had already emailed him to tell him of my arrival, ending the email, as I later saw, with the brief description "she's a class act". Similarly with Harry, he was curiously both avaricious, yet philanthropic, occasionally pugnacious, yet often extremely courteous – a man who never forgot anyone's name and would greet both his benefactors and key staff with equal warmth.

Mercedes was one of the main sponsors of the festival and we were meeting to discuss which models they would loan us for the duration of the festival. While they really did not need to promote their products – after all, anyone who is anyone in LA has one – the West Coast regional office felt that it was not just a synergistic partnership, more one which exuded status, due to the festival's growing pulling power in attracting the top stars, and recognition by Variety magazine, one of the entertainment industry's bibles', as having "a featured role in the awards season ... its Awards Gala dovetails with Oscar balloting."

And in power-hungry, status-riddled LA, that means everything. Harry opened the meeting by outlining the festival's marketing plans and promising that the festival's LA-based PR agency would ensure photos of the A-List stars getting out of the cars would be on the front pages of the LA Times and USA Today, as well as on the wire to news agencies worldwide.

Ed, who did what only Ed does best, casually dropped names of all his friends and contacts who would be attending as freely as if one were writing out a grocery list, and so putting Eddie from *Absolutely Fabulous* in the shade.

Duly impressed by 'the names', it was a done deal within minutes and we had twelve S-Class Sedans for the Opening and Closing nights, plus the first and last weekends; additionally, they offered two Maybachs for the Awards Gala ceremony.

'We'll need more than two,' I said, probably a bit too quickly. 'We've got some stellar names coming in, at least twelve of which are receiving or presenting awards at the Gala.'

Mercedes' Vice-President looked at me for a second, then Ed, Harry and Duncan, before alighting back on me. Like Kane Eppstein, he was obviously not used to being challenged.

‘And who exactly have you got coming in, by that I mean *confirmed* as attending?’

I reeled off the list of the stars’ attendance whom the studios had confirmed in writing, as well as those names we were still awaiting confirmation – but who had been verbally promised to Duncan by either their agent or studio that they were “ninety-nine percent sure of their attendance”.

‘My God, you guys have scored this year, that’s a pretty impressive line-up.’

‘Yes. So you see, we really could use another couple of Maybachs.’

I knew I was out on a long line, but an impressive American I had worked with in London years before, bemused by my British reticence about asking for anything, had always said, “if you don’t ask, you don’t get”, and I had since followed his mantra.

‘Okay,’ he said slowly, as if for us to savour the impending announcement. ‘We’ll agree to your request for four Maybachs, but on the condition they are used only for the top A- List.

‘And I want to know which stars will be having the Maybachs and which ones will be in the S-Class Sedans,’ the Vice President intoned. ‘We also need to have copies of driving licences and social security numbers of drivers you assign to our cars, and only those drivers, once designated, are to drive the cars. No exceptions.’

Everyone agreed and I made a mental note to email my Transport Manager, whom I had yet to meet, with this directive.

As we wrapped up the meeting and left the offices, Ed turned to me. ‘Good work Vanessa. This is the first time we’ve even been able to get the S-Classes, so getting four

Maybachs is a real coup. Welcome on board. Let's see what else you can do for the festival...'

Without finishing the sentence, he and Harry roared off in his Ferrari towards Santa Monica airport and to his private jet which was waiting to fly him home.

No sooner had Duncan and I got back to the office, some two-and-a-half hours later, I found a bank of phone and email messages for me, eleven of which were from Ed, via his Blackberry. Had we asked this person?, who was doing hair and make-up for the awards ceremony host?, had we set up separate suites at the host hotel for the TV crews?, what were we doing for celebrity wallpaper this year? (a term used in the industry to denote C-list and beyond celebs who had once been fêted, but whose star had now waned), who was dealing with Barbro?, which talent would be at the receptions for our key sponsors?, had we organized a private jet, in case a star felt it was too far to drive?

Oh dear Lord, had we done this, had we done that, and had we jumped backwards through enough hoops?

'You're on his radar now,' said Duncan. 'Better watch out, he'll have you organizing his personal Chairman's Cocktail Party the night before the Awards, and travel for all his personal guests from LA, on top of everything else you have to do.'

And so it was to be. The start of the tsunami.

CHAPTER FOUR

It had been fortuitous that I had been to see all the hotels on my first day and had met either the General Manager or the Sales Director. I had called the General Manager of the Spa Resort to give him confirmed dates of Lawrence Eppstein's visit and how many nights he would need; I had assumed that there would be no problem and that it would just be a matter of saying which suite we wanted and giving the dates.

As it turned out, the hotel was, unfortunately, hosting a poker convention during the period of the film festival and was, the GM told me, "completely sold out" and could not accommodate Mr. Eppstein.

'OK, no problem, we'll put him into the Four Seasons,' I said, oblivious to the nuclear fallout this would create. 'Thanks for your time.'

'Sorry the timing sucks,' he said, by way of apology. 'Any other time, you can have whichever suite you want.'

I immediately called Charles Rutherford at The Four Seasons. 'Hey Charles, how are things? I'm calling for two reasons. One, can we fix a date for that fun lunch, which I am already in need of, and two, and the real reason for this call, can I have an extra villa for Lawrence Eppstein?'

Charles was in a frivolous mood. 'Well, first things first. Lunch next Wednesday, twelve-thirty. I'll meet you in the bar with a glass of champagne. As for Mr. Eppstein, sure you can have an extra villa. Just email my Sales Director with the dates and we'll take care of everything.'

Breathing a sigh of relief that this had been sorted quickly and relatively easily, I made a start on the next major task: the ubiquitous goody bags. Having looked at the log for last year, the 'goodies' had seemed pretty pedestrian. Since the stars had not been of the same calibre, I reasoned that perhaps this was why the items were more of a token than a gift. This year, however, with names like Olivia Lautner, Liam Taylor, Lawrence Eppstein, Barbro Innes, Daniel Eversleigh, Taylor Quentin, Cody Quinn, Nancy Demainne, Kevin Upstone and Ed Tyler, the gifts had to be far superior.

Duncan had told me that the studios were a good place to start, as they were often willing to throw in their new Blu Rays and DVDs, and that Sharper Image Design would usually offer their latest electrical gizmo. But what does one give the star who has everything?, and particularly when one cannot afford – as the festival could not – to pay for the latest must-have toy? That was the dilemma I was facing and I had set my sights higher up the food chain than a Blu Ray or DVD. But beggars can not be choosers, even when it comes to smoothing the ruffled feathers of Tinseltown. My gifting ideas, though, were more along the lines of luxury goods, coupled with upscale quirky, and thereby more unusual, gifts.

The two other main sponsors complementing Mercedes-Benz were Tiffany and Saks Fifth Avenue and they each had a large store on State Street, the city's own 'Rodeo Drive'. Tiffany was sponsoring the Awards Gala and had already agreed to place a present – gift-wrapped in its signature Tiffany box and white ribbon – on each place setting at the dinner. As we were expecting one thousand, seven-hundred people at the Awards Gala, this was already an exceptionally generous gesture. Would I be pushing it by asking for more? Tentatively, I put a call into the PR Manager at each store and asked if I could come and meet them, briefly outlining the reason why.

'Sure, how about tomorrow at ten o'clock?' said the Saks Fifth Avenue lady.

'Yes, that's good for me. Thanks, I look forward to meeting you then.'

'I could do three o'clock on Thursday,' said the Tiffany executive, to which I intoned the same response.

My direct line phone rang. It was Kane Eppstein.

'Is everything sorted for my dad at the Spa Resort?' he asked abruptly.

No good morning, no how are you.

'Actually, I was about to call you,' I lied. 'There's a small problem with the Spa Resort. They've got a poker convention on at the hotel for two weeks while the festival is on and they are completely sold out. I did try my best with the GM and explained it was for your father, and thought he might juggle something, but he just said he couldn't do anything.'

A deafening silence, but I pressed on. 'This isn't a problem Kane as I have already booked your father into The Four Seasons and he has one of their private deluxe villas, with its own butler.'

I had stupidly thought this would pacify him. A roar bellowed down the phone. 'I told you my dad only wanted to stay at the Spa Resort. Which part of that statement did you not understand? He *will* stay at the Spa Resort, so you had better sort something out. NOW.'

He slammed down the phone; now I knew why everyone

had commiserated with me in having to deal with him.

Feeling as if a wet fish had just been slapped across my face, I again called the General Manager of the Spa Resort. 'Look, I'm really sorry, but I've just had Kane Eppstein on the phone and he isn't happy that his dad can't be at your property. Isn't there *any* way at all that you could move a couple of guests around, so that Lawrence can be with you?' I pleaded.

'Sorry Vanessa, but like I said, we're completely sold out and with guests who are paying top dollar for their rooms. This is serious revenue for the hotel, while you are asking for a comp suite for five nights. Sorry, I'd be happy to help on any other occasion but no can do for the dates you are asking.'

'OK, I understand. Thanks for your time.'

In the course of only a few minutes, while I was on the phone to the Spa Resort, Duncan had appeared in front of my desk, looking annoyed. 'What's the problem with Lawrence Eppstein?'

I told him and said that it was under control as he was now at the Four Seasons. Duncan shifted uneasily.

'I've just had Ed on the phone, because Kane has just been onto him, bitching about how incompetent this office is. Kane, being Kane, went stratospheric. We need to sort this somehow.'

I told him again that I had.

'It's not your fault Vanessa, it's just that Ed gets edgy when studios or publicists start bitching, and then it all comes down to me. And Lawrence does like that hotel, he's known it for ever, so its kinda like a home from home for him.'

As I was explaining that I had begged the General Manager to move guests around to try and accommodate

Lawrence, Anna came to the doorway separating her and Duncan's office suite from the 'Hollywood Hills'.

'Ed's on the phone for you Duncan,' she said nervously. He took the call at my desk, holding the receiver about a foot away from his ear. We all heard it; Ed had personally called the General Manager and it appeared that there *was* a suite available after all, though not the one Lawrence usually had. 'I thought you said this girl was savvy,' screamed Ed. 'She can't even get a frigging suite for a top Hollywood legend. There'd better not be any more f***-ups like this.'

He, too, slammed down the phone. I was incensed, not with Ed, but with Kane for going behind my back and making me look like an idiot in front of both Ed and Duncan. I vented my spleen to Duncan.

'I will not stand for that. I will not tolerate anyone treating me like that, whoever the hell they are. He knew that I had really tried with the GM twice to get the suite. It's not my bloody fault that the hotel is staging a frigging poker convention and they are sold out. What am I supposed to do, call the GM a liar and demand that he conjures up a suite, along with a hat and a rabbit in a puff of smoke? If this is how Kane is going to behave, he can go screw himself. I don't give a damn that his father is so-called Hollywood royalty.'

Rather than being angry, Duncan looked bemused. But within two seconds, my direct line phone rang; it was Ed.

'I've had Kane on the phone and I've now sorted out the suite. You don't tell people like Kane in this town that you can't get them what they want. For God's sake, come to me first if there's a problem. I know enough people to fix things.'

'Thanks Ed,' I said icily, before explaining exactly what had happened. He softened, realizing that I had tried my best and that Kane was on one of his usual orbits.

'OK, no big deal this time, but just remember who you are going to be dealing with as we start finalizing everything for the festival. These people are used to getting what they want, when they want.'

After about twenty minutes, I called the General Manager. 'I gather you have now managed to find a suite for Lawrence,' I said dryly.

'Yeah, we had a cancellation just come in.'

'Oh, *r-e-a-l-l-y,*' I said, somewhat sarcastically. 'That's good. So we're all sorted for Lawrence. Which suite have you allocated to him?'

'I've moved some guests around, so he's got a good one.'

'But he must be in the Penthouse. For all five nights? And with a Butler?' I demanded.

'OK, OK, I'll sort everything.'

'Good, can you email confirmation and a reservations number. Oh, and contact name of whomever at the hotel I should now be dealing with as regards Mr. Eppstein and his suite.'

I thought about slamming down the phone, but guessed there would be many more similar conversations with many more people.

I called Charles Rutherford at The Four Seasons straight away. He sensed from my voice that something was up.

'Hey, any chance our lunch can be brought forward, to today. I need some immediate succour. Oh, and I'm sorry to mess you around, but I also have to cancel the villa for Lawrence Eppstein.'

Charles knew the workings of the film festival and how tensions ran high at times. 'Darling, of course. I'll cancel my lunch date, so just get your pretty little ass over here as soon as you can.'

The Concierge looked horrified, as though I were trailer trash, when I pulled up at the *porte-cochère* in the Dodge pick-up – not quite how one usually arrives at this swanky hotel. I quickly explained who I was and apologized for arriving in a Dodge, saying I was picking up items around town and it was the easiest vehicle to use, at which he breathed a palpable sigh of relief and beckoned to one of the Valet Parking guys to quickly remove the offending vehicle.

Leading me inside, he directed me to the main Reception desk where they called Charles's office. Attempting small talk, I asked if they were busy. 'Oh yes, we're full right now. Lot of high fliers who want to get out of LA for a long weekend.'

'Anyone of note?' I enquired casually.

'Oh yeah, and a couple of them are in the restaurant now, so you'll get to see them.'

Charles appeared, dispensing air-kisses as he looped his arm through mine and led me straight to the Terrace Bar at the side of the restaurant for a much needed glass of champagne.

'OK, what's happened?'

I told him the story and he did not look remotely surprised.

'You'll get used to it. This industry has way, way, too many egos and everyone thinks they're at the top of the pile, even the wallpaper, who really should be grateful they even still get a look in!'

Giggling like a pair of school children, we sipped our Roederer Cristal and, duly fortified, made our way to our table, en route passing two recent Oscar-winning directors lunching together, a well-known TV actress with her agent, a high-profile TV producer and his scriptwriter, who had written one of the most compelling American TV shows ever, and a supermodel with her equally well known husband. At least the next two hours would provide some respite.

Back at the office more volunteer staff had begun arriving, together with a core band of freelancers who did this gig, and several other major film festivals across North America, every year. Among the new volunteer arrivals were two guys who would be in my team: a lovely teddy-bear of a guy called Dino Inglemann, a recent law graduate from Yale – one of the US's top Ivy League colleges – and Mike, who became known as Mike 2, who had worked at the festival the year before and, as with child birth, had obviously forgotten the pain he endured. His knowledge of the brickbats that were to lay ahead proved invaluable and even when tensions were at their zenith, he remained an oasis of calm and support, despite our disagreeing on some aspects of the execution of the role.

Dino, whose gentle manner belied his extraordinary brain-power, became my rock. He managed to slice through the hissy-fits and tiara tantrums that soon engulfed us in the 'Hollywood Hills', much of which came via the studios and the publicists, though a great deal was also from Mike 1.

Assigning Dino the task of managing the hotel grid for the filmmakers, studio executives, publicists and celebrity wallpaper, I knew this would require enormous reserves of inner strength and diplomacy in dealing with the hotel General Managers and the guests themselves once they found out they were not staying at The Four Seasons or The

Ritz Carlton. I, myself, would handle the hotel reservations for the A-List stars at The Four Seasons, together with any other last-minute key celebrity invitations.

I knew that Dino and Mike 1, the 'goblin-like' character who had taken up residence in the corner, would not get on, for they were the antithesis of each other, so I set Dino up at a desk next to me at the far end, for I did not care much for Mike 1 either. (He later proved to be a snake in the grass and was fired, but we all had a festival to get through first.)

Some of the core freelancers were doing the rounds of the office to vet the new arrivals such as myself and check that their desks were as they were last year. Among them were Hannah Upton, a Canadian Programming Manager who had worked very closely with Christian for a number of years in selecting the myriad US and foreign movies; a Programmer from Chicago called Alicia Timms, who always had a smile and a warm welcome; Alexis Davidson, a delightfully quirky gal from San Francisco who would be in charge of Print Traffic – the department responsible for getting the cans of film reels shipped in from all over the world – and Alan Tighe, a Film Data Co-ordinator who, while friendly most of the time, would often be heard to scream at the 'Hollywood Hills' on a daily basis, 'Will you shut the f*** up, I can't think straight', and which naturally always provoked a suitable response from the gay 'goblin' in the corner.

Hannah was the one who had nicknamed the Guest Services area the 'Hollywood Hills'. I felt it only appropriate that the Programming Department – adjacent to us but screened by a thin wall covered in slips of paper which were constantly moved around as they got confirmation that (a) the film cans had arrived, (b) the director had accepted the invitation to attend, or (c) the reels had been checked for tears and general quality – should also have a suitable soubriquet.

As we looked after the celebrities and filmmakers, it was fitting that Guest Services was known for the area where most of them lived; Programming, being on a slightly lower level, became known as 'The Valley' – as in the San Fernando Valley. Thus, whenever Hannah and, in time, Christian, Alexis and Alicia, walked by, she or they, would dutifully trill, 'Hello Hollywood Hills,' and, depending upon which crisis we were dealing with at the time, we would respond in unison, 'Hello Valley Guys.' Puerile to the extreme, but it got all of us through the long days and evenings, and often nights.

The frivolity of our mutual admiration society was soon shattered by another call from Kane Eppstein. This time he wanted to know what was happening about a car for this dad. I said I had arranged for a Mercedes S-Class Sedan, as instructed, and a dedicated driver. Naturally, this was not good enough.

'He will want his usual driver,' he boomed. *Grrr*, I was to be a mind-reader now as well.

'Fine. I can easily change that. However, as I don't know who your dad's usual driver is, would you mind telling me his name and giving me his number, so I can see if he is available?'

'He will be,' came the riposte.

'I still need to have this information Kane, otherwise I can't do anything. Please can you just email it to me soonest, OK?' I said wearily, hoping against hope that our future conversations would not be this tiresome.

Mike The Goblin was now having the first of his many tiara tantrums: the office of Armando Aguilar, a well known Spanish film director, had emailed to advise that he was bringing an actor with him, also Spanish, and could we re-arrange his flights from Argentina, where he was filming, and a flight from Madrid for the actor Jaime Bardeles. Yelling over the wall to Christian and then scurrying around it, The Goblin demanded to know why he had not been told and what was the protocol for invited extra guests, as the two-hundred identified guests had already been issued with their invitations. After intense consultation, which involved Duncan as it was a budget issue, Christian sauntered over to my desk.

'Mike's gonna get an extra flight sorted, so can you arrange a limo to meet Jaime Bardeles at LAX and also a room in one of the better hotels. Suggest you put him in the same one as Armando.'

This was a statement, not a request. 'Who the hell is Jaime Bardeles?' I asked.

'Who knows, who cares, but if Armando is requesting to bring him, we accommodate him. End of,' hissed Christian, spinning on his heels before he had even finished the sentence.

Without looking back, he tossed another riposte over his shoulder, 'Oh, and he doesn't speak any English, so you'll need to find a Spanish speaker to accompany him all the time.'

I muttered something about all this fuss for a complete unknown, until Carl witheringly looked back at me. 'It's for Armando.' Of course it *was*, how stupid of me not to have realized.

As the day drew to a close – normal working hours of nine to six in the *first* week – more and more assorted characters wandered into the office to announce their arrivals, several of whom looked extraordinarily gothic and grungy.

'Ah, that's pretty much the Pacific Northwest look,

particularly around Seattle,' explained Diana when I shot her a quizzical glance as the troupe meandered in. High-fives and punching of the air ensued as they re-acquainted themselves with people they had worked with at other festivals.

'Hey Dude,' was the tribal call of these urban warriors to both known individuals and to complete strangers, such as myself.

'Oh hello, it's nice to meet you,' I replied teasingly in my best Queen's English. That stopped them in their tracks and about eight of them collected around me for further inspection.

'Hey, you're Australian! What's your role here?' said the ringleader, obviously incapable of working out for himself what it might possibly be.

'Actually I am *not* Australian', I answered indignantly. 'I'm English. I'm Head of Guest Services, so in charge of the hospitality suite, all the celebrities and other VIP guests.'

'Hey, our filmmaker guests will love you with *that* accent,' observed another guy with a beard that made him look like a ZZ Top band member, but who turned out to be a gem of a guy called Frank. 'And so will *we*. By the way, has anyone ever told you that you look like Cher? or Angelica Huston?'

Diana returned to collect me, shutting down my computer before I could do anything else and announced that we were going to The Mountain for cocktails with Duncan, Anna, Christian, Hannah, Alexis from San Fran and a couple of the other staffers.

We drove off down Main Street with the palm trees gently swaying and the fairy lights adorning them twinkling, the sun slowly setting behind the mountains and the lights of the city coming on. At The Mountain Bar and Restaurant, itself half way up one on the outskirts of town and so affording the most magical views, we settled into a corner booth and ordered what seemed to have become our customary drinks: large margaritas in enormous bowls and a couple of bottles of Merlot.

As would usually happen, the wind-down drinks swiftly turned into a debriefing session, which was no bad thing. Duncan and Christian were upbeat as they had just secured a couple more movies, bringing the score sheet to two-hundred-and-thirty movies from seventy-five countries worldwide.

The Opening Night gala presentation, followed by a massive invitation-only party, was a US movie from Paramount Studios and with the lead actor being honoured at the Awards Gala ceremony with the Career Achievement Award. Five major new international films, making their US or world premieres, would comprise the International Gala section, with its director and/or major talent (actor) in attendance at a reception to follow each of the screenings; there were some thirty-five movies in the Cine Latino category from Latin America, Spain and Portugal; there was a Virtuoso New Visions section, with a juried competition for about a dozen debut works by first-time filmmakers; and a Documentaries category, with over fifteen entries this year; while the World Cinema segment would showcase a sampling of "essential" new films from around the world.

In homage to the sexual orientation of the majority of the entertainment industry, there was a Gay-La category; aditionally, in preparation for the madness that is 'Awards Season' in LA – among them the Golden Globes, Screen Actors Guild Awards, Directors' Guild Awards and the Academy Awards, or Oscars – there was the Awards Buzz category, the considered frontrunners for Oscar hopefuls in two arenas: the Foreign Language Oscar Submission (some forty-one films) and Documentary Shortlist (some twelve films). Finally, there was the Closing Night Gala presentation, again followed by another considerable invitation-only party.

'We've even dedicated the Closing Night to the UK, just for you Vanessa,' trilled Christian, looking overly pleased with himself.

'Oh yeah?' I replied casually. 'What's the movie, who's the director, is he coming over and are any of the lead cast coming over too, if they're well known, that is?'

'Oh, you know him,' said Duncan. 'And you'll be looking after him.'

'Who is it?' I asked urgently.

'It's Daniel Eversleigh,' squealed Christian.

Hmmm, that was OK with me. 'But I haven't seen his name on the list?' I quizzed Duncan.

'That's because I only got the heads-up this afternoon from his West Coast agent and I had to run it by Ed. He had to sign off for the transatlantic flight which, of course, will have to be First Class, and then there's the limos…'

'Oh, that's my job. I'll take care of all of that and the hotel and make sure he has everything he needs!'

A heart-throb actor turned director, this movie was his directorial debut and was already garnering acclaim on both sides of the Atlantic from industry veterans at private pre-release screenings.

Several more rounds of fishbowl-sized margaritas were ordered; I was looking forward to meeting Daniel Eversleigh, but had not, for one moment, expected that our first meeting would be in his hotel bedroom. But more of which later….

CHAPTER FIVE

The sprinklers were in full force as I turned off the main thoroughfare into State Street and drove the four blocks until I reached Saks Fifth Avenue, itself taking up an entire block. Manicured lawns and immaculate flower beds encompassed all the deluxe shops along this road – dubbed the 'alternative Rodeo Drive' by a leading Hollywood television entertainment presenter – and I marvelled at how spectacular it all looked before realizing, when looking at the prices in the window displays, just why it did all look so spectacular.

Walking into the Saks store was like walking into another world; a bank of four huge glass and gold-coloured metal doors, with the familiar black logo etched on each, opened onto an array of luxuriant carpet, armchairs, gleaming counter tops and sales assistants who looked more like Ralph Lauren models than ordinary mortals.

The Concierge directed me to the Public Relations Department. Once through the Executive Offices' doors separating the well-heeled shoppers' rarified world from normal life, I was met by PR Manager Antonia Hoyle and Jefferson Maynard, the store's Director of Merchandise, himself also looking more like an Armani model than a retail manager. I outlined the reason for my visit, realizing it would be a more difficult 'sell' than I had anticipated.

I had expected them to be pleased with the roll-call of A-List and celebrity names I proffered – it was the most impressive to date for the film festival – but they, in turn, wearily advised that they get asked *all* the time to support events in the area and with the same calibre of names.

Antonia advised me, as if I did not know, that as a major sponsor, they were already getting the press exposure in LA of being a partner and there was, in reality, little I could offer them. This was indeed true; getting ready to move off the achingly comfortable sofa, I said I understood, thanked them for their time and that I would look forward to seeing them again at the Opening Night party.

'Wait,' said Jefferson. 'We simply can't do two-hundred goody bags, but we'll donate something for the A-List goody bags of those attending the Awards Gala ceremony. I think you said it would be twenty in total?'

'Yes, but I would need an extra gift please for a very well known British actor turned director, whose new movie has been chosen for the Closing Night screening and he is now coming over for it.'

'Fine, we'll throw in an extra couple and make it twenty-two in total. We have some extremely nice sterling silver key rings and some fabulous new crocodile tote bags just in from our New York store. They won't be at any of our other branches on the West Coast until late Spring, so they will be a unique gift for your celebrities. Naturally, they will come in our deluxe gift-wrap. Does that sound acceptable?'

'Do you have a picture of the totes?' I enquired, wanting to ensure that they would look good enough for the A-List swag bags. A brochure of a sumptuous tote was duly produced. 'Yes, that would be very generous of you. When should I have them picked up?'

'Give us about four days, as we have to get them from our warehouse. I'll call you when they're ready,' said Antonia. 'And I'll need a list of the final A-List names, just for our records.'

'No problem,' I said, again thanking them for their time. One luxe retailer down, about fifteen more to go.

The mercury was rising back at the office. More cans of film reels were constantly dropped into Reception by FedEx and yet more peripatetic volunteer staff kept arriving – most of them involved in the Box Office and operational side of each of the fifteen auditoriums that would be showing the movies. The reception area and outer lobby began to resemble a warehouse, as Ingrid's myriad special events set props were delivered. We were tight on space as it was in the offices, so to have hundreds of packages and boxes lying everywhere soon made it near impossible to easily walk to other people's desks.

The Goblin was muttering to himself in his corner and dispatching verbal orders to Dino which I had to quickly countermand; I had also been quietly told that he was writing a blog on his computer, rather than sorting out flights. A spike full of phone messages and around fifty-eight emails greeted me – and I had only been out of the office for one-and-a-half hours.

Duncan was in a foul mood due to one of the studio's demanding the earth, moon and everything in between; Kane Eppstein had called again and demanded I return his call "immediately"; two of the hotels had told us they could not offer any more comp rooms; the host hotel had left a message for me advising that they would be charging for computer set up in the hospitality suite and that if I wanted a separate room for media interviews, that too would be an extra charge.

Sam Devane, a Festival Board Director and also a Hollywood agent, wanted to know how many rooms I had allocated for celebrity wallpaper; two restaurants, who had agreed to provide food for the hospitality suite, now said they had "re-considered" and felt unable so to do; my Transport Manager could not arrive for another two days; the car rental company, who would be providing a fleet of cars for the myriad LAX pick-ups and returns, had decided "sorry, can't do this year", and Christian was jumping about like a Mexican bean demanding to know where *his* filmmakers would be staying, even though most of his guest list had still to RSPV.

Grabbing a large Latte and some cookies from the kitchen, I went to the Marketing area to seek solace with Diana.

'Hey, Vanessa, how'd it go with Saks? Oh, and this is Jean-Pierre, who does all our local PR and marketing, but we just call him JP. JP, this is my friend I was telling you about, the one from England.'

'Hello, great to meet you,' I said to JP, realizing at once that he was far too good-looking to be straight.

'Hey, welcome to the craziness that is film-fest! Let me know if there is anything I can do for you,' he replied in the most gorgeous chocolate-brown voice.

I briefed Diana on the Saks meeting, asking both her and JP if they thought the silver key fobs and crocodile totes would be OK?

'I'll have those,' they chorused, adding, 'always try and get a couple of spares, so we can have something too.'

'Sorry, told Saks the correct number of celebs.'

'Oh well, if the three of us manage to get invited to the Awards Gala, we'll have the Tiffany's gift on our place setting,' said Diana.

‘Is that likely?’

‘Nope, but I guess if anyone gets the chance, it’ll be you. Guess you’ll be doing the whole red carpet thing at the ceremony anyway, so I’m sure you’ll get a seat at the high alter. I’ll mention it to Duncan,’ as she scribbled another note on her huge notepad, the ‘to do’ list already spread over three pages.

Diana resumed checking the proofs for the official programme, a forty-page guide which would be distributed with the local paper about ten days before the festival started. It detailed all the movies to be shown, both alphabetically and by country, an overview of the different movie categories, how to purchase tickets in advance and at the Box Office, and half-page profiles on the Opening and Closing Night movies, plus messages from the Chairman, Ed, and the Executive Director, Duncan, as well as logos of all the sponsors in their differing financial contribution categories.

She was on a tight deadline and several sponsors’ logos had still not come in yet, despite repeated calls and emails. Dispatching JP to go and physically get them on a disc and bring them back to the office, I saw an opportunity to try and reel back in the two restaurants who had “re-considered”.

‘Diana, I need a favour. Can we give the Guest & Industry Suite sponsors a logo in the programme, rather than just simply stating their name? That way, I can get these two high-profile restaurants back on board, which we desperately need, and use it as a hook to go back to the other sponsors to get more out of them.’

‘Yeah, I think that’s a good idea, but I’ll have to run it by Harry. It’s his baby. I’ll get back to you.’

Returning to the ‘Hollywood Hills’, I surveyed the

detritus that was my desk. Oh God, where do I start? I called The Goblin and Dino over.

'OK, a quick where-are-we-with-things meeting. Which filmmakers and industry guests have RSVP'd and given us travel dates?; who has RSVP'd but not yet given any travel dates?; who have we booked flights for?; if the flights have been booked, have they been allocated a hotel? And Dino, I'd like to work closely with you on that, as we'll need to ensure some film directors and studio heads are accommodated appropriately, with spa treatments etc. As for the hospitality suite, Dino can you follow up on the stores and restaurants that I have called with a formal letter to thank them and confirm what they have offered, and what we have agreed to give them in return.'

'What have we agreed to give them?'

'Still working on that with Diana, but hopefully a logo in the official programme guide, but leave that bracketed in the letter until I get word from on high.'

The Goblin, doodling furiously on his notepad, growled. 'Who the f*** is the transport person and where the f*** are they?'

I explained that Lizzie Nicholson could not be here for another two days as she was shooting a commercial in Pasadena and that we would have to cover her work for forty-eight hours.

'Oh terrific, we've got a mini movie-star to do what is arguably the toughest job in Guest Services,' snorted The Goblin.

'She knows what she's doing,' I said impatiently. 'She's worked here many times.'

We ran through everything we had at that stage; worryingly, only some thirty of the two-hundred invited guests had replied to confirm their attendance and available dates. I could see that the next couple of weeks would be hell as the other one-hundred-and-seventy-plus would, no doubt, have some extra last-minute additions which would roll in like a wall of sea.

Quickly deciding that we should work on the basis that all two-hundred would be attending, we would work in reverse, as far as the hotel rooms went, and free up a room if the person was not attending; that way, I explained, we could now input into Dino's hotel grid the key film directors, studio heads and key talent into the higher-end hotels and private apartments, and then work down the 'pecking order' by allocating rooms to the mainstream guests. The issue of rooms for celebrity wallpaper would pose a problem.

'We only have ten rooms as contingency over and above the two hundred,' I told Dino. 'Not sure how we're going to play the whole celebrity wallpaper thing. Sam Devane is coming in tomorrow, so we'll have a clearer idea of what he is planning, but I fear that as he has been an agent forever, he'll want to invite all his clients, past and present.

'Mike, I think we need to send chaser emails to the one hundred-and-seventy-odd who haven't responded. We need to start getting seats booked on the flights before they sell out.'

'You don't have to tell me how to do my job,' he snapped.

'Well, might I suggest that you go and get on with it. Dino, can you start the grid and we'll sit down again tomorrow, once Sam has been in.'

A quick injection of caffeine and a call to Kane Eppstein. 'Hi Kane, I got your email. What can I do for you?' He wanted to know about the car and driver for his dad.

'Your father is confirmed in the Penthouse Suite at the Spa Resort. It has a master en-suite, two further double bedrooms, separate bathroom, a dining room and two sitting rooms. Oh, and a dedicated Butler and Concierge. I think he'll be very comfortable. I've also got a Mercedes S-Class for him and, as requested, his regular driver is available and signed up. I have forwarded his driving licence details to Mercedes for their authorization. It's just a formality, so everything is in place as regards accommodation and transport.'

There was silence. Oh dear God, what was coming next?

'At last, some good news. Thanks. Nothing else needed for the moment, but I'll call you when it is.'

"Find another car rental partner" was scrawled onto a Post It note and slapped onto one of the piles of papers on my desk, each designated 'to do', 'to do now', 'priority', 'urgent', 'urgent priority' and, finally – and nearest the phone – *'Absolute Bleeping Priority'*.

By now, just about everything was having to be moved from the 'to do' and 'to do now' piles to the 'urgent priority' pile – with a couple of items, such as cars and extra hotel rooms for the celebrity wallpaper, moving straight across the chess board to the *'Absolute Bleeping Priority'* pile. Strictly speaking, this was a job that would have been covered off by the festival's Business Development Director, but she had been off sick for several days and this could not wait.

I called most of the leading car operators and was met with the usual response: "Would love to work with you guys, but we need more notice to run it by head office". I had Hertz left to try and my heart was sinking fast. If we could not get a vehicle supplier on board, we were sunk;

we had two-hundred-plus guests to ferry from LA to the festival and back, all at differing times of the day and night and so could not rely on contract taxis. I dialed the number.

'Hi, could I speak to your regional manager please. I'm calling from the film festival offices,' I said breezily, trying to mask the desperation in my voice.

'Hold for a moment, I'm connecting you to Martin Ellmore.' I held on for what seemed forever until he came on the phone.

'Hi there, what can I do for you?'

Quickly introducing myself and the festival, I launched forth, spinning an economy of the truth, knowing that if I was completely honest, they would feel insulted about being asked at the last moment.

'We're looking for a new car rental partner this year as we weren't very happy last year with our usual supplier,' I said in a measured tone.

'We have around two-hundred guests coming in from all over the world, a mix of key film directors, actors, studio heads, journalists, publicists and up- and-coming new filmmakers, and we need to be able to transport them from LA and LAX to the festival and back again. In addition, we obviously need to ferry them around the city during the festival, to take them to screenings, invitation-only events, judging panels, Q & A sessions and the like.'

Without giving him time to say "sorry, no can do", I continued. 'We obviously want the best for our guests and so I thought of you guys. We've got some stellar stars attending, including Olivia Lautner, Liam Taylor, Lawrence Eppstein, Barbro Innes, Tommy Kane, Kevin Upstone, Taylor Quentin, Nancy Demainne and Cody Quinn, to name but a few.

'We'll obviously give you as much in return as we can which, at this point, would be a colour logo on all collateral material such as banners, flags and posters throughout the city in the run-up to, and duration of, the festival. You would also have your logo and company strap-line in all programme guides and catalogues; be stated in all press materials as being a major sponsor and get a complimentary quarter-page advertorial in the local paper.

'And, the best bit is you'll get a table for ten at the Awards Gala. I promise you'll be near the front by all the stars' tables.'

I was going out on a limb with the latter promise, as Harry had complete control over the table plan for the Gala and not even Duncan, as Executive Director, had any sway over who sat where. But I also knew that Harry would be the first to ignite if we did not have cars for our guests. I was also nervous about reeling off the stars, as while I had not categorically stated that we would use the cars for them, it had been implied and I knew that Martin Ellmore would have assumed that as well.

After what seemed another eternity, I proffered a new carrot. 'This would be incredible PR for your company, as not only is the local paper covering the run-up to the festival with full features and then daily front-page new stories and photos, but the LA Times is also running a special pull-out edition on the festival the day it starts. Further, about eight major TV networks are covering the event, as well as all the local regional networks. Oh, and not forgetting Entertainment Tonight, of course.'

A long pause. 'Yeah, this sounds like it could be of interest, but you haven't given me much time to run it through corporate HQ. What car model and size would you be looking at? I'd have to run a track on inventory to see what we'd have available, if we did decide to help.'

'Obviously the best saloons and SUV's you can do.

Hey, if I put everything I've just said to you on an email and ping it off right now, can you forward it to HQ and perhaps let me know by, say, tomorrow, whether you think, in principle, it's a deal? I have a couple of other companies that I could call, whom I know from previous years want to be our partners, but we have decided we would really like to work with you guys.'

'OK, give me until close of play tomorrow.'

I decided to try a local company as well; even if Hertz came on board, they may not offer enough vehicles and it was a good idea to have more than were actually needed; as it turned out, a correct assumption.

Fred Lipsey, the manager of Classic Limousines, was delightful. 'Hey, I was kinda wondering why you guys hadn't called us already?'

'I'm so sorry, you've been on my list for a week now and I was just awaiting final confirmation of the A-List stars coming in before I called you.'

Repeating an edited version of what I had spun to Martin Ellmore, I was surprised to get an immediate, and enthusiastic, answer.

'Sure, we'll give you three mini-buses, with dedicated drivers, to do LAX pick-ups and returns, they each hold about twenty-five passengers, and we'll lay on ten Chevrolet Camaro saloons for general taxing around the city. Does that sound a deal?'

'Sure does,' I replied, breathing a sigh of relief, for even if Hertz did not come up trumps, this would just about cover it, albeit with some very careful planning. 'I'll email you the paperwork in a few minutes. If you could review, print off and sign where marked and then get it back to me soonest, that'd be terrific. But can I just double-check now. We do have a deal, right?'

'Right. We do.'

A call came through from Ed as I was working my way through the rest of the day's problems, flagging up potential ones with Dino and The Goblin.

'What the hell have you done to Kane Eppstein?' he asked in a flat tone so as not to give any clue as to whether he was happy, merely OK or generally pissed off.

'Oh God, what have I done now?' I implored.

'I don't know,' said Ed, 'but you've sure done something. Kane is delighted and rang me to say how impressed he was. And he never, ever, ever, does that. So, what *have* you done to, or should I say for, him?'

I told him about managing to change the suite to the Penthouse, arranging for a dedicated Butler and Concierge, getting Lawrence's preferred driver signed up and getting Mercedes to authorize the S-Class saloon for Lawrence's personal use during his visit.

'Good girl. Kane, like most Hollywood players, can be difficult at times and particularly when he doesn't know someone. But I think you'll find him to be OK from now on. He seems to trust you now.

'Oh, and as a gesture of thanks, because I don't like people being mad at me, particularly at festival time, I'm inviting you to the Benefit Screening and private reception afterwards that I'm arranging for Friday night. It's 'Blind Islands' and Michelangelo Delucca is coming in for the reception. Similarly, on Sunday afternoon I'm having the Chairman's Private Pre-Festival Screening of Leonie Cayzer's new movie 'The Pain Room' which is up for an Oscar Best Picture and she'll be there.

'Raine Daysen, the top publicist in Hollywood, is organising them for me. You'll also be working with her regarding the Awards Gala, so it'll be a good time for you to meeet her. In fact, there'll be lots of key players from the city and LA at both, so it's a good opportunity for you to meet a lot of people you'll be dealing with over the next few weeks. Bring a friend if you want to.'

There was a muffled click as I said, 'Thanks Ed, that would be really nice and I look forward to it.' The muffled click turned out to be Duncan who, unbeknown to me, had been hooked up to Ed's call. He appeared, leaning against the archway separating the 'Hollywood Hills' from his office suite.

'Well young lady, you really are on his radar now. I'm the only festival staff person he ever invites to his Benefit and Chairman screenings, so you've made your mark quickly. But beware, I've already warned you that he'll have you organizing his Chairman's Cocktail Party next!'

And with a wink of the eye, he turned and walked back to his office, his desk already awash with his own piles of 'Absolute Bleeping Priority'.

Before I could even put the call through to The Wyndham, my direct phone rang again. It was Ed.

'Vanessa, come to my office tomorrow morning at eleven. I'm planning on doing a cocktail party the evening before the Awards Gala, i.e. on the Friday, and I will need someone to organize it all for me. As you are the point-person for all the celebs, it'd kinda make sense if you helped me with this. We'll go through the guest list in the morning.'

Duncan had been right. I had no idea how I was going to fit in all the extra work, but it would be a great networking opportunity as it would bring me into personal contact with all the Board Members and leading city players, not to mention many of the A-List stars and key studio executives who would have arrived that day. I felt upbeat as I dialled

The Wyndham.

'Hi, what can I do for you?' said Jon Bauer, the General Manager.

'I'm calling about a message I've received ref computer set up charges in the hospitality suite, plus a charge for the extra room we need for press interviews,' I said, sounding somewhat peeved. 'This was never part of the original discussions and, as you know, the *raison d'etre* of the festival... erm, I'm sorry, one of the main thrusts of the festival is to boost tourism to the region, thereby filling the city's coffers and bringing business to your hotel.'

There was a pause; I guessed he was not used to people questioning him, but I felt buoyed by Ed's call and that he would be on my side if there were going to be any problems with the hotel. After all, it was in Ed's interest to ensure that the hotels gave us the best deals and facilities for our guests. Dino was watching me with interest, wondering if I would win this particular battle.

'OK, we usually charge a set up fee for the computers and modems, but I'll waive it on this occasion,' he said, sounding distinctly hacked off. 'But we have to charge for the room adjacent to the suite.'

Knowing full well that it was never part of the original contract, I again challenged him.

'Oh, that's a pity, because I was told that we had that room for media interviews. We do need a quiet area right by the hospitality suite to do media interviews, not just with the film directors and studio heads but, more importantly, with the key A-List celebrities receiving honours at the Awards Gala. You know the names we have coming in and, as I'm sure you are also aware, we have Entertainment Tonight doing a special, as well as NBC, CBS and ABC broadcasting daily news updates from the festival, so it would also be showcasing The Wyndham. That's thousands of dollars-worth of prime time TV exposure you'll be getting for little outlay and …'

Before I could finish, Jon responded, with more than a hint of exasperation. 'OK, OK, I guess I can waive that charge too. You're sure one persuasive lady. I don't do this for other folks.'

'Thank you very much,' I replied triumphantly. 'I'll drop a letter in to the hotel this evening outlining our conversation. If you could let me know when you have signed it, as confirmation, I'll come over and pick it up. By the way, who are my contacts for the suite, for banqueting and all technical matters?'

He gave me the names, which were added to the cast of thousands in my Day File; I had to keep him on side as I knew I would be going back to ask for more complimentary rooms as we got closer to the festival.

Rushing to the other end of the office to invite Diana to Ed's two private screenings, I felt strangely elated, but knew that there were still way too many burning hoops to jump through yet.

CHAPTER SIX

Ed's office was in the old part of the city, located at the junction of Main Street and Canyon Drive, each lined with boutiques, specialty food shops, bars and restaurants. It was a vibrant part of town, teeming with residents and visitors and there was a real buzz in the air, as if some sort of conspiracy was being concocted. The entrance to the office was dominated by a small piazza with a large fountain, behind which lay impressive double-height and double-width doors to the lobby area. Running up the stairs to the mezzanine level, I stopped to check my hair before pressing the chrome button on the entry-com system.

'Hi?' enquired a voice.

'Hi, I'm Vanessa Vere Houghton. I've got an appointment with Ed at eleven.'

'Oh, OK, come on in.' The door swung open to a huge, luxuriously-carpeted hallway with windows dressed in great swathes of silk curtains, replete with swags, tails and supremely-large tie-backs, and chandeliers. 'It's through there,' said a young, stereo-typical LA girl: tall, blonde, tanned, white teeth and sculptured chest.

I walked into Ed's inner sanctum and met Miranda, his secretary of twenty-eight years and who knew exactly which closets hid which skeletons. She was not someone to be trifled with.

'Hi Miranda, I'm Vanessa,' I said proffering my hand. She did not return the gesture, remaining firmly rooted to her chair and computer.

'He's expecting you. Go on in, it's that office.' As I turned to go in, I heard a scream of laughter emanating from his office, plus a cry of exasperation from another blond woman at the desk in the opposite corner to Miranda, furiously thumbing through the local newspaper. 'F***-ing paper,' she seethed, 'why can't they do the f***ing edits when I tell them.'

Walking into Ed's office, I found the owner of the laughter. 'Hi Vanessa, meet Jacky Florschon. She's an old friend of mine from LA days.'

'Yeah, but I live here now,' she said, forensically examining me to see if I fitted the bill.

Ed continued, 'She knows everyone in this town, so if you need any help, ask her.'

Jacky and I continued to survey each other. She was an interesting looking person, dressed circa 1967 in a white leather front-zipped catsuit (and with zip down to display her ample cleavage), thigh-high stiletto boots and layers of chains and beads around her neck. Her long black hair was brushed off her face with a row of kaleidoscopic combs, her eyes dramatically outlined with layers of kohl and her eyelashes were weighed down with false ones drenched in lashings of mascara, while her glossed lips had obviously been injected with collagen. She looked as though she had just come off the set of Valley of the Dolls.

I did not initially take to her, but as the festival prep period cranked up several gears, I found that, under the chameleon image, there was a genuinely nice person, and she did come to my rescue on more than a few occasions.

The peels of laughter, I discovered, came from a story in the LA Times about a guy – whom they both knew well, but despised – who had been done for both DUI (Driving Under the Influence) and using the services of a prostitute while wearing some juicy gear.

'At last, he's got his payback,' chuckled Ed. 'Serves him right. He was always a total a***hole.'

Jacky got up to leave, kissing Ed on both cheeks and tapping me on my arm. 'See you tonight at the Benefit. We'll go party afterwards.'

'OK business,' snapped Ed, the niceties of the day over as he threw a wad of papers at me. 'A few years ago, I used to hold small receptions for a few friends the night before the then much smaller awards ceremony. I want to do that again this time, but make it much bigger and exclusive. We've got a stellar line up of talent coming to the ceremony and many of them will have arrived the night before. It's a way of saying thank you to them for attending but, more importantly, it'll give all our main sponsors – Tiffany, Mercedes etc. – a real buzz to be invited to a private party with the stars.

'So I want you to work with me on this. We need to reserve somewhere at The Four Seasons from six to eight-thirty p.m. so that invitations, which are at the printer in draft form, can be printed as soon as possible. They'll need to be ready to send out early next week. So, where are we with talent, wallpaper and the studio heads?'

I explained that we had confirmation from nearly all the key celebrities of their attendance, but had no idea, at this stage, of when they would be arriving. This would become my 'urgent priority' task for next week, along with all the others. I suggested we drew up a guest list, split into A and B, and email a Keep the Date invitation out on Monday and

Tuesday to all the key guests; that way we would know if they were available. Then we would follow it up with hand-delivered and posted invitations. All RSVP's would come to me – Ed quickly rang the printer to instruct that amendment – and I would keep a running list of acceptances and declines.

'You mean regrets,' said Ed. 'People don't decline invitations in this town unless it is absolutely unavoidable.'

Ignoring this perceived riposte, I continued, 'Because of the calibre of stars we have at the festival, the event itself has to be spectacular, not just a cocktail party.' He looked up at me for the first time, his brow furrowed.

'What's the most iconic logo in the world?' I asked him, assuming he would answer immediately.

He thought for a while. 'Disney or Shell, I guess.'

'No, it's Chanel. And it's power lies in its simplicity: two colours, two letters entwined. It's elegant, it exudes class and in terms of brand awareness, there isn't another one to beat it. I think we should theme your reception along the same lines. Black and white, but shot with some red for vibrancy, and the red carpet, of course! The walls should be adorned with giant-size black-and-white photos of Oscar winners from Hollywood's golden era. The table linen should be white floor-length oblongs with a black band around the outer edge and with black over-lay squares and the cocktail napkins should be a mix of black and red.

'Champagne will be served in ultra-long-stemmed flutes, wines in goblets and soft-drinks in hi-balls. The plates could be those funky-squared white ones you see in Crate & Barrel, with red-handled cutlery. The canapés and finger-buffet items must be one-bite sized and should be presented on black slate oblongs placed on crushed ice and rock salt on bamboo platters and adorned with Swarovski crystals and black pearls.

'Bonsai trees on each table, but there should only be white flowers: orchids, peonies – they are, apparently, the signature flower of Tom Ford – calla lily, roses, gardenia and sweat peas for scent. The waiting staff should be dressed in black trousers and white linen shirts. Oh, and there must be a decent gift for everyone to take home.'

I gasped inwardly as I said this, for I knew that this meant a second set of goody bags to be organized, and so more pleading and begging.

A smile broke out on Ed's face. 'Do you know,' he chuckled, 'most of the volunteer and temporary staff we get each year haven't a clue what I mean about things. But you, you speak my language. Sounds good to me. Go for it. Perhaps we'd better have a meeting with Charles at The Four Seasons to see if this can be done.'

'Leave Charles to me, I'll sort it,' I said, knowing this was the perfect reason for another heroic lunch.

'OK, that's it for now. I'll see you tonight at the Benefit screening.'

I rendezvoused with Diana at Flemings for a quick hamburger, telling her about my meeting with Ed.

'OMG Vanessa, you are going to be slammed. You won't be able to juggle all of this. Next week is the deadline for the studios to give us their talents' travel requirements. Have you any idea of what it will be like when they all start kicking in next week?'

I muttered that it would all have to get done somehow and that Dino, 'nice Mike' and The Goblin would have to step up to the plate. Back at the office, I briefed Duncan.

'What did I say? You do realise you'll soon be working twenty-hour days.'

I thought he was joking, but I was soon to find out that he was not.

Sherri, the Receptionist, pitched her head through the lobby door and yelled along the corridor to me, 'Sam's here for you', reminding me that it was 'wallpaper' time. Walking briskly to the lobby, I found Sam Devane scrutinizing a box of festival-logo'd T-shirts that had just been delivered.

'Hey, you must be Vanessa,' he said, peering at me over his bifocals. 'Nice to meet you, sweetie.'

'Yes, hello. Come on through to the chaos that is currently Guest Services.'

I led him around to the Hollywood Hills, where Dino and The Goblin were having a *contretemps* over hotel allocations, not that this was anything to do with The Goblin as flights were his domain; Christian was screaming at Alexis and Damien from Print Traffic that the films were not getting here quickly enough; Alexis screaming sarcastically that, for some inexplicable reason, she had no control over FedEx and UPS; while Duncan was in full flow chewing the head off some poor minion about something that was probably fairly inconsequential.

Duncan, ever the mercurial character, had the propensity to erupt at the slightest thing and be charming the next minute – and with a vicious tongue for those who really got on the wrong side of him – but he did have a lot on his plate and I knew it would only get worse.

Cutting off the lava flow to the minion, Duncan acknowledged Sam – not with a greeting but with a growl – about why the Board still had not yet signed off on the final budgets for the Awards Gala, and Opening and Closing Night receptions. 'We're coming right up to it Sam and I still haven't got a f***-ing clue as to what I have to play with. I can't tell the studios anything, I can't tell Programming whether we can invite more guests, Vanessa's gonna have to buy stuff for the hospitality suite and it'll be a given that we have to buy in more hotel rooms. I'm just not getting any response from Harry, as usual, and I'm f***ing pissed off about it all.'

Re-routing the lava flow to now engulf Sam, he retreated to his inner sanctum, slamming the door behind him so hard that the whole office reverberated and the film cans and screeners – new movies put onto DVD by the studios to send out to press for previews – came tumbling off the shelves.

'Oh, that's just Duncan, sweetie. Take no notice of him,' said Sam, turning back to me and assuming I needed an explanation. I did not like to tell him that this happened periodically and I had been briefed that the eruptions would get worse as we got closer to the festival.

'OK, wallpaper,' I said briskly. 'Let's go through that now.'

Sam was very much movie industry 'old school': a charming gentleman in his mid sixties and with exemplary manners – something I had not seen for the past week. He was still an agent in Hollywood, but his *métier* had long passed and he had quickly been overtaken by the new breed of cutting, thrusting, chew-you-up-and-spit-you-out hotshots that now ruled Tinseltown. His contacts book and implacable courtesy did, however, mean that he still commanded respect from his industry peers and he had retained many of his 'older' clients, even though he now missed out on the more recent waves of new A-List actors who all flocked to the multi-million-dollar deals marketing agencies such as Creative Artists Agency (CAA), United Talent Agency (UTA) and William Morris Endeavor.

Sam pushed a piece of paper towards me. On it were the names of about fifteen people – his clients, our 'wallpaper' – that he wished to invite, not just to the festival Opening and

Closing nights, but to the Awards Gala as well. Skimming over the list, I recognized only a few names. Not wishing to upset Sam by showing him that I had no idea who the others were, I said simply, 'I'm going to have to run this list by Duncan as the hotels this year have cut back on the number of rooms they're giving us, and we've only got enough for the two-hundred invited industry guests.'

'But my dear, they *must* all come, *all* of them. I simply cannot not invite them and most of them have been given the nod anyway,' he cried anxiously.

'Well, then I need to talk to Duncan as I guess this becomes the budget issue that he was referring to a few minutes ago. Leave it with me Sam. I promise I'll do my best.'

My phone rang. 'Sam, excuse me for a moment, it's Ed.'

Grabbing the receiver and pinning it between my right shoulder and ear, I heard Ed demand to know what had been agreed at The Four Seasons for his cocktail party.

'Hold on a minute Ed, I've come straight back to the office for a meeting with Sam who needed to discuss wallpaper. I haven't had a chance to call Charles yet, but it'll get sorted, don't worry.'

Before I had even drawn breath, he shot back: 'Brief me tonight, before the Benefit.'

'But I won't have had time to see Charles…,' I wailed as the phone was put down on me.

'I'll leave you sweetie, you're busy. But I do need to have my guests authorized to attend and rooms booked for them – and there may be one or two more that need to be invited.'

I shot Sam a look that was a mix of panic and astonishment. '*No more* Sam, we haven't got rooms at the moment for this lot. If you absolutely need to invite others, you'll have to swap some names on this list. Sorry, but we're maxed out for rooms.'

Looking like an admonished puppy, he picked up his super-sized Filofax-type desk notebook. 'I know you'll figure something out, Vanessa. Oh, and please ask everyone here not to refer to them as wallpaper. They may not be the Angelina Jolie's or Brad Pitt's of today, but they were once names and should still be accorded with some respect.'

I nodded. 'Will I see you at the Benefit tonight?'

'Yes, why, will you be there? Ed doesn't invite staff. Duncan is the only person who gets an invite.'

'Well, he has invited me, so I'll see you tonight. Thanks for your time Sam.'

I still had not got around to the issue of resolving the problem with the two restaurants who had left messages to say they had "re-considered". If I could get that sorted this afternoon, it would round off the week well. I called Saigon Wang first as this was a key one to have on board: hip, modern, Asian-fusion food, and it was also the one who had initially promised to do a full supper buffet for five nights out of the ten nights of the festival. If I lost this one, I was in deep trouble.

'Hello Mr Wang. Variety and Entertainment Tonight are both looking to do receptions at the beginning of the festival with the studios who are coming in, and that would include their talent and many of our A-List celebs. It'll be one hell of a photo opp for you. ET will obviously have a crew there to cover it; Variety will have a staff photographer and we'll have someone from Getty Images who can send shots out on the wire to absolutely everyone.

'They'd be paying for the reception, so we're not asking for comps, and if I get one of them to agree to do it at Saigon Wang, will you come back on board for the five nights, as previously discussed and agreed?'

My heart was thumping, my throat was bone dry. I could not lose this restaurant and there was no way I could find five others to replace it. After what seemed an hour, but was only a few minutes, he eventually said, 'OK, bring us that party and we're back on board.'

Elation, tempered by the fact I knew I had to get Duncan to persuade ET and Variety, I marched straight in to his office. He was sitting at his computer desk – his own proper desk buried under a ton of papers, emails, contracts and general detritus working his way through myriad emails that had just popped into his Inbox.

'Jeez, only one-hundred-and-forty-seven in the last hour,' he said, half-laughingly. 'Just where the hell am I supposed to start?'

This was probably not a good time but, because of his workload, it never was with Duncan.

'Have a slight problem,' I ventured.

'NO problems. Got enough of my own.'

'Well, this could become one of your's if we can't fix it now.'

He looked up. 'OK, you've got three minutes of my time. What's up?'

I told him about Saigon Wang and how I had reeled them back on board, explaining that there was no venue yet decided for the Entertainment Tonight and Variety receptions, and that Saigon Wang would be the perfect venue for one of them. It was new, hot, hip and the reviews had been ecstatic. Could he pitch it to ET and Variety that this was the perfect venue?

'Yeah, I agree it would be perfect. Can they do the Monday night and shut the restaurant to the public?'

'Yes, they said they were OK for the early part of the week, obviously they wouldn't shut for a Thursday through Saturday night, but they will for a Monday to Wednesday event,' I said somewhat confidently, and nervously, for this point had not actually been rubber-stamped.

'Sure, leave it with me and I'll put in the calls, but it'll be Monday morning as I'm slammed right now and we've got the Benefit to go to in just over an hour.'

'Thanks Duncan, you're a star.'

'OK, guys, I'm outta here,' I said to no one in particular, although there were throngs of people milling about. 'Have a good weekend and I'll see you all on Monday.' Duncan was striding through the office, simultaneously putting on his leather jacket and shades. 'C'mon Vanessa, we're gonna be late.'

Christian appeared in the archway. 'Where are you two off to?' he demanded.

'Ed's Benefit screening,' I responded breezily, not realizing that it would irritate the hell out of him.

'*What!*' he shrieked. 'How come Hannah and I don't get to come? We're the frigging Programmers and without us, there's no frigging festival for Ed to have.'

'Haven't you watched enough movies this year, in order to select the ones we're showing at the festival?' I nonchalantly purred.

'Yeah, but this is the Chairman's Benefit and I want to come to the party afterwards,' he said truculently.

Duncan was impatient. 'Hey Christian, just meet us at the party and I'll get you in. In fact, Anna, call Miranda and just have her put Christian's and Hannah's names on the guest list. C'mon Vanessa, we really need to get outta here.

Like now would be good.'

The car park at the movie theatre was already jammed as we joined the line of cars on Main Street, waiting to pull in. Approaching the entrance to the theatre, I noticed that the local TV station had already set up their cameras, the red carpet was down, the local paper had two reporters and two photographers strategically positioned, and the Entertainment Tonight outside broadcast van was pulling up at the main entrance – all of whom were being briefed by Raine Daysen over covering the arrival of Michelangelo Delucca. As Duncan and I walked into the already heaving lobby, a tray was immediately brandished in front of us, bearing sparkling wine and canapés. The arc lights for the TV crews were strong, but through the glare I spotted Harry with some suited gentlemen.

'Who's that with Harry?' I asked Duncan.

'Oh they're Mark Olsen and Hayden Morrison. They're on the Board.'

'Perhaps a good time to gently nudge Harry about budgets,' I joked. 'He might be more agreeable in a social setting.'

As we approached, Harry turned to greet us. 'Budgets,' said Duncan. 'We've got to sort them out on Monday morning. I've got the world on my case over them. Need to get it sorted.'

Out of nowhere appeared Jacky, the lady I had met at Ed's that morning, still looking like a sixties rock chick and still in a cat-suit – but this time it was black leather and, coupled with white stiletto cowboy boots, she was not going to fade into the background.

'Hey Duncan, hey Vanessa, glad you're here. Come and meet Rory Cohen, he's with NBC and knows absolutely everyone in LA.'

Duncan made his excuses as I dutifully followed Jacky. Mr Big Shot was like the majority of studio executives that I would stumble across in due course: bloated ego, no finesse and only wanted to know someone if they could do something for him. The premise that somebody could just be liked because they were a nice, decent person with integrity neither entered his, nor his industry peers', orbit. I shook hands with him and true to form, he had turned away before I had even finished saying that it was nice to meet him. Unlike most 'LA hopefuls' who would fawn and put up with this behaviour, I made my excuses and, spotting Ed pacing nervously near the main entrance, walked over to him. 'Anything I can do?'

'No. Thanks. It's just that Michelangelo is running late, which means I've had to put back the intro's and screening by thirty minutes and people are getting impatient. The TV stations want to start their interviews now, in order to get them back in time for the seven o'clock show and the main evening news bulletins. And I don't have my star here.'

As if on cue, Raine, trailed by two cameramen and two reporters appeared. 'We can't wait any longer Ed, we gotta shoot now and go with what we can. Sorry.'

Ed did his piece to camera, starting with Entertainment Tonight, which went out each evening at seven o'clock, followed by the local station for its seven- and eleven-o'clock news bulletins. He was a consummate professional and I watched in awe as he delivered an artful and eloquent reason for the Benefit – for the local Aids Foundation – and a succinct, but compelling overview of the festival and why everyone should be buying tickets for all the movies.

Just as everyone in the lobby was being ushered into the auditorium and Ed was finishing, the star guest arrived.

'Hey my friend, what took you so long?' Ed joked as

he slapped Michelangelo on the back. 'People have been asking, but at least you're here for the reception. Come on through.'

'H-e-y Michelangelo, can we have a quick word before you go in,' chorused the two camera crews. And so he did his piece to camera, the crews got the footage they wanted and Ed walked into the auditorium and onto the stage with his special guest.

'My guest needs no introduction and I'll let him tell you about his new movie and how it came to be made, but I'd just like to say that we are honoured and delighted to have him here tonight, especially as he is in pre-production talks right now for his next movie. Ladies and Gentlemen, please stand and welcome Mr Michelangelo Delucca.' Upon that command, the entire auditorium rose to its feet and applauded Michelangelo.

The movie, a dark thriller centering around the disappearance of a murderer from a hospital for the criminally insane, was excellent and Michelangelo delivered a blistering performance, as everyone sycophantically told him afterwards at the reception. He stayed for the pre-requisite time and then departed with Raine and his bodyguard before the guests had realized they were not even going to get to mingle with him or take a shot of him with them on their mobile phones, despite having paid top dollar to attend.

My introduction to Raine Daysen had lasted a full two minutes.

'That's all most people get, unless you're a major star,' Ed shrugged. 'But she's one of the best in Hollywood, so we just let it go.'

Diana and I mingled with the guests for about another hour and then decided to head home, via a quick detour to Tommy Bahama for a couple of celebratory "you've-made-it-through-your-first-week" cocktails. I had made it through my first week; I had enjoyed it, despite the odd moments of frustration, but I still had no idea of what lay in store.

My tsunami was only just waking up on the ocean floor.

CHAPTER SEVEN

The sun was already streaming through the shutters and although it was only six-thirty a.m., I leapt out of bed, ready to start the day, *my* day, for it was the weekend. The difference to my psyche following a week of wall-to-wall sunshine, heat, clear blue skies and the cityscape's vibrant colours was unbelievable, and here I was raring to go at this ungodly hour.

'OMG, you're up already,' coughed Diana as she appeared in the kitchen. 'I think we need coffee. If you want a lemon for your morning detox, just reach out of the window and grab one off the tree.' She cranked the Nespresso machine into gear.

After breakfasting by the pool on scrambled eggs, toasted brioche and honey, and lashings more coffee, we planned the day. We would both have a mani-pedi, lunch at The Yard House, some retail therapy at the mall, go to a new teas tasting at Starbucks on State Street, and then Happy Hour and an early supper at The Cliffhouse, before finishing up at the EOS Lounge to see a band. The day sounded good to me, but first I had to have a swim.

The day went exactly as planned, though a very late night and too many margaritas had not been factored into the equation; with aching heads the next morning, we set off at Sunday lunchtime to drive into town for The Chairman's Private Pre-Festival Screening.

The movie, 'The Pain Room', was an emotionally intense drama following members of an elite US bomb disposal team; it's director, Leonie Cayzer, had crafted a sharp thriller which also delivered a powerful and often haunting critique of the addiction to danger. Despite its perceived political overtures, the film had already garnered rave reviews and was up for Best Picture at both the Golden Globes and the Oscars, with the smart money in Hollywood trumpeting that it would win both awards.

As Leonie Cayzer and two of the leading cast characters were in town for the screening, a repeat performance of Friday night followed, with photographers and media all jostling for prime space on the red carpet. Raine Daysen had invited several of her celebrity clients and friends: there was a 'hot' leading prime-time TV actor, who was reportedly starting a romance with an equally 'hot' TV actress and thereby making this visit an instant news story; a top Hollywood producer who had a second home in the area and had had huge success with a recent movie trilogy; a presenter on one of Tinseltown's leading entertainment news shows, sporting the most amazing pair of diamante-tipped false eyelashes I had ever seen; the daughter of a top Hollywood director and who herself was considered a 'rising star' and an A-List actress and her daughter, also an actress, who were both considered as 'hot' as each other.

It was amusing to watch the guests, and the broadcast and print media – each with their mobile phone cameras and large, sophisticated A/V cameras – jostle for their pictures.

'If you think this is fun, wait until the A-List walk the red carpet at the Awards Gala,' laughed Diana. 'It's a zoo, complete madness.'

As we took our seats in the auditorium, Jacky Florschon rushed over.

'Hey, how'ya doin?' she asked and, without waiting for an answer, 'I need to have a list of *all* the celebs coming into town for the festival for my radio show. And I'll pick out who I want to interview and then you can drive them down to the studio. OK? And I need that list tomorrow for our production meeting and I want to know where everyone is staying. Oh, and goody bags. I want to know *exactly* what is going into them and who is getting what.'

Dear Lord, obviously no such thing as a day off at a film festival.

Tiffany's PR Manager, who had had to postpone our meeting last week, called first thing. 'Can you do either eleven this morning or tomorrow at two?'

'Yes, this morning is fine. I'll see you at the store.' Better to do it now, I reasoned; tomorrow would be another day of the carousel of demands, hassles, revisions and revised revisions.

'OK, everyone listen up. Staff meeting in two,' yelled Anna over the already incessant din of conversations, phones and arguments; it was only five past nine.

Filing into the Boardroom and taking our seats around the huge table, we waited anxiously for Duncan to come to his throne. I had expected the meeting to be an intense briefing, given that we were only two weeks away from opening, but Duncan – though visibly stressed – merely asked each of the Department Heads for an update.

I told him about my Tiffany and Saks meetings, the hospitality suite food sponsorship to date, ideas for the goody bags, having to source two new car rental partners and the extra work involved with Ed's personal cocktail party the night before the Gala. I also voiced my concern over the sheer volume of emails and calls from the studios and publicists, the perceived lack of support from the host hotel, the issue of celebrity wallpaper and the fact that we were about to go over budget on unplanned extra air fares and hotel rooms.

Diana voiced her concern over the printing deadline for the Programme Guide; Christian said he needed to add some more guests to the master invitation list ('we *could* get more hotel rooms and air seats, *couldn't we?*'); while Alexis railed at the amount of film reel cans that were being lost in shipment and attendant costs of retrieving them. Surprisingly, no one else ventured much information and neither did Duncan in response, except to say that he was hoping to add a 'surprise presenter' to the Awards Gala listing, that budgets were being 're-crunched' and that we *would* be ready for the festival's opening. 'Even if it means working 24/7.'

Arguments over, I went straight to the Tiffany meeting, parking the white Dodge pick-up about a hundred yards from Tiffany's store on State Street as it would appear somewhat out of place among the Ferraris, Porches and Mercedes convertibles.

Walking into the large, voluminous store, with its chrome-framed floor-to-ceiling windows draped with grey and taupe silk curtains and a luxurious grey-white carpet, I was greeted by the Concierge who checked my name off his list. He immediately called up to Rebecca Madden, the PR Manager, who appeared from the side of the store and led me to her opulent office behind a showroom wall laden with sparkling glass cabinets ornately displaying Paloma

Picasso and Elsa Peretti custom-designed ranges of gold and silver jewellery.

'As we're already a main sponsor and donating gifts for the Awards Gala, which will amount to some one thousand-seven-hundred items, I am not sure if we can really go much further for you guys in terms of the goody bags, especially as you're A-List will already be at the Gala.'

I nodded in agreement, understanding her predicament. 'However,' I said slowly, 'and please don't think me rude, but I wonder how much notice they'll take of that gift, given that they'll see everyone else on their table and neighbouring tables, having the same or similar. And they'll be distracted by the whole process of their going on stage to receive their awards.'

I waited to see if there was a response before continuing. 'I know Tiffany is being exceptionally generous with gifting the entire ballroom, but I was really hoping that we could also give the A-List, and one or two other key celebs, a Tiffany gift in their goody bag which was more, how shall I put it, exclusive? It would be more personal, and they would see that.

'Look, I don't want to overstep the mark here, but you and I both know that the gifting industry in LA is all about PR and brand awareness. I wouldn't be here asking you if we didn't have the stellar names coming in. Would you at least think about it and talk to your boss?'

'Sure Vanessa, will do. Why don't we go and look at some items in case he signs off on this?'

An Aladdin's Cave awaited us. Not knowing where to start or stop, I made a list of possibilities which included the Tiffany Signature ring in gold and silver, the stunning Twist Knot earrings in eighteen-carat gold, an Elsa Peretti 'Diamond-by-the-Yard' bracelet, a Tiffany 1837 business card case, the Paloma Picasso Groove sterling silver cufflinks with red enamel finish, theTiffany Blue leather journal, the Tiffany 1837 suitcase key ring in sterling silver and the Pure Tiffany eau de parfum and Tiffany for Men cologne atomiser.

'When do you think you can let me know?' I asked, as we walked to the door.

'Hopefully by mid-week, is that OK?'

'Well, ten minutes ago would have been better!' I laughed. 'OK, sure. As soon as you can.'

I could not even get into the lobby when I returned to the office; piles of steel cans were covering every inch of floor and desk space, eclipsing the long-suffering Sherri. Walking around to the rear entrance, I found Duncan puffing furiously on a cigarette as he paced up and down.

'What's up?' I asked nervously.

'What isn't up,' he growled. 'I still can't get a frigging budget out of the Board, three studios are constantly changing the goalposts, there's a question mark now over whether Olivia Lautner can even make it to the Gala as her filming schedule keeps changing, Christian's invited more guests and so wants more air seats and Alexis tells me that there's a courier strike in New York, so we probably won't get all our movies shipped in time. What's not to like about that lot?'

I said Reception was awash with film cans and, as if on cue, Alexis flung open the door. 'Bloody Israelis,' she screamed. 'They're saying we have to pay for shipment of the movies if we want them. That's gonna cost close on a thousand dollars. What do you want me to do?'

'Have a frigging cigarette and chill for a second,'

growled Duncan. The three of us sat on the small wall pondering this little predicament before I briefed Duncan on my meeting at Tiffany.

'Nah, they won't give us any more, why should they? They're already doing seventeen-hundred gifts at the Gala.'

I looked him straight in the eyes. 'Oh ye of little faith! Let's wait and see.' Christian sauntered out. 'What's the prob with the Israeli movies?' he demanded. Alexis repeated her dilemma.

'God-damn-it, we have to have those movies. Has everyone forgotten that a large section of the festival is devoted to up-and-coming directors from Israeli cinema?' he seethed. 'Just get them here for Christ's sake. And where are we with the thirty-two-odd Latino movies?'

'Have you *seen* Reception?' I breezily intoned, trying to break the ice.

'Oh, that isn't a quarter of it yet,' he snapped at me, as if to say *'how little you know'*.

'OK, smoke time over, back to work everyone,' snapped an equally testy Duncan. 'Alexis, just pay for the shipment and get those f***ing cans here – and in time for the run-throughs.'

Returning to my desk to start again on the goody bags, a well turned out woman in her late forties flew into the office, threw her things onto the only empty desk in the 'Hollywood Hills' and sank into the chair. The Goblin, Dino and I all looked up in animated formation; it was Lizzie Nicholson, my Transport Manager, who had done the job for the previous three or four years.

'Hi, sorry I couldn't get her last week. The shoot in Pasadena took longer than planned. Guess you're Vanessa?'

I smiled and half-nodded. 'And I guess you're Lizzie?' More nodding. 'Well Lizzie, this is Dino, who's doing hotels, and Mike, who's in charge of flights, and there's another Mike who isn't here today, but you'll get to meet him tomorrow. And that's the team to do all this crazy work.'

'So, who's my assistant?' she demanded. 'I've done this job many times and don't need you to tell me what to do, but I can't do it single-handedly. I need an assistant. And I don't report to you, just Duncan.'

As I explained that we did not have the luxury of having assistants, even though we could all do with one, and that she would, in fact, be reporting to me, I could see Anna out of the corner of my eye with her index finger against her temple as if a gun were being held to her head. I knew instantly what she was trying to tell me – that Lizzie,while experienced, was going to be trouble, though as I got to know Lizzie, both professionally and socially, I really warmed to her. It was just that she was too similar to me – neither suffered fools nor took prisoners.

Having briefed Lizzie on the staff meeting and situation with both Mercedes – who had just emailed Ed and Duncan authorization for twelve top-of-the-range S-Class Sedans and two Maybachs, but not the four we had originally been promised – and the car rental partner I was still chasing, I left her to sit down with The Goblin; we needed a preliminary LAX and local airport pick-up programme, mapped out on the flights information we already had and what we expected the arrivals to be. I wondered whether she and The Goblin would get on; as I suspected, they did not.

'No way,' said Dino, knowing exactly what I was thinking, as he came and sat next to me to run over the hotel grid. Within five minutes, Lizzie and The Goblin were arguing over some trifling matter.

'Lizzie, shut the bleep up, you're doing my head in

already,' yelled The Goblin for the entire office's benefit. 'There'll be plenty of proper stuff to argue over in the next couple of weeks and I'm in charge here, so you do what I say anyhow.'

Dino tapped my calf with his right foot as if to say "this is going to be fun if we have this crap going on all the time". I got up and walked over to The Goblin's desk.

'OK Mike, cut the attitude. We've got enough to do without petty histrionics and I hate to spoil your afternoon, but you are not in charge of Guest Services. That's my role, as well you know. So may I suggest that you both apologize to each other now and let's work as a team.

'Lizzie, I know you've done Transport here for several years and have a wealth of experience, so Mike and I will be relying heavily on your judgement to dovetail flights and pick-up's. But if there are any problems at all, either with cars or people, you come to me, OK? And if either of you have a problem with me being in charge of the department, then you can go to Duncan, although with what he is juggling at the moment, I don't think he'll be impressed or amused if you did go to him. Are we clear?'

'I get to allocate the two Maybachs and the S-Classes, don't I?' asked Lizzie.

'Erm, no, sorry, that's my job. The Maybachs are only for the A-List on the Awards night and they're my responsibility, so I decide which two stars have them. As for the S-Classes, we'll need to work together on that as we'll use them for the remaining A-List on that night, as well as key film directors, producers and studio heads. We'll work together on deciding which guests need better cars for airport transfers and, for the remaining guests, you can decide whether it's the rental cars or the S-Class. But just keep me in the loop at all times.'

She looked disappointed, but understood my reasoning.

'Why don't you draw up a list of all the volunteer drivers from previous years that we are likely to have and email or phone them to get them on board?' I said with an encouraging nod of my head. 'We need to have those names ASAP.'

'I'll do it tomorrow, I have to go home and check my stuff has arrived from Pasadena,' she said tersely as she scooped up her belongings.

'One tricky dame,' chuckled Dino, as Lizzie flounced out.

'Yes, but she has got the worst job in Guest Services and she knows the ropes and where the skeletons are, so let's give her some leeway,' I said, suddenly feeling hugely sympathetic for the poor woman.

There was still an inordinate amount to sort out for the hospitality suite, let alone flights, cars and studio demands, which were beginning to pour into my Inbox. I baulked when I had finished my list of items for the hospitality suite under the headings Technology, Decor, Catering, Publications, Volunteer staff and General.

There was the small issue of which publications and glossy magazines we featured in the suite; it went without saying that obviously Variety, The Hollywood Reporter and Screen International would be there as they were the 'industry bibles', but we had been approached by Entertainment Weekly, People, USA Today and Harpers Bazaar, to name but a few.

I took a visibly deep breath.

Today I could at least look forward to lunch with Charles at The Four Seasons to discuss Ed's cocktail party. But before then, I had to get on top of the goody bags and the hospitality suite situation or, to use its proper name, The Guest & Industry Suite. I put in a call to Jon Bauer at The Wyndham.

'Hi, could I come and see you later today. There are a few things I need to run by you in terms of our requirements, and also agree what the hotel can provide and what we need to bring in ourselves.' There was the usual pause.

'What is it that you need to discuss?' he said in a tone which indicated a meeting was the last thing he could be bothered with.

'There's too much to run through in a phone call and it would be very helpful to have the Conference & Banqueting person in on it as well so we can just get everything signed off today,' I said firmly.

'OK,' he said reluctantly, 'how about four?'

'Perfect, see you then. And you'll have your C & B Director there?' I repeated again, so that he got the message that this person was more important to me on this occasion than he was.

I enlisted Dino's help with the goody bags as the other Mike – the nice one, to be known as Mike 2 – was now needed back in New York until next week. We both looked at last year's 'swag' list with disdain, for it was distinctly unimpressive and unexciting, though we both knew we could not compete with the Oscars goody bags which were rumoured to contain gifts worth over $100,000.

The whole goody bag culture has an interesting history; created in the early 1980s, the Oscar bag was designed as a token of appreciation for some forty key production staff. Growing incrementally over the years to encompass all the other film and music awards ceremonies, movie premieres and celebrity book launches, it has mushroomed into the 'beat-this-if-you-can' freebie culture that is testimony to the relentless growth of star power.

As such, the goody bag (or 'swag') has become a core ingredient of the star system, serving simultaneously as an advertisement, a bribe and a measure of celebrity; the bigger the star, the better the gifts must be.

As I was explaining to Dino that the gifts are donated by companies who are anxious to 'buy into' an event's glamorous association – such as the Awards Gala ceremony – and that the celebrity endorsement, however low-key in photographs, was regarded as a valuable marketing tool, Duncan walked by and, overhearing our discussion, told us with glee that there were 'people in LA with entire closets, bathrooms and family rooms filled with free stuff.'

Finding our goody bag task more interesting than re-doing the budgets, he slumped into a chair and continued.

'The excess has gone stratospheric, it's kinda become bag porn now. At a recent Academy Awards, the bags included a $6,000 wide-screen digital TV and a week-long Caribbean cruise. And at Sundance, they went as far as having a swag-house where the stars weren't given a bag, they simply grabbed whatever they wanted from the gift room. The only condition being they had to be photographed with the product.

'You know, people used to go to events and parties wondering who they'd meet and, hopefully, score with. Now they just want to know *what* they will leave with. It's crazy, and the worst thing is that now the publicists all ring up and want to know what's in the bag.'

I laughed nervously. 'So, Duncan, no pressure then on us to come up with a half-decent goody bag!'

Dino and I set about making two generic lists: one for the Awards Gala – the A-List receiving and presenting the awards, but which also included the English actor-director coming out for Closing Night, plus a spare bag (twenty-two bags) the other list for the two hundred filmmakers and industry guests.

The priority was to get the A-List bags done first. I ideally wanted such items as a Tiffany gift, a Mercedes-Benz gift, a rose gold Montblanc fountain pen, a small leather item from Hermés, a pair of Louis Vitton iconic Soupçon oversized sunglasses, the latest iPhone, the Sony HD Handycam, billed as the world's smallest high-definition camcorder, a three-night stay with spa treatments at the sumptuous Parrot Cay resort in the Turks & Caicos, the latest Frédéric Fekkai age-defying hair product, something from Smythsons – the upscale English stationers who was all the rage in LA following its store opening on Rodeo Drive – and a weekend in the Kennedy Cottage of the hip San Ysidro ranch just outside Santa Barbara.

My blue-sky-thinking was now so far off the radar that I wanted to include the world's most expensive hand-made chocolate, The Madeleine, a combination of French Valrhona cocoa powder rolled over a French Perigord black truffle and sitting on a bed of sugar pearls in a silver box wrapped in ribbon. As each chocolate costs $250, I figured the makers, Chocopologie by Knipschildt, would summarily decline my request.

I also wanted some smaller, funky items such as the Kerstin Florian Myrrh Nail Oil, the Ciroc Vodka 'strobe-effect' flashing ice-cubes and Bath & Bodywork's fabulous Eucalyptus Spearmint Sugar Scrub.

For the industry filmmaker guests bags, our list earmarked a Cavallini Moderno journal from Lincoln Stationers, Evian face spritzers, Kerstin Florian Spa Face Lipo-Marine Crème and Sun Spa sunscreen, Frédéric Fekkai hair products, a travel alarm-clock from hip electrical supplier Sharper Image, specialty chocolates from Godiva, a high-end photographic book of the city and a couple of new Blu Rays from the studios. We would also try and persuade Mercedes to give us a further two hundred pens

Surveying the list, Dino said to me, 'You know what we haven't included? What about hangover gear, you know, for all the headaches they're gonna have each morning.'

My eyes widened. 'Good thinking Dino. Delighted to see your parents' vast fees for Yale were well spent! What do we need? Tylenol, Berocca, eye gel, breath freshener, a detox drink… what the hell, let's see if someone does a Bloody Mary kit. Hair of the dog is always the best remedy in my book.'

Christian, who had decided he needed to be part of this conversation, popped his head over the wall and commanded, 'Better get a bunch for all of us too. We're gonna need something to get us through this festival.'

Lists done, we now had the Herculean task of pitching our donation requests to the relevant companies. It was going to be a hard sell as we were neither the Cannes nor Venice film festivals – nor even Sundance or Toronto – but Variety magazine had said in a recent editorial that the festival "… has made a mark during Oscar season …", so I reckoned we had a chance of securing some of the A-List items. While it would be one thing to get the A-List gifts, it would be quite another to ask a company, some of them small ones, for two-hundred-plus items (knowing that many of the festival's core staff would want one).

'Jeez, that's ambitious,' gasped Duncan as he swung by again. 'If you get *any* of that lot, make sure there's an extra swag for me.'

The three Valet Parking guys looked faintly amused as I roared around the turning-circle, replete with requisite fountain in the middle, and pulled up at the *porte-cochère* in my Dodge pick-up. This was definitely not what The Four Seasons was used to.

'Hi, I'm in charge of celebrity guests for the film festival,' I said, confidently tossing the keys at one of them, just so that they did not think I was some bag-lady. 'I'm having lunch with Charles Rutherford. Guess I'll be about an hour.'

As if on cue, they chorused, 'Of course, madam, we'll take the utmost care of your car,' as one of them jumped in and drove it away to the car park at the rear while the Concierge hurriedly flung open the doors and half-bowed his head as I walked through. As I was soon to be visiting The Four Seasons on an almost daily basis, this pattern of reverence from all of them became something of a joke and was incrementally exacerbated with each visit – for both sides' amusement – so that, by the time the stars had all departed from the hotel, the bowing and scraping had reached epic proportions.

Charles had witnessed all this from the lobby, where he was bidding farewell to some exceedingly rich guests – a couple, both of whom were draped in furs, diamonds, Oyster Rolexes and bespoke apparel by Briony. Finishing his conversation, he walked over and gave me a hug. '*What are* you doing to my staff?' he quizzed, laughingly. I gave him a kiss on both cheeks.

'Oh Charles, they know *who* the most important people are, even if one does arrive in a pick-up!'

We walked through to the Terrace Bar where a glass of Roederer Cristal champagne was immediately produced. 'I assume this is what you'd like?' Charles quipped.

'More than that, my darling, it's what I *need* right now,' I laughed, 'as you'll see when we talk over lunch.'

After quickly catching up on the latest industry gossip and *affaires de coeur,* I began with my list for the festival, feeling that the requirements for Ed's cocktail party would require further fortification for both of us from the Cristal bottle.

'Just need to absolutely double-check that we have twenty-two Deluxe Villas for two nights and six Junior Poolside Suites for eight nights. If needed, we could also request six Deluxe Lanaii king-size rooms for five nights?' He nodded.

'Great. Now, spa treatments. Can the A-List have complimentary spa treatments while they are here?'

'Yeah, sure, but only the AA-List!' he laughed, 'those that are being honoured at, or are presenting at, the Awards Gala. For the other celebs, the A-minus-one-List as I call it, we'll give them fifty per cent off.'

'OK, cool. Now, in the villas for the key celebs, the AA-list as you call them, I'd like to have a really decent white floral arrangement, a basket of fruits from Whole Foods, a bottle of Roederer Cristal, the Godiva Chocolate Truffles Gift Box and some Provence soaps. Is that OK?'

Charles looked momentarily askance. 'Boy, you don't want much do you?' he grinned. 'OK, OK, as it's you. I'll get Stephanie, our Special Events executive, onto that.'

I suddenly thought of something else. 'I assume the villas do have Broadband in them and they're Wireless enabled?'

'But of course,' said Charlie, raising his eyebrows at my doubt. 'We'll ensure they are not parted from their laptop, iPhone or BlackBerry at any time.'

Moving through to the poolside terraced dining room, I forewarned Charles about Ed's cocktail party.

'You know that Tiffany is also hosting its own reception and has taken a suite,' he said. This rather important detail had not made its way to me in the office.

'Well, I assume Ed must know that as he'll be on the guest list. What's the date of it? Ed's is the night before the Awards Gala and is essentially for the A-List, studio heads, directors and key city dignitaries. I assume Tiffany is doing it more for their key customers and business partners, so they shouldn't clash too much.'

Charles fired off a quick text on his BlackBerry. 'Should have the date in a minute.'

Settling into the Zoffany-covered chairs, I broached the subject of the cocktail party. Charlie, as he had now become, was being far more sensible. 'Let's order first, then we can get down to business. If you like fish I'd recommend the coconut shrimp for an appetizer, the seared scallops and Dungeness crab cakes with baby fennel and blood oranges for the entrée, and then the petit tiramisu in espresso cups for dessert.'

How refreshing; a man who takes control. We ordered and then returned to the nerve-racking subject of the cocktail party.

I outlined to Charlie what I had suggested to Ed and waited for his reaction, expecting him to blanch visibly before me. Completely nonplussed, he said the hotel could organize all of it, even down to the red and black voile cocktail napkins and black slate oblong servers, and suggested that we hold it in The Grand Ballroom.

'A friend of mine runs Huntingdon Catering in Hollywood. They cater for all the absolute top parties in LA. I'm sure I can persuade him to come and do this gig – and for a greatly reduced fee as there'll be so many stellar names there.'

'That's great. Charlie, you'll go to heaven,' I leapt up and gave him a huge hug and kiss.

We began our lunch and, as he promised to show me The Grand Ballroom after dessert, there was now only one more favour I had to ask.

'I'll need a villa again towards the end of the festival for about five nights. We have a very well-known British actor coming out. His directorial debut is our Closing Night movie.' Charlie nodded approval while delicately extracting the tiramisu from the espresso cup. 'And while he wouldn't necessarily be on *your* AA-List he is, nonetheless, a key celeb both in the UK and here, and he needs to be accorded the same treatment and gifts as we are doing for the Awards Gala stars. Is that OK?'

'Who is it?' asked Charlie, suddenly looking interested.

'It's Daniel Eversleigh and sorry, but he isn't gay,' I reproached teasingly.

As we were leaving to go and see The Grand Ballroom, I suddenly spotted a familiar face. 'Isn't that Kate Berryman from "Frenemies". And who is she with?'

Glancing over, Charlie confirmed it was indeed whom I thought and said casually, 'Oh, I think he's some musician. Apparently, she's been seeing him under the radar for a while. Probably just trying to win back her ex-husband, not that *that* will work.'

The Grand Ballroom would be perfect; large enough for around one hundred guests, small enough to be intimate, and flanked by the pool and the rose garden. The doors on both sides opened out onto the pool terrace and garden, which could be adorned with fairy lights and hurricane lamps to add cosy lighting.

'Charlie, this is fabulous. Can I book it right now so that I can tell Ed it is confirmed?'

We went back to the Front Office where Charlie personally logged in the booking.

'All done and Stephanie will now be your point-person for the event. She'll liaise with Huntingdon Catering and anything else you need. Just call her directly.'

I drove back to the office to pick up messages – a stupid mistake as there was a ton of them – and then went off to The Wyndham for my meeting with Jon Bauer.

Waiting in the vast lobby area for him to come down, I ruminated on how I was going to approach this Herculean task, for he was not a particularly receptive person and certainly not in the same league as Charlie in terms of General Managers; he did not seem that bothered about helping the festival, even though it was a high profile event for his hotel. I kept glancing over to the two connecting banqueting rooms which would be our hospitality suite for ten long days, mentally visualizing what the lobby would look like once we got going.

Jon appeared after a fifteen-minute wait. 'Sorry, Corporate HQ needed to run through some things urgently, not least of which was the festival.' He proffered a hand which I shook firmly.

'Thank you for your time in seeing me. I think it'll be to our mutual benefit if we can cover off quite a lot of elements now.'

I followed him up to the Executive Offices, where we launched straight into battle.

'I have a list here of what we *absolutely* need in the hospitality suite,' I said firmly as I pushed the sheet of paper towards him. It was covered from top to toe with bulleted items; as he perused it, his brow furrowed repeatedly.

'I hope I haven't forgotten anything. I'll also need to know the extension numbers of each of the ten phones, so that I can give them to everyone that might need to contact us urgently. And then there are other elements which we don't expect the hotel to provide, but which we'll need to bring in from outside.'

'That's quite a list you've got here. Are you sure this is *all* you need?' he said, sarcastically. Ignoring the brinkmanship that appeared to be in play, I simply replied, 'Yes, I believe so at this point. But if there is anything else, I'll be sure to call you.'

Before he would agree to anything on my list, he wanted to know what the 'outside' items would be.

'Oh, you know, décor. We'll need drapes and piping to mask the trestle tables, at least two three-seater sofas, four or five armchairs, two tall, free-standing lamps and a few table lamps, which hopefully you can provide, two large floral arrangements for the central room columns and about ten floral arrangements for the tables, plus some artwork for the walls.

'And we need to clarify now that the hotel will allow us to serve Starbucks coffee at breakfast, rather than your own. I quite appreciate you may not like this as you'll be losing F&B revenue, and we'll also be serving Teccino's herbal coffees and teas during the day. We'll also need you to sign off on our bringing in food, wines, spirits and soft drinks, all of which will be kindly donated by local grocery stores, restaurants and distributors.

'And, finally, there is the small issue of which publications and glossy magazines we can have in the suite. I'm assuming you'd have no objection to Variety, Hollywood Reporter, Screen International, People, Harpers Bazaar or USA Today?'

Clicking his pen with one hand while tapping the desk with the other for what seemed an interminable length, he surveyed the list again and again, finally raising his head slowly.

'Well, you drive a hard, if not overly ambitious, bargain.'

Ignoring the sarcasm, I asked if this meant he was willing to sign off on the list and the outside items, gently reminding him of the PR and kudos his hotel would be gaining.

'Corporate has sunk a heck of a wedge of money into this festival in terms of donating guest rooms, meetings rooms and services. I can't say I necessarily agree with it, but it's a done deal and so I have to deliver a return. So yeah, you can have what's on your list, but only because I believe it will help the return on investment.'

Before he had a chance to change his mind, I pushed the piece of paper back towards him, indicating that he write either 'OK' or ' Agreed' on the sheet and confirm it with his initials and date.

'And what about Starbucks providing coffee and bringing in our own food items and drinks?' I asked nervously, for this would be a deal-breaker if he refused.

'I'll make an exception on this occasion, but keep it discreet. I don't want Meetings Planners in the locality thinking they can save money by bringing in their own supplies. It's only because the festival is a not-for-profit organization and it brings in tourism dollars to the city that we're even allowing this.'

Thanking him again for his time and, more importantly, his largess, even though it had taken almost two hours, I confirmed I would put the contents of our meeting on an email that evening and asked that he could reply by return to again confirm all the points.

Stepping out of the elevator, I spotted Diana in the

lobby talking to a woman. I walked over to her.

'Hey, didn't know you were here,' she cried. 'What have you been up to?'

I started to explain, but she cut in, 'Sorry Cathy, this is Vanessa Vere Houghton, my friend from England I was telling you about. The one who is heading up Guest Services and looking after all the key celebrities.'

'Hi,' said Cathy, 'Good to meet you.'

Turning back to me, Diana continued, 'Vanessa, this is my friend Cathy who works on the Daily News Press. She's in charge of the editorial content of both the festival programme guide and the daily news reports. And she's married to the editor, so a key person to know. We thought we'd run through the programme guide away from our offices and over a drink. Fancy joining us?'

'Hi Cathy, it's good to meet you also. Sure, I'd love to join you. I've just had a pretty tricky meeting with Jon Bauer, but got everything we need for the hospitality suite, including his agreement for us to bring in outside food and beverages.'

'Hey, good work,' said Cathy. 'I trust the paper will have full access to the suite and its treasure trove?'

'But of course,' Diana chipped in, 'Vanessa will make sure of that.'

'Then I think the paper would want us to have a glass of champagne,' grinned Cathy.

'Or two or three,' mocked Diana, as we walked over to the elegant lobby bar, already heaving with people.

Three tall, dark-haired, good-looking guys huddled over scripts commanded one end of the long bar. They were dressed in Rock & Republic jeans and Armani shirts to display their impressive tans. One was tapping furiously on his laptop, while the other two interjected with pitch ideas.

'Mr Laptop' was particularly attractive – a doppelganger for Bradley Cooper. Cathy saw that my eyes had alighted on him.

'Do you want to meet him?'

'Do you know him?'

'Yes, he's Rob Palmer. On Hollywood's radar as one of the most creative new screenwriters. I've met him a few times, so I can easily go over.'

'Oh, he wouldn't be interested in meeting me.'

'A sassy English gal like you. Of course he would. Anyway, I want to interview him for the paper, so that's a good reason to go over to them and then I can casually introduce you and Diana. And we'll see what happens.'

Cathy walked over to them and, after a few minutes, Rob followed her back to our table.

'Rob, this is Diana, the Marketing Director, and Vanessa, who's in charge of all the A-List celebs and filmmakers. Come and join us, I want to pitch an interview idea to you.'

Deciding that my role might be of value to him, he pulled a chair up next to me, rather than taking the empty one by Diana, while Cathy outlined her proposed article. Business concluded, Rob turned to me and, locking his piercing blue eyes onto mine, wanted to know everthing I was doing at the festival, how an English girl had landed this 'amazing gig', which directors and producers were coming in – and could I get him into the hospitality suite and various parties.

We talked earnestly for a couple of hours, oblivious to Cathy's and Diana's presence. He told me about his privileged childhood in Malibu, his Ivy League college, how he wanted to be an actor but failed all the auditions and so turned to screenwriting. He had crafted two scripts and now needed to get them in front of a key director or producer – which is where I came in.

Suddenly remembering I had to go and do the email to Jon Bauer, but not wanting to tear myself away, I gave him my card as I got up, saying a little flirtatiously, 'I'm sure we'll run into each other during the next few days.'

Rob pre-empted my wish with the suggestion of a 'pit-stop lunch' the next day at Flemings – no doubt so that he could try and find someone to pitch to – and we settled on twelve-thirty. He returned to join his friends and I walked out of the hotel as if on sunshine. Though not for long.

It was after eight-thirty when I got back to the office and I was surprised to see a few stragglers still at their desks. Scanning my Inbox and telephone spike, the ton of messages from earlier that afternoon had doubled, with many from the studios marked 'urgent', but I really could not face dealing with them. They would have to wait until morning. I carefully composed my letter to Jon Bauer, detailing exactly what had been discussed, agreed and confirmed, and emailed it to him, marking it 'High Priority'. It was after ten o'clock when I left, consciously noting not to make this a habit.

But I was soon to discover that ten o'clock would be an early day.

CHAPTER EIGHT

Driving to work in the wall-to-wall sunshine, I marvelled at how beautiful everything was – mountains with a sprinkling of summit snow, majestic palm trees lining the boulevards, manicured lawns and immaculate flowerbeds, ritzy, private, gated communities with perfectly-timed fountains, ûber-luxurious hotels, impossibly-perfect golf courses with their exclusive residences, and swathes of Ferraris, Porches and Mercedes sports models. Even the Hummers were attractive. It sure as hell beat my previous London commute on the Underground to Covent Garden.

Eight-thirty a.m. and already there were problems; people rushed around, yelling and waving sheets of paper at each other – the most vociferous being the Print Traffic Department's supremo Alexis, her assistant Damien, Bud the Transport Manager and Hannah. Negotiating my way through the fluid mountain of movie reels that now occupied every conceivable bit of spare floor space, I found The Goblin in a tirade; an independent production company – an 'indie' – had emailed overnight with required flight changes for their party of five guests.

'Don't they f***-ing well know how f***-ing difficult it is to get flights in the first place, let alone make f***-ing changes?' he screamed, staring, in turn, at me, Dino, Hannah and Christian who had arrived, as if on cue, clutching a very large coffee. 'They're only a f***-ing small indie, it's not as though we're dealing with The Weinstein Company or DreamWorks here.'

Christian looked bemused as if, in a perverse sort of way, he was pleased things were starting to go wrong, for the hardest part of his job was now over. He had the movies he wanted for the festival and he could now, more or less, sit back and enjoy everyone else's miseries and frustrations in getting their assignments done, and on time.

'You think the big guys are not going to give you grief? Just you wait,' he said, as if he was the headmaster lecturing his band of naughty pupils, before sashaying off around the corner to his den – via Duncan's office for a quick early-morning general bitch.

'How's the grid looking Dino? And have you and Mike sent the email chasers for RSPVs?' I questioned urgently. 'We must have the invited guests pinned down as soon as possible, so that if they cannot attend, we can then move onto the B list.'

He nodded to affirm that they had sent the chasers. 'But only a couple have come back, so we're working on those now.'

'If people have not responded within forty-eight hours, you and Mike must send a second chaser, marked Urgent and sent as High Priority, saying that if we do not hear from them within the next forty-eight hours, we'll assume they are unable to attend and their allocation will be passed to another guest.'

'You can't do that,' yelled Christian, periscoping his head over the wall now nicknamed Mulholland Drive, 'they're *my* guests and it may just be that they're out of their offices this week. You must leave them all as they stand.'

The Goblin, having decided he really did not like me and was not going to do anything I asked, agreed loudly with Christian. Hearing the rising voices from the Hollywood Hills, Duncan appeared in the archway.

'Hey, I'm with Vanessa. She has a point. We're three weeks out, we've got a major holiday coming up which will close most offices and we have to know whether people are attending or not. I'm not running a god-damn festival on the basis that some frigging filmmaker might deign to turn up or not. Mike, Dino, send the chasers in forty-eight hours. And that's that Christian. Period.'

Christian shot me a withering glance, whereupon I shot back an equally lacerating one, though this was no time to be smug. There was a ton of stuff to get through and it was building incrementally. I decided to leave the studio emails until the after my pit-stop lunch with Rob – in hindsight, never a good policy – and pulled out from the bottom of the pile the folder marked 'Hospitality Suite Food & Beverages', tossing it onto the only part of the desk that was not already covered by the ubiquitous little 'Absolutely Bleeping Urgent' Post It notes.

Though the two restaurants were back on board, meaning that most of the evenings were covered with proper suppers or fork buffets, the hoary chestnut that was the confirmation and signing of the contracts for the staple food donations was growing by the day. I again enlisted Dino's help.

'Hmm,' he said, flicking through last year's donation log, 'they didn't seem to bother very much with anything last year. In comparison, you look as though you're trying to run a Michelin-starred restaurant.'

Supper, under the banner heading of 'Cocktails' was to be the main event; the suite would serve cocktails, wines and spirits from five o'clock onwards, with hot dishes being delivered around six o'clock so that everyone could start eating around six-thirty and be out in time for the plethora of receptions, private screenings and parties that dominated each evening's calendar. Cocktails were supposed to finish at eight o'clock, but if someone did not have a party to go to that evening, they could always linger in the suite until around nine-thirty; we always had myriad items to run through and check off for the next day, and it was easier to do it in the suite when all the core and volunteer Guest Services staff were there.

For the evening bar, we would have Bloody Mary's by the gallon – a very prescient choice as it turned out – wines from Napa Valley, Chile and Argentina – the latter to please a director being honoured at the Awards Gala – Coca Cola, mixers and beers, plus Red Bull to keep energy levels up for the heroic partying that most guests indulged in.

Leaving him as he drew up another of what would become Dino's famous grids – in fact, by the time we got to the eve of the festival, there was almost a grid for breathing and sleeping – I made my escape to meet Rob.

Sliding onto a bar stool on the outside terrace, I noticed a black Porsche Boxster pull up and park in one of the only four spaces at Flemings. Out stepped Rob, looking every inch the Hollywood star, not a fledgling screenwriter. He did seem to have a lot of money for someone purportedly making their own way without family support, I mused, as he glided in, ordering two glasses of champagne – to accompany a burger!

'Hey you, wasn't sure if you'd show.'

'Neither was I, but only because work is beyond crazy. I'll need to be quick.'

Wolfing down our burgers and champagne, there was

just enough time for Rob to tell me he had to go to Mexico at the weekend, but would be back next week.

'What's in Mexico?'

'Oh, just some unfinished business, but it should be worthwhile. If you weren't working, you could come down with me.'

'Sounds a plan! Perhaps we can take a raincheck and do Mexico after all this mayhem is over.'

I later dialled the Business Development Manager, a strange woman called Hayley Conway who was your new best friend one day and had no idea who you were the next. I later learned that she was gay and, as I did not know any lesbians, wondered if this was one of their peccadilloes. She was obviously having a bad hair day. 'Yup,' she snapped.

'Hey, Hayley, how are you today?' I said, determined to swop some basic pleasantries before we started the gritty business of sorting out alcohol.

'Whad'ya want?' she snapped again.

'I need to know where we're at with drinks donations. Do we have the Ciroc vodka and wines? I've had an email from Harry's secretary asking for quantities. I've calculated that we need five hundred red and five hundred white, assuming half a bottle per person times ten days.'

'Don't be ridiculous,' she hissed, 'there's no way on earth we can ask for that and we don't need that much anyway. You Europeans drink far too much!'

Treating this remark with the contempt it deserved, I blithely ignored her and carried on. 'We'll need at least five bottles of vodka per day, so that's fifty bottles of Ciroc, or Grey Goose, but we really want the Ciroc so we can have their stupendously wonderful flashing ice cubes. For the beer, Red Bull, mixers and water, assuming twenty-four in a case and allowing for one per person per day, that's eighty cases – so let's make it one-hundred cases of each.'

There was an audible sigh, one of a pained expression. 'Are you crazy? We're never going to get this much and I'm not going to ask Harry for this amount. You're going to have to scale right back and that's that.'

Tensions were starting to run high and it was only mid afternoon.

'Fine. I'll go to Harry if you don't want to. But I cannot scale back as this is already bare bones. And I am not going to have a hospitality suite where there's no frigging hospitality to be had. That rather defeats the object, doesn't it?' I said impatiently. 'And you know as well as I do that Duncan, Christian and Hannah will go ballistic if they haven't got a decent hospitality suite. Let me know what you can't be bothered to do and I'll do it myself.'

I took a deep breath before resuming with Dino, working through the rest of the afternoon, putting in call after call and following up successful contacts with emailed letters of confirmation for their signature. By about six o'clock, I could no longer leave all the dreaded emails from the studios, and so started pouring over them.

I now had one hundred-and-forty-five and, while it initially looked ghastly, I soon realised that, given the American propensity for CYA (Cover Your Ass), the majority of the emails were 'thoughts' of myriad people to whom the original email had also been copied. Now came the annoying task of scrolling back to the beginning of each email to see what the original question or statement was, then filtering through all the cc'd responses to see if we could all arrive at one universal agreement. As I was soon to discover over the next couple of weeks, that in itself was something of a joke.

Scrolling back to the beginning of my Inbox for

yesterday's influx and speed-reading my way through them all, it quickly became apparent that the studios' marketing and publicity executives were not emailing me to help me in any way, such as to advise when their 'talent' would be available so that, God forbid, we could begin to start making the necessary travel plans. They were, in fact, all emailing me with more questions: at what time *exactly* would (star name) be going up on stage to receive the award?; who *exactly* would be presenting the award?; how long *exactly* would the award presentation speech be?; how long *exactly* was (star name) expected to be on stage; how long *exactly* was the award acceptance speech expected to be?; who *exactly* would be writing said acceptance speech?; how long *exactly* would they be waiting in the Green Room?; please confirm there would be a Green Room; who *exactly* would accompany (star name) in the Green Room?; who is the wrangler? (showbiz speak for a person who temporarily "handles" a star's needs for a specific event, such as an awards ceremony or film premiere); could I confirm that the show host was Natalie Immber, one of the key anchors on Entertainment Tonight?

And so it went on and with each extra person cc'd, so extra questions – or 'thoughts' – were added to the fray. To compound matters, the CYA brigade also cc'd Duncan who, in his haste to get through much the same exercise with all his mail, merely forwarded his cc's on to me, thus mushrooming my Inbox five-fold.

The problem was that none of this had yet been finalised with Rocco Tramanti, the Awards Gala Producer. Although he had crafted this show for numerous years and naturally had an outline framework in his mind, he nonetheless would not even have any idea himself about the running order and timings until about a week beforehand, as he adapted, corrected, changed and again re-worked the whole event.

I started emailing replies to this effect to everyone and, within the space of about five minutes after I had hit the Send button, there was a reply in my Inbox! Oh God, about another ninety emails – most of them saying just 'thanks' – but some asking more questions and, of course, each email had to be read through again in case there was the faint possibility of someone actually giving us information. It was a deeply arduous and deflating task and one which was to be repeated about ten times every day from hereon in.

It was about eight-thirty when I had finally finished addressing all the emails and subsequent responses that had arrived during the past forty-eight hours. I had advised the studio marketing and publicity executives, as well as the publicists I knew of at this stage who personally handled the stars, of the *proposed* running order of the Awards Gala: start times for red carpet arrivals, cocktails, Green Room, escort to table, dinner, the show, actual presentation on stage, very approximate length of acceptance speech, time of photocall, rough timings for post-show media interviews in the Green Room and roughly when the ceremony would end.

I had not stipulated the actual running order of the stars being called up on stage to receive their award as Duncan and Ed were still negotiating with two studios over a couple of key A-List ones they wanted as presenters. Until we had this nailed down, Rocco could not work out the order of the actual presentations as it would depend on how 'big' the stars were that were presenting. We had to be mindful of the studios' egos, in terms of their talent's position on the running order and try not to put anyone's noses out of joint. Poor Rocco, the Awards Gala was just one long juggling act, with everyone around him railing over some minor dispute or other; it was, as I soon discovered, a minefield and how he negotiated his way through it each year without being torn to shreds I shall never know.

I repeated the caveat that this running order was extremely tentative and that the show producer would only have it finalised about seventy-two hours out – obviously omitting the fact that we were still trying to tie down certain stars' agents over their presenting appearances, and that the producer deemed it *his* show and so what *he* said went and that it was non-negotiable.

I had thought that this would be enough, but, no. Back the emails came, streaming in like the Angel Falls, this time asking detailed questions such as: what time would the limo pick-up be from the hotel?; what type of limos were they?; how long would it take from the hotel to the Gala venue?; who were the drivers?; would they have the same driver for return to the hotel as to the Gala?; how long would the photocall be?; who were the photographers?; how many media interviews would there be in the Green Room?; how quickly could they (their star) get away?; and during the Gala itself, where was their talent's table positioned and could they approve the positioning before it was confirmed?

The problem now was that the first cast of thousand who had been copied in on the CYA emails had, in turn, decided to copy everyone they seemed to know at their respective studio; the Angel Falls gathered momentum and soon became the raging torrents of the Zambezi River. They had all, well the majority of them, also forgotten to ask first time around ... when could they have a copy of the entire show script because they needed one now to run by their Business Affairs Department.

Oh. My. God. I looked in utter disbelief as I watched, at

nine-thirty, this surge of emails cascading into my Inbox. Where the hell was a Microsoft crash when one needed it! Just as I was putting my index finger to my temple in mock suicide, Ingrid roared in, evidently in a foul mood and, throwing her bulging Armani tote onto her desk, screamed at the entire office.

'God-damn frigging people. The f***-ing props company is now saying we can't have the stuff I ordered weeks ago because, apparently, some stupid little arse of a girl has already booked it out. What the f*** am I supposed to do now? Those props were for the Opening Night party, the Starbucks party at The Palms, three of the Consul events and the Gay-La party. Jeez, will someone help me with an idea of how to get out of this cluster-f***?'

We all had our own minor crises to deal with, so there was not much of a response. I ventured that she try Movies Props Magic in Culver City as I had read an article in the LA Times about them and, although small and run by two young guys who were both ex 'wannabe actors', appeared lean and hungry. They would, I was sure, be the answer to Ingrid's dilemma.

'Call them now,' I urged her.

Needing a distraction from my tsunami of emails, I swivelled my chair over to Ingrid's desk where we Googled Movies Props Magic, browsing all the props and paraphernalia we could buy or hire.

'Look, there are autographed movie scripts, life-size cardboard stand-ups, vintage movie posters and celebrity autographed photographs,' I said, feeling rather pleased with myself at remembering the article and company name.

'This is a real find, Vanessa, it's like an Aladdin's Cave. I think we ought to concentrate on the autographed movie scripts, but also get a couple of stand-ups and a couple of signed photographs. Which ones shall we go for?'

'You know, you could always try Paperbag Princess, if you wanted a fashionista approach.'

'What the hell is that?' she asked, giving me a resigned look.

'My God, you don't know? It's the most to-die-for shop in LA. It's in Beverly Hills and is the most wonderful, just the most fab, high-end 'thrift shop'. But they have everything, and I mean everything, not just designer gowns worn by stars to the Oscars and Golden Globes, but handbags, boots, shoes – including Jimmy Choos and Manolo Blahniks – evening and day dresses, jeans, coats and so on…'

Ingrid's face lightened. 'H-e-y, we could do a sort of fashion approach for the French Consul party. Like where you're coming from, Vanessa. Thanks. Can't be arsed to look at their website tonight though, I'll do it tomorrow. Remind me.'

Having had enough of a distraction to temporarily no longer wish to commit suicide, I returned to my Inbox, inwardly cursing whomever it was who had invented the whole concept of electronic mail. The Zambezi was nearing the end of its journey and the emails were, thankfully, now just trickling in. It was after ten o'clock and time to go and hook up with Diana, JP and Cathy for a restorative glass or two of Merlot. I shut down my computer, yelled 'Goodnight' to those remaining and walked out to the car park. The night air was crisp and clear, there was a full moon, stars shone brightly, the fonds of the palm trees swayed gently in the still-warm evening breeze, and the blue hues of the mountains could still just be seen in the moonbeams.

This job was not going to be a walk in the park. It would

be tough and frustrating most of the time, I would probably lose my patience five times a day and I would no doubt die of exhaustion before the festival ended. But, I reasoned, for all the hassles and aggravation that would come my way, this *was* a once-in-a-lifetime opportunity. I would do the best I could, give it one-hundred-and-fifty per cent and just hope that I did make it through to the end without some studio minion demanding my head on a platter.

I pushed open the doors of Midnight Rescue and picked my way through the hip, young crowd towards the bar where I found Diana, JP and Cathy in heated conversation about the Programme Guide – and who had, by now, been joined by Joanna Escondio, the Design Manager on the local paper – and Alexis and Damien from Print Traffic.

Reading my mind, Diana handed me an extra large glass of Merlot.

'Had a good day at the office?' she asked in mock sarcasm, to show that she knew I was in need of some TLC. I told them briefly about it.

'*Arrgh,* you wait!' exclaimed Alexis, clearly fortified after a couple of prior margaritas from another bar. 'This is nothing. The week before is the worst. If you can get through that, you can get *through anything*.'

Cathy interjected, with too much glee, 'Yeah, you should see the hoops we have to jump through just to get the frigging paper out every day!'

Their comments did not improve my mood, but as the Merlot flowed we all mellowed and chilled sufficiently.

After all, tomorrow would surely be a better day?

CHAPTER NINE

The pace stepped up several gears as the week wore on. We were all expected to start running – often literally – to keep up; the workload increased substantially, with the usual tripwires and nooses along the way, and everyone's angst, both within and outside the festival, increased exponentially, as did The Goblin's strange behaviour. He had now decided that he held the trump card in that flights were *so* important that, without him, the whole festival would implode – and that he needed to be treated with the utmost respect and showered with gratitude. This attitude did not go down at all well with Duncan, who had already decided something was not quite right with this guy, even though he had been recommended by Christian.

The sponsorship of the hospitality suite, in terms of food and beverages, proved irksome beyond belief. Yes, they would be happy to donate 'X' they said; then a few hours later, no they could not donate 'X' but would we accept 'Y'? At last I won the battle, though not the war, and we ended up with a roster of delicious, interesting and unusual food items, even if they were not the epicurean delights that Alain Ducasse or Heston Blumenthal would have demanded.

And so it went on, day in, day out, evening in, evening

out. Dealing with The Lesbian was also difficult, for while I have no problem at all with gays – most of my male friends in London are gay – I had never felt comfortable with female gays, lipstick or otherwise, and on a professional level (for I was the 'Type A Personality' who did not take "can't get", "no one is available to speak to" or "no" for an answer), I found her damned awkward. We wanted – no, we *bloody well needed* – the Ciroc vodka, the wines and the beers and so I did go over her head to Harry to enlist his help. Cue another battle, of which more later.

There were hassles galore with all the hotels, aside from The Four Seasons or The Wyndham. They now could not give the requisite number of rooms they had previously promised; they now could not, or would not, include breakfast; they now wanted a written contract stipulating that a 'star' or 'stars' who would be staying there would be photographed at the hotel in return for all the rooms they had originally agreed; they wanted assurance that they could photograph said 'star' or 'stars' with the owner or General Manager; they wanted to know this, that and everything else – all of which had been clearly laid out in our original letters, multitude of conversations and ensuing contract letters. But no, we had to go through it all again.

'What the heck do we do about the stars issue?' I wailed to Dino. 'We never once said that specific stars would be staying with them, it was just a general view that we had film directors, producers, studio heads and some really great A-List names coming to the festival. How do we get around this? We can't afford to piss off anyone, as I know we're gonna need more rooms.'

Dino and I spent days calling the twenty-two hotels to placate them, side-stepping the issue of the celebrities by saying that we were still awaiting travel plans from the studios – thankfully not a blatant lie – and, with the exception of the budget hotels that, yes, we would ensure that a key personality would be staying with them. What we did not say was whether the 'key' in question would be an actor, director, producer or publicist.

The goody bags still had to be done. Having compiled a highly ambitious list, we had begun making the calls to the suppliers; the usual response was a rebuff delivered in an icily dry tone, but occasionally we struck gold, punching the air with relief when we did. The list had to be revised pretty smartly and downgraded to more realistic gifts, for we were not, after all, the Oscars, Golden Globes or Emmys – we were merely a film festival, however stellar the 'names' of some of our guests. Days were spent phoning, leaving messages, phoning again, leaving more messages, phoning again, screaming at the phone, throwing the phone at the wall, and then putting it back together again, and phoning again, persevering with gritted teeth and a mountain of 'comfort' cookies on our desks to console us.

The one thing I have learnt about working within the LA entertainment industry is that *no-one* ever returns calls. To an English person brought up in a certain background and with the mantra 'manners maketh man' drummed into one since childhood, it still came as quite a shock to me that no-one had the courtesy of returning a call; the entire week was spent shackled to my desk with a phone glued to my ear by day and, more often than not, my festival mobile phone in the same place during the evenings.

Had we forgotten the celebrity wallpaper? Of course not, we were just trying to avoid this little issue, but Sam ensured we would not. He, too, was on the phone and in the office day after day, augmenting his list with, 'my dear, she *simply must* be on the guest list' or 'my dear, you *do know* who this person is, don't you?'

The wallpaper, as we shorthanded it – for we felt that the moniker 'celebrity' no longer applied here – grew too long and I was having to enlist both Duncan's and Ed's help to override Sam; this in itself was difficult as he was a Board Member and, like Ed, knew a lot of people in Hollywood and could call in favours when really needed. The wallpaper drove us to distraction, along with everything else, and it took on the surreal elements of a game of chess. It was another battle of wills, for Sam was determined to have his wallpaper – *each and every one* of them – and Duncan and I were determined to ruthlessly trim the list, thankfully with Ed's blessing.

By mid-week, we were at our forty-eight hours time limit for chasing the guests regarding their attendance, and thereby, the necessary notification of proposed travel plans.

'Mike, Dino, send out those chaser emails today,' I shouted, above the cacophony of the Programming Department and Special Events. 'Please make sure you put, in bold at the top, that we must have an answer as early as possible and by Monday latest next week. State that if they don't respond by Monday, we'll assume that they are unable to attend and will give their place to another guest on our list. I suggest that you also finish off with the fact that once we have re-allocated their place to someone else, that they cannot, repeat cannot, come back to us and say they are now attending.'

The Goblin composed the chaser email. He was in his usual stroppy mood and it would, therefore, be very firm in its composition; I vetted it for any profanities before The Goblin and Dino sent them off, duly carving up the database list between them.

Most of the new peripatetic volunteers were like the

first bunch I had met during my first two days: edgy and trying so hard to master the grunge and gothic look but, sadly for them, not quite pulling it off.

The one new person I did like was David Donally, the Special Events assistant. He was a solid, decent guy with a very cheerful disposition and who had time for everyone; he was also straight, which was unusual in this environment, and sported a wonderful smile which creased his whole face. It was a delight to have him working a few feet away from me and he balanced perfectly the atmosphere in that department where Ingrid was – due to the nature and stress of her role – fairly moody most of the time.

Frank, my 'Z Z Top man' who had arrived with the first batch of 'grungees' – as Diana and I nicknamed them – now took to hanging around the office more than he needed to under the pretext that he was there to see Hannah, Bud or Alexis about a particular film; had it come in?; where was it?; could he take it down to the movie theatre to check for quality? I mused to Anna at the water cooler that it was either because it was warmer in our office than the Production Suite (even though the office roof was full of holes and every time it rained we tripped over buckets and saucepans), that we had loads of cookies in the kitchen or that, possibly, he fancied Alexis – or even one of the guys!

'Wrong on all counts Vanessa,' she said, kicking the cooler to get the last remnants of water out. 'We think it's you he hangs around for.'

Frank and I had hit it off when he arrived, for he was charming and fun and we had become firm friends, to the extent that we frequently joked about getting hitched and living happily ever after in Santa Barbara. It was pure acting and simply a way to ease the tensions of the ridiculous workload, but some of the 'grungees' thought this was all for real.

'What!' I exclaimed, also kicking the cooler for good measure. 'No, we're just friends, that's all. Anyway, I've started seeing this gorgeous screenwriter guy, Rob. Well, seeing as in the few nano-seconds of free time I have! The getting hitched thing is just a joke, a failsafe to stop us blowing when the overload switch is on.'

She did not seem convinced, but it was not that important; as it turned out, the reason Frank kept hanging around was because he had an issue with Hayden – the 'head grungee' in charge of operations at all the movie theatres – over how the movie reels would be delivered to, and stored at, the theatres and who would be responsible for setting them up on the 35mm projectors?

There was one brief respite in all this chaos and stress. The Senior Account Director and the Account Executive from the festival's LA-based PR agency came into town for a meeting with Duncan; they needed to run through the final press releases to announce the A-List presenters and 'honourees' – the recipients – at the Awards Gala, and confirm the final number of movies being screened, so that they could start a media blitz to promote the festival and get their requisite column inches and 'opportunities to see' marketing points.

Ric Isaacs and Shane Yateman were slick operators with an impressive contacts book. Their agency, one of the bigger players in LA and owned by a global advertising agency, handled the publicity for a number of high-profile stars; the media came to them for industry business stories – such as a studio's new big budget movie – and the daily trivial feeds about the stars' life and relationships, as well as salacious gossip.

Shane would be the mainstay during the festival and

disseminate the daily photographic and editorial feeds to the wires and any LA-based media that had not made it to the event, while Ric's role was primarily the red carpet media placements at the Awards Gala. They would bring in a photographer from one of the main wire agencies to cover not only the Awards Gala and the Opening and Closing Nights' receptions, but also the entire festival in terms of the other parties – where the media may get an 'off-message' photo of a key personality in full party mode, thereby further boosting the festival's press coverage.

Duncan had told them that I had a marketing communications background and so, after an hour into their meeting, I was summoned to his office. I felt an instant synergy with them both and we soon fell into a conversation about the whole advertising world. After a few minutes Duncan, increasingly bored with PR and ad-land talk, swivelled three-hundred-and-sixty-degrees in his chair and said mockingly, 'any chance we can all get back on the same page? We're running out of time here and I really don't give a damn if XY buys Z or not.'

Taking my cue, I got up, playfully tapping Ric on his arm as I instructed him, 'come and see me on the way out.'

The daily deluge of emails from the studios, with the cc'd people now mushrooming like an atom bomb; the almost daily calls from Kane Eppstein about this, that and everything else and how quickly could I get it done? and the now thrice-daily calls from Ed regarding just about everything, meant I now seemed to be his information point. This was amusing, given that most of the time none of us in the office was being briefed about anything. Still, it was good to know that I was on his radar, even if it meant being in a state of permanent high alert.

Was everything sorted for his cocktail party? Pretty

much. What had not been done? Well, the Swarovski crystals and cultivated black pearls had not yet been ordered, but they were a next day delivery, so not a problem, but I had not had time to source a gift. Had the invitations gone out? No, they were still being printed. Had the guest list been drawn up? No, I had not had any time to do that, there were a few other things regarding the festival (remember, Ed, we *were* also staging an entire festival). Had the bonsai trees and flowers been ordered? Yes. Did we need to have another meeting to run through everything? No, not this week, maybe next week. And so on.

Kane had, at least, become calmer and we enjoyed what could be described as normal conversations; he had dropped the demanding bark and now adopted a more positive tone, probably because he at last realised that, on this occasion, he needed me more than I needed him.

As if we did not have enough to do, Duncan decided that Guest Services could also handle the Industry Accreditations received from people who were not one of the two-hundred invited guests, but were in the industry – and usually at a junior level or even just not important – who felt *they* should be part of the action. This mundane job was usually processed either by Duncan's assistant, Anna, or someone in Programming and, naturally enough, there were no volunteers to undertake it. Tossing a huge black Lever Arch file at me, Duncan simply said, 'can you do these now darlin', I need them for a meeting in a couple of hours', as he walked swiftly back into his office, assuming I would know what to do with them. I looked blankly at the clutch of forms, many of which contained photographs and saw that one or two had been graded A or B.

'What the bleep do I do with these?' I groaned at Anna as she ran past me, yelling at several people at once that

Duncan wanted to see them *now*.

'Sorry Vanessa, can't stop. I'll try and help you later.' But later was no good.

Christian, who always felt that it was *he* who *really* ran the whole show, and that he should be the one in charge of *everything*, came to my rescue. He explained that all I needed to do was to call each person – there were about a hundred already – and verify (a) they were who they said they were as 'so many people want to be part of the whole film festival circuit that they pretend they are someone else in the industry'; (b) what they would be doing at the festival (making contacts, looking for a distributor or writing articles?) and (c) check that they would be paying their own way (flights, hotels, subsistence) as they were not formal guests of the festival. If they had not supplied a photo for ID purposes, then they had to email one straightaway.

'Once you've done all this and marked it on each page, give the file back to me so that Duncan and I can grade the person A or B.'

The A grades would definitely get passes – the Industry Accreditations – which would also give them access to certain parties and events during the festival, while the B people would have to try again next year. Dropping everything else, I worked my way through the file, thinking that this was all of them; I soon learned that the applications piled in thick and fast, and each day's mail brought another bagful.

We were all, by now, doing unrelenting twelve-hour days, and soon enough these would be considered 'short days'. There was no time for lunch, even running out to grab a sandwich at the store opposite and eating it at our desks took up far too much precious time, and no time to sit back and evaluate whether what one was doing was even going in the right direction. More often than not, no time to even go to the bathroom – we would suddenly remember that three hours ago we were heading there before being waylaid by yet another phone call.

Even Rob had to come to the office for a few snatched minutes – I was not about to let this budding relationship fall through the cracks – but it was to his favour, as he often ran into a producer visiting Duncan and it afforded him the chance to pitch his movie.

Everything was done 'on the hoof ', including meetings which invariably took place running around the office after Duncan, Ed, Harry, Sam, Christian, Diana, JP, Alexis, Ingrid, Anna, Bud or The Lesbian. We began living on coffee, cookies and pastries and adrenaline.

And so the whole merry circus rolled on.

And on.

CHAPTER TEN

'You're trying to do way too much,' said Diana on Saturday morning, stabbing the power button on the Nespresso machine with one hand and leaning out of the window to grab a lemon with the other, while I propped my eyes open with matchsticks. 'You'll be worn out soon and nobody will give you any thanks. We're all expendable, so just pull back a bit.'

We both knew this was not going to happen, for I could hardly say no when asked by the Chairman or Executive Director to do something; I would just have to find a way to get through it all.

A therapeutic visit to Sea Spa was called for to have Papaya-Oxygen facials, detox massages, seaweed wraps and Hot Stones therapies. After a blissful six hours, rejuvenated and totally relaxed, we had forgotten all about the festival's mayhem and its eclectic coterie of staff.

We moved seamlessly to Elements for cocktails, where Rob joined us, then onto the Coast Restaurant to meet up with Anna, JP, Alexis, Damien, Dino, and David for dinner. Rob was an instant hit with them all, swopping Tinseltown gossip and regailing them with tales of his 'wild trips' to Mexico – one of which ended up with him on the set of the Michael Douglas/Benicio del Toro quadruple-Oscar-winner movie 'Traffic' as a production assistant.

'And did you manage to bring anything back,' everyone chorused, each knowing full well what was meant.

'Erm, no. But I learnt how it was done!'

We put the world to rights over glasses of margaritas and bottles of Merlot. Mercifully, the Valet Parking guys were willing to forego their gratuities and called us cabs instead.

Rob and I spent a blissful Sunday with breakfast and a medicinal 'hair of the dog' Bloody Mary by the pool; lunch at The Yard House, a spot of retail therapy at Neiman Marcus, tea at the delightful Wolfgang Puck café and then back to Diana's house to crash on the sofa with the LA Times. Life had returned to some semblance of normality; but that, as with everything else, was short-lived.

It was the week before Christmas, but there was no let up in the preparations at the fun factory as we all knew that, despite the fact that America Inc. only has Christmas Day itself off, LA is a different land altogether; the whole city – as in all the entertainment industry – would shut down between Christmas and the day after New Year.

It was, therefore, vital to try and get as much done as possible this week and scored through on the jotter pad. There would not be any time to be excited about Christmas, to go Christmas shopping, to write cards or decorate the house, nor even think about my trip to Arizona where I was spending the holidays with great friends in Scottsdale. No, the merry-go-round continued and, like a carousel, one had the highs occasionally, and then plummeted back down more often than not when the goalposts were re-arranged and then put back to their original location – and then re-arranged again.

The work and projects continued apace from where they

had left off last week, but we had to step up several gears to cram what was essentially two weeks work into four days, as most people were planning to leave at lunchtime on Friday to make it to their respective destinations the next day for Christmas Day. As if this was not bad enough, a couple of 'situations' occurred to ensure we all remained in a state of high alert and the blood pressure remained at the systolic end of the chart.

The first was the hotel flyer, which had been put together a few weeks ago by Joanna Escondio, the graphic designer. I now discovered that, at the point of it going to print, The Wyndham had not formally agreed to be the host hotel, due to all the cripplingly-expensive hoop-jumping that went with it and so it had not been flagged up on the flyer as the host hotel, as it should have been. There was much wailing and gnashing of teeth from Programming.

While we were all juggling our many balls and trying to keep them all airborne, The Goblin decided that, in the spirit of keeping the mayhem alive, he could also do a bit of stirring. Christian had gone to The Goblin's desk to ask why The Wyndham was not listed first? The Goblin decided to email Duncan and Diana – but not me – with this dilemma, suggesting we re-design the whole flyer with The Wyndham at the top. Not knowing that it had been drafted weeks ago, and before my arrival, he helpfully added that he wondered why I, as head of Guest Services, had not done the flyer. Was it not leaving it all a bit late? How could *he* help to save the day?

Diana, never a person to cross, exploded at receiving this email and seeing the number of people it had been CYA'd to – though not sent to his boss, me, who should have been a key recipient – and at his insolence. She immediately fired a broadside across all bows, kindly copying me in so that I knew what The Goblin was up to.

'Direct all Creative Services questions my way please. Way, way too many cooks in the broth on this one!' she commanded, before telling The Goblin in no uncertain terms that she, Duncan and I would decide whether a re-design and re-print was required. Duncan also exploded, telling The Goblin to 'just f***ing stick to doing the god-damn flights and don't interfere in things that don't concern you.' I, in turn, had my knuckles wrapped by Duncan for unwittingly allowing The Goblin to encroach onto what was my and Dino's territory.

The second 'situation' was Davina Isner, who went by the rather important-sounding job title of Awards Gala Volunteers Manager but whom, in reality, was simply in charge of procuring volunteers to help out at the ceremony by escorting the stars, plus their handlers and publicists, to their respective tables.

She was, in fact, a very elegant and extremely nice lady who took her job a bit too seriously. She waltzed into the office one day and suggested it would be prudent if we were to have a meeting there and then. Sensing that it would be diplomatic if I did drop everything and meet her, I ventured into the Boardroom where she was waiting. She wanted a finalised list of the *exact* presenters and award recipients (honourees), the names of all the approved celebrity wallpaper, the key studio executives and the stars' publicists – all of whom would need 'kid-glove escorting' to their tables.

I explained that, while the honourees were pretty much set in stone, Duncan was still negotiating with some studios and agents over some of the presenters and that this would not, in all probability, be finalised until the New Year, or even a couple of days before the festival started.

She looked askance. Was this really not all finalised?

My brow furrowed for a moment, for I knew that she knew, that in the land of this particular film festival, nothing as important as an awards ceremony would be ready until the eleventh hour, as changes, adjustments and tweaks were continually made, even when there was no call for them to be done. I had been told, for example, that Harry *never* finalised the seating plan for the Awards Gala until about forty-five minutes before guests started arriving. So, no, this was not all ready now; we still had two weeks to go, for heaven's sake!

This was obviously not what she had set out to achieve by coming into the office. While I saluted her professionalism and dedication to the role, I also knew that her angst was partly down to stress, which we were all suffering. She reclined into the chair to formulate her thoughts.

'OK, I know this stuff doesn't get done quickly and there are so many changes. We never seem to know what the heck is going on, but when I report back to Andrea, she sure as heck is not going to be pleased.'

Who was Andrea, I enquired? 'Ah, you haven't met Andrea yet?' she smiled very slowly, as if to warn me of impending danger. 'She's a producer in LA, a friend of Ed's and, for the Awards Gala, assists Rocco with the whole show. She's quite a gal.'

I instantly understood from what Davina *had not* said that I was to be prepared.

The Exocet landed the next day in the form of a tall, immaculately-groomed and elegant woman called Andrea Carnegie. Davina had obviously reported back to her in the negative and Andrea decided she would come and sort it all out. She was a consummate professional, if rather icy in manner initially, and certainly did not believe in wasting the time on any pleasantries; it was a case with her of setting the course directly to target without straying.

She asked all the same questions that Davina had asked the day before, though why I would never know, especially as Davina had given her all the answers, and then demanded to see the hotel listing for all the A-List stars and celebrity wallpaper. She was, however, only interested in talent, not the mere mortals comprising the bulk of our guests.

When I told her that we were still finalising the list of presenters, that there was now also an issue over whether one of the honourees could attend due to new filming commitments, that the wallpaper was still being thrashed out between Sam, Duncan and Ed, and that, until we had a clearer idea of it all – particularly regarding wallpaper – we could not progress properly with the hotel grid, she looked at me as though I was stark raving mad.

'I want to know where everyone is staying and I want to know *now*. I want a hotel list.'

As I was explaining that the A-List were all booked into The Four Seasons, she interrupted immediately with, 'Barbro Innes won't stay there, so where is she booked into?' Ignoring the interruption, I continued, saying that in the next few days I would draw up a draft hotel grid to also include the one or two wallpaper names we thought would be attending. She got up and left as quickly as she had arrived, without saying 'thank you', 'see you soon' or even 'goodbye'. I was suitably on my guard.

'Oh, she's an industry girl,' said Anna, witnessing my expression as the Exocet sped to its next target. 'You'll soon realize that in LA people only want to know you if you can do something for them. If you can't further their career, magic up a box office smash or provide mega-bucks for a film project, they don't want to know you.'

I looked even more shocked. 'That's appalling! What happened to common courtesy and sincerity?'

Now Anna looked bemused. 'Hey, we're talking La-La Land here. You'll get used to it.'

As I was walking back to my desk, feeling as if the Exocet had actually exploded on impact, The Lesbian raced around the corner and shot me a withering glare. Ah, I reminded myself, I need to have a meeting with Harry regarding the booze for the Guest & Industry Suite.

I placed a call to his long-suffering secretary, who wearily told me that it would not be possible this week. I told her, politely but firmly, that it *had* to be possible, otherwise we would not have a suite; it would only require one phone call from Harry, but I needed to talk to him about drinks and Mercedes-Benz.

She slotted me in at seven o'clock the next evening. 'Come over here and don't be late. He's got another meeting at seven-thirty and then one at eight.'

Once more into the breech, I thought, as I put down the receiver.

The official Programme Guide was due at the printers in two days' time, so there was the small matter of getting it signed off. I knew from the puffs of blue air emanating from the Marketing area that Diana and Christian, not to mention The Lesbian – and Cathy, when she came into the office – were all in a state of discord over the conceptual layout. Cathy was naturally coming at it from the local paper's perspective, which was simply to sell copies, Diana was obviously treating it as a valuable marketing tool to boost Box Office revenue, while Christian and The Lesbian just wanted a fun festival item, without too much thought as to why we were even doing it.

There had, for example, been furious debate over the

running order of all the various sponsors' logos. Aside from the specific category sponsors, such as Mercedes-Benz being the Official Car of the Festival, or Tiffany being the Awards Gala Presenting Sponsor, there were myriad other Sponsor categories. Then there was another exchange over whether the films should be at the front and logos at the back, or vice versa; then were there too many advertisements?

'We do have to make this pay,' said an exasperated Cathy. 'Would it not be better if the listings of festival staff and Board of Directors were on the back page, rather than the first page?'

Duncan, who had the final say on everything, had been reeled in to resolve the squabble, albeit there was still the odd sharp intake of breath.

The final proof came in from Joanna around nine-thirty on Tuesday evening. Diana printed it off and, deeming it approved, took it to Duncan's office, whereupon he merely said, 'Chuck it on the desk honey, I'll take a look at it in a moment.'

Duly doing as she was directed, she tossed it onto the mountain of paper that was his desk – but not before placing on it a yellow Post It note with several asterisks to denote its urgency. Exiting in reverse, she said firmly, 'Need to have approval by tomorrow morning latest. It's got to go to print by tomorrow evening, otherwise we've missed the printing slot and it won't be done for the January Third edition of the paper. I'm getting quotes for having it on Electrobrite paper, but I need you to authorize the over-runs. Fifteen-thousand.'

He did not look up and she knew, from old, that that was the cue to get the hell out.

There was an almighty ruckus the next morning. The mercurial Duncan was in a particularly filthy mood, screaming at everyone who entered his orbit as he marched around the office waving the Programme Guide proof.

'Christian, Hannah, Diana, get the hell into my office. NOW.'

Immediately dropping everything, they nervously made their way into Duncan's office, sensing this was real trouble.

'This is total crap. What the f*** do you guys think you are playing at? We went over this yesterday for Christ's sake. I specifically said that the films listing *had* to be at the front and the logos at the back. Which part of that instruction did none of you understand? The Chairman's and Executive Director's messages have been changed. And the editorials for the Opening and Closing Night screenings. Hannah *what were* you on yesterday evening? It's complete garbage. A kid of six could have done better. I want an explanation and I want it now.'

Deciding that passing the buck was their best option, Christian and Hannah turned towards Diana with a look that said, "you had better deal with this". Diana duly stepped up to the plate.

'We all agreed with you Duncan, but Harry said last night that he wanted the logos at the front, and he insisted on the changes to Ed's and your messages.'

'Well f***ing change it back to the way I wanted it.'

'But Harry will override you again and we *have* to get it to print by early evening, otherwise we miss the print slot and it won't be out with the paper on January Three.'

'I don't give a f***. This is a piece of s***,' he screamed, now incandescent with rage as he hurled the proof pages at Diana. 'Get the hell out of my office now you silly little bitch and go sort it. The way *I* want it.'

Diana, who had never had much time for Duncan's management style and vituperative nature, erupted as she scooped up the papers from the desk and floor.

'You may know everything there is to know about world cinema, but you have absolutely no idea how to manage people or get the best out of your staff. What am I supposed to do when Harry countermands your instructions? Tell him to f*** off instead? You know something, you and Harry are the god-damn kids around here. And you know something else Duncan, you are a f***ing a***hole. I'm going home. No one talks to me like this. You can sort it out with the design department and printers, and then you'll see just how much work goes into this.'

Hurling the pages back at Duncan with equal force, Diana stormed out of his office, slamming the door so hard that Anna dropped her phone in shock, and repaired to her desk simply to tell JP that she would be at home, but only if there was 'a proper crisis.'

It got worse. I then had Ed on the phone. 'Come over straight away,' he snarled.

I jumped into the Dodge and raced to his office, taking the stairs two at a time as this was obviously very urgent.

'Do you have *any* idea who Andrea Carnegie is?' he thundered, as I walked into his office.

'No, I don't,' I replied glibly. 'Who is she?'

'She's a producer, she's a key player and a movie she's just co-produced has been given an Oscar nod. What the hell do you think you're doing telling her she can't have a hotel list for a few days. If she wants it now, she gets it now. Clear? Go back and get the god-damn list to her immediately.'

I tried to explain what I had said to Andrea – that I was

on overload, that I would get her the list as soon as possible and that, realistically, it would be in a couple of days. I was not trying to be obstructive or difficult; we just did not have all the information ready yet.

'Just do it,' he upbraided, not even looking at me as I was given my marching orders.

The day did not improve much, for in among all this anguish was the usual round of phone messages and emails to change things, to verify conversations which had already been verified countless times before, to chase, chase and chase. I still had not heard from Tiffany about a gift for the goody bags, so that *was* a priority to chase; there was still all the technical equipment to sort out for the suite, as well as the décor, and I had to pull the white rabbit out of the hat for Andrea.

Dino and I sat down and looked at the hotel grid. There really was not much more that could be put on it that I had not already told Andrea, but I had to produce something and fast. We had all the A-List in The Four Seasons and I had now been told that Barbro Innes would want to stay out of town at The Ritz Carlton, so we added that hotel into the grid. The plethora of wallpaper we knew of at this stage, although unknown as to whether they would remain on the guest list, were allocated rooms across three hotels – The Wyndham, the Hyatt and the Hilton – depending upon their current star 'currency'.

I asked Dino to email it on my behalf to Andrea and Ed, copying it also to Sam and Duncan, with the caveat that the wallpaper names were not confirmed as attending and that this was still be to be finalised during the next few days. He punched the Send button with glee. 'Job done.'

The atmosphere in the office had been tense all morning following Duncan's nuclear fall out; everyone was still walking on eggshells when Diana swept back in around the middle of the afternoon. She strode to the kitchen, opened the bottle of wine she was clutching, grabbed a glass and proceeded to her desk where she defiantly sipped the Merlot as she again corrected the proofs and apologized to the printers for the continued mayhem concerning the Programme Guide.

'Duncan called me at home and apologized for his outburst,' she informed me triumphantly when I went to Marketing to ask why she had returned. 'He blows hot and cold all the time. It's his modus operandi. He's mega-stressed, I'm mega-stressed,' she grinned lifting her glass to me in a salute, 'and I guess your pretty damned stressed too. Go get a glass and have some while I get this baby sorted out and off to the printers a.s.a.p.'

I left the office at six-thirty for my meeting with Harry. One of the city's leading philanthropists, he was a consummate money-maker, with fingers in many pies and a burgeoning business empire on both the West and East coasts encompassing marketing and restaurants. As Managing Director of the festival's Board of Directors, he kept a razor-sharp eye on income and expenditure though, it had to be said, was far more relaxed when it came to advertising his business interests in the local paper.

He did not believe in subtle or clever advertising and used the medium simply as a direct 'call to action'. He did his own media buying for space on TV and in the papers and, as such, believed he knew more about marketing than anyone else, which irked Diana to the core. Despite this, he was a courteous man who always found time to greet the key festival staff – those that would assist him in delivering a phenomenal monetary success – by their names and ask how they were.

'Hi Vanessa,' he said, swinging around in his over-sized desk chair. 'Come and have a seat. What do you want? We also need to discuss the Mercedes deal. I've got all the authorizations through now, so we can decide which talent gets which car.'

I advised him on the looming problem with the drink for the suite, specifically that firstly, we were still waiting to see if we would get anything at all and secondly, the quantities. I told him about my exchange of words with The Lesbian regarding how much we needed and her total rebuff. I explained that Dino and I had worked our butts off to get all the food items, including getting two restaurants to come in and cook the suppers, but that I was very concerned that we would not have any drinks for cocktails and supper, before finishing with the fact that the suite was a showcase and 'damn well had to work'.

He nodded approvingly. 'Jeez, we can't have a cluster-f*** like this. Who's she going to for the vodka and other stuff?'

I muttered a name I thought was the company, but said I was not sure.

'Don't worry, I can fix it with a few calls and get everything.'

While I was thankful, I explained to Harry that we had to have Ciroc vodka, both for the suite and the other special events parties, 'for their fabulous flashing ice cubes'. He looked at me in bewilderment until I showed him a sample I happened to have. 'Jeez, they're good. OK, I'll get my man to make sure its Ciroc. While you're here, you might as well tell me how much you need of everything.

I rolled off the numbers; he did not seem at all fazed

and scribbled all the figures onto a pad, pulling off the sheet and tossing it into his out-tray for his secretary to deal with in the morning.

'Right, Mercedes. They're not gonna give us four Maybachs, we can only have two. As they're four-hundred-thousand dollars-worth of car, I guess we're lucky to have two. So, who're you gonna give the Maybachs to?'

I said Duncan had already shown me Mercedes' email and that, at this stage, I was planning on Olivia Lautner and Liam Taylor.

'What about Lawrence Eppstein?' he shot back. 'He's getting the Lifetime Achievement Award. Shouldn't he have one?'

I related my numerous telephone conversations with Kane, saying his dad did not like limos and had expressly requested a Sedan, and that I had allocated one of the S-Class models to him. Harry seemed content with this. 'OK, but keep me in the loop at all times.'

I said I would as I bade him goodnight but, before walking out of the door, took the opportunity to ask if there would be any possibility of my being invited to the Awards Gala itself, given that I was looking after all the A-List and would have to be there anyway to ensure everything ran smoothly.

He laughed. 'We'll see. The numbers are heavy and I don't know how we're gonna get everyone in. I won't know until that afternoon. But you can always bring your pretty frock to the office, just in case.'

Damn right I would, and the five-inch heels.

The rest of the week was its usual frantic self. The Industry Accreditations applications poured in, with all the people having to be verified before passing to Duncan for grading. We needed to sort out the décor for the Guest & Industry Suite and so I put in a call to the showroom that Duncan had suggested, which had some beautiful and unusual furnishings, and asked if I could go over and meet the owner.

Within an hour of being at the shop, we had settled on various items to furnish the suite – a Robin Day Hille teak sofa, two retro Pieff leather two-seater sofas, two ClassiCon Mole Lounge chairs, two Norman Cherner chairs, two Castiglioni-inspired floor arc lamps, two Guzzini-style table lamps and a wonderfully over-the-top art deco mirror.

Finally, my eyes alighted on two absolute must-haves – a large four feet by two feet Andy Warhol art print of his 1967 '10 Marilyns' and a smaller square print of his 1964 'Shot Blue Marilyn'.

The list of what I had selected was printed from the computer, I signed for it and arranged delivery to the suite the day before the festival started. Why was not everything to do with the festival as easy as this? But another call was now required, of course, to check with The Wyndham that we would have access the day before. Back at the office, I duly put in the call to the Conference & Banqueting Director to be told, by his secretary, that we only had access to the suite from four o'clock onwards.

'But that's ludicrous!' I shrieked. 'We need access the entire day before, and preferably from four o'clock the day before that. There's no way we can get an entire suite set up for two-hundred guests if we can only get in at four, even if we worked until midnight. You must see that!'

She was either too stupid to see my point or too petulant to make any concessions, so I demanded to speak to Jon Bauer; reluctantly, she put me through and I was greeted with the same weary tone as always. I really got the feeling that he did not want the festival happening at his hotel, even though it brought great kudos to his property and, thereby, to him.

'We have a meeting already booked forty-eight hours before the festival starts,' he pronounced triumphantly.

'What time does it end?' I asked urgently.

'Erm, lunchtime,' he replied, not quite so triumphant now.

'Then we can get in at, say, two o'clock to start our set up,' I shot back. 'I don't care if your cleaners are in there, we can work around them, but we have to be able to start setting up that afternoon, and have that evening and all of the next day. Sorry, but this really is non-negotiable.'

Another wearied 'OK, OK' and the phone was once more put down on me.

I swung by Duncan's office, popping my head through the door. He, Christian and Diana were all huddled over what seemed to be the millionth programme guide proof, pens furiously making yet more corrections for, having missed the printer's deadline of the previous evening, it now had a non-negotiable, *absolute final* deadline of this evening. I breezily told Duncan about my conversation with Jon Bauer, hoping it might improve his mood, which had not changed much since yesterday morning. He looked up, his eyes brightened while his jaw dropped.

'You did what, darlin?' he said in feigned amusement. 'That's the way. Do you want to take over all my studio calls?'

I knew he was joking. 'No, thanks, got quite enough of my own.'

I showed Duncan the final proof for the Guest Services Guide; he haphazardly flicked through it. 'Do I need to proof-read this before I sign it off, or can I hope that one person in the god-damn office can do something properly?' he asked, weary from working sixteen-hour days all week.

'Not unless you really want to.'

'OK, darlin, just get it off to print. Let's get one damn guide done.'

'I need to see it *as well*,' Christian cried petulantly. 'After all, my name is on the front page along with Duncan's.'

Pursing my lips at Duncan, I tossed it over to Christian. 'Need to have it back within two hours, otherwise we miss our print slot. There *shouldn't* be a need for any corrections, Christian. After all, Duncan is *happy* with it,' I retorted sarcastically.

The flights scenario remained problematic in that many of the guests were travelling in from Europe, Central and South America, Israel, India, South Africa and Australia; trying to confirm the arrival times at LAX and co-ordinate cars to pick up groups at a time gave The Goblin, Lizzie and I numerous headaches.

Cars also continued to be a hassle. The guy from Hertz, who had promised to get back to me 'before close of play tomorrow' – last week! – still had not responded, despite my chasing. I put in yet another call; he was very apologetic about his tardiness, but the good news, he said, was that they would be delighted to be a festival partner, as long as they were the only major car rental company. I assured him that they were adding, by way of courtesy, that there was also a small local outfit who was supplying three mini-buses for LAX pick-ups and ten Chevrolet Camaros for general ferrying around of the majority of the guests.

'We need your cars for the more important guests,' I said, 'you know, stars coming from LA, film directors, key studio execs. That's why we need high-end, reliable vehicles. And a hybrid, such as a Prius, would be great, as one or two of the stars attending are keen on these cars.'

Not wanting a vehicle committed to paper that I did not think was suitable, I quickly asked him what models they had in mind.

'Oh, you know, we'll make available a mix of Audi TT Coupe 2.0, Alfa Romeo Brera, VW Beetle Cabriolet, Jaguar X-Type 2.0 V6 and the Toyota Prius,' he said, assuming this was the end of the conversation.

'How many of each?' I immediately enquired, trying to cross all the t's and dot all the i's in one go. 'And can we have a couple of Cadillac Escalades and/or SUV's?'

I knew I was pushing my luck here. There was an ominous pause.

'Erm, I guess. How 'bout five of each saloon models, one Escalade and two SUV's?'

Punching the air with palpable relief and frantically waving at Lizzie to get her attention, I quickly carried on before he could change his mind.

'That'd be just great. Thank you so, so much. As I'm sure you're aware, as a major car partner you'll get tickets for the Awards Gala itself, so you'll get to see, maybe even meet at the cocktail party beforehand, the A-List stars that are coming in for the ceremony. I hope your guy from Corporate HQ can make it down. I'll need to know names after Christmas of who will be attending from Hertz.'

True to his word, an email dropped into my Inbox within the hour to confirm all the points discussed. I beckoned to Lizzie to come over and read it.

'Hey, we're not used to having such good cars, it'll spoil our guests! Perhaps we should also throw in a little Estee Lauder amenity bag on the back seat,' she giggled mockingly.

'Well, at least you'll have enough cars to play around with. We've got the heirs and spares,' I laughed as we high-fived.

'What's going on?' demanded Christian, as he stood on his chair to peer over the Mulholland Drive partition wall.

'Oh, nothing much Christian. Just getting *our* jobs done. How's your's coming along?'

To partially ease the stress, I would often walk over to the Print Traffic office and marvel at 'Alexis' Wall' as it became known. She had plastered an entire wall of her office with paper and A5-sized envelopes, upon which the names of all the two-hundred-and-thirty-odd movies were written in black felt pen, and roughly how many cans each one would be arriving in. When a movie was delivered to the offices, she would check the number of cans against her manifest and then put a huge green tick on the relevant envelope if the whole movie was there.

More often than not, though, the envelopes contained red and green scrawls to denote that only 'x' number of cans had arrived and not the whole consignment; it was not unusual to discover that, when the boxes were opened and the numbers of cans were checked against the shipping document, there would be one or two cans missing – usually the middle parts of the film. So more frantic calls, more emails, more translation costs and more holes in the budget were required to locate the missing cans and get them shipped from half-way around the world. And it naturally meant a hell of a lot more stress for all of us.

Lizzie decided that the only antidote to combat the sheer aggravation of the week was to throw a party. She was, however, sensible enough to know that the real stress had not even begun. She dutifully walked around the office, dispensing a hand-made invitation depicting a photograph of Sarah Palin, with the words "Eliminate…" on the front, and inside "the stress and frustration that is Filmfest and party with me at my place. Thursday, 7pm until whenever…"

It was a much needed fillip and there was no cajoling required to get us there. I checked whether she had asked The Goblin. 'No way Jose, you've got to be kidding. But do bring Rob if you think he can cope with us crazies!'

Rob met me at the office and we drove to Lizzie's place, arriving at seven on the dot. It was a pretty three-bedroom, two-bathroom, two-garage-plus-pool house in 0.75 acre of grounds that is standard for the area. Lizzie had gone to town on the food, for there was not an inch of the extended table in the hallway that was not covered with shrimp Tempura, mini-hamburgers, pizza squares, guacamole, chilli con carne, rice, diced turkey, chicken wings, fried onions, coconut shrimps and salads.

The drink flowed freely while we all kept telling ourselves, as if it were a mantra, that it *was* needed and, therefore, medicinal. Stresses and differences of opinions from the office were soon left behind and we partied hard and fast and long into the night – thanks to Rob's surprise contribution of some superb hash and cocaine.

My head the next morning, Christmas Eve, told me it had been a good night. Dino, JP, Alexis and Christian happened to be the first people I saw when I walked into the office; their faces confirmed that they, too, had had a good night. It had had the desired medicinal effect, for everyone, including Duncan, was in a much better frame of mind, although I assumed it was partly down to the fact that they knew they had a day off the following day.

Seizing upon Duncan's increasingly rare good humour, I breezed into his office to ask if I could be indulged with having the day after Christmas Day off as, being English, it was also a major holiday for us, plus I was going to Arizona for 'The Holidays'.

He feigned horror for a few minutes and then laughed. 'Sure, darlin. You'll need a rest before next week.'

Oh dear God, what did that mean? I worried momentarily about this as I kissed him on both cheeks and then darted around the office with my sprig of mistletoe, kissing and hugging those I wanted to, exchanging presents with the favoured few and merely tapping a cursory greeting on the arm to those whom I did not particularly care for. The Goblin and The Lesbian got neither.

I climbed into the Dodge, put on my Raybans, turned on the ignition and headed towards the Interstate. The traffic was already building, but soon I was in the outside lane with the warm wind blowing through my hair and sweeping away the tensions and stresses of the previous weeks.

I had no inkling of what was to come when I returned to the festival; but for now it was Christmas. I was going to be with two of my dearest friends and their two adorable sons.

It would be a glorious respite.

CHAPTER ELEVEN

Christmas with Robert and Juliana Renke in Scottsdale had been simply perfect; their abundance of love, hugs, presents, fabulous food, champagne and fine wines provided a welcome respite. They had two adorable boys, Alex and Robbie, and a divine Labradoodle called Rusty. Being half English and half Italian – and with that a love of wines and food – Robert has instigated a tradition in throwing open his house on December 26 for a Boxing Day party. This ritual continues to amuse all his American friends and work colleagues, none of whom could understand why, in days gone by, the English Upper Classes would use the day after Christmas to give food or gifts, in boxes, to their servants and the 'lower orders' in the community. But it was a damn good excuse for another party and none of us was complaining.

Christmas came to an end far too soon; after only a sixty-hours break, I was heading back along the Interstate and to the 'joy' that awaited me at the festival's offices.

Mike Katz, or Mike 2 as he became known, had finally returned from New York; an astute guy in his mid-twenties, he had just finished a post-graduate course in media studies at Columbia University. As he had worked in Guest Services the year before, he both knew the ropes and many of the staff. This would be a huge help to me, especially when the tsunami arrived the day before the festival opened and I was desperately paddling to stay sane, as Mike 2 was able to take control of the final set-up stages of the Guest & Industry Suite and man it once it opened.

He did not have any time for The Goblin, but got on well with Dino and Lizzie and was more than willing to do any of the assignments thrown his way. I immediately passed him the job of completing the goody bags, for they had rather got pushed to the bottom of the pile with the myriad aggravations of the prior week. Dino and I briefed him on what we had managed to elicit thus far and I asked him to start with chasing DreamWorks and Sharper Image, plus the other potential suppliers – though we soon discovered that La La Land was soundly asleep until New Year.

This in itself posed a real problem for me; while on the one hand the flood of emails from the studios before Christmas had been ridiculous, I now needed them, and with answers about their relevant star's attendance time and required travel details.

Before Mike 2 and I discovered that LA had closed down for the Christmas holiday and would not be up and running again until the New Year, I had fired off a blitz of emails to all the relevant studio marketing and publicity people, as well as to the stars' own personal publicists, to ask for this vital information so that Lizzie, Dino and I could allocate cars, drivers, hotels and any other specific needs. I had been sent a full list of all contacts and telephone numbers by Raine Daysen and, when no response was forthcoming, started making phone calls. It was then that I discovered from the voicemail that no one was in town; everyone, bar one or two, seemed to be skiing at Lake Tahoe or Mammoth Lakes, as evidenced by the automatic replies to my emails from their BlackBerrys.

While we could not move forward with a lot of the A-List specifics, much to my frustration, we did, however, seem to be bogged down with what we did not want – the dreaded celebrity wallpaper. The emails with their names just kept rolling in, from Sam, from Ed, from their agents and, soon enough, the wallpaper *themselves* were asking for friends to be included. This had to stop. We were in danger of diluting the power of the stellar A-List names and other key showbiz luminaries attending the Awards Gala.

I went to Duncan with my concerns. He concurred, but was, as ever, drowning in his own minutiae – at that precise moment, he was tweaking the final 'contractual letter' for two key A-List stars to present gongs at the Awards Gala, so I left him to it.

The Four Seasons was a model of efficiency and had pulled out all the stops for Ed's party, but dealing with some of the outside contractors to provide décor, flowers, cutlery, glasses and food proved irksome beyond belief. Just these tasks alone took an inordinate amount of calls, emails and more chaser calls to complete and secure their commitment. It would be forty-eight hours before the festival started that all the elements for both Ed's party and the hospitality suite were finalized and signed off.

Two more staff meetings still failed to provide a proper briefing at any of them; it seemed to be more a vehicle for Department Heads to let Duncan know that everything was on track, rather than for us to receive a detailed briefing and flag up any possible problems on the horizon – which, of course, there were plenty.

Tensions ran high all week. It was as though everyone was in a permanent state of high alert; each department having their own mini crises and trying to outdo everyone else in the tantrums stakes. The sheer volume of flights to be booked was beginning to have an effect on moral within Guest Services; The Goblin was struggling to keep up, but would not admit to not being up to the job and, as the flights were booked, emails whistled over to Dino and I to book the hotel rooms.

If truth be known, we were all struggling to keep up, as it was never just one job to do. We were fire-fighting, but without extinguishers, and everything, but *everything*, was on a deadline – none more so than getting the flights booked before the airlines withdrew their agreed promotional rates and seat allocations.

We had had to send another chaser email after last week's chaser to get responses about their attendance. Finally, the RSVPs started coming in by email, but it was never straightforward; a film director would want to know if he could bring two other guests; a producer would ask if he could change his (already booked) travel date; another film director wanted to know if anyone from his Consulate had been invited and, if not, could we please send an invitation to Mr X, which had to be passed by Duncan for budget approval; a studio executive wanted to know, while on vacation in the mountains, if we could get an air ticket outside the allotted time-span of travel in order to accommodate an actor's filming schedule in Europe; or an agent – also vacationing in Aspen and deeming his BlackBerry to be under utilized – would ask if it was possible for us to re-route his client on the outbound leg so that said client could stop off in New York to do some shopping.

In among all these somewhat trite emails, one caught my attention; it was from The Goblin to Daniel Eversleigh, the director of our Closing Night movie. Daniel had emailed the office to ask if he could come out a few days earlier as it was 'damn cold here in London and I could do with a couple of days of sun', whether he could have a limo transfer from his London house to Heathrow and whether there would be any spa treatments available during his stay at The Four Seasons?

I told The Goblin that as we had purchased a full fare First Class return ticket on Virgin Atlantic for him, a limo was already part of the package and that, yes, I would sort out whatever spa treatments he would want. To my horror, The Goblin fired off an email to Mr Eversleigh, ending the response with the words… 'our Guest Services Director, the delightful Vanessa Vere Houghton, will personally take care of all your needs while you are in town.'

I yelled over to him, 'How could you say that? The innuendo implied is *so* embarrassing. Really, it's not particularly professional.'

I was furious, but it had already gone and there were myriad other distractions.

Kane Eppstein regularly rang to ask for something else to be actioned for his father's visit, usually to do with his driver or the hotel suite. On one occasion, as I was feeling particularly battered by a rude and arrogant supplier, Kane called asking if I could make a reservation at Bouchon for his father and seven other guests on the night before the festival opened.

'But he is supposed to be at Ed's cocktail party,' I said, perhaps a little too briskly. After some light-hearted brinkmanship, Kane agreed that his father would attend the cocktail party before dinner. Though Kane had been very brusque to begin with, his whole demeamour had now changed and whenever he did telephone, he was far more courteous and friendly, even prefacing his requests with 'Vanessa my dear, would you mind …' or 'could you do this for me please, Vanessa.' Duncan and Anna were dumbstruck with the transformation from grizzly bear to contented pussy cat.

'What have *you* done to him?' asked Duncan in amazement. 'No one before you has managed to tame him.'

In fact, Kane turned out to be a very charming man; he even invited me to his house after the festival ended and was helpful in giving me names of people in LA to approach with a project I had in mind.

As if there was nothing else to do, Ed would ring up four or five times a day to appraise himself on his cocktail party, particularly with regard to the guest list; Andrea Carnegie would want a hotel update each day; Christian wanted to know, usually twice a day, who was arriving at LAX on which days and at what times – he, of course, did not need to know this information, merely that his guest was attending. The roster of drivers that Lizzie had drawn up unraveled by the minute, due to forgotten family anniversaries or such like on the days they were allocated to do an LA or LAX run; Davina Isner wanted to know, daily, if the Awards Gala honourees and presenters had been finalized, so that she could allocate her chosen volunteers to escorting the stars to their tables; and the drinks sponsors, the ones who had finally been nailed down by Harry, kept calling to see if they could donate something other than what we had requested, and in differing quantities.

And so the whole merry carousel went around and around, picking up speed with each circumnavigation and with all of us clinging on to the outside poles by the skin of our teeth.

There was, however, one aspect of tension distillation among the mayhem. Alexis had returned from her Christmas break – all of one day – with three ducklings which she brought into the office. They lived on her desk in a large

FedEx shipment box and, in between sleeping and quacking at Alexis for food, hopped out through the carefully crafted doorframe and waddled about the desks, busily scattering the manifest papers and shipping documents that were, in essence, the lifeblood of getting the festival off the ground.

They grew inordinately quickly as the days went by and soon were waddling around on the floor, often happily relieving themselves on the carpet. We now had a new hurdle to negotiate, that of not treading on the ducklings as we all flew around the office at supersonic speed.

'Great!' said Diana, as she gingerly picked her way along the corridor past Alexis' office, 'we've now got duck s*** everywhere!'

But the ducklings – Henry, Bordeaux and Paris – proved a great hit, melting even the most hardened heart, and they did inject a brief measure of sanity into the proceedings.

It was 9.28 pm on Friday evening when my mobile rang. 'Where the hell are you?' asked Diana tersely.

'I'm in the office, of course, where else would I be!' Normally this was where I always was to be found, as Diana knew only too well, except this evening was New Year's Eve.

'Get back here right now. We're going out to celebrate and Rob and his mates are joining us.'

'Oh God, I feel so shattered, I don't think I can. I just want a glass of wine, a hot bath and bed,' I whimpered pathetically.

'Oh for God's sake. It's New Year's Eve. Just get back here and you'll feel fine. We're going to Arnold Palmers and we're going to have some fun for a change.'

Tossing my mobile into my tote, I quickly finished

what I was doing. I was not alone in the office, for Ingrid and David were emailing the caterers about the first five receptions and parties to be catered for; Anna was checking replies against the guest list for the Opening Night reception being held at the city's main art museum; The Lesbian was harrumphing in her office over some sponsor who still had not affirmed their commitment; Dino was re-arranging the hotel grid to see if there was *any* way we could accommodate everyone (we could not); Alexis was re-arranging the envelopes on her wall as more now had red strikes on them; Duncan was skimming through his emails; and The Goblin was furiously pounding his computer – but did not seem to be producing any confirmed flight bookings. We found out why the following week.

'OK guys, I'm going to get a life for once, and I suggest you all do so as well. See you all tomorrow,' I said to all and no one in particular. Pausing outside in the cool evening air, I took several deep breaths, clambered into the pick-up and headed back to Diana's house. The thirty-minute journey was just enough to marginally de-stress and, after a glass of wine gulped in a bath brimming with essential oils, I felt revitalized.

'OK, let's go party,' I said, as a very glammed-up Diana and a moderately scrubbed-up self climbed into her SUV. We drove across town to Arnold Palmers – a *tres chic* restaurant and bar which styled itself more as a nightclub than just a restaurant and was, naturally very popular with the high-end golfing crowd.

The Valet Parking guys looked at us in mild amusement when, at eleven o'clock, we told them that we had not booked and they quietly suggested that we "might be disappointed", though, of course, they were more than happy to park the SUV in return for their expected gratuities.

The place was heaving and there was no space. But Diana knew everyone that mattered in the area and so she asked for the manager, who came down and greeted her like a long lost friend. After scanning the reservations book, she found a space for us, but it would have to be at the bar, although we could order off the full menu. Escorting us to the long bar adjacent to the main restaurant, we found two seats jammed in among the throng of second-sitting revellers waiting to go to their tables as soon as the first-sitting had vacated them.

It was a hip place and there were quite a few 'society faces' which I recognized from the local paper; it was elegantly decorated and the bar tenders were amusing – even though they all thought they were auditioning for the re-make of the movie Cocktail. The food was sublime and the drinks kept coming. What more could a girl possibly want, except, perhaps, some 'new blood' to talk to.

This soon presented itself with Rob and his two friends who had been with him at The Wyndham bar when I met him. Aaron and Mitch were also budding screenwriters, but conceded creative force to Rob. They were amusing, irreverent, tall, athletic and good-looking – Aaron was a Rob Lowe-lookalike, while Mitch bore a passing resemblance to Kevin Bacon. Together with Rob, they stood out like a beacon and it did not escape my notice that almost all the 'cougars', many with fat, balding men way past their sell-by date, were eyeing Diana and I with contempt.

The five of us chatted animatedly for most of the night; I noticed that Mexico cropped up a lot, but didn't give it too much thought, and then it was almost midnight.

The sixty-inch UHD wall-mounted television dutifully informed us that in five minutes it would be a new year. The bar tenders leapt into frenzied action and within seconds there were pyramids of champagne flutes positioned along the bar and side chests flanking the restaurant. With just two minutes to go, corks popped in a crescendo and the bottles' contents were adroitly delivered into the flutes; they were then placed on silver salvers and taken to all the diners, with one pyramid left on the bar for the bar-flies. We each grabbed our flute as the TV screen beamed earlier images from New York's Times Square where the celebrities *du jour* had counted down the seconds to midnight three hours earlier. Ticker tape streamed down as clocks all over the West Coast struck midnight and we all wished everyone around us a "happy new year" with hugs and kisses – the cougars making a bee-line for Rob, Aaron and Mitch.

The jazz band hired for the night swung into action, tables were pushed back against the walls and revellers crammed onto the small dance floor which reminded me of Annabel's, the London nightclub which has a similarly miniscule dance floor, though this has never detracted it from being London's top night-spot.

Rob pulled me onto the dance floor, where we showed the older crowd how to move; no one else at the restaurant was planning to go anywhere. We all stayed until five o'clock, by which time I had 'hit a wall' with exhaustion. Rob asked when we could next meet, despite knowing the work vortex and that I would not have a second for the next fifteen or so days. Giving him a lingering kiss, I joked that he would at least have time to go on vacation in Mexico.

'But I want you to come with me.'

'I can't honey. I am just jammed until after the festival.' Squeezing his hand, I said I would call him when I had a spare nano-second, before giving him another final kiss.

The Valet Parking guys promptly brought Diana's SUV around and she gave them a very generous tip and several Merlot-fuelled kisses. God, it had been good to do something other than emailing, phoning, arguing and fire-fighting. But it would be back to all of that tomorrow – no, later today! For, in the land of premier film festivals, and with one coming up so quickly, there was no such thing as a New Year's Day holiday.

Saturday morning, New Year's Day. While most normal people were at home in bed nursing a suitably decent hangover, I was in the office by nine-thirty – late by everyone else's standards – and nursing my own crushing headache, when there came a bizarre call.

'Debra Haynes is on the line for you,' Sherri, the Receptionist, trilled down my phone.

'Who's she?' I asked, not feeling at all like having any more work thrown my way.

'She's from the Daily News-Press.'

'OK, put her through.'

A charmingly soft voice came on the line. 'Hello, is this Vanessa?'

'Yes, it is. Hi. How can I help you?'

She explained that the paper's editor had thought a behind-the-scenes article on what we all did to make the festival happen would be a great feature to run on the day the festival started. 'You know, a sort of spotlight on all the backstage hands that makes this happen.'

I was horrified. Let the paper into our offices to see what *really* went on in here to get this show on the road.

'Erm, let me run this by our Executive Director and I'll get back to you in five.'

I dashed to Duncan's office where he and Christian were finalizing the movies playlist at each cinema on a large poly-board – Christian's own version of the 'Alexis wall'.

'Duncan,' I called urgently. He looked up.

'What's up darlin? No problems I hope, my head just won't hack it this morning.'

'I've just had a call from the Daily News-Press and they want to do a feature article on us and everything we all have to do to get this show on the road.'

He grinned. 'Yeah, just had an email from Ed about it. He thinks it's a good idea and says we must do it.'

'What!' I shrieked. 'It's a terrible idea. We're all totally stressed and overloaded and it will come across like that. It'll end up a hatchet job.'

Duncan was unusually nonplussed. 'Nah, darlin, it'll be fine. Our papers are way tamer than yours in England. They don't do hatchet jobs here, they do nice. Call her back and see when she wants to come in, but try and push for tomorrow, it'll be the last down-day we have.'

Down-day? What on earth was that?

I called Debra. 'Hey Debra, sorry to keep you. We're happy to help you, although when you come into the offices you must excuse the mess everywhere. As you can imagine, we have a ton of stuff constantly being delivered for the movie theatres and host hotel, so we look as if we are a loading dock at the moment.

'Any chance you could come in tomorrow, then you could meet all the key players – Duncan, the Executive Director, Christian, the Programming Director, his assistant Hannah, Diana who does all the marketing and programme guides, Ingrid, who heads up Special Events, and myself, I'm the Guest Services Manager, How long do you think you'd need?'

An almost ecstatic 'Oh, about four hours in total, say

forty-five minutes per person. I don't want to hold anyone up.'

'Sure, let's start at, say, eleven o'clock.'

'Hey, really look forward to meeting you tomorrow, and Ed says I should start with you.'

Diana was not amused when I rang to tell her she was required in the office tomorrow but, under duress, said she would come in only if she followed me in the interview running order and that Duncan then took us out to lunch. I told her there was no chance of that as we were all still totally overloaded. She snorted an agreement of sorts and announced she was going back to bed. Sensible girl, I thought, as I returned to my daily detritus.

There was, thankfully, some good news. Three hair and cosmetic giants, Frédéric Fekkai, the fabulous Smashbox and Aveda, plus two studios, Universal and DreamWorks, had emailed with confirmation they would donate to the goody bags, plus Saks Fifth Avenue had sent a brief message to say that the crocodile totes and the sterling silver key rings had arrived from New York and were ready for collection over the weekend. Kirsten Florian and MetroMint also both confirmed they would donate to the 'swag'.

Frédéric Fekkai was offering Ageless Overnight Hair Repair for the A-List goody bags and Ageless Damage Defence Capsules for the other two hundred bags; Smashbox was donating its award-winning Halo Hydrating Perfecting Powder for the A-List bags and its Naked Beauty Lip Gloss Collection, in eight colours, for the remaining ones; while Aveda was giving two hundred tubes of its body moisturiser for the industry guest bags.

Universal and DreamWorks each stated they would courier over their about-to-be-released Blu Rays for the industry guest bags – we had not asked them for anything for the A-List bags – and Kirsten Florian advised it would donate Myrrh Nail Oil for the A-List bags and Spa Face Lip-Marine Crème & Sun Spa Sunscreen for the industry bags.

During the course of the weekend, we got word from the sublime San Ysidro Ranch that they would donate a two-night stay in the Kennedy Cottage to the A-List bags – more punching of air in glee as we worked out it was worth approximately $8,500); Louis Vuitton said it would donate their iconic Soupçon sunglasses to the celebrities' bags, and Smythson advised it would love to donate its Portobello Desk Diary – which we had asked for. Mercedes also emailed to say they had already shipped over two hundred and fifty illuminating pens for the bags. Things were slowly coming together on the 'swag' front.

Debra Haynes duly arrived at eleven o'clock the next morning, though I could not fathom why a journalist would want to work on a Sunday morning. She was a delightfully sincere, warm and amusing lady in her mid-forties. There was no agenda; she just wanted to do an honest portrayal of what it took to put on a major film festival and get the calibre of stars we had coming in. She said the paper simply wanted a good colour piece to portray the significance of the event in the local region and thought that, by leading with office staffers, it would present a more personalized overview.

What she had not told us, though, was that she was bringing a staff photographer with her, who duly turned up ten minutes later, to take some general shots to add visuals to the editorial.

She quickly averted my fears over the resulting article

resembling a 'hatchet job'. We got along swimmingly and I soon found myself relaxing in her presence, explaining my role and its tasks – both the expected and the more unusual – that I and my team had to undertake, answering all her questions and telling her odd juicy bits of industry gossip.

Dino had also come into the office to do more on the hotel grid and so we both showed Debra the flights and hotels grids, the gift ideas we had planned for the goody bags, the plans for Ed's cocktail party at The Four Seasons the night before the Awards Gala – and the whole hospitality suite manifest, from breakfast muffins and cocktail hamburgers, through to the Asian-fusion menu and the proposed décor.

She spent over an hour with Dino and myself and seemed suitably impressed that twenty-five hotels and over eight-hundred-and-thirty room nights had been allocated for the festival's celebrities and VIP guests; that we had secured Mercedes S-Class Sedans and two Maybachs; that Tiffany was leaving a small gift on the table setting for every guest at the Awards Gala; that we were handling over two-hundred flights from Europe, Central and South America, Israel, India, South Africa and Australia, in addition to Canada and internal US ones. She particularly loved the titbit that the complement of chauffeurs engaged were adept at speaking Spanish, French, German and Portuguese.

After interviewing Diana, she moved on to Duncan. He kindly underscored the fact that his staff had been working fifteen- to twenty-hour days to make it all happen, that we had two-hundred-and-thirty movies from seventy-five countries – many of which were having their world premieres at the festival – and that he projected an audience of around one-hundred-and-twenty-five-thousand. Debra then met Christian, Hannah and Ingrid, the latter regaling her with details of the various receptions, parties and venues and the fact that we had forty caterers on hand, but that "the trick is to have fun and stay cool", but if something went awry, "we smile and put on more lipstick."

Alexis tossed in a couple of blinders, such as the fact that the schedule called for as many as four-hundred-and-sixty screenings across fifteen cinemas and that the festival stood head and shoulders above others because it insisted on showing 35mm films "because that's the crème de la crème. It's still the global standard."

True to her word, Debra was not obtrusive and did not seem fazed by all the film reels and boxes of promotional items stacked all over the place. She only 'held us up' for around fifty minutes each and we were soon able to return to the chaos that engulfed us. We had all liked her and felt that our interviews had gone well.

If we had thought that the rest of the day would be marginally more relaxing – it was a *Sunday*, after all – we were in for another surprise. Diana, who had sensibly taken her hangover to The Yard House at lunchtime for a hair-of-the-dog Bloody Mary, returned to the office at the end of the afternoon, having been summoned by Harry.

'He wants all the proofs for the Awards Gala programme emailed to him in New York this evening,' she muttered as she slammed her bulging tote onto her desk. 'Frigging nuisance, I thought we had this one away and I just know he will make changes for the sheer hell of it.'

Being the money man, Harry was obsessed with just two things – revenue generation and sponsors' logos. Forget incisive copy and arresting images, as far as he was concerned logos were the only item on his radar and the only element that mattered within any of the festival's guides, and the Awards Gala programme was the touchstone.

By about seven o'clock, Diana, having re-worked, re-sized, re-positioned and re-formatted just about every logo and sponsor name – apart from the sacrosanct Tiffany & Co. and Mercedes-Benz logos – leant back in her chair and exhaled deeply.

'OK, you little bugger. Off you go,' she said slowly as she emailed the considerably revised proof to Harry.

I said I would wait with her as I had more than enough to get on with – the goody bags really did need to be finalized, so yet more begging emails needed to be dispatched. We cracked open a bottle of Prosecco and drowned our sorrows while Diana paced the office and generally harangued Duncan, Christian and Hannah. I, in the meantime, continued to hammer my keyboard.

The call from Harry came through at nine-thirty.

'Hey Diana. Where's that god-damn proof I asked for about five hours ago?'

'I emailed it to you over two hours ago. Haven't you even bothered to look at it?' she snapped. 'I need to get it to the printers sooner rather than later, so a green light from you would be good Harry.'

'Haven't got it. Send it again. Oh, and I have just completed one of the biggest deals of my life, so I'm off to the 21 Club with my colleagues to crack a few magnums. You're gonna have to wait in the office until we're finished. Guess it'll be another good few hours.'

'*What!*' exploded a visibly enraged Diana. 'For Christ's sake, it's nine-thirty here. You think I am going to sit in the god-damn office all f***ing night for the peanuts the film festival pays me while you are out partying at 21 Club. I'm going home in fifteen minutes. I'm not waiting here until you deign to call me with your approval. I'm done for the day. And don't bother to call me at home either. You are so full of s*** sometimes Harry.'

'OK. OK. OK. Frigging calm down. Email the proof now and I'll call you back in ten.'

Diana knew that Harry knew that she was, at that moment, more important to him than vice versa. And sure enough, the call came through in ten minutes, but it was not what Diana had hoped for.

'OK, most of it looks fine, but I need to make a couple of calls to double check a few things. We may have another sponsor. I know you're pissed with me, but you are just gonna have to wait for a couple of hours and there is nothing else to it. I have to take these guys to 21 now. Period. I'll call you back in a couple of hours. Wait at the office.'

Shaking her head in disbelief and speechless with rage, Diana threw the phone back onto the receiver while slamming her fist onto the desk and emitting an ear-splitting *'Grrrgh'*. She knew she had no alternative but to wait.

It was one o'clock in the morning when Harry finally called, sounding as though he was suitably refreshed.

'OK honey, we haven't got that other sponsor so you can send it to the printers and then you can go home as soon as you've done that.'

'Oh *thank you so much,*' Diana spat through clenched teeth, 'and I'm not your honey, so don't ever call me that again.'

On the way home, we mused over Debra Haynes' interviews and how the Daily News-Press feature would turn out. The litmus test, however, would be what appeared in the paper on the day the festival opened, which was now only four days away.

CHAPTER TWELVE

La La Land's entertainment industry was now back at work and the emails were taking on leviathan proportions. There were emails to again ask most of the questions from two weeks ago: to whom was their star presenting the award? (even though Duncan had advised their bosses in the initial negotiations); which media were covering the event?; what type of cars did we have? (I read this as were they *good* enough?); who were our drivers (ditto interpretation); how long had we allowed for transport between the hotel and the Awards Gala venue?; who would be the driver for that run?

There were emails asking for reminders of the timings concerning just about everything to do with the Awards Gala: would there be a Green Room?; who was handling red carpet escorts?; was the star expected to be at the cocktail reception immediately before the awards ceremony or could they go straight to the Green Room?; how many places on the tables?; when did I need to have the list of the star's invited guests; who was handling security for the ceremony?; would there be a suitably experienced hair and make-up person on hand?; how many people in total would be attending the Gala?; who were the dignitaries within this audience?, when could they see the script for the show? The questions were unrelenting.

I, in turn, also had to email them all to ask if the respective star would be able to attend the Chairman's Private Pre-Festival Cocktail Party at the Four Seasons the night before the Awards Gala – assuring them that this was a small and *very* exclusive affair – and could they please reply to this as soon as possible. This provoked a flurry of worried emails! They were not sure, they said, if their talent would be able to be in town the day before, as "filming and other prior commitments, you understand"; they would check and come back to me as soon as someone could get hold of the star. And so a third of the next few twenty-hour days were spent going back and forth over this single subject alone.

'Hey Vanessa, we're gonna have to change Xavier Torres' flight. He's been delayed in post-production and he can't get out of Rio until the weekend,' screeched Christian in near-hysteria as he rounded the corner from Duncan's office and ran up the steps of the 'Hollywood Hills' to slump on the edge of my desk.

'But for Christ's sake, make sure you get him in here by Monday night latest. *Absolute* latest. In case you've forgotten, we're giving him the International Filmmaker Award at the Cine Latino Gala on Wednesday night, so he *has,* but *has,* to be here for that. Just get the flights changed.'

'Yep, and the limo, the driver and the hotel', I muttered.

As The Goblin, Dino, Lizzie and I all huddled at one end of the Boardroom table and poured over our grids to ensure there were no yawning chasms we could all topple into, Hannah swept in with a near repeat of Christian's earlier diktat.

'Hey guys, really sorry to dump this one on you, but I've just had an email from Armando Aguilar's people and he and Jaime now can't leave Madrid until tomorrow, so you're gonna have to change the flights. But as Armando's a presenter, you've got to get them here by Friday latest!'

My jaw, along with The Goblin's, hit the table.

'But they're booked on the flight this afternoon!' I screamed at Hannah. 'It's not just a question of us changing everything, the airline may not allow it. Has anyone *thought* of that? And we're messing the hotels around as well, with now empty rooms that they could have sold.'

'Yeah, I know,' she said, backing out of the Boardroom as quickly as possible, 'that's why you gotta move fast.'

Shaking my head in disbelief, I looked at The Goblin. 'Go. Now! Do Armando and Jaime first, then Xavier Torres. Any problems, back to me immediately. And this is the last time we are changing flights.The domino effect is too bloody time consuming and one thing we haven't got is the luxury of time.'

Looking thunderous, The Goblin scuttled off to his desk, re-emerging an hour later with his blackmail; he had, by the skin of his teeth, managed to change the flights, so now we all owed him with passes to most of the receptions and parties. Telling him to get over himself, I asked Dino to do suitably apologetic notes to the hotels in which our three delayed guests were booked.

This soon became the pattern over the course of the next three days. Nothing remained in place, particularly when it came to those attending the Awards Gala. As soon as I had arranged something, it was cancelled, re-scheduled, re-cancelled and re-scheduled – all in the space of about half a day; as we were doing twenty hour days, these ten hours were more than most peoples' full day. There were moments when I thought it would have been more sensible not to do anything at all and just arrange everything right at the last moment, but that would, of course, be impractical and would have had us all jumping out of windows like screaming banshees.

Email, after email, phone call after phone call. I was drowning and the only way to try and keep on top of all of this was to have some admin help – even if only to just answer my phone while I got on with the emails. I called Ed.

'Hey Ed, you know you said for me to call if I needed help. Well we're absolutely swamped here and I could really use one of your ladies to come over and help with the phones. Any chance?' I implored.

'What the hell do you think I'm running here, a god-damn secretarial bureau?' he barked.

'Well you did say to ask for help if I needed it, and I *really* need it now. So, any chance?' I retorted, equally briskly.

'See what I can …' He hung up the receiver without bothering to finish the sentence.

I was not amused, given the fact that I was working my butt off to do his damn cocktail party over and above my role which, I had been reliably informed by a discreet insider, was usually fulfilled by two to three people. But, within the hour, the cavalry arrived in the form of Cindy and Marjorie, with 'valium sandwiches' and flasks of Starbucks Latte Mocha.

'Thank God you are here!' I exclaimed, sounding like Custer in the final throes of the Battle of Little Bighorn. 'Please can you just man the phones and take detailed messages. It's complete madness, as you will soon see.'

Though Ed himself was a powerhouse, his main secretary Miranda handled most of his work and so Cindy and Marjorie were not used to much pressure. The poor souls soon wilted, furiously scribbling messages for me and, as the phone lines raged, the messages became more and more ragged and illegible as they attempted to keep up.

The need for Prozac was extending to other departments, particularly Print Traffic which I felt was on a par with Guest Services for stress-induced meltdown. Poor Alexis spent the whole of the next three days tearing her hair out – 'Alexis' Wall' still had some glaring omissions – the envelopes were not all ticked green, as she and Christian had expected at this stage of the game. Frantic phone calls were placed to all the major FedEx and UPS offices around the *entire* country in an attempt to locate the missing component. One, for example, was found in a warehouse in Texas – it was reel number four of six from a French film that was produced in Pakistan.

Diana, whose main job was now over and, as such, could languish in luxury at the spa, was rudely jolted out of her sleep-inducing massage by a call on her mobile from The Lesbian, who was incandescent. The official Programme Guide had appeared this morning in the local paper and it was not on Electrobrite paper, nor were there enough run-on's. Diana, who also did not much care for The Lesbian, fired back a withering broadside.

'Oh for God's sake, is that all you've got to be worried about? Duncan and I agreed before Christmas that the budget couldn't stretch to Electrobrite, and the run-on's are being delivered this evening. *So sorry* no one has told you. OK. Bye.'

It never ceased to amaze us all how people generally could not manage to read what was in front of them, be it an email or in a newspaper. As with Guest Services' raging Zambezi of emails, poor Sherri was swamped with calls from the public about the screenings, the timings, the cost and how could they buy a ticket, even though it was all clearly stated in the official programme guide. I felt for her, as I knew only too well what it was like and so I offered Cindy to help with the reception phones. But before we knew it, the cinema-going public were pouring through the office's main entrance and flooding reception with a barrage of questions and demands which made it impossible for any of us to enter or leave, take deliveries of missing film reels, or even deal with them.

The guide, intended to make life easier for everyone – particularly those manning the Box Offices at the movie theatres – appeared to have the opposite effect, as the sheer volume of calls that day for tickets jammed the lines and crashed the reservations computers, both at the theatres and the main one at the office. While the festival's accountant rubbed his hands with glee, it proved a logistical headache for the Theatre Operations staff.

One of my gazillion emails stopped me in my tracks. It was from Focus Features, stating that its key star – who was receiving an award at the Awards Gala – would do neither the red carpet, the reception nor the Green Room. He would arrive at the rear of the venue – we had to agree the rather unglamorous loading dock as the rendezvous point – and simply be escorted backstage to await his call on stage.

He would receive his award, make his speech and then leave the proceedings via the loading dock. He would do neither media interviews, nor photographs and this was all non-negotiable.They also asked for extra security on the night and suggested that we consider engaging the services of the Los Angeles Police Department and, possibly, the FBI.

I read, re-read and again re-read the email in utter astonishment, finally taking it to Duncan, who erupted into mocking laughter as he read it.

'Oh dear God, the crap we have to put up with. Well, darlin', I suggest you get onto the FBI.'

Assuming he was joking, I went back to my desk and carried on scanning the subject headlines, secretly wishing I could just highlight the lot and hit delete.

Another one caught my eye; it was from Liam Taylor's publicist, advising that he went under the alias of 'Mr Malden' when travelling and could his hotel reservation be made in that name? It also detailed the name of his security man who would also be attending the festival. I shot back a reply, thanking her for this information but that, unfortunately, the hotel reservations were made two weeks ago and that he was booked in under his real name, as were all the other stars. There would be several more emails like this over the next couple of days and they all elicited the same response, though a couple of the recipients were not amused to be told this and demanded the reservation be changed. By now, my patience was wearing very thin and I took great pleasure in deleting those ones.

At just past midnight, Andrea Carnegie had emailed appropriate staff members requesting their attendance at The Wyndham this afternoon for a gala rehearsal. Dropping everything else, and with Ed's words "did I know *who* she was" still ringing in my ears, I shot over to the hotel at the appointed hour.

The show producer, Rocco Tramanti, was there, as were representatives from the Los Angeles Times and Entertainment Tonight, the latter taping the show to broadcast it on the following Monday evening. We went through absolutely *everything* from the room layout for the cocktail reception and dinner seating plans; which star was to be the first on the red carpet and how long it would, or *should,* take each star to walk it; through to the running order and timings of each award presentation and acceptance speech; how long Natalie Immber would be on stage and how many video clips would be shown, and which volunteers would escort the A-List and other celebrities to their tables. Last but not least, came the format for getting the A-List out at the end of the ceremony and over to the after-show party at The Four Seasons.

We ran over lighting, set décor, off-stage voice-overs, audio feeds and video rolls. We debated how we would cue the hotel staff to set and clear away the meal courses, as well as the intricate task of coordinating close up and zoom angles on five or six video cameras. Rocco had a draft script of the show, written to a minute-by-minute format.

Nine awards were being handed out and the recipients all had to be cued in; to keep us on our toes, one of those being honoured would then be called back to the stage to present the Lifetime Achievement Award. It had to be immaculately timed and there was no room for error; hence this rehearsal was the first of several over the following three-and-a-half days.

'When will the Step and Repeat Wall be ready?' Ric Isaacs from the PR agency called me, as he was leaving the underground car park of his LA office to drive to the city. Oh My God. Who was supposed to be organizing the Step & Repeat Wall? (An integral component of all red carpet events, it is a large format banner onto which sponsors' logos are printed in order to gain maximum brand exposure when the celebrities are photographed walking the carpet or at the post-event media interviews.)

'Erm, have no idea Ric,' I said slowly, trying to buy

time to figure this one out. 'Not sure who's even handling this one. Leave it with me and I'll call you back in five.'

I raced to Marketing; JP was on the phone, but mouthed "no" when I asked if he was handling it. I called Diana at home; no, she said she had not been asked to do one, although she had brought it up at one of the first staff meetings. I ran to Anna's office; no, she knew nothing about it, but nodded over her shoulder towards Duncan's office. He just shook his head; no, he was not handling it, but added somewhat tersely, 'I hope to God that someone is, otherwise we're really gonna piss off Tiffany.'

It must be Ed, I thought, calling his office. 'No,' said Miranda, 'Ed had not requested one, but yes, we need one, so who is organizing it?' I ran around the corner to The Lesbian's office; no, she snarled, without even looking up, not her remit. I called Harry's office, a wave of relief flooding over me when he said he had emailed a local production company to make one, but had forgotten to tell any of us that he had done so. No one from his office had followed through and no one seemed to know if it had even been put into production.

'Jeez, give me the name and number now and I'll follow up.'

Heart pounding, I called the number, only too aware that if they had not started the wall it would now be too late and the proverbial s*** would hit the fan in several shades. The Creative Manager came on the line.

'How can I help?' he asked casually, not realizing that his answer could destroy someone's career in a second. I took a deep breath and tried to sound calm.

'I was just wondering if the Step and Repeat Wall for the film festival was ready, or nearing completion?'

After an eternity, I could hear him walking back to the

phone. 'Yeah, last coat's still drying, but I guess it'll be ready in thirty-six hours. Where do you want it delivered?'

A deep exhalation of breath. I suddenly realized I had not been breathing during the conversation. 'The main ballroom at The Wyndham on Saturday. But it absolutely must be there by two-thirty as we have a final walk-through with our star host from Entertainment Tonight and the show producer.'

He was so laid back compared to my near-meltdown. 'Yeah, that's cool. It'll be there.'

One crisis averted, but there would be more. The next one awaiting me as soon as I got off the phone was computers and modem layout at the host hotel; their tech guy had called to say they could not put in the required modem lines and phone jacks. I leapt into the Dodge and drove over as fast as I could, for all the tech equipment had to be installed today as Guest Services would be moving into the suite tomorrow afternoon and we needed the computers up and running in order to continue working.

There was also the monumental task of co-ordinating the bulk of guest arrivals at LAX with mini-buses and limo drivers, and we could not possibly do that without computers and phones.

Throwing my keys at the Valet Parking guy, I raced into the lobby, almost flattening Jon Bauer in the process, and dashed sideways into the suite. It looked a mess, having been 'taken down' from a previous meeting and I wondered how on earth we would transform the cavernous room into an ambient, stylish and relaxing salon.

Pushing thoughts of interior design to one side, I sought out whom I assumed to be the head of IT. He was a charming man, more than willing to help out and very apologetic for the fact that one of his staff had sent me hurtling into a corkscrew spiral. I laid out the plan of the room I had sketched in the office at one o'clock last night, and said we simply had to have all the lines, jacks and computer points.

'I've got four full-time staff who'll each need a computer, plus two part-time volunteers who need to share one computer. Then we need at least three computers dispersed throughout the room for our guests to access the internet, and a further two computers, plus an ISDN line, along that wall for the PR agency,' I said, stabbing my finger at each of the blocks on the layout. 'And in the connecting room, which is where we'll do all the media interviews, we need ISDN lines to be able to do live feeds.'

He looked at me and smiled. 'You don't want much lady, do you.'

'So, you can do all this for me?' I asked, not daring to yet feel relieved.

'Yeah, but it'll take a while.'

'How long?'

'Umm, guess a couple of days,' he said, obviously not having been told when the festival started.

'Oh my God, we've got to have this all in place by tomorrow mid afternoon latest,' I shrieked. 'The festival starts the day after tomorrow. Didn't anyone here *tell* you that? If necessary, you're going to have to draft in more guys, start right now and work through the night. But this has just got to be done. Sorry, but it's non-negotiable.'

He looked pitifully at me. 'Seems your under a lot of pressure lady. OK, we'll try and get it done in time.'

'By tomorrow, three-thirty absolute latest,' I yelled, running out of the room.

Back at the office, there was more grief awaiting me.

The Goblin gleefully advised that, while he had

managed to change the flights from Rio for Xavier Torres, and Madrid for Armando Aguilar and Jaime Bardeles, it had cost us an extra $300 apiece to do the change. We were now over budget by $1,000 and still being asked to change flights; yet another problem to sort out with Duncan who, as a walking movie encyclopaedia, was not remotely interested in budgets at the best of times, least of all when he was only thirty hours away from opening one of the biggest film festivals in the country.

Just so that I had not forgotten them, the Zambezi emails from the studios' marketing and publicity executives and the stars' publicists were still surging ahead towards the whitewater rapids that was rapidly becoming my head.

There were reams of stars' guests names for the Awards ceremony; could we book hotel rooms for them – ten per table x nine stars being honoured equalled an extra ninety people for which they, the studios, would pay, but we still had to find the time to see if there *were* any rooms left in town and book them; was the script for the Awards Gala ready yet and if so, could I email a copy to them?; addresses for limos to pick up the stars on myriad different times on Friday and Saturday; aliases that many of the stars liked to travel under; yes – 'x' star could attend the Chairman's cocktail party; no – 'x' star could not attend; what were plans for inclement weather? – something we had not factored into the equation!; if so, which was the nearest private airfield in which to land the studio jet? And so it went on. And on. And on.

The emails tumbled in with such speed that it was impossible to keep on top of them; no sooner had I penned a quick response to one, about twenty more had dropped in. And Ed, too, was emailing me about his cocktail party which, with the broad scope of the whole festival, seemed to be of paramount importance to him. That night, I counted over one-hundred-and-sixty-eight new emails arriving since the middle of the day. It had become sheer madness.

Meanwhile, we still had to cancel and re-book hotel rooms for Xavier Torres, Armando Aguilar and Jaime Bardeles. We had to finalize which driver and car to use to pick-up Daniel Eversleigh at LAX; make a reservation at The Ritz Carlton for Barbro Innes – whose office had just called to confirm that she wanted to stay there as it was further out of town – and find a room in town for her publicist.

As many of our two-hundred guests were now starting to arrive at LAX, though the majority would be arriving tomorrow, Lizzie, Dino and I began calling drivers into the office, handing them car keys and giving them a detailed brief about whom they were collecting and which hotel to take them to. It was a good rehearsal for tomorrow, which would test our sanity to the limits.

I finally left the office at one-thirty in the morning and drove back to Diana's, taking care not to wake her as I crept into bed. It hardly seemed worthwhile as I would be up again in four hours.

Countdown day. The festival started in twenty-four hours; after just a few hours' sleep, I was back on the hamster wheel. Although feeling absolutely shattered, I had to be in fifth gear, for not only was Lawrence Eppstein arriving today, but the Guest & Industry Suite had to be ready and fully operational by tonight.

Ed constantly phoned and emailed me about his party, for which he had now directed that all RSPV's came to me; the wallpaper issue had to be resolved today; the PR agency arrived in force – Ric and Shane bringing with them their assistants and a couple of other junior executives; all the A-List's guests names for the Awards Gala had to be emailed over to Harry's office for him to do the seating plan, and the 'Hollywood emails', as I now dubbed them, still flowed in from the studios.

The walkie-talkies and keybox for the cars still had not arrived, the goody bags had to be made up and the Welcome Packs had to be finished; the majority had been done at midnight, but the Guest Services Guide had only been delivered at seven o'clock this morning.

Kane called. 'My dad's arriving in a short while. Is everything ready at the hotel?'

In the frenzy of all the work still to be done, I had forgotten his arrival time.

'Hey Kane, I was just on my way over to the Spa Resort to double check, but yeah, everything's sorted.'

I grabbed my keys, plus Dino and Mike 2 as I figured that we could all drop off a few things at The Wyndham en route back – and headed over to the Spa Resort.

I ran into the lobby; rudely pushing in front of another guest at the Concierge Desk, I breathlessly asked to be taken up to the Penthouse Suite and to meet its dedicated Butler. After five minutes of explaining who I was and why I was there in such a frazzled state, I was escorted to the top floor. It was a stunning suite and would have comfortably accommodated my English cottage twice over. The Butler was charming and efficient, and I briefed him on his 'V-VIP' guest, giving him my mobile number in case there were any problems. He assured me there would be none.

Relieved, we headed back to the fun factory, via The Wyndham, to find out what the next little crisis was in store.

It was Lizzie, pulling her hair out as the majority of

the two-hundred guests were arriving today. There was a constant loop of runs to LAX by the mini-buses, limos and cars to meet and greet the guests and safely deliver them to their respective hotels; we had left a welcome letter for them and to request that they came to the Guest & Industry Suite in the morning to collect their personal Welcome Packs which would contain all the information that they needed. But all the invitations to the various receptions and parties still had to be placed inside the Welcome Packs. This was not as simple as it sounded, for while most of the two-hundred guests received an invite to the Opening and Closing-Night receptions, only selected industry guests – mainly established film directors, producers, studio heads and key executives – received invitations for certain parties. These had to be carefully checked and put into the correct Welcome Pack, which meant putting personal labels on each pack, so that the right invitations got to the right person. It all took time.

My four assistants started moving across to The Wyndham, a feat in itself when they were continually having to answer emails and phone calls and solve problems, while I, at Ed and Duncan's suggestion, would remain at 'base camp' with a computer and phone whose signal would not be interrupted. I spent the entire evening with the team setting up the suite and adjacent media room, and sorting out the squabbles as to who was to sit where. Finally, just after eleven-thirty, we all agreed it looked fabulous and congratulated ourselves on a job well done.

I told the others to go home and get some sleep, for they had to be back in the suite at seven o'clock the next morning. Lizzie remained shackled to her computer, as there were a few glitches still to be sorted out due to a last minute re-scheduling of an arrival early the next morning.

Crawling back to the office shortly after midnight, I was met with another hell of a ruckus, and was soon to find out why. It had been brought to Duncan's attention by a friend in LA that someone at the festival office was writing a blog, and not a complementary one at that. Alan, our geek Programming assistant – the one who constantly yelled at me over the 'Hollywood Hills' wall to lower my voice – had traced the blog back to The Goblin. Now it made sense, for several of us had wondered why he spent almost 24/7 at his desk when the level of flight bookings were not commensurate with the amount of time he was buried at his computer.

Duncan was incandescent with rage. 'That's it. He's fired. Get him over here now,' he yelled at me.

'But Duncan, it's nearly twelve-thirty and I sent him home twenty minutes ago,' I said, taking a step back from the tornado that was flattening me.

'I don't give a flying f***, just get him here now. He's out and he can damn well leave town tonight. You'll just have to manage without him.'

Secretly rather pleased, for The Goblin had not been a particularly pleasant character, I called him on his cellphone, enjoying the moment of *schadenfreude*.

'Hey Mike, sorry to hassle you at this time, but something urgent has just come up and we really need you in the office. Duncan needs to run it by you now. Can you get over straight away?'

He obviously had no inkling, as he casually replied, 'Do I have to? Oh-kay, be there in five.'

Ping. Ping. Ping. Three texts from Rob rolled into my phone. "Hi lovely, how'ya doin'? I'm just outside Culiacán with my good friend Javier Pajares and his mate Manuel Sinalopéz. After we've sorted a few things, we're gonna fly back to Tijuana and then Santa Monica in Javier's Cessna. Should be back in a week. Stay cool!"

I didn't pay too much attention to the part about a plane, as I had heard about Javier and his privileged lifestyle, although Rob had never explained the derivation of all his wealth.

The Goblin strolled into Duncan's office, can of Becks in one hand and a roll-up hanging out of the side of his mouth.

'Hey, what's up? I was just getting to sleep. You know that word, Duncan. Sleep. What none of us has at the moment.'

His execution was swift; he naturally tried to deny it, but Duncan had the blog up on his computer. There was no way out for him except to pack his bags and get the hell out. We all knew that he harboured an ambition to move to LA and work in the industry, so the sting in Duncan's scorpion-like riposte as he walked towards the door was to the point.

'Don't even think you'll get a job in LA or at any other film festival in North America or Europe. I will personally see to that. Now get out and never let me see your pathetic face again, you little piece of s***.'

The Goblin was consigned to history.

The entire office was feeling ragged and it was beginning to show; tempers were frayed and conversations were conducted in varying pitches of angst and hysteria. We were "running on empty" – to quote the immortal title from the classic Jackson Brown song – living purely on adrenaline and working simply crazy hours.

But we had ten days of a festival to still get through. Would the world ever return to normality?

CHAPTER THIRTEEN

The first day of the festival. At seven o'clock, the Guest Services team were in the suite, double-checking everything was in place; the Welcome Packs were laid out on the main trestle table in alphabetical order of guest names, while the goody bags were carefully hidden underneath to eschew people helping themselves to more than one.

Duncan, Christian and Hannah appeared about fifteen minutes later, seemingly pleased with the suite layout and décor, and congratulating us all on a job well done. By eight o'clock, the coterie of suite volunteers began arriving to await the imminent onslaught of the guests. Our collateral materials had stated that breakfast would be available from nine until eleven o'clock, but we knew that they would immediately want their Starbucks.

A couple of minutes later, the PR agency arrived in force and the assistants immersed themselves in the designated media area at the far end of the room, positioned so that they had some relative peace and quiet. Among them was an attractive guy whom I had not seen before and with the most uplifting smile I have ever seen. He came over and introduced himself to me.

'Hi, I gather you're Vanessa. I'm Dominic Steinberg and I'm helping Ric and Shane do some media stuff, though PR isn't my background. I'm a writer and producer and I've just completed my first short feature. Actually, it's being screened at the festival, so I am here as an official guest, but I like hanging out with these guys.'

I was captivated by this gorgeous guy.

'I'll be over on the Media desk if there's anything I can do to help.'

I was soon jolted out of my trance by Ric and Shane in Scud missile-mode, making a direct hit on Duncan and almost emptying his coffee into his lap as they dropped copies of today's edition of the local paper onto the table, whooping with delight. Debra Haynes' behind-the-scenes article was the lead feature in the Life section, but it had also been flagged up in a shaded box on the top of the front page, just under the masthead: "We've got the scoop on the behemoth tasks needed to put on the successful festival and the hundreds of staff members and volunteers who make it all happen."

Duncan looked momentarily askance. 'Do I need to be worried? I've got enough to cope with already, without negative press.'

Ric beamed from ear to ear. 'Oh per-leez. It's great, it's terrific, actually we couldn't have done a better job. There are great references to you and Vanessa. Go on, read it now. It will *so* improve your day.'

We each grabbed a copy. Headlined 'Working outside the Spotlight', it did portray, in a positive light, the sheer amount of work and people needed to make it happen. "The film festival has become one of the major industry showcases"... it started, thereby pleasing Duncan immeasurably, before going on to say "… galas, 230 films from around the world and a bevy of celebrities with whims that would thaw an icy-swizzle stick in a martini before it hits the glass". Duncan shot me an enquiring glance.

'I didn't say that!'

'Hey darlin', it's a good line. I must remember that one.'

Using quotes garnered from influential dignitaries within the city, it went on "... and is one of the most prestigious film festivals in North America. It has achieved recognition from the international community that festivals from other countries only dream of."

Turning to "the workforce who makes this happen", the article revealed ... "Their roster of duties is mind-boggling; their pace without slack." The next paragraph started with me, though with a variation of my job title ...

" 'It's complete madness,' " said Vanessa Vere Houghton, Concierge of VIPs. "But if the silky-voiced, English-accented Vere Houghton was on overload, she didn't show it"... before moving on to describe the flights, hotels, limos and goody bags ... "she's gotten sponsors to donate upscale items, including a mock-crocodile Saks Fifth Avenue tote for the goody bags..."

The article even included an interview with the local Police Chief, "...he assigns a police sergeant to assess all VIPs to take away any potential for stalkers. 'We're not enamoured by the celebrities,' " he said. " 'We're more concerned with those who are enamoured with them.' "

This triggered Duncan to ask me, 'You did call the FBI yesterday, didn't you?'

'No, of course not. I thought you were kidding.'

He looked at me, narrowing his eyes. 'Darlin, he may be one of the biggest names in Hollywood, but he doesn't have a huge fan base following his political views. I'd suggest you contact this police chief and see if they've been contacted by either the FBI or LA PD. If they have, then we're clear and the venue security is their problem. Also, call Raine to get her take on it.'

He had not been joking and I had not followed through. I was a huge admirer of the star in question, for he was an exceptionally talented actor who had become an exceptionally talented director, though if press reports were to be believed, often difficult to work with. I immediately called the Police Station, explained who I was and why I was calling, and was put through to the Police Chief's assistant. Yes, they had been contacted by both the LA PD and the FBI and "were on the case." They would have a complement of officers working alongside officers from the other two law enforcement agencies and were, at that moment, evaluating the need for sniffer dogs.

Raine tersely advised she had already organised a bodyguard for Taylor Quentin.

This was becoming surreal, as if it were a Hollywood movie in the making. I appraised Duncan but, before he had time to respond, our first clutch of guests arrived.

It was show time.

I suppose the guests had all thought that if they got to the suite early, it would be less of a mêlée to pick up their Welcome Packs and get the best pickings for breakfast; even before the Welcome Packs were opened, the guests examined their goody bag first, before bagging a table and chair and heading over to the breakfast counter for the much-needed caffeine injection.

The suite soon resembled a cross between a deluxe hotel restaurant and a private members' club and, by nine o'clock, the official opening hour, it was full to capacity; in the past hour alone we had checked off one-hundred-

and-sixty-five guest names, and they were still coming in. Press and TV crews also started arriving, setting up mic's and video cameras in the corner by the PR desk to catch any 'off message' moments to add colour to the pre-booked media interviews.

I stayed for another hour, mainly to ensure that Lizzie and her volunteer assistant were on top of the remaining airport runs that morning, before heading back to the office to coordinate Olivia Lautner's flight.

Raine, Ed and the studios were in full flow as usual, wanting their check list updates and my Inbox was already at capacity. There were emails from Ed requesting an update on his party guest list. Had the wallpaper guest list been finalized? Check. Would Charlie Rutherford be on hand at the party? Check. Raine asked if Barbro Innes – scion of another Hollywood dynasty – had confirmed attendance? Check. Where was she staying? Check – at the Ritz Carlton. Did we have hotel reservation confirmation numbers, name and numbers of the local transport company we were using? Check.

The studios repeated their requests for copies of the Awards Gala production script; what was the *exact* timeline for the ceremony?; could we confirm that we had the correct pick-up locations in LA for the stars? Check. When would we ship them the B-roll video tape of the Gala?, plus emails detailing travel arrangements for those stars wanting to make their own way to the festival.

There was an email from Rocco Tramanti, the Awards Gala producer, saying that Raine and Ed had thought it would be a good idea if all the award recipients and presenters remained on stage after the last award had been presented – the Lifetime Achievement Award to Lawrence Eppstein – for a group photograph, and could I email all the studios and publicists to ask them if they could ask their star if they would agree to this. Duly firing off this email, I waited for the fifty or so replies that would flood back in.

Lawrence Eppstein was already in town. I rang Kane to check that his dad was happy with everything and to enquire if there was anything else we could do for him.

'Hi Vanessa, yes everything is just fine, thank you. No, we don't need anything else right now.'

I had come to really like Kane and assumed that this was his real nature – but he was so different from the first time I had met him.

I dashed to The Four Seasons to do a quick check on the room for Ed's cocktail party and the villas and rooms for the A-List stars who would start arriving tomorrow. The Villas and Junior Suites all looked immaculate, as if they were being photographed for a spread in Vogue, and the items I had requested be placed in them – Roederer Cristal champagne and two Waterford crystal flutes, a deluxe fruit basket from Whole Foods, a Godiva Chocolate Truffles Gift Box and Provence soaps – were all elegantly arranged, replete with hand-written welcome notes from Charlie Rutherford and myself.

The oversized vases of peonies and white trumpet-shaped lilies would be delivered to the rooms an hour before the star arrived so that they were at their peak. I was pleased with the way it looked, and at least one aspect was going according to plan. I had also taken over the goody bags and given them to Charlie to lock in his office; they would be taken, with the floral arrangements, and placed in the sitting rooms just prior to the star's arrival.

Satisfied there would be no glitches, it was straight back to the office to carry on with the emails and phone calls. Cindy and Marjorie, having each survived a total of just fourteen hours, had fled in panic at five o'clock on Tuesday – only half way through the day for the rest of us – so I was back to being a one-man band. I had watched in wry amusement at the beginning of the week as their eyes widened in sheer terror at the amount of emails and incessant phone calls, and how their messages became shorter and shorter as they lost the will to live.

They were frustrated because, as they answered the phones for me, I was unable to take the call as I was constantly on my own line. It was an impossible way to work, for the role really needed two, or even three, people to fulfill it properly, especially when the Chairman suddenly tosses his own personal cocktail party into the mix. I had no alternative but to continue fire-fighting on my own.

The office felt strangely quiet, for everyone else bar Duncan, The Lesbian, the accountant and Alexis, had moved out to their respective locations for the next ten days. Christian and Hannah, as both Programmers and 'ambassadors at large', were in and out the whole time, either overseeing operations at the movie theatres or having meetings in the Guest & Industry Suite. Duncan, too, was out a lot, meeting, greeting and spending time with the filmmakers of the movies he had watched at festivals all over the world during the prior twelve months; while Alexis, whose stress lines had visibly reduced now that her main job was done – her 'wall' was, at last, complete – was able to relax for a few days, attend to her ducklings and go and watch movies.

As the day progressed, the hotels started filling up, the movies started screening, the shuttle buses began running between the hotels and movie theatres, the festival Board members came and socialised at the suite, the filmmakers among the two-hundred-odd guests began their pitches to the independent studios for distribution, the studio executives started their purchasing negotiations, the major sponsors made an appearance – and the festival staff continued to tear their hair out.

Feeling exceptionally ragged, but having an Opening Night movie and reception at the Art Museum to attend, I decided to steal away from all the madness and get a much needed mani-pedi and shoulder massage. In England I probably could have got away with the way I looked, but in California grooming is the absolute Holy Grail. I called Lin, the lovely Vietnamese Manageress at Happiness Nails, begging her to fit me in that afternoon.

'You Dinla friend from Engrand?'

'Yes,' I said, reminding her that I had been in three weeks earlier. She duly commanded I report for my rejuvenation at three o'clock.

Before that, though, I had to call The Ritz Carlton and check the requested suite was ready for Barbro Innes' arrival later tonight, and that one of our driver's had picked up the Mercedes S-Class Sedan and knew her address in LA from which to collect her. I had to check that the cocktail mixes and appetizers would be delivered to the suite at four-thirty; that Dino and Mike 2 were coping in the suite; and the weather, for there were reports of a powerful storm in Alaska and the Yukon which was projected to surge down the west coast as far as Oregon and northern Californian before turning eastwards to blow itself out over Idaho and Nevada.

The hotel was fine, the driver was fine, the appetizers and cocktail mixes would be there, Dino et al were fine – but the weather was not.

Scanning The Weather Channel there was, indeed, a filthy storm which had emanated over the Bering Strait and had now swathed mid- and southern-Alaska. The website stated that the system was set to move south over the next forty-eight hours into Washington State and Oregon and, as predicted, Northern California, before turning inland. It looked bad for the weekend and, if true, we would need to have some contingencies in place for the Awards Gala.

I rang Ed to alert him to the fact that his precious ceremony might be engulfed in torrential rain. He had heard the reports, but thought it would move eastwards and blow over before it got anywhere close to us. I told him the satellite images suggested it looked bad, but he was engrossed in negotiations to "borrow a private jet, so that we can fly Olivia Lautner up" and we ended the conversation without having any contingencies resolved.

I had made an appointment for Diana to also have a mani-pedi and she met me at the salon. After lying on the powerful vibrating massage chair-bed for forty-five minutes while having an Indian Head Massage and a Dead Sea salt scrub on my hands and feet, together with the manicure and pedicure, I again felt human.

We both selected OPI nail varnish; Diana, in more daring mode than I, chose a fabulous dark grey varnish for her nails called Suzy Skis in the Pyrenees, while I opted for a safer, but sublime, pink called My Chihuahua Bites. I was kneaded, pummeled, scrubbed and buffed and re-appeared, suitably rejuvenated, to face the world and the Opening Night extravaganza.

'OK, let's go party,' said Diana. 'We've damn well earned it.'

The enormous trolley-mounted searchlights panned across the night sky, summoning the guests as the PAR floodlights (Parabolic Aluminised Reflector Lights) rotated 360 degrees while simultaneously moving up and down so that the festival logo was clearly illuminated on the façade of the museum. The flank of steps leading up to the main entrance was adorned with a cerise carpet – not red, as that would detract from the Awards Gala – and slow-burning church pillar candles amid bundles of terracotta pots filled with gardenia, sweet peas, jasmine and roses.

Inside the glass-fronted doors, temporary black walls had been erected to give the semblance of a narrow corridor, upon which a tableaux of blown-up images depicting the various movies to be shown throughout the festival beckoned the guests through to the main auditorium. There, waiters stood to attention bearing silver trays laden with sparkling wine, Ciroc vodka, Merlot from Argentina and Cape Point Semillon – in homage to our South American and South African filmmakers – and soft drinks.

Here the great and the good of the city would rub shoulders with the great and the good of the creative, production and financial sectors of the entertainment industry – where egos could, and would, spar and clash in an appropriately glamorous mileau.

The Opening Night movie, from the Paramount Studios stable and based on a true story, was deemed an enormous hit, and that it would probably get an Oscar nod. The studio top brass had brought the real life main character of the movie to the screening and party, as well as the director – though this was little consolation for the 'social x-ray' guests, with their plate of just two rocket and radicchio leaves, who had come to see *the* star. His filming schedule meant that he would only come in for the Awards Gala, and promptly leave straight after.

Gucci and Briony loafers quickly side-stepped Jimmy Choos, Manolo Blahniks and Christian Louboutins, while chiffon designer gowns swirled and trailed past Roland Mouret 'Galaxy' and Hervé Léger 'Bandage' dresses. Botoxed earlobes stopped heavy diamond chandelier earrings from making the ears droop, diamante-tipped false eye lashes fluttered, white teeth dazzled and lip gloss shimmered on pouted lips as ambient millionaires and their wives vied for attention around the crisp white linen- and voile-covered buffet tables. The cocktail waiters serenaded the crowds with their precious cargo perched high above their shoulders, liberally dispensing bubbles and happiness in equal measure.

Staying long enough to get a good look at the city's icons and key society players – those with the largest cheque books as opposed to accidents of birth – I made my way back to the office at around eleven-thirty as Ed had emailed, saying there were 'one or two extra, but important, guests for both his cocktail party and the Gala which need accommodating.'

We had neither room allocations nor budget left, so it was a question, at almost midnight, of calling The Four Seasons and The Wyndham to see if they could give me a decent room at a hugely reduced rate. I also needed to check that Barbro Innes had arrived safely.

An email alert the next morning from Rocco Tramanti, designated 'Urgent', flashed up on my screen. I pulled it up right away, the subject heading appealing to my sense of humour, "this-is-as-final-as-it-gets". He had attached the planned, as of thirty hours beforehand, Awards Gala script, the timeline of which also spelt out, down to a nano-second, all the show elements, including off-stage voice-overs to be done by Ed's friend, Jacky Florschon, logo and lighting sequences, orchestra and conductor cues, video clips, opening credits and camera pans for the autocue shots.

Every single activity, be it a video tribute, an announcement, the presenters' or award recipients' speeches, the escorting of stars to the Green Room for photos after the award and then back to their tables in the ballroom, or even when the various dinner courses would be served to the tables, were timed with the utmost precision.

I quickly read the script. The stars' designated time allocation for presenting, and receiving, most of the awards was set at two minutes, with an accompanying video clip of much the same duration, while the major award – the Lifetime Achievement Award, being presented by Barbro Innes to Lawrence Eppstein – was allocated a lengthy twenty minutes for the intro's, video tribute and the star himself. I was not quite sure how much more 'final' this could get, assuming that it must be immutable but, as with everything else in the run-up to the festival changing by the minute, I suspected this would also. There was, after all, still twenty-eight hours in which everyone could change their minds.

Alongside the script was another attachment – the timeline for the stars' collection from The Four Seasons, plus the other two hotels where Lawrence Eppstein and Barbro Innes were staying, and transfers to the Gala. It, too, was timed down to the last second and detailed the order in which the stars were to be collected as there was a strict protocol for the red carpet arrival. This attachment was marked for me only and was not to be distributed further. I printed it off and put it with the sheaf of papers I had already in the folder marked 'Awards Gala – Bleeping Urgent'.

I emailed the script to the stars' publicists and studios' marketing and publicity people, and hoped for the best. No sooner had I done this than the phone rang. It was Barbro Innes' publicist, a girl called Laura Glassmann, whose unfriendly, actually downright rude, manner immediately hauled up the drawbridge. She was dictatorial and full of herself, thinking that just because she worked for Barbro Innes, she could demand, and expect, the earth, the moon and everything in between.

'You're going to have to change the pick up time from the hotel tomorrow. It has to come forward by thirty minutes and I want to know the name of the driver and have his mobile number. Oh, and I assume you have booked me into The Ritz Carlton as well?'

No pleasantries, no courtesy, just a demand. I bit the inside of my cheek, saying I would re-schedule the driver and no, she was not at The Ritz Carlton; she was at the Hilton. She was not happy with this, but I had neither the time nor the inclination to change it.

I was in the middle of a call to Cate Phellim, Olivia Lautner's publicist at PMK – one of LA's largest and most revered PR agencies – advising that we would fly Olivia and herself from Santa Monica to the city in a private jet, and that I would have the Presidential Suite at the Hilton for Olivia to relax and refresh herself before transferring to the Awards Gala, when my mobile rang. This was becoming the norm now, concurrently having conversations on a landline and a mobile. It was Raine Dysen.

'Natalie Immber is bringing her own hair and make up people. They'll need rooms tonight and you'll need to book a suite at The Wyndham for them to do Natalie's make-up right after the rehearsal is done.'

An email from Duncan to all of us advised that he had had final confirmation that the ensemble of the recent hit musical 'Hairgloss' would be attending and with the possibility of an open-air performance; of the two lead stars, only Kevin Upstone would be coming and he would just do the red carpet and Awards Gala stage appearance.

But this meant begging another room at The Four Seasons.

Oh good grief. It was going to be another ridiculous day in the fun factory. Ed's cocktail party was tonight and the celebrity wallpaper names – this issue never had been fully resolved and we ended up finding hotels rooms for about sixteen of them – kept being added to the guest list, as did friends of Ed's and Harry's.

Liam Taylor was arriving today from London, where he was directing a play, and would check into The Four Seasons this evening, hopefully in time for the cocktail party; one of our Mercedes S-Class sedans, replete with one of our most trusted, and smartly dressed, drivers, was dispatched to LAX to collect him. Also arriving today on the Madrid flights we had miraculously changed were Armando Aguilar and Jaime Bardeles. They, too, had to be 'Mercedes-met' at LAX and transferred to The Four Seasons. And I still had to get rooms for Ed's three extra guests.

The emails poured back in from the studios regarding our request for a group photo at the end of the awards ceremony but, naturally, there were umpteen questions attached. Emails rolled in from Raine, Ed and Harry to check, no double-check, guest names for the Awards Gala seating plan, and who had bought entire tables – especially those near the front of the stage and, therefore, next to the stars' tables. Emails romped in one after the other to change a star's guest name which, of course, meant more emails to Harry's office, with an FYI copy to Ed and Raine, to advise and amend the plans.

Miss Dictatorial, *aka* Barbro Innes' publicist, was constantly on the phone demanding this, that and everything else; the latest being that Barbro simply *had* to have hair and make-up done at two-thirty tomorrow, I *must* book the best hairdresser in town, and he *must* go to her.

Oh, and I must do this straight away, as it was important. As if nothing else was!

What was more important was finalising the private jet for Olivia – Cate had now emailed me with the time that they could get to Santa Monica airport – and, ignoring Miss Dictatorial for a few minutes, I called Harry to ensure we could use his jet and obtain the name of the contact at Santa Monica Airport that I would need to liaise with. And I still had to go over to the suite and check everything was OK, though I had total faith in Mike 2 and knew that if there were any issues, he or Dino would alert me.

Duncan happened to be running through the office just as I put the phone down on Miss Dictatorial and I told him about her increasingly rude demands.

'Ah, darlin', I did warn you about the publicists. Most are fine, but one or two are the ones from hell,' he said sympathetically. 'Here's the rub. The stars themselves are great and actually don't ask for things. It's their publicists who, in the main, are so terrified of keeping their jobs and constantly looking over their shoulders at whose gonna pinch it, that they're the ones who demand everything, just to try and prove to their boss that they can get them whatever they want.

'Now, the exception to the rule are Raine Daysen

and the publicists for Olivia and Liam Taylor. They are professional, courteous and a delight to deal with. And as a result, they get their star the works and the moon.'

I concurred as, during my dealings with the publicists and studios, I had found both Cate Phellim at PMK and Stephani Yorke at Polaris, Liam's personal publicist, to be both charming and consummate professionals. But Miss Dictatorial clearly thought her boss was the only star in the galaxy.

Duncan, seeing that I was already on my knees with exhaustion, valiantly decreed that I should book myself into the Hilton for the next four nights so that I was on the spot as, he told me with relish, 'you're gonna be on call 24/7.'

The Four Season's *porte-cochère* was bedecked with tiny white fairy lights and the main entrance doors, flanked by towering flame torches, were swathed in great bolts of red silk and velvet. I pulled up in the 'Goods Only' car park to the far side of the hotel so that Ed and his guests could not see me climb out of the Dodge pick-up. I had hastily changed in the office into a favourite Azzedine Alaia cocktail dress and four-inch scarlet suede court shoes. Already late, I finished dressing – diamond stud earrings, 9-carat gold fob-watch chain worn as a necklace, an antique 22-carat gold bracelet that had belonged to my great-grandmother, my new Gucci watch and a generous spritz of Chanel Allure – as I made my way to the entrance.

The Concierge, who knew me by now, beckoned with a warm smile as he held open the door for me and the cluster of people behind, all clutching their stiff white invitations to The Chairman's Private Pre-Festival Cocktail Party.

Inside, in the middle of the lobby, stood Charlie Rutherford, guiding guests towards the party in the ballroom. I darted down the length of the lobby to peek inside the ballroom before retracing my steps to give him a huge kiss.

'Darling boy, the entrance and ballroom look just *absolutely* fabulous. You and your staff have performed nothing short of a miracle.'

Just as he proffered his arm for me to take, Jacky Florschon hoved into view from the far corner of the lobby and made a beeline towards us. She was dressed in a white Hervé Léger 'Bandage' dress that was the current rage in Tinseltown with all the A-List – which showed off her size zero figure to perfection – and a pair of vertiginous Christian Louboutin crocodile evening sandals that stretched her already 5 ft 11 inch frame heavenwards. Her long brunette hair, ironed for the evening, was pulled back with a wide Swarovski-encrusted alice-band, falling loosely down to her waist. In short, she was not someone you would miss in a room, and she knew it.

Entwining her arms with ours, she steered us towards the ballroom.

'Darh-lings, sooo exhausted, been in Gala rehearsals all afternoon. What a wonderful party. Everyone is having such a good time and have you seen all the Tiffany stuff? Can't work out whether there's more in the display cabinets or adorning the wrinkly necks and fingers of the matrons of this city!'

Jacky had a sharp, if acerbic, wit and was pretty non-PC; she was not afraid to say it how it was, which is what I found so appealing about her. She broke loose once we were inside, air kissing the matrons she had just derided, making sure there was at least two inches of air between their cheeks as they bowed their heads in greeting – so as not to disturb the recent nips and tucks – before alighting on the Eppstein clan, Lawrence, his wife Angela, Kane and his wife Jenny, who were just "stopping by en route to dinner with old friends." Stopping by was good enough for Ed, who positively beamed that the main star being honoured at the Awards Gala the next night was here, at *his* party.

Charlie and I grabbed a flute of Cristal and a Saigon ricepaper roll from the passing canape tray and amused ourselves 'star-spotting' among the assembled crowd's patina. Natalie Immber, one of the key anchors of Entertainment Tonight, was in deep conversation with John Haines, the Los Angeles Times' showbusiness editor, and Raine Daysen, who had just arrived from LA. Armando Aguilar and Jaime Bardeles, who had checked into the hotel during the afternoon after their flight from Madrid, were immediately pounced upon by the LA networks and photographers for, while few people in the US or UK knew at this time who Jaime was, and he hardly spoke any English, he had won Best Actor in the European Film Awards for a searing movie about human frailty and which was also nominated for an Oscar in the Best Foreign Language Film category.

The acclaimed film composer Irving Tremshore, also another award recipient, and his wife were among the crowd, as were singer Curtis Nicklelow and heavy-weight Hollywood producer Kyle Yablonski, both of whom had second homes nearby. The corporate hierarchy of both Tiffany and Mercedes-Benz were clearly happy to be clinking glasses with Hollywood royalty and ambient millionaires, and were even more delighted when asked if they would mind posing for a photograph with Lawrence Eppstein, Natalie Immber and Ed.

While the potent mix of A-List stars would not be in this

room until tomorrow night – at the post-Awards Gala after-show party – there was, nonetheless, enough fodder for the media to keep them happy for the morning's editions.

'Liam Taylor arrives in about an hour,' Charlie whispered. 'Do you want me to signal to you when he does?'

'You bet. I have left word with the Front Desk for them to let me know when he does get in. After all, it is my *duty* to ensure he has arrived safely and that he is happy with the room. We'll escort him to the villa together.'

As I was giving this instruction to Charlie, there was a brush against my arm. It was Kane.

'Hey Vanessa, great party. Sorry we have to leave, but we have dinner reservations. See you at the show tomorrow.'

I knew they had reservations, for I had made them! 'Sure will,' I smiled, not wanting to admit that Cinderella still did not know if she would be going to the ball. 'Have a great dinner. I hear the Bourbon and Maple Glazed Duck at Bouchon is amazing. Your father's driver will pick him up at the hotel at four-forty-five and, at this point, it is planned that we'll take him directly to the Green Room so that he doesn't have to do the whole red carpet routine. The two tables directly in front of the main stage area are designated for your group.'

Charlie, who had disappeared, suddenly re-appeared in the doorway and urgently waved at me to come into the lobby. I knew what this signal meant as I rushed over to him.

'Where is he?'

'He's just going over to his villa now,' said Charlie, with an amused look on his face.

'Why didn't you call me when he was checking in?'

'Erm, that's because he refused to do check in now. Says he'll do it tomorrow. He did look very tired. Actually honey, he didn't look that good at all.'

Charlie started walking down the lobby towards the doors leading out to the Rose Garden and the private villas beyond.

'Can I come with you? After all I am supposed to be looking after him and so I should at least come and say hello and ask him if there is anything he needs.'

Charlie grinned again. 'Oh, I don't think he needs anything else at the moment. He's got a *young* companion with him. Let's just leave it at that.'

Reluctantly, I went back into the ballroom and attempted small-talk with the guests, but I was annoyed at not meeting Liam myself when he had arrived, especially as I had specifically asked the Front Desk to alert me; I reasoned that it was probably his security man who had told them there was to be no fanfare. I would get to meet him tomorrow before the Awards Gala.

It had just started to rain quite heavily as I drove over to the Guest & Industry Suite to check everything was in order. Mike 2, Dino and a couple of the PR agency staff were finishing the last remnants of vodka and beers from the evening before starting to clear up for the night; by all accounts it looked as though our filmmaker guests had had a good evening in the suite. I cast a quick glance over our work desks to see if there were any problems, particularly with the limos and drivers for the next day. It all appeared to be fine, apart from one folder on which had been written What The Bleep Is This?; inside were some hastily scribbled names and telephone numbers, and I made a mental note to ask Lizzie in the morning.

Feeling utterly exhausted, I swung by the office to

check on my emails. A big mistake, for I counted over one-hundred-and-eighty that had come in since four o'clock. I was far too tired to even contemplate scanning the senders' names and subject headings. They would all have to wait until tomorrow morning.

Hearing the rain falling heavily on the office roof, I checked the weather report and took a sharp intake of breath as I read it. The storm that was coming down from the Pacific North West – and forecast to start moving eastwards by the time it reached Oregon and Northern California – had changed course.

I quickly fired off emails to Ed, Duncan and Harry, as well as ringing their mobiles to leave voice-messages about the storm.

It was heading straight towards us.

CHAPTER FOURTEEN

A 1972 hit song says it never rains in southern California, but let me assure you that it does; admittedly not that often, but when it does, one certainly knows about it. And the lyrics of that song go on to warn us that, sometimes, it doesn't just pour, but man, it pours.

And so it was that the powers that be up in the heavens decided that the weekend of the Awards Gala ceremony – *the* most glamorous and financially important event of the festival – would be the time to test our nerve and take us to the wire with the worst storms mid- and southern-California had seen in twelve years.

It was certainly testing Ed for, having been quite adamant that the storm would veer off and not touch us, he had to admit he had been wrong in neither heeding the weather reports nor my frantic phone call and email late last night. He was in melt-down, firing frenzied emails to all the staffs' mobiles to get awnings and canopies put up around the Convention Centre, get the red carpet inside (thankfully it was still rolled up in its huge canvas case), cover the floodlights and signage, go and buy umbrellas and put waterproof sheeting over everything.

When it was reported back to him that there were no umbrellas to be had in town, for they had all been bought yesterday by tourists and residents alike, his meltdown went stratospheric. He summoned Hayden, the Head of Theatre Operations, to his office and, in a voice pitch 'off radar', demanded that he and six of his staff drop everything *immediately*.

'Go to every single country club and resort hotel in the valley and demand, not ask, that they loan the festival their golfing umbrellas.'

In terror and bemusement, Hayden fled the office to obtain what Ed deemed that day to be the holy grail.

By mid morning, the heavy rains of the previous night had now become torrential, exacerbated by strong gusts. To add a layer of irony to the proceedings, the office roof began to leak – not just in one place, but in six. Duncan and I, by now both fielding frantic calls from the studio heads about how their precious stars would get to the Awards Gala, sat surrounded by mini waterfalls and overflowing saucepans as we mobilized contingency plans.

Alexis from Print Traffic was also in fight-or-flight mode, for the cans of film reels of the movies to be shown over the next three days had been stacked outside, waiting to be delivered to the respective movie theatres. She drove into the office parking lot so damn fast that we wondered whether she would even manage to brake in time. Leaping out, still in her pyjamas and with a BlackBerry clamped to her ear, she yelled into it for Damien to 'get you're a*** over to the office right now.'

Her concern was warranted; with the average one-and-a-half-hour movie shot on 35mm film, where about two-thousand-feet of reel lasts only twenty minutes, this was a priceless commodity. She had to get the cans water-proofed in a matter of minutes before the reels inside were ruined. Grabbing a box of black bin-liners, she started chucking the cans into them, not caring that they were now all out of sync, as Damien swept into the parking lot, also still in his pyjamas.

'Just get them into the frigging bin-bags,' screamed Alexis. 'We'll sort them later today.'

It took them four hours to complete the task – given that one movie comprised some eight cans – and with ninety movies to be shown during just the next three days, it equated to some seven-hundred-and-fifty cans. I felt sorry for her but, in a perverse way, it was de-stressing to watch them, drenched to the skin and in, by now, near see-through pyjamas, battling the elements with nothing more than bin-liners.

The de-stress was, however, short-lived. The studios were now changing weeks, if not months, of carefully crafted organization. Granted, the weather did warrant some of their requests, but it was deeply depressing, to put it mildly, that everything we had done was unraveling before our eyes at the rate of knots. Among the myriad changes, Paramount decided that there was no way they were risking their key star in a two- to three-hour limousine journey, so after endless conference calls with their Marketing and Publicity departments, they decided they would fly Tommy Kane up in the studio's corporate jet.

Within twenty minutes an 'urgent' itinerary flashed into my Inbox from the Marketing Director, detailing the twelve studio executives, along with Tommy and his wife, who would be flying up. This entailed Lizzie and I cancelling the limos and drivers assigned to collect Tommy in LA, organizing stretch limos to meet them at the airport – assuming they could land at either the airport or one of the city's private airfields – and laying on one of the Mercedes Maybachs to take Tommy and his wife to the hotel. There was also an interesting aside; an instruction that the Mercedes driver was to present himself to a certain studio executive before he went anywhere near Tommy Kane. I never did find out what that was all about.

Ed, by now in def-con mode and barking instructions to any staffer who had a nano-second to answer their mobile, arrived at the office to continue directing his battle plan, presumably so that Duncan and I could see how much work *he* was doing, as he obviously thought we had nothing to do. He seemed momentarily perplexed when he saw me at my desk with a landline phone clamped to each ear and a mobile phone under my nose, and with all three ringing continuously.

Seemingly unaware that I was drowning with all the changes to the stars' travel itineraries that day – not to mention whether any jets we laid on would even be able to land at the airport – he demanded to see the stars' final guest list for the Awards Gala tables seating plan, asking why he had not seen it by now. Printing off another copy, I told him, firmly but politely, that I had emailed it to both his and Harry's offices yesterday, with a copy to Duncan.

'Well, I haven't seen it,' he snapped.

'Sorry, not my fault,' I retorted, in between confirming hair and make-up details on one landline, new limo arrangements on the other and timing of the red carpet arrivals on the mobile, immediately followed by the next set of three concurrent conversations – delivery of the Awards Gala programme guide, notification of the tail number of the Lear Jet we were using for Olivia Lautner, and the planned start time of the after-show party at The Four Seasons.

Lizzie squelched into the office looking like a drowned rat, her highlighted blonde hair scrapped back in a pony tail, mascara 'going south' and with her new Rock & Republic jeans and Converse sneakers soaked through. I had asked her to come and work out of the main office with me, rather than staying in the hospitality suite, as today was going to be a tough call and we would need to liaise very closely. She did a double-take as she spotted the waterfalls and saucepans, and Alexis and Damien in their pyjamas stacking the bin-liners of reel cans in the main corridor, effectively ensuring that nobody would now be able to get past them.

'Oh My God, what the hell has happened here? We can't work in this bloody mess!'

I glanced up, letting a landline slip from my shoulder in the process. 'Hey Lizzie, we ain't got a choice I'm afraid. As long as we don't electrocute ourselves, we've just got to get on with it. Here's a quick de-brief of what's happening.

'OK, first up. Cancel the limos for the Tommy Kane and Olivia Lautner LA pick-ups. They're both flying up, Tommy in the Paramount corporate jet and Olivia in the Lear we've borrowed, but we'll need Maybachs to meet them at the airfields though, as yet, I don't know which ones they'll be coming into. Ditto for Kevin Upstone as he is now flying himself in, but again, we'll need a Sedan to meet him at whichever airfield he comes into.

'Taylor Quentin's and Nancy Demainne's people have asked that the pick-ups be brought forward and I've agreed with them one hour earlier.'

As I was about to get onto the thorny issue of who had Maybachs and Sedans, Duncan came bounding out of his office with something quite rare of late – a smile.

'Hey darlin', just got confirmation of our surprise presenter for tonight.'

I shot him an anguished look. 'W-e-l-l, that *is* a surprise.

I didn't even know we were having a surprise presenter! Did I need to know about this possibility, in case he or she needs a flight, hotel, limo pick-up or hair and make-up by any chance? Do they? Lizzie and I are *really* looking for some extra work right now.' The trace of sarcasm now patently obvious.

'Nah, he's flying in from his vacation home in the Caribbean and staying with a producer pal of his, so no hassles and everything is sorted. Just be your usual charming, classy and welcoming self.'

'Now who's being sarcastic,' I laughed as Duncan's mobile went off for the umpteenth time. 'And do we have a name?

Duncan feigned shock. 'Darlin', it wouldn't be a surprise presenter if we all knew his name, would it?'

I assumed he was going to tell me, but there was a pause. A long pause.

'Oh for God's sake, come on. Who is it?'

Still he would not give up his annoying little secret.

'OK, I don't really care who it is anymore. We've got enough grief to sort out right here and now.'

By now Harry had also come to the office, ostensibly to calm Ed but, in reality, to dispense more anxiety and stress by announcing that the awards themselves – unique gifts and bronze statuettes – had been delivered to the printers by mistake.

'So who exactly is going to go and pick them up and take them to the Convention Centre?' he rasped. When none of us volunteered, he called Andrea. 'I'll call Diana and get her to do it,' I heard her say on the loudspeaker. Oh dear God, I thought to myself, Diana will be really thrilled.

Lizzie and I spent most of the day – up until two hours before the Awards Gala reception was due to start – with a landline clamped to each ear and a mobile under our noses, conducting two, sometimes three, conversations concurrently to make all the necessary changes. I also had to check that Barbro Innes' hairdresser had arrived at her suite at two-thirty p.m. to do her hair, and that the hair and make-up people for Natalie Immber had arrived at the suite at The Wyndham to be ready post rehearsal.

Olivia's publicist Cate Phellim and I were on the phone every thirty minutes or so throughout the day, up-dating each other on arrangements and timings. She was a joy to deal with and her professionalism, like Stephani Yorke, who handled Liam Taylor's publicity, made the day almost bearable. However, at the other end of the spectrum was Laura Glassmann, *aka* Miss Dictatorial (Barbro Innes' publicist) who was already on the phone at twelve-thirty p.m. to demand that the hairdresser *would* be at the suite at two-thirty p.m. to do Barbro's hair and that the chauffeur needed to "arrive an hour later to pick up Ms Innes".

When I told her that would not be possible, due to the carefully planned red carpet timings, she went into orbit and screamed down the phone that I was to follow her instructions. Although extremely annoyed by her manner, I calmly told her the chauffeur would be at the hotel at the time originally advised to her and Ms Innes, and that there would be *no* change.

As there were so many A-List stars coming in for the Awards Gala – Kevin Upstone, Taylor Quentin, Cody Quinn, Olivia Lautner, Liam Taylor, Lawrence Eppstein, Tommy Kane, Nancy Demainne, Barbro Innes and Ed Tyler to name but a few – there was to be one final Awards Gala rehearsal early in the afternoon. We had already had a two-hour rehearsal yesterday afternoon and Rocco Tramanti was now saying we needed another hour-and-a-half-long one to 'batten everything down'.

Lizzie and I really did not have time, but it was important, particularly to co-ordinate the timings for the limo transfers from the hotels and arrivals at the red carpet and, for me, the length of time allocated for each star to do media interviews along the red carpet and expected arrival time at the main doors for escorting to their tables.

As we drove to the Convention Centre, Diana called. She was incandescent; Andrea Carnegie had ordered her to go to the printers, pick up the awards and take them straight over to the Convention Centre.

'What does she frigging well think I am? The god-damn delivery man. And then when I get to the printers none of them – *not one* of the awards – is even protected with any wrapping. Can you believe it? So I go to the office and ask Anna for some help and she tells me she's too busy. So I wrap up the gifts and statuettes myself with T-shirts and bubble wrap and put them all on the front and back seats of my SUV, in the pouring rain I might add, and I'm driving the f***ing precious cargo over to the Convention Centre right now.'

Awnings and canopies had been erected around the Convention Centre's main entrance and a canopied tunnel had been installed along the route of the eighty-eight-feet-long red carpet, as well as a 'roof' over the paparazzi pens to try and keep the floodlights and the 'paps' themselves dry – a pointless exercise as it turned out. The cordons and posts were in place, albeit under plastic sheeting and the sacrosanct red carpet was just inside the main doors, still rolled up in its canvas casing and where it would remain until the last possible moment before it had to be rolled out. Stacked in the corner by the main doors was an enormous pile of colourful umbrellas; the Theatre Operations team having managed to beg, borrow or steal just about every single golf umbrella from the nearby golf and country clubs. I grabbed two in case of emergencies for stars' or media use.

Entertainment Tonight co-host Natalie Immber was already on stage doing her rehearsal, though she looked so different without her TV make-up. While her camera crew were setting up, Rocco and his production team were running at full throttle to gauge and adjust each and every possible camera and lighting angle, orchestra cues and back-stage voice-overs, and triple-check the bank of stage video screens. The venue's banqueting staff, having already set up the tables, were hastily arranging the place settings for seventeen-hundred guests, while the bar staff transformed the 'wings' of the main entrance lobby into two behemoth cocktail lounges. They knew that the seventeen-hundred guests would all arrive at the same time – people in this town liked their cocktails promptly at five o'clock and would want as much 'star spotting' time as possible.

Andrea knew that Lizzie and I had to get back to the office as quickly as possible. We ran through the hotel transfers and red carpet arrivals first, as I was given a sheet detailing – with laser precision – the rotational order that the stars would be picked-up from the hotels and arrival times at the start of the red carpet, together with appointed length of walking time down the carpet to the expected time of arrival at the main doors.

Ric and Shane from the PR agency were also there to advise on the agreed media interviews at the start of, and along, the red carpet and anticipated time required for photo-calls. With the media's best interests at heart – and thereby the festival's – they requested changes to the precisely-planned running order of talent arrivals on the carpet and so, just for a change, we made fresh amendments to the zillionth copy of our carefully executed itineraries which, in turn, required changes to the roster of volunteer staff who would escort the stars either to the Green Room for media interviews or directly to their tables.

While we were tearing our hair out over the revisions, I noticed a mass of black on the far side of the road in front of the venue. I watched, with incredulity, its velocity as it approached the main glass-fronted entrance and change from a blurred outline into a 20/20 visual; in front of us were some twenty FBI and LA PD officers, dressed in flak-jackets and replete with Glock semi-automatic pistols and Remington sniper rifles, and accompanied by bomb sniffer dogs.

I remembered the conversation I had had forty-eight hours earlier with both Duncan and the local Police chief, but had not thought for one minute that this would actually be taken seriously. But here we were, rehearsing for a star-studded awards ceremony with, by now, dogs sniffing every nook and cranny. Just to ensure the law enforcement officers knew we were to take this seriously, they also positioned snipers on the roof. Just how much crazier could this all get?

By two-thirty p.m. and with my brain 'fried' with all the information I was having to assimilate, Lizzie and I repaired to the office to jump back on the absurd merry-go-round that had become our life of twenty-hour days and no proper food. I had not had one second to deal with my Inbox and looking at it – another one-hundred-and-seventy-two emails having arrived since the morning – decided I still did not have time to deal with them; in any event, most of their content was now coming in by phone from the studios and publicists, so they were being dealt with, I told myself.

A call came in from Cate Phellim, confirming what time she would get Olivia to Santa Monica airport. I called the airport to discuss the proposed flight plan with pilot Mark Partlin – a charming man whom the studios used frequently for aerial sequences in movies and who would be flying Olivia Lautner up in the Lear jet. I could tell by the tone of his voice that something was wrong.

'Hey, what's up Mark?' I asked, trying to sound calm.

'The weather's worsening here and its moving your way. I can get out of Santa Monica OK, but I'm not sure how easy it will be to land at your end. Let me work on it a little more and I'll update you in about an hour.'

Oh. My. God. 'Mark, I understand safety is paramount, but you *have* to get Olivia here. She's one of the main award recipients and we have all the main TV networks coming in to interview her. Please, please, don't tell me you're even thinking you can't get here at all?'

Pausing ominously, he said in a measured tone, 'Oh, I can get her there, but whether it will be in time for your awards ceremony is another matter. I'll call you back in an hour.'

I asked him to call earlier if he could, explaining that the Awards Gala reception began at five o'clock, with the seventeen-hundred guests being seated by six o'clock and that a call at three-thirty p.m. would not give me any time at all.

He hung up but I held onto the phone for another few minutes, willing him to ring back and say it was all a mistake and everything would be fine. The jet was our limousine contingency, but we had not factored a contingency for the weather preventing a jet landing. Another call quickly followed from Kevin Upstone's people to say that he had changed his mind and was not flying himself up; instead, he and his agent were already on the road.

Call after call came in from the studios' publicists, many travelling with their talent, to check, every few minutes, on the weather situation and condition of the roads. I assured them all that, while it was exceptionally heavy rain, the roads were good, there was no need to worry and they would get here in time. What I was actually saying was 'please stop calling every two seconds, I haven't got time.'

Miss Dictatorial's pace did not slacken, with calls to demand why the chauffeur had not arrived to pick-up her boss as she had clearly instructed (obviously having forgotten our conversation of only four hours prior) and The Wyndham called to say they would have to charge us for the suite being used by Natalie Immber's hair and make-up people; I was too exhausted to argue with them, so limply agreed to be billed. Andrea called to say that the awards themselves had still not arrived, so I chased Diana. Clearly still incandescent, she bellowed at me, 'Tell that god-damn woman I've got the awards, but in case she hasn't noticed, we've got the worst storm California has seen in twelve years and I'm in grid-locked traffic. I'm gonna need help when I get to the venue, as one or two of these awards are pretty large. And you can tell Harry and Duncan that I damn well expect a seat at the ceremony for all this crap I'm doing for them.'

As if on cue, an equally harassed Duncan appeared from his office. 'Where's the f***ing seating plan? I've got Fox Searchlight on the line wanting to know their table number for a guest who's gonna be late, and Raine says she hasn't been told her table number.'

I shot in Diana's request for a seat before he could say anything else.

'Ask Harry, I haven't got time for all this f***ing crap!' he snarled.

I hastily called Harry who, with Ed, has sensibly fled the chaos and hysteria that masqueraded as our office and had repaired back to the sanctuary of his own, to ask him the status.

'Don't bother me now, we're working on it,' he fumed.

'When will it be ready?' I pressed further.

'When it's f***ing done,' he screamed.

'When *exactly* will that be?' I asked, ignoring his mini-tantrum. 'We need it now, as the studios and the talents' publicists are asking us and, if you don't mind me saying, we're looking a little stupid in not being able to tell them.'

My remark sent him into orbit and he slammed the phone down on me; too late to ask him if Diana or I could have a seat at the ceremony.

'Hey Vanessa, remember to breath!' Alexis and Lizzie chirped in unison, trying to lighten the situation. I took a singularly long, deep breath. 'Well, it's bloody ridiculous to not have the seating plan done by now. I just hope to God that after tonight, it calms down a little, otherwise there's no way we can get through another eight days of this festival in one piece.'

Glancing at the clock, which showed three-fifty p.m., I suddenly realized that Mark Partlin had not got back to me. With trepidation, I called.

'Hey, what's the situation Mark?' I asked, trying not to sound as stressed as I was feeling.

'Just filing the flight plan now. We should be taking off within the next twenny or so minutes, or as soon as Olivia Lautner and her publicist get here. Our Tail number is N1519R. Not sure yet which airfield we'll land at, depends on the conditions when we get closer.'

He gave me his mobile number and that of Andrew, the ground control operator at the city's main airport.

'Thanks Mark, please keep me in the loop once you're airborne. I need to know of any delays or problems, plus where you will be landing, as I shall have a Maybach awaiting your arrival.'

'Will do.'

Four o'clock and one hour to go before the scrum on the red carpet and the Awards Gala reception began.

Unlike most women going to a major work event, who would allow themselves enough time to change and freshen their hair and make-up, I did not have such luxury. If I was lucky, five minutes in my hotel room would be the most I would have.

Lizzie and I quickly arranged to have a Maybach at two of the seven private airfields surrounding the city, and a Sedan at each of the other five; we had no idea which one Mark Partlin or the Paramount corporate jet would land at, so it was a pure stab in the dark as to which ones to send the Maybachs. That done, I dashed over to The Four Seasons to check that all the Awards Gala recipients and presenters had arrived – luckily everyone had, aside from Olivia, Tommy Kane and Kevin Upstone whom we knew about – and to double-check that the new limo departure times for the red carpet had been delivered to their villas and suites.

Andrea's assistant Mitch Stanley was in place, walkie-talkie super-glued to his mouth and stop-watch in hand as he confirmed to Andrea that the Golden Globe-nominated British Director Keith Yates would be the first to depart and would be at the start of the carpet at five o'clock sharp, followed – at three minute intervals each – by Lawrence Eppstein and Barbro Innes from their respective hotels, Tommy Kane, Liam Taylor, Ed Tyler, Nancy Demainne,

Cody Quinn, Kevin Upstone and, finally, Olivia Lautner.

Olivia was perceived to be the 'shining star' of the night due to her Oscar success and the fact that she had made advertising history by starring in a three-minute commercial that was not only the most expensive one to have been shot, it also resembled a micro-movie. She would, therefore, be the last to arrive to keep the screams of the fans going until the last possible minute. It was prescient that she was scheduled to be last as we needed all the extra time possible to allow for any landing problems with the jet.

Taylor Quentin never 'did' red carpets and rarely agreed to the usual hoopla of awards media interviews, so we had arranged for him to be driven directly to the rear of the venue where I – or a colleague if I was held up with meeting Olivia – would meet him on the loading dock; not terribly glamorous, but that was the way he wanted it. Our surprise presenter, about whom I had had a sixth sense, turned out to be Conrad Young and he also would not be doing the 'formal' red carpet foray; we had agreed that we would drive him to a side entrance and escort him directly to the Green Room where he could meet up with the other stars once they had stepped off the carousel that was the red carpet media circus.

I shot back to the office at around four-thirty p.m. – half-an-hour to go and I still had not changed. Calls were still coming in from the studios about the road conditions and had their talent arrived at the hotel? I had thought that their publicists would have advised them of their arrival, but I confirmed everyone was in, except Tommy Kane and Olivia Lautner, who were both flying up.

Having double-checked the Hilton's Presidential Suite was ready for Olivia's possible use and, confident that we were almost ready and that I could go and change, there came a call to send my stress levels into stratosphere.

Liam Taylor's security guy – whom Lizzie had been liaising with all along – decided suddenly that Liam could not possibly have a car that someone else would also be using. He had to have his *own* car for the *whole* evening. This was not a request, it was a statement of what *would* happen, whether we liked it or not. I advised him that we had allocated Liam a Maybach, but that it was currently picking-up Tommy Kane from an airfield; however, once Tommy was at the hotel, the Maybach would be Liam's personal car for the rest of the night.

Oh good God, this whole day was turning into sheer lunacy. Lizzie and I scrambled to change the cars manifest; Liam would keep his Maybach all evening (which meant someone else would not get the pleasure of riding in one), the other Maybach would meet Olivia at whichever airfield she would land at, transfer her to the hotel and then on to the red carpet. Lawrence Eppstein would keep his S-Class Sedan all night with his own personal driver and everyone else would be chauffeured in a mix of CL-Class Coupes and S-Class Sedans.

Having done that, I dashed to the Hilton at five minutes to five o'clock to change into the only dress I had had time to grab the day before when I left Diana's house. It was a very pretty, figure-hugging coral-coloured cocktail dress by English designer Emilia Wickstead – perhaps now a little too figure-hugging after a diet purely of cookies and coke for the past five weeks. Quickly pulling it over my head, I slung on a pair of coral suede evening shoes which would, of course, get ruined in the wet, frantically applied more foundation to my face, quickly flicked some mascara onto my lashes, ran a brush through my hair, dabbed blusher on my cheeks and applied lip gloss. It would have to do, for there was no more time. My mobile rang. It was Mark Partlin.

'It's not good up here, but we're about four minutes out and I'm gonna land at Millionaire.'

'Thanks Mark,' I yelled, simultanously ringing the Maybach chauffeur whom I had sent to a closer and more likely airfield, telling him to drive like hell to Millionaire Airfield. My mobile rang again; it was the Marketing Vice President of Paramount Studios, saying they had just landed at Millionaire. I quickly called the other Maybach chauffeur, who was at the neighboring airfield, to advise him that Tommy Kane had just landed at Millionaire, and followed this with a call to one of the other Sedan chauffeurs, telling him to come over to Millionaire in case some of the Paramount executives wanted to drive into town alongside Tommy Kane. I then called the drivers of the Sedans at the four other airfields and told them to return to the hotel.

I called Duncan and Lizzie to advise them that Tommy Kane had landed and that Olivia Lautner was about to. Just as I came off, my phone went again; it was Cate Phellim.

'Hi Vanessa, we've landed and we're getting into the Maybach now. Thank you so much for arranging this. The car is great. And we'll go straight to the red carpet as we are already ten minutes behind schedule.

'Oh, and Vanessa, please will you meet Olivia and I at the red carpet and stay with us on the carpet while Olivia does her media interviews, so you can take us straight to her table.'

I had not expected this, but was hugely flattered to have been asked to do so.

'Sure, no problem, I'll see you there in about five.'

Tossing my phone into my bag, I yanked off my shoes, tucked them under my arm – for I only had a small evening bag already stuffed with my walkie-talkie – and ran, barefoot, from my room, through the hotel lobby, along the vast connecting corridor to the Convention Centre, through the annexe chambers and outside into the rain-sodden street, so that I could come around to the front – to the start of the red carpet – without any TV crews or photographers having witnessed a barefoot runner with a plastic bag over her head, but who had an Access All Areas badge around her neck!

The rain had, thankfully, eased off a little and now was no more than a heavy shower. Turning the corner onto the boulevard at which the main entrance was located, I paused only to put my shoes onto my thoroughly wet feet, take the plastic bag off my head, check my hair was reasonably OK and that my mascara was not walking down my face.

I took several deep breaths as I approached the security cordon at the red carpet.

It was show time.

Let the magic begin.

CHAPTER FIFTEEN

A line of Mercedes convertibles, Lincoln Town Cars, Porches, Bentleys and the odd Rolls Royce snaked along the boulevard, crawling towards the barriers at the main entrance. Their contents, merely the great and the good of the city, would, however, have to wait to be waved through to a side road by Security, as the road and parking area immediately in front of the Convention Centre was cordoned off for the exclusive use of the A-List stars – and where a huge detail of police officers and security men ensured that anyone who was not supposed to be there gained access.

As the celebrity wallpaper began strolling the eighty-eight-feet-long red carpet, the first of our S-Class Sedans, with their identifying sticker on the windscreen, had already dropped off a star and was turning to go and collect the next one. My walkie-talkie burst into life. 'Lawrence Eppstein and Barbro Innes nearing end of carpet. Escorts come forward,' I heard Duncan's assistant, Anna, instruct. 'Tommy Kane on carpet, approx. three minutes to entrance. Escort be ready.'

It was five-fifteen p.m. and most of the seventeen-hundred guests, who had walked along their own 'red carpet' – some five feet adjacent and a shade of red more resembling muted raspberry – were clinking glasses of champagne in the cocktail lounges inside the palm tree-lined entrance and straining to catch a glimpse of the stars, many in the misguided hope that they would be schmoozing with the talent.

Men in tuxedos, some in white-tie, though it was not a formal occasion, and spit-polished Gucci loafers and Bottega Veneta brogues downed wines and Beach Blonde ales, while the sea of haute couture gowns and current trend of one-shoulder designer dresses laid rest to any notion of a world recession. Armani Privé, Oscar de la Renta, Lanvin, Roberto Cavalli, Carolina Hererra, Zac Posen and Elie Saab gowns all swirled past each other, the bodices and skirts so tight on some that one wondered how the wearer could even exhale.

As with the Opening Night reception, the diamante-tipped false eyelashes fluttered and the lips shimmered under a heavy coat of lip-gloss, though unlike that reception, here the necks were adorned with heist-worthy diamonds and sapphires, ears groaned under the weight of oversized chandelier-style diamond and platinum earrings and, on one guest, at least a fifteen-carat diamond ring meant she could hardly lift her glass of 'fizz' to her mouth.

As I approached the start of the red carpet, a security man blocked my path. 'You ain't allowed in here lady.'

'I'm festival staff and in charge of the celebrity guests. Here's my ID. I have to be here to meet Olivia Lautner who is arriving at any moment. Her publicist specifically asked me to meet her here. So, actually, I *am* allowed in here.'

He scrutinised my AAA badge and reluctantly pulled back the cordon, allowing me to take my position next to Raine Daysen and Ric Isaacs from the PR agency on the road just in front of the red carpet.

My first thought was the carpet. Although we had erected

a canopied 'tunnel' over its path and it had only been rolled out at five o'clock, it was already sodden and memories of a similarly rain-soaked BAFTA Film Awards in London – where someone had shampooed the carpet in readiness but had not rinsed it properly, resulting in the celebrities all squelching through soap-suds – came flooding back. I knew that this carpet was a new one, so there would be no problem with soap-suds, but their shoes would be ruined and, if they were wearing full-length gowns, the bottom of their dresses would be wet and clammy for the rest of the evening. But there was nothing we could do about it.

The 'seating plan' for the red carpet followed a strict protocol. At its start were the key showbiz programmes and TV stations – Entertainment Tonight, The Insider, Extra, Access Hollywood and the news channels of the main networks NBC, ABC, CBS, Fox and CNN; then came the main wire service, Associated Press, and one of the main LA television stations, KTLA. After them were the other local network affiliates, plus the key industry and celebrity magazines – Variety, Hollywood Reporter, Screen International, Entertainment Weekly, Moving Pictures Magazine, People, US Weekly, In Style, Star, In Touch Weekly and Harper's Bazaar – and newspaper reporters, who would immediately make their way to the Green Room once the red carpet hoopla was over.

Next came the staff photographers, again in priority order – Associated Press, LA Times, Wall Street Journal, USA Today – and then key cities mainstream papers, such as the San Francisco Chronicle, Chicago Sun, Boston Globe, Philadelphia Inquirer, Miami Herald and, finally, all the freelance journalists and photographers.

In all, there were around two-hundred-and-fifty media and they naturally all wanted a slice of the action – the exclusive picture and quote from the celebrity – and trying to keep them in their allocated seats was not always possible. But that was Raine, Ric and Shane's job, and thankfully not mine.

Liam Taylor climbed out of one of the Maybachs and immediately was confronted by Entertainment Tonight and the main network news channels for a 'piece to camera' before walking down the carpet to a crescendo of paparazzi flashbulbs. Another S-Class Sedan pulled up and, as the doors were opened and the passenger stepped out, near hysteria erupted from the fans, the majority of whom filled the large canopied grandstands – the Bleacher seats – on the opposite side of the road and the smaller ones lining the barricades flanking the red carpet. It was Kevin Upstone and they cared not one jot that they were getting soaked.

'This will take forever,' groaned Raine. 'Every media outlet here tonight will want a piece of him. Expect the red carpet process to take at least forty minutes.'

I called Anna on my walkie-talkie. 'Still waiting for Olivia. Kevin Upstone's just arrived and Raine reckons it will be around forty minutes for him to get down the carpet. Who's in the Green Room?'

She buzzed back, 'Keith Yates, Lawrence Eppstein, Barbro Innes, Tommy Kane and Liam Taylor is just coming through the main doors. What news on Nancy or Cody Quinn?'

'Another Sedan is just pulling up, so it will be one of them. Let you know in a minute.'

I switched channels to call Mitch Stanley at the hotel to check on Taylor Quentin. We had changed his departure time to be at least ten minutes after Olivia's, on the assumption that Olivia would have been leaving from the hotel, as he was going to arrive via the loading dock to eschew the media and red carpet.

'He's hanging out in the bar, he's cool,' he said. I told him that everyone was here except Nancy, Cody and Olivia. 'When did Nancy and Cody leave?' I asked.

'Nancy about five minutes ago and Cody's just gone. The limo drivers' are saying they're having difficulty in getting through the traffic, but they should both be there in a minute. Someone needs to meet Cody at his car. He hasn't got his publicist with him.'

Advising Ric was here with me, I said we would handle that and the media interviews. Quickly checking the roster of escorts, I saw that my divine new friend, Dominic Steinberg, was down to be Cody's escort. I called Anna. 'Can you get Dominic Steinberg down to the start of the carpet now. He's Cody's escort.'

'Sure, he's on his way now.'

As I was saying this, two Sedans pulled up simultaneously. Nancy Demainne – probably the most successful female artist in the music industry – stepped out of the first car, accompanied by her handler. I do not know if it was my imagination, but she seemed a little unsteady on her feet.

'Is she OK?' I half whispered to Ric.

'Oh probably not,' he replied nonchalantly. 'You know what these divas are like.'

The fans yelled, whistled and chanted her name. She swung around, tilting precariously as she grabbed for her handler to steady herself.

'Hi everyone. It's great to be here.'

And with a wave which almost toppled her, she began a rather precarious walk along the red carpet, grinning broadly as the sea of light bulbs flashed and popped.

The contents of the other Sedan caused even more uproar among the crowds, for it was Cody Quinn, arguably

Hollywood's hottest star and one half of LA's golden couple. The explosion of flashbulbs, clapping, ear-piercing screams, wolf-whistles and general near-hysteria was testament to the fact that he was worshipped across the land by media and ordinary people alike.

We stepped forward to greet him. 'This will take forever as well,' Raine quickly whispered as she positioned Cody in front of the first of the TV crews.

I called Anna. 'Quick heads up. Nancy is on the carpet, but looking a little spaced, and Cody has just arrived and doing the TV pieces. What's going on at your end?'

Just as I said this, I noticed a guy leap out of a Sedan and sprint up the carpet, cheerily dismissing any offers of greeting or an escort. He looked familiar, with his recently balding pate and slighter physique, but for a minute I could not place him, and then it hit me. It was Conrad Young, our surprise presenter and who was supposed to be arriving at the side entrance to go straight to the Green Room. He happily waved to the cheering crowd as he almost ran along the carpet and was out of sight in a nano-second. Before Anna had had time to respond to my question, I continued, 'Conrad Young has just arrived and is almost skipping up the carpet. Expect him in about three minutes.'

'What's the thing with Nancy?' she asked.

'Not sure, she looks as though she's been drinking. Dominic's here for Cody. Oh, got to go. Olivia's here.'

The Maybach pulled up in front of the carpet and two Concierges each opened the rear doors. First out was Cate Phellim, who walked around the back of the car to stand beside Olivia as she stepped out to a rapturous applause from the crowd, accompanied by a blinding flurry of flashbulbs. I went forward to meet Cate, who greeted me warmly and thanked me for all the festival's assistance in getting them to the Gala. She then introduced me to Olivia who, despite a rather gruelling journey, was also extremely warm, thanking me for all the arrangements and being very apologetic about not using the Presidential Suite I had organized.

She was beautiful, with porcelain skin and strawberry-blond hair, elegantly dressed in a chignon, and so much prettier in real life than her press photos; she looked stunning in a strapless dark creamy-beige chiffon gown with a wisp of a chiffon train cascading down her back to the floor.

We chatted for a few minutes before Cate said Olivia needed to start the press interviews. 'Oh God, I'm taking up your time. I think Entertainment Tonight is getting a bit snippy,' I laughed.

As Olivia turned to the cameras, Cate said, 'Vanessa, you will stay alongside us on the carpet and then escort us to Olivia's table, won't you?'

Assuring her I would, I dutifully stepped back five paces and out of camera shot.

Looking ahead, I could see Cody and Dominic slowly making their way along the carpet as the paparazzi kept calling him to come over to them or to look their way. This was lucrative fodder for the myriad celebrity magazines worldwide which sated our incremental thirst for knowing every minutiae of the stars and their gilded lives, and the 'paps' – as they are known – were going to get *that* picture, at any cost.

As with Kevin Upstone earlier, it took Cody about forty minutes to just get past the media before he had to run the gauntlet of the screaming fans positioned beyond them. 'Cody, Cody,' they yelled. 'Cody, over here,' they screamed. 'Cody, please, please,' they begged, waving mobile phones, notebooks and T-shirts in anticipation of getting his photograph or autograph.

To his credit, he was very relaxed about it all and went over to them, shaking their hands, saying hello and signing autographs on as many items thrust into his face as he could. As he worked the line, girls with mobile camera phones clicked madly, as did the 'paps' – realising that a photograph of Cody Quinn signing a T-shirt while still on the girl would make for a thousand-dollar photo. And then came one of the most charming moments of the evening; as he worked his way along the line of adoring, hysterical fans, a girl in her mid-twenties was on her mobile to her mother in Idaho shouting above the din.

'Mom, I'm standing in line and Cody Quinn is coming towards me!'

As he approached her group, she thrust her phone out over the cordon, screaming, 'Cody, Cody, will you say hello to my mom?'

Without any hesitation, he took the mobile from her hand and said, 'Sure, what's your mom's name?'

'Oh my God, Oh my God, it's erm, Gloria,' cried the girl, now sobbing in disbelief that Cody Quinn had stopped to talk to her and that her mom was actually going to be *talking* to Hollywood's hottest star.

'Hi, Gloria, this is Cody Quinn and I'm at the film festival talking to your daughter.'

Even a couple of feet away, Dominic could hear the response. 'Oh. My. God! Is this *really* Cody Quinn?'

'Yeah, sure is,' replied Cody, followed by a loud thump which Dominic presumed was the mother fainting in disbelief that she had actually just had a split-second conversation with Cody Quinn himself.

A feeding frenzy of 'paps' flashguns ensued and

Dominic went to grab Cody's arm to lead him to another live TV interview, but the lights were too intense.

'Hold on a minute man, I can't see anything,' implored Cody.

I shadowed Olivia and Cate as they did all the media interviews and photo-ops, meeting them at the end of the carpet to escort them directly to their table, Cate having already indicated Olivia did not want to go to the Green Room.

It was now five-fifty p.m. and most of the guests were slowly making their way from the cocktail lounges into the auditorium, negotiating their way around one-hundred-and-eighty tables to their own ones – the seating plan having only arrived from Harry's office forty-five minutes earlier.

The stars' tables were in the centre of the auditorium, set out in front of the stage in a column of five across by four deep. They were, in turn, flanked by tables for the studio heads and guests who had paid over $5,000 each for the privilege of sitting near them. Guests who could only afford $1,000 for the hottest ticket in town that night were spread throughout the middle section of the auditorium, while those who had paid just $300 were relegated to the far sides and rear section.

I led Olivia and Cate to their table and waited until they were settled before dashing to the side goods entrance to await the low-key arrival of Taylor Quentin. His limousine was just pulling up at the loading dock as I got there, and when he got out I immediately sensed he did not want to be here. I escorted him to the backstage area – Taylor's people having advised that he would not do the Green Room either – where he would wait until he was to be called on stage to receive his award; I knew the wait would be punctuated by several visits back to the loading dock for a smoke.

I called Anna, 'OK, everyone's here. I'm going back into the auditorium.'

As I approached Liam Taylor's table, one of his security men stepped forward and told me, in an exceptionally blunt manner to, 'Step away from the table.' I did a double-take, telling him, possibly a little too curtly, of my role and that I was simply checking everything was in place. He was non-repentant and ordered me to, 'Step away.' Good God, who do these people think they are? I suggested he 'got a life' and edged towards the stage and the front row of tables.

Kane Eppstein, whom I had not heard from in several days but had seen briefly last night, broke off from his conversation at the adjoining tables linking the Eppstein clan.

'Hey Vanessa, how are you doin?'

'I'm good thanks Kane,' I replied, trying to sound neither stressed nor exhausted. He smiled. 'Have you met Dad yet?'

'Yes, of course, but only briefly to check on arrangements, so not properly. Is everything still to his satisfaction?'

'Oh, sure. Come and meet him properly.'

He led me to the centre of the tables to where the legendary actor himself was sitting.

'Dad, remember Vanessa who has organized everything for your visit?'

I learnt forward to shake his hand. 'Mr Eppstein, it's an absolute joy to see you again. I do hope that you are happy with everything?'

He took my proffered hand, cupping it in both of his. 'My dear, everything is just perfect. Thank you so very much.'

In an instant, I felt completely humbled by his graciousness and warmth.

'It's my pleasure, and please do not hesitate to ask Kane to call me if there is anything else at all that you and your wife need or want.'

A booming voice offstage suddenly rippled through the auditorium. 'Ladies and Gentlemen, please take your seats. Dinner service will begin in five minutes.'

I took my leave and made my way towards the rear of the room, stopping en-route to where Diana was frantically beckoning me to an empty seat on the table at which she was already seated.

'OK, let's get this ego-trip started,' she quipped, grabbing the bottle of Merlot in front of her and liberally dousing our glasses. 'This should be an interesting evening.'

It was six o'clock and there was still a long way to go yet.

The lights dimmed slowly as the offstage announcer's voice commanded, 'Ladies and Gentlemen, please be seated. Dinner will begin promptly.'

Guests swapped business cards and entered phone numbers into their BlackBerrys and iPhones while forensically studying the menu – micro-field greens encircled with parsnip chips and edible flowers, phyllo-wrapped tenderloin of beef with red wine poached pear, artichoke and wild mushrooms and, for dessert, tiramisu topped with powdered chocolate and fresh berries – to ensure that they would not be adding one single ounce to their already taut frames. Satisfied they would not, they started on the appetizer.

The wine waiters circled the 'ordinary' tables, disgorging the contents of their bottles in torpedo-like fashion, while a small posse of Sommeliers grandiosely delivered, to the talents' tables, sterling silver engraved wine buckets full of bottles of Roederer Cristal, Krug and

Chablis, plus silver trays of Chateau Pétrus and Chateau Latour. Two minutes later, the orchestra struck up as the film festival logo, and then the opening credits, rolled on the bank of video screens at the back of the stage, followed by video clips from the attending talents' various movies.

Just forty-five minutes had been allocated for the trivial pursuit of eating the appetizers and entrées before the serious business of ego-pandering and back-slapping began; by six-forty-five p.m. precisely, the banqueting staff, who had already whisked away all the crockery and cutlery, had started serving dessert. We were ready to go.

The offstage voice summoned everyone's attention. 'Ladies and Gentlemen, please give a warm welcome to our Academy Award winners and celebrity guests.' As the names of the awards recipients and presenters were read out, the video banks in the centre of the stage flashed up super-sized pictures of the stars, with the side banks of screens depicting clips from some of their more recent movies.

This was followed, at seven o'clock precisely, by host Natalie Immber's arrival on stage. Looking resplendent in an Ali Rahimi for Mon Atelier couture gown and with full hair and make-up, she cut a glamorous figure as she approached the microphone. After a brief preamble about the Awards Gala celebrating cinematic milestones and the festival now being viewed by Hollywood 'as a legitimate precursor to the Academy Awards', she welcomed on stage Tiffany & Co.'s US Chief Executive Officer to a rapturous applause – for there had been a stunning gift in the iconic blue Tiffany box at each place setting – before continuing.

'Please direct your attention to the video screens for a salute to the timeless elegance of Tiffany and a sampling of our talents' movies that may well be the big hits this year.'

Coffee, liqueurs and Godiva chocolates were expediently served while the video screens engaged and delighted the audience, and the first of the celebrities to be on stage, as either a recipient or presenter, was discreetly collected from their table and escorted backstage in preparation.

The format for the ceremony was simple. Natalie Immber would announce the presenter, naturally hyping up any awards nominations recently accorded to the star – Golden Globes, Oscars, Emmys, Screen Actors' Guild, Directors' Guild of America or BAFTAs. The presenter would then come on stage and talk, for a maximum of two minutes, about the award recipient's career highlights; this would be followed by a video tape, usually three minutes in length, of said star's movies, old and new.

The presenter would then say, 'Please welcome (*x star*)'; the star would walk on stage and go over to the presenter who, by now, had been handed the actual award to be presented, all amid much pre-recorded backstage 'ballyhoo' to ramp up the atmosphere.

The presenter would then briefly explain why the particular award was being given to the star – Lifetime Achievement Award; Visionary Award for Acting, Directing and Producing; Career Achievement Award: Actor; Director of the Year Award; Outstanding Film Score Award and the Chairman's Award – and give the award to the recipient. In turn, the recipient would deliver an acceptance speech designed to be no longer than two minutes – though one or two turned into ten minutes. Interspersing the awards would be brief speeches of thanks for the largess of various city luminaries by Ed (as festival Chairman) and Harry (as festival Managing Director and 'bankroller'), and, to underscore the importance of its independent spirit, Duncan as festival Executive Director – each welcomed to the podium by Natalie Immber, whose smile never faltered for one minute.

Simple enough and there should not have been any hiccups or gasps from the audience, but Diana's comment 'this should be an interesting evening' had been prophetic, even if she had not realized it. Just as the Stage Manager was preparing to cue the first presenter, I slipped out to the loading dock to see if Taylor Quentin was OK. He seemed agitated and was pacing up and down the ramp.

'Hi, are you alright?' I said breezily.

He looked up. 'Do you smoke?' Replying that I did not, he looked even more dejected. Noticing that Ed's chauffeur was behind the wheel of his limo at the far end of the parking bay, I dashed over.

'Could I please have the packet of cigarettes?' I pleaded and, without waiting for an answer, learnt forward and grabbed the Marlboro Lites; seeing that there was also a packet of Kool on the dashboard, I grabbed them too. 'Sorry, an emergency. Oh, and I also need your lighter.'

The poor chauffeur looked startled as I hijacked his only form of succour that evening and ran back to the loading dock. Proffering the first packet of cigarettes, I asked Taylor Quentin if he smoked that brand. 'No,' he growled.

'What about these?' gesturing the other packet towards him.

'No,' he again growled.

He clearly wanted to be anywhere other than at this awards ceremony. Suddenly, I had hit a wall of exhaustion and said, perhaps a little testily, 'Well, you have a choice of either these two brands, or nothing. Up to you, but the Chairman's chauffeur has donated them to you, so I'd suggest you put your preferences to one side and enjoy them. It's all you're going to get tonight. Well, at least until we get to the after-show party.'

He looked up again, with a faint trace of a smile. 'I'm sorry, I've got a lot on my mind at the moment and could do without being here. Thanks for the smokes. They'll both be fine.'

I said I would leave him in peace and return in about twenty minutes when his escort, who was waiting inside the loading dock doors, would need to escort him backstage.

Back inside the auditorium, the fanfare was in full swing and two awards had already been presented. Natalie Immber reappeared. 'Ladies and Gentleman, will you please welcome legendary Hollywood producer Kyle Yablonski to present the Visionary Award to the BAFTA award-winning British Director Keith Yates, whose latest movie is garnering lots of buzz for Golden Globes glory in a few weeks.'

The first hiccup of the evening. As Keith Yates took possession of the rather cumbersome award, he looked somewhat sneeringly at the gift and quipped laconically to the microphone, so that absolutely everyone could hear, 'It's not *quite* what I was expecting. I have absolutely no idea what this thing is or what I am supposed to do with it, or how I'm even going to carry it onto the plane, but thank you anyway.'

Unfortunately, the creator of the large hand-blown glass vase – for that was what it was – was none other than the internationally celebrated American glass sculptor Dale Chihuly (who had transformed the lobby ceiling of the luxurious Bellagio hotel in Las Vegas into a work of art) and who was sitting at a table three rows from the front. Sensing the perceived slight and ensuing awkwardness, Natalie Immber breezed back on stage with a joke, while speedily ushering both Kyle and Keith off stage.

Luckily, the next presenter was Hollywood's hottest star, so the audience instantly forgot the awkward moment and a revered hush descended.

'To present the Ensemble Performance Award, please give a very warm welcome to Cody Quinn.'

The room erupted in applause as Cody came on stage and, before he announced the name of the recipient, video clips were run to much cooing and sighing as the recipient was revealed to be Kevin Upstone. Cue more applause as Kevin bounded onto the stage, grinning from ear to ear. I had heard he had been charm personified as he had walked the red carpet, chatting to fans and signing photos, and he seemed utterly at ease, even bemused, with this award for his role as a woman in a musical.

Thanking the festival, he said, 'I've come full circle with this award, for I started my career in musicals, although I was a man then, and now some twenty years on, I'm back to musicals, albeit as a woman!'

A roar of approval swept through the room, accompanied by thunderous applause and wolf-whistles. But as the evening was precisioned-timed, Kevin was quickly ushered off and we were onto the next award.

Liam Taylor, himself a recipient, was the next presenter, giving the Career Achievement: Actor gong to one of Paramount Studio's leading stars, Tommy Kane. I dashed to the loading dock to take Taylor Quentin and his escort backstage, as he was up next with our surprise presenter. Back in the auditorium, it was time to see whether there really had been a need for the FBI, the LA PD and bomb sniffer dogs.

Natalie Immber swept back on stage. 'Ladies and Gentlemen, it's now time for one of the major awards tonight. Director of the Year.' A ripple of applause broke out. 'Neither our next presenter, nor recipient, need any introduction, for they have both raised the bar in Hollywood. Our surprise presenter tonight has kindly cut short his Caribbean vacation to be with us and present this award, so would you please give a rapturous welcome to Conrad Young.'

The orchestra again struck up as Conrad bounded on stage, grinning like a Cheshire Cat, in much the same way as he had skipped along the red carpet.

'Hey everyone,' he waved to the assembled throng, 'Isn't it good to be here tonight?'

A roar of 'yeah' and 'sure is' rolled back from the tables. Clutching the award to be handed over – this time a more suitable bronze statuette – he held it up above the microphone and proceeded.

'As Natalie rightly said, the next recipient *really* needs *no* introduction. You know him through his many movies as a particularly talented actor and you may know him as a great writer. You know him as a perfectionist and someone who is not afraid to take on challenging roles or projects. You know him as an American film icon in a career spanning three decades. But, more recently, we have seen him as an exceptionally gifted director who takes cinematography to another art form. Let's take a minute or two to see the genius of his work.'

The video clips finished to a standing ovation from the room, the atmosphere was electric and my heart was racing. I was an avid fan of his. Spotlight back on Conrad, he continued, 'Now you can see why he is being honoured with this award. Ladies and Gentlemen, please welcome one of the most original and imaginative actors today, an amazingly creative director and two-time Academy Award winner, Taylor Quentin.'

A trumpet fanfare heralded Taylor Quentin as he walked on stage, cigarette in one hand and a glass of Jack Daniels in the other. This was not the usual way to come on stage and accept an award, but then he was very much his own man and did not care much what people thought of him. He looked more at ease than five minutes earlier on the loading dock.

'Hey, what's up? Think anything is going to make YouTube tonight?'

Another prophetic statement, as it turned out. As Conrad hugged him and handed over the statuette, Taylor put his drink down on the podium, quipping that his intention of receiving his award 'in absolute sobriety' went the way of 'the best laid plans.' He then flipped the statuette over to his right hand and triumphantly held it up in the air, as if in defiance to some of his detractors, of which there were plenty in Hollywood.

Upon being conferred with the accolade of being "the best actor today, who is now also directing movies" by a top Hollywood director – who delivered this impromptu statement from the audience – Taylor, in a rare display of humility, said 'this was a lie. The British actor Daniel Day-Lewis may very well be the greatest actor ever recorded on the screen. His performances makes one want to be an actor and try harder.'

A resounding applause, probably as much for what he had just said as for him himself, broke through the room and continued after he had left the stage. As the clapping died away, Natalie came back on stage to announce the next award – the recipient of which would provide our 'gasp' for the evening and turn Taylor's joke about YouTube into reality.

‘Our next recipient is one of the biggest names in the music business. A multiple Grammy award winner, now turning her hand to acting, she has delivered a noteworthy performance in her first role in a gritty, edgy new movie about a teenager’s life of poverty and hopelessness. To present the award is the movie’s director, Mike Edelston. Ladies and Gentlemen, please welcome Mike Edelston and Nancy Demainne.’

A more upbeat orchestral arrangement cued Mike out first, followed by Nancy who sauntered onto the stage wearing a tight, low-cut, black-beaded full-length Hervé Léger gown, and promptly fell into the director’s arms, giving him a long, emotional hug. It was, however, immediately apparent that she was having ‘difficulties’. She kept fanning herself and repeating ‘Oh my goodness!’ several times before launching into what became a four-minute rambling, disjointed acceptance speech. The audience was clearly not impressed.

Trying to compose herself, she said, ‘Please forgive me, because I’m a little bit, erm …’.

A guest sitting at one of the $15,000 ‘Star’ tables at the front (so named as they were the closest ‘ordinary’ tables to the A-List stars) finished her sentence for her. ‘F***-ed up.’

So out of it that she had not properly registered the comment, she quipped, ‘Yeah!’, reeling with laughter.

The audience, in an unforgiving mood, tired quickly of her party attitude and slow-clapped both her and Mike Edelson off the stage before her acceptance speech was over. It later transpired that an audience member had captured her acceptance speech on their phone camera and the clip appeared the next morning, firstly on CNN and then on numerous cable channels and web sites, giving the festival column inches so yearned for by the PR agency, even if not for the right reason.

Frivolity over, it was back to the serious awards and, in an attempt to make light of Nancy's protocol gaff, Natalie Immber chirruped, 'Who says we don't have fun here?', before quickly leading into the next award.

'To present our next award, The Visionary Award for Acting, Directing and Producing, will you please give a warm round of applause for one of Hollywood's most enduring actors and who is currently enjoying something of a renaissance with the hit TV series about family wealth, greed and feuds on Park Avenue. Ed Tyler.'

Ed bounded on stage, still cutting the dashing figure from when we first saw him in the mid Sixties; his piercing blue eyes and now silver-grey hair only adding to his sexual magnitude.

He paused momentarily to acknowledge the audience's rapturous welcome.

'Hey, I've got the easiest job here tonight. I'm introducing someone who needs no introduction. The recipient of this award is a two-time Academy Award winner, his range and diversity of acting methods and vocal skills has ensured roles on Broadway, in dozens of films and a mega new TV hit series. His artistic direction has enthralled audiences across the pond and we are fortunate that he can join us here tonight. The video montage will provide us with a brief overview and highlights of his career and will, I'm sure, underscore why he is being given this prestigious award.'

Lights dimming, the orchestra revved up, the video screens came alight and, for four minutes, the audience sat in hushed silence.

Spotlight back on Ed Tyler, he turned to the room. 'Please welcome this year's recipient of the Visionary

Award for Acting, Directing and Producing – Liam Taylor.'

An ecstatic reception greeted the actor as he walked on stage and immediately displayed evidence of his comedic versatility.

'Usually when you're up here receiving an award, there's an orchestra behind you ready to cue you off before you've said anything!'

He then began what turned out to be an emotional ten-minute acceptance speech, dedicating it to 'the team that makes what I do possible' and expressing gratitude for being able to thank all his business associates in public, whom he considered 'family' and many of which had helped him since his early days as a stand-up comic in New York.

He then delivered a rare rendition of his impressive skill as an impressionist, ranging from actors Jimmy Stewart and Jack Lemmon, Christopher Walken and Al Pacino through to a pitch-perfect President Bill Clinton. The audience was enthralled and could not get enough, with cries of 'more, more,' as he finally left the stage, statuette held triumphantly aloft in his right hand.

The atmosphere had now swiftly moved up to fifth gear and the audience was keen to get to the final award. But there was one other to be handed out first. Natalie Immber, back on stage, trilled that the next award – The Chairman's Award – 'is designed to acknowledge actors who take risks in their selection of roles. To present this award, please welcome the multi-talented director and producer, Armando Aguilar.'

He ran onto the stage, hugged Natalie and, grabbing the microphone, breathlessly addressed the audience.

'A diverse career and the courage to continually explore the frontier of one's acting skills sets her apart from many actors of her calibre. It is no wonder that she is an Academy Award and Golden Globe winner. As she was handed her Best Actress Oscar, a contemporary quipped "... and the winner is Olivia Lautner by a nose!" Audiences can look forward to even more from this adaptable nose in her upcoming roles. Ladies and Gentlemen, please point *your* noses towards the video screens for a glimpse of the exceptional talent of Olivia Lautner.'

A four-minute tribute flashed on the screens and, as the lights returned to a dimmed level, Armando shouted, 'Please welcome Academy Award winner Olivia Lautner.'

A crescendo of applause and wolf-whistles greeted Olivia as she walked serenely onto the stage. I watched in awe at how she had managed a seamless transition from travelling in a jet, jumping into a Maybach and treading a very damp red carpet, to walking on stage looking absolutely immaculate.

Taking the award from Armando – another exquisite Dale Chihuly hand-blown glass ornament – she expressed her thanks by saying simply, but eloquently, 'It is an enormous honour to be given this award, but I love acting, absolutely love what I do. To receive an award for something you love to do, well it doesn't seem fair. Thank you so much. Thank you.'

Cognizant of the fact that timings had overrun, she walked towards the back of the stage, turning twice to acknowledge the audience's salutation – many of the guests having, by now, risen to their feet to clap their hands above their heads in tribute.

Maintaining the momentum of the moment, and in homage to the next recipient, the orchestra played the opening chords of Khachaturian's instantly-recognizable *Adagio of Spartacus* as Natalie Immber came back on stage, amid a swirling dance of spotlights, to announce the key award of the night.

'The Lifetime Achievement Award is reserved for a lifetime of exemplary work. Tonight, we are honoured to have, as the award recipient, one of the giants of cinema. He has played a rogue, a hero, a family man and a cowboy.

He has acted with virtually every major actor and actress of his day. In short, he is a Hollywood legend. To present the award, please welcome a scion of another Hollywood dynasty, Barbro Innes.'

More applause and wolf-whistles as Barbro took the microphone to deliver her eulogy.

'It is amazing to be involved in a family affair such as this, for this family is truly one of the great performing families in America. The Eppsteins, like the Barrymores, the Hepburns and the Fondas, form part of American cinema legacy.'

She paused briefly to check she was holding the audience's attention. 'Sadly, Nate Eppstein is unable to be here tonight as he is on location, so please direct your attention to the video screens for his message.'

The lights dimmed as the screens relayed a very personal message from his most famous son and Hollywood heart-throb. A resounding cheer emanated from the audience as Nate echoed the sentiments of an award justly deserved. Barbro again took up the reins.

'The Lawrence Eppstein legacy is legendary. His acting career has spanned seven decades. Yes, seven. And his latest movie premieres at this festival. Please direct your attention to the video screens once more for a glimpse of the work of Lawrence Eppstein.'

Once again, the video screens roared into action, starting with clips from his earlier historical adventure epics and running through a pastiche of his myriad film, television and Broadway appearances, before culminating in his more recent work. Barbro returned to centre stage and, despite all the hoopla, simply said, 'Ladies and Gentlemen, please welcome the recipient of the Lifetime Achievement Award. Lawrence Eppstein.'

The guests watched in revered silence as the great man himself, now in his late nineties and who had battled back from the brink of a severe stroke some twenty years earlier, walked unaided onto the stage.

In the preparations for the Awards Gala, we had factored in the possibility that his health might not allow him to stand for three to four minutes to deliver his acceptance speech, so a chair and a walking cane had been placed discreetly to one side of the stage in case such a need arose. He surprised us all by not needing the chair, standing as he delivered an acceptance speech a full eight minutes long. He appeared to be loving every minute and the only sign of his failing health was his faltering speech.

'When I came to Hollywood from Broadway, I wanted to see the stars, but I didn't see any until, one weekend, someone brought me to this city and then I saw Edward G. Robinson and Errol Flynn at the Racquet Club.'

As he continued with his speech, Barbro – who had remained on stage – beckoned to a stage assistant for the rest of the award recipients and presenters to come on stage and join Lawrence in a surprise tribute. She slowly walked forward and, when Lawrence had finished, took his arm to support him and told him that there were some people who wished to join him on stage in recognition of, and as a tribute to, his lifetime's achievement.

The other recipients, followed by the presenters, returned and surrounded the great man; overcome with emotion, and now with the need for the chair, he slowly sat down while the honoured stars fêted him – and then the entire audience paid their own homage, scattering chairs as they leapt to their feet for an emotional standing ovation that lasted over six minutes. There was not a dry eye in the house.

Seemingly unwilling to bring the proceedings to a halt, but knowing that the audience would be keen to get to the after-show party, the preternaturally enthusiastic Natalie Immber, who had kept the whole ceremony moving at an even canter, swept back into the spotlight. Now joined by Ed and Harry, they warmly thanked all the honourees for taking time out of their hectic filming commitments to attend, the sponsors for their generosity and the guests for their largess in contributing to the fundraiser.

The message of thanks over, the orchestra began its final piece, the lights dimmed to a warm glow, the guests put away their tissues and gathered up their precious Tiffany gift.

It was time for the after-show party.

The rain had finally eased and was now just a light shower as Diana and I drove over to The Four Seasons, this time in her car and not the Dodge pick-up that I usually drove to the hotel. The Valet Parking guys, seamlessly relieving the owners of their cars, guided the crowd through the huge entrance doors into the lobby and out into the Rose Garden. The gravelled pathway leading to the bay-fronted Grand Ballroom was lined with hurricane lamps and verbena-scented rocket candles. As I walked into the Grand Ballroom, my mobile rang. It was Cate Phellim calling from the Lear jet as they taxied down the runway to return to Santa Monica; I darted back into the garden.

'Vanessa, thank you for all your arrangements and all your efforts in ensuring the evening went so smoothly. I really appreciate everything you did for Olivia tonight.'

I was very touched by this and certainly had not expected a call – an email in a week's time, perhaps – but not a call straightaway.

'All part of the service. It was a pleasure meeting you both and I hope that you have a better flight going back than you did coming up.' I could hear shouting in the background.

'Vanessa, can you hear Olivia? She's shouting "thank you" to you,' screamed Cate over the roar of the engines thrust as they took off.

'Say thank you to her, and I hope to see you both in London sometime,' I yelled back as the Lear jet soared into the clouds.

Back inside the heaving party, I wandered over to the cordoned VIP area to see who was there. Raine Daysen, Ric and Shane were with several journalists who were chatting to Keith Yates – himself still trying to work out what his Dale Chihuly award was actually supposed to be – about his clutch of upcoming Golden Globes nominations and whether this would translate into Oscar victory, and to Ed Tyler about his new hit TV series. Barbro Innes was there with her husband, Kevin Upstone was with his actress wife and Conrad Young was with his new, young, wife, while Cody Quinn conversed studiously with his agent.

There were, naturally, plenty of directors, producers and studio heads in the closed-off area; it was fascinating to see 'the lesser mortals' visibly tense in the presence of the A-List, reacting with the measured casualness of the famous confronted by celebrity of an entirely different order.

Lawrence Eppstein, Olivia Lautner and Tommy Kane had all left immediately after the Awards Gala – Tommy also back to LA on the Paramount jet – and so I looked around for Liam Taylor and Taylor Quentin. Waiters clad in white military-style jackets and skinny leg black trousers glided around, as if on invisible roller skates, bearing trays of champagne, Dirty Martinis, wines and acai berry martinis, plus shot glasses of white corn and roasted bell pepper chowder, Roquefort tartlets, Tempura shrimp, bite-sized crab cakes and mini Kobe cheeseburgers. Rob should be here, I thought, as I grabbed a Dirty Martini from a passing silver tray.

As I walked past Keith Yates, who appeared to be overly-confident of both Golden Globes and Oscar success – some unkind Academy voting member had earlier labelled him "arrogant" – I quietly said to him, 'It's a vase. Hand-blown by Dale Chihuly, one of America's most fêted artists. They sell for thousands, so you're actually quite fortunate to have been given it, though I do appreciate it will be a hassle when it comes to hand luggage!'

He looked around sharply, surprised more at the cut-glass English accent than anything else. I smiled and wished him luck for the awards season and walked on, not wanting to interrupt the media's time with him more than I had done already.

Dirty Martini replenished and wanting some air, I walked out into the garden. There, in deep conversation with his agent and smoking furiously, was Taylor Quentin, looking visibly more relaxed. Iaine Yardley, who had left Miramax to set up his own eponymous company, was chatting to Liam Taylor and a clutch of his friends – his business associates whom he had referred to in his acceptance speech as "his family" and which included his publicist, Stephani Yorke. I said a quick 'Hi' to Stephani as I circled around them and made my way back to the party, almost colliding with Cody Quinn and his agent as they were leaving. I escorted Cody back into the main part of the hotel as he had an early morning departure for LA, before re-joining the party.

Diana sauntered over, a margarita in one hand and an acai berry martini in the other. 'Hey, try this!' she shouted as she thrust the acai berry martini into my hand. 'It's really cool. I've never had one before. Think they've created them just for the party.'

It was indeed good and as we pushed our way to the bar to refill ourselves, Dominic Steinberg joined us.

'Do you know something, he was really cool, really relaxed, really happy to chat to the fans and sign autographs. I was *so* impressed,' he said.

'God, did you see the way he was happy to talk to a fan's mother, on her mobile!' trilled Diana. 'Stars just don't do that. *That* was so cool.'

As we debated Cody's red carpet behaviour, Taylor Quentin and his agent came back inside and leaned up against a tall bar table, helping a passing waiter to lighten his load by taking several martini glasses and a small plate of canapés.

'Oh. My. God. It's Taylor Quentin! I want to go and say hello,' squealed Diana, sliding off her seat in excitement.

'Oh for God's sake, be a bit cool and leave the poor guy alone. I don't think he wants to be here as it is,' I retorted sharply.

'Yeah, he's looking for an exit strategy alright,' Dominic pronounced seriously.

But Diana would not have any of it and, like a heat-seeking missile, made straight for the poor guy.

'Hi Taylor, I just wanted to say congratulations on Director of the Year. I'm a huge fan of your work.'

Taylor, obviously now feeling far more chilled out, graciously said to Diana, 'Thank you, I appreciate that.'

Taking her cue to leave, she spun around and fixed her stare plus the widest grin imaginable – upon Dominic and I, as if to say, 'See, not *that* hard!'

It was now almost two o'clock and the party had begun to thin out. The stars – those that had stayed the course, either through the need to relax or have yet another meeting with their agent – had begun to leave, as had many of the older guests, the patrons of the festival.

Raine tapped me on the arm as she left. 'I'm leaving early, so shan't see you tomorrow. Thanks for all your help.'

'See you in LA in a week or so,' I said cheerily, not knowing that this would never happen.

I, too, had hit another wall of exhaustion; grabbing one more acai berry martini 'purely for medicinal purposes' as Diana put it, I made my way over to the main hotel, spotting Ed Tyler and Liam Taylor in animated conversation at The Terrace Bar. The Valet Parking guys, having had a stupendous night in terms of tips, kindly called me a cab; within thirty minutes I was back at the Hilton and cocooned in the luxurious Egyptian cotton bed linen.

But respite would not be for long. Tomorrow was Sunday, but it was a normal working day at the festival and I would have to be up after the usual four hours' sleep and be in the Guest & Industry Suite at seven-thirty a.m. to help set up breakfast, and catch up on what had been happening there during the past three days under the aegis of Mike 2 and Dino.

A text from Rob said he and Javier had concluded their business and were flying back to Tijuana from Manuel

Sinalopéz's ranch on the outskirts of Culiacán.

I was too exhausted to realise what this text actually meant, or its implications.

CHAPTER SIXTEEN

The hotel lobby was already buzzing at seven-thirty a.m. with cleaners and night staff handing over to the regular day staff as I walked through to the Guest & Industry Suite. The room was empty and, apart from a bit of debris at the bar area, it was clean and tidy; fifteen minutes later, Dino and Mike 2 walked in, both looking the worse for wear.

'Hey guys, had a good night?' I smiled, as they clutched their heads and begged for Tylenol.

'Oh God, Vanessa, don't talk too loudly,' pleaded Dino.

'Ah, you should have kept some extra hang-over cures for yourself that you sensibly put into all the guests' goody-bags.'

I unlocked the First Aid cabinet and rummaged for the Tylenol.

'How was your night?' asked Mike 2.

'Interesting,' I replied slowly, as if to labour the point. 'Actually, it was great. Not without a few hassles here and there but, overall, everything went according to plan. But, my God, you should have seen Nancy Demainne. She was out of it. I think her handlers will be regretting that they didn't stop her from swigging the champagne, and whatever else, before she even hit the red carpet.'

They concurred quietly, which was about as much as

they could manage, as the hotel banqueting staff arrived to set up breakfast, clanging trolleys, banging trays and sifting cutlery with gusto.

'Are either of you OK to drive? As in now?'

A look of panic flashed across their faces.

'Erm, guess so,' said Dino hesitantly.

'Good, then can you go and get breakfast. Quick though Dino, our first guests will be here in about thirty minutes.'

'Need a hair of the dog, Mike? I could easily rustle up a Bloody Mary, but if you do want one, you've got to promise me that you won't tell a soul.'

The poor boy's face lit up, for he clearly was suffering. 'Awesome!'

'I take it that means yes!' He nodded animatedly as I went to the back of the storage room and unlocked the cupboard housing the spirits. I whipped up two Bloody Marys – though not proper ones as I had neither Lea & Perrins nor a stick of celery – but it would, nonetheless, hit the spot and provide a degree of succour.

The breakfast bar was soon set up with all its goodies as guests started trickling in at eight-thirty a.m. – most of them looking as though they had had as good a night as Dino and Mike 2. (I later discovered that there had been an impromptu and unofficial 'gay-la' party at one of the nightclubs in town; unofficial as there was an official Festival Gay-la party scheduled for later in the week.) Satisfied everyone seemed content, I walked over to the far side of the room to the bank of computers and phones which comprised our work station. After the tsunami of the past four days, I wondered if today I might possibly have a chance to catch my breath and get some down time. Remembering that Xavier Torres was arriving today from Rio, I quickly glanced at the flights and airport pick-up rosters and saw that he was due in at LAX at twelve noon. Just as I was scribbling a note to Lizzie to ensure that one of the chauffered Lincoln Town Cars met him at LAX, Christian appeared out of nowhere, also looking the worse for wear.

'Hey, don't forget that Xavier Torres arrives today,' he snapped in a somewhat stressed state as I shot him a resigned look. 'What time will he be here, I need to meet him personally.'

Without answering him, I held up the note I was writing to Lizzie, so that he could see it was already in hand.

'Call me when the driver has picked him up at LAX, and ask the driver to call you when they are thirty minutes away from arriving, so that I can be at the hotel to meet him.'

'Good God, he's just a film director. Anyone would think it is the President or Royalty arriving for a state visit,' I muttered deprecatingly.

Christian was not amused. 'These people, whether leading actors or directors, *are* our royalty in *our* world,' he hissed.

'Oh, per-leeze,' I shot back witheringly. Seeing that he was now clearly agitated and, needing to diffuse the situation, I quickly added, 'He will be met at the airport by a chauffeur, driven back here to the hotel in a Lincoln Town Car. You will personally meet and greet him at the hotel; he will then be personally escorted, by the hotel general manager, to his private villa, which comes with a butler, and offered any amenity or service that he requires, which includes the use of a limousine and driver at any time during his time with us. I think that pretty much covers the royal visit.'

Shooting me an equally withering look, he spun on his

heel and flounced out of the room. It was already shaping up to be the usual crazy day in the kooky world of film festivals.

I noticed our four Chinese filmmakers – two directors and two producers, each with a film being shown at the festival during the coming week – at a table in the centre of the room, trying to simultaneously eat their breakfast and conduct an animated conversation. But, by the looks on their faces, something was clearly worrying them; within the hour, we would find out.

It transpired that the Chinese government – aggrieved at learning that there was a 'pro-Tibet' documentary film following the Dalai Lama during the protests in Tibet, the Beijing Olympics and talks with China, being screened at the festival – had applied pressure on Duncan to pull the screening.

When Duncan had politely, but firmly, said the festival would not do this, citing that 'its mandate was to present as broad a spectrum of films and points of view as possible', the Chinese Vice Consul in LA allegedly said that the documentary had to be withdrawn as it was 'riddled with lies and that the Chinese government and the Chinese people in China would be very unhappy with the festival presenting it.' He also threatened to pull their two Chinese movies in protest.

Duncan, having consulted the Board, who stood behind his decision to support his staff's dedication to artistic freedom, would not be swayed. He told the Vice Consul that, while he understood their concerns, the festival attached a much higher degree of value to freedom of expression.

Clearly rankled at their demands not being immediately met, the Chinese government responded by pulling their two films and ordering the directors and producers home.

The filmmakers, excited at the opportunity of showcasing their first feature films at a major international film festival, looked first downcast and then utterly dejected as their mobiles rang constantly and the story unfolded.

By mid-morning, they came to the travel desk to explain that 'for unexpected personal reasons, they were having to leave today' and could we change their flights back to Beijing and arrange transport to Los Angeles. They were also 'so velly solly' for all the trouble it was causing us.

The suite filled up with guests, many of them nursing hangovers from too much partying the night before; they wanted nothing more than Tylenol, coffee, and more Tylenol. A few die-hard ones, however, decided that the age-old cure of a Bloody Mary was the *only* way to get them out of their morass, so like a couple of old bartender pros, Dino and I opened up the drinks cupboard for the second time, liberally pouring vodka and tomato juice over crushed ice into large Hi-ball glasses, replete with celery tree-trunks, and proceeded to dispense medicinal happiness to those in pain, much to the consternation of the hotel breakfast servers.

Dominic, who the evening before had been Cody Quinn's escort at the Awards Gala, was milling around our work station while he waited for the PR team to arrive.

'Hey, how's your head today?' he asked, beaming from ear to ear. 'And what did you make of last night? Wasn't Nancy a riot? Talk about a train wreck!'

I smiled back at him and gave him an impromptu kiss on the cheek. 'My head's fine, thanks. It's everyone else who seems to be suffering today. Did you go to the gay-la party after the after-show party?'

His smile gave away the fact that he had, and had obviously enjoyed it a little too much.

'Any Tylenol left Vanessa?'

Reaching down into the cabinet hidden under the linen drapes covering my desk, I grabbed one of the last hang-over cure boxes that Dino had assembled for the goody-bags. 'Have it on us.'

As Dominic was getting his hands on that morning's holy grail, Ric, Shane, and their assistants, walked in. Shane was his usual bouncy self, but Ric looked tired having, he explained, been up most of the night fielding media questions about the personal life of another showbiz client who was on location in Thailand and clearly enjoying some of the local produce.

The conversation reverted to Nancy, for it had been brought to Ric's attention fifteen minutes earlier that it was now splashed all over CNN. The four of us sprinted to the adjacent media room and, grabbing the remote, Ric clicked through to CNN. Sure enough, on the rolling 'ticker-tape' Breaking News feed at the bottom of the screen was the headline: 'Nancy Demainne allegedly drunk while accepting award at film festival'.

We waited impatiently until the main international and domestic news stories were done and watched, with mouths open, as it came up.

The news anchors, clearly delighted with this story, gave it the full treatment for about five minutes. Showing the film festival logo, clips of her stumbling on the red carpet, the clip of her performance in the new movie and then, in all its glory, the Awards Gala guest's mobile phone camera video of her acceptance speech. Clips over, Ric punched the remote.

'Oh well, the festival's made it onto CNN, even if not for the right reason! What with all the other cable channels it will feed into and the print media that will pick it up today, I reckon we're looking at nearly two million media impressions, which would be worth some forty million dollars in advertising spend. That should keep Harry happy!'

News story over, we repaired to the main suite.

'Was she on drugs as well?' asked Dominic.

'Who knows, but she'd certainly been on the juice when she arrived at the carpet and she knocked back the champagne in the Green Room,' said Ric. 'She even asked me to fix her dress for her before she went on stage, because it was riding up around her hips!'

We looked at him incredulously. Feigning shock and cupping both hands around his cheeks, Shane shrieked, 'And *did* you?'

'Of course not,' squealed Ric. 'You really think I'm gonna go up to Nancy Demainne while we're in the Green Room and start re-arranging her dress! I asked one of her handlers to do it for her.'

The Nancy saga was halted by the arrival of two gentlemen, both of whom we all instantly recognized and whom Ric and I had seen last night engulfed in a sea of beautiful people in the VIP area of the after-show party. One was Iaine Yardley, one of Hollywood's most influential power-brokers, who had left production and worldwide distribution company Miramax to set up his own eponymous production studio; the other was former fashion designer Vere Gough who, during his fourteen-year tenure at one of Italy's foremost luxury goods companies, had turned the ailing label around to become one of the world's most commercially successful fashion houses.

I had read that both men had known each other for many years, having met at a film party in London some twenty years ago and, as Iaine's wife was a fashion designer with her own label in New York, there was an obvious synergy between the two men. I also knew, from Ric and Shane's plethora of press releases which weighed down my Day File, that Vere was here for his directorial debut with his first feature film. He had set up his own production company in LA and, having adapted a novel for the screenplay, had himself directed and co-produced the movie.

Ric, knowing there would be substantial press column inches to be gained, especially if a distribution deal was struck, went forward to greet them. I followed, beckoning Dino and Lizzie to join me. Iaine and Vere were both charming, albeit keen to get on with their own meeting and, introductions and offers of any assistance at any time dispensed with, they quickly walked over to the art deco sofa at the far end of the room where they could talk in relative peace – although their time was punctuated too often by sycophantic guests, eager to shake the gilded hand of LA's newest, and most media-hyped, director.

Turning my attention back to more mundane, but pressing matters, I rang LAX to check that the American Airlines flight from Rio had landed and was informed that it had. I called the chauffeur to check that he had arrived at the airport, advising him that the flight had landed and double-check he had collected the VIP sign bearing Xavier Torres name on it.

He was there and had the sign; good, ticks to those three boxes. I reminded him that he needed to call me as soon as he had Mr Torres in the car and again when they were thirty minutes from arriving at the hotel.

Scrolling through my emails, now luckily only trickling in, I noticed one from Daniel Eversleigh, who was flying out the next day. I immediately replied; no sooner had I pressed the Send button, back came a reply.

'Greetings from a very cold London. Thank you for your note. I am very much looking forward to coming to the festival and getting some sun – and a massage or two.'

There was also an email from Anna, asking me if I could attend the two Consulate receptions with her this evening. Checking the Special Events listing, I saw that one was at Le Manoir, being hosted by the French Consulate, while the other was at The Upper Deck and hosted by the Israeli Consulate; emailing her back to confirm I would join her, I realized I would be missing the screening of Vere Gough's debut movie and accompanying Q & A session with him afterwards.

Sudddenly remembering Rob's email of the early hours, I scrolled back to re-read it, my eyes widening as I now understood what it possibly – probably? – meant. I knew Rob ran with a wild crowd in LA and San Diego, and had experimented with numerous drugs; I knew he smoked dope and regularly took cocaine – as many in Tinseltown did – but this email inferred something more dangerous. He couldn't be running drugs across the border, could he? It would explain, in part, his wealth without any apparent source of income. But I couldn't think about this now.

The suite was, by now, humming with aspiring filmmakers rubbing shoulders with studio executives, seasoned directors and producers, many of whom had started out in the same way – as a complete unknown, submitting a first feature film to a film festival for consideration – and, as such, they were willing to share insider tips on how to work the festivals circuit, get their movie noticed, meet the right people and strike the deals.

In Tinseltown, closing the deal is high on the priority list, but as far as the studios are concerned, it is *only* about Box Office receipts; how much money it will gross, thereby recouping the studio's production costs – normally hundreds of millions – plus returning a hefty profit.

As they came and went, iPhones and BlackBerrys clamped to their ears, I mused on how surreal this all was, particularly the Awards Gala yesterday. It were almost as if I were dreaming and I would awake to the real world in a moment.

I was stirred from my reverie by Dominic, who had pulled up a chair in front of my desk and thoughtfully placed a glass of wine between my keyboard and the computer screen.

'You need to try this one. It's from Napa and getting rave reviews in the LA Times. Let me know what you think of it. Go on, try it. Now.'

I looked at him for a moment; it was such a shame he was gay. 'Or do you need a hair of the dog?' he laughed.

'No, no, I'm fine, just really beat,' I simpered. 'Actually, it's beyond exhaustion, but there's almost a week to go yet. Not sure how I'm going to get through it, but I guess the adrenaline will keep kicking in. How are you doing with all your media guys?'

I took a sip of the wine as he feigned a winced expression. 'Oh, you know, the ones at the top of the pile, the pro's, are great to deal with, but the ones on the way up, well, they're all a bit up themselves. They think it's their right to have a one-on-one interview with the A-List and, quite frankly, they're all a bit kooky.

'We had a guy in yesterday, who'd been credentialed, insisting he had an interview with Nancy Demainne, and it turned out he was from some soft porn internet site! You just have to smile, try and give them what they want and then go to the Restroom and scream at the wall.'

How true I knew this to be.

As we immersed ourselves in our wine tasting, Ric came over and excitedly pointed out that three other guys had joined the art deco sofa meeting. Did this mean what we all thought it might mean?

'Only one way to find out', Ric whispered conspiratorially, beckoning Shane over.

'Shane, go and pull up the Getty images from last night on the computer by the sofa. Spend a few minutes selecting the best shots for us to use, but listen to what they're saying. When you've got about twenty shots selected, wave for me to come over.'

Looking bemused, but wanting to get in on the act, Shane sauntered over to the computer; after a few minutes, he turned and beckoned Ric. They both huddled over the computer as Ric selected the shots from the thirty-odd ones that Shane had pulled up and studiously wrote down the image numbers, before returning to the Media desk and sat down, grinning from ear to ear. Unable to contain ourselves, Dominic and I took our wine tastings over to them.

'Well?' demanded Dominic.

'I can't be sure, but I think Yardley has just agreed the rights to Vere's film,' said Ric. 'If that's the case, it'll be great PR for the festival and we could get a release out on the wire today.'

I looked at him quizzically. 'Hey, you're going to have to wait until they make some sort of an announcement and then see if they even want you to do that. Not wishing to teach anyone how to suck eggs, I'm sure they'll both want their own PR machines to do it. But there's no harm in seeing if they'd let you do it on behalf of the festival.'

The consensus was for me to casually walk over, ask if there was anything they needed and simply remind them that if they needed any press assistance, the Media desk was here for that purpose. As instructed and, after circling the room and chatting to some other guests, I returned to the Media desk.

'They thanked me, said everything was in hand, but would call upon you if they did need any assistance. I think that's all we can do for now.'

Just as I was cramming my Day File and laptop into my tote, a call came through on the main suite phone; thinking it was Xavier Torres' driver, I looked expectantly at Dino. He shook his head, curling his lips down at the corners in mock disgust as he mouthed 'It's The Lesbian' to me.

'Oh God', I muttered, for I was on call to do movie announcing and was already late. Dispensing with the social niceties of being addressed by one's name, she merely bellowed down the phone, 'Hey, we need a wrangler tomorrow afternoon, about four. Can you do it?'

'Who is it? And I'm curious to know why are you asking me, rather than Hannah or Christian?'

'Look, can you do it or not?' she snapped.

'Yeah, yeah. Tell me who, where, what, the time, and for how long.'

The who? was Tamara Danzig, still riding on her success in the massive TV hit drama about political life in Washington DC; the what? was meeting and greeting her at her car and escorting her into the movie theatre for her new movie screening and Q & A afterwards with the director; the where? was the Arlington theatre; the time? was three-thirty p.m. and the for how long? was one hour.

'I'll be there,' I said as I pulled my diary out of the tote and scribbled in the entry. 'Got to go. I'm already late for some announcing. Bye.'

Turning to Lizzie, who was giggling at this, for she, too, had no time for the "jumped up little Lesbian", as she often referred to her, I asked her to have one of the Mercedes Coupes available to collect Ms Danzig from her hotel, bring her to the theatre, wait and take her back again about an hour later.

'Already done!' she cried, as she logged it into the computer and punched the air.

I drove over to the Regal cinema for my first attempt at movie announcing. This had come via Davina Isner, whom I had met last week, though that now felt like six months ago when she came into the office to discuss volunteer staff for the Awards Gala. Davina was in charge of the movie announcers and had thought that my "posh sounding" English accent would go down a storm with the audiences. Always one to take on a challenge and curious as to what it actually entailed, I agreed to do some announcements – about four as it turned out.

The film I was announcing was *Before The Rains*, a story of forbidden love in the dying embers of 'The Raj', the British colonial rule of India; directed by the acclaimed Indian filmmaker, Santosh Sivan, its stunning cinematography was very much the hallmark of Merchant Ivory.

My mobile rang just as I came off stage; it was the driver saying that he would be dropping Xavier Torres off at the hotel in twenty-five minutes. I immediately rang Christian to advise him of this, ending the call before he could issue me with any further instructions.

I met Anna in the suite at five-thirty p.m. to go to the first of the Consular receptions. We drove in her car to Le Manoir for the French reception at six o'clock. These receptions were not onerous for the film festival as they were organized, in the main, by the Consulates in LA and our involvement usually only ran to advising them of the movie being premiered from that country, arranging interpreters, if required, and ensuring that Duncan, Hannah, Christian and key festival Board members, as well as the film's director and leading actor(s), were all present.

There was already a line for Valet Parking when Anna and I arrived and, as we ascended the wide staircase – lined with lit Diptyque scented candles interspersed with baskets of lavender and lemon-scented votive candles wrapped in pine sprigs – we could see the restaurant's terrace bar was packed with wall-to-wall Chanel. Trays of Porcini mushroom tartlets, baby artichokes stuffed with crab salad, warm camembert with wild mushroom fricassee and grilled bacon-wrapped figs passed by, while waiters who looked as if they were dressed by Givenchy circled bearing glasses of prestigious champagnes – Krug, Roederer Cristal, Dom Perignon and Bollinger – while, for the wine buffs, there was Chateau Pétrus, Chateau Lafite and Chateau Latour, plus, to salute the event, glasses of Calvados.

'I'll need your help in making sure the Consul meets the key festival benefactors,' said Anna, 'particularly the Rhodes, the Rosenthals and the Blumbergs. If you see them, can you steer them towards the Consul and we'll wait for an appropriate opportunity to do the introductions.'

I nodded. As we weaved our way among the throng, picking out Board members, key benefactors, Ed and Harry, and steered them towards the Consul, we realized that the sole topic of conversation was not about the achievements of the French director whose movie was premiering that evening, but of the Chinese pulling their two films from the festival in protest at Duncan keeping the Tibet documentary in the schedules.

The Consul, charm personified, congratulated Duncan on his handling of the whole *'l'affair difficile'*, while his wife, dressed from head-to-toe in haute couture, exuded the effortless chic that is the hallmark of patrician Parisian ladies.

After two hours, we bade our *'adieus'* and drove across town to The Upper Deck for the Israeli reception. There was an evident security presence, which was somewhat unnerving, and it was a much more muted affair with none of the trappings of the French reception.

Again, Anna and I weaved through the room, sliding our arms into those of the chosen few who would be brought forward to meet the Consul, while waiters proffered trays of mini Reuben sandwiches, Matzo Ball soup in shot glasses, bite-sized potato knishes and smoked salmon with Yukon Gold potato chips – all accompanied by flutes of Herzog Brut, glasses of Chateau Yon Figeac and Pardess Heron Merlot, and hi-balls of Goldstar and Maccabee beer.

It was nearly ten-thirty p.m. as we pulled out of the parking lot, ostensibly to go home. Anna had finished for the day, but I still had things to do.

'Hey, you know we missed Vere Gough's debut movie tonight. I'd have really liked to have seen it, but it's only down for one screening,' I said, dejectedly. 'And he was doing a Q & A afterwards. I wonder if Christian and Hannah had to decorate the stage with white peonies!'

'Yeah, it was a pity to have missed that. But I'm sure we could get a screener and watch it later on in the week, when things start to calm down a little.'

I turned to look at her, hanging my head down to emphasis the point that I was questioning this statement. 'Erm, exactly *when* will anything start to calm down? Even when the festival is finished, we've still got to get everyone home, take down the suite and media room, clear up all the general detritus and return stuff to those that loaned us items. Oh, and when all that *is* done and dusted, we then have to do the wrap reports!'

She laughed. 'OK, OK, we'll watch the screener in about three weeks time!'

'Hey, do you mind swinging by The Four Seasons so that I can check if Xavier Torres is OK and see if he needs anything for his screening and Q & A panel tomorrow?'

We pulled up at the entrance where I was, by now, on first-name terms with all the Valet Parking attendants and the two Concierges; walking through the lobby to the Front Desk, I asked for Mr Torres. The Night Receptionist, who looked as though he had stepped straight out of a Dolce & Gabbana commercial, told us that there was a note in the system to advise that, should anyone need him urgently, Mr Torres was at the Guest & Industry Suite.

'Thanks. We're on our way there anyhow, so we'll catch up with him there.'

As we walked back towards the entrance, I spotted Kane Eppstein and the TV actress Suzanne Tomey, plus spouses, emerging from the smaller lobby bar.

'Hi Kane. Is everything OK? Does your father need anything?'

He smiled at me as he patted me on my shoulder. 'Everything's just fine Vanessa, thank you. In fact, Dad keeps saying he doesn't want to go home, so I think that's probably your fault!'

I bade them farewell. 'Well, you have my mobile number if you do need anything. Don't hesitate to call.'

He nodded. 'Thanks, will do. Come and have a drink at the house when all this fun is finally over.'

Anna looked at me incredulously. *'W-h-a-t?* You are the only person in the office who has ever, and I mean ever, managed to get any civility out of him. What *have* you done to him?'

I shrugged my shoulders. 'Oh, you know, it's just my English charm. Or something! As you well know, we did have a run-in at the beginning and I think that, in a perverse sort of way, he liked the fact that someone stood up to him because, ever since that point, he has been absolutely charming. I really like him.'

The suite was packed when I got back at eleven-thirty p.m., though it should have closed at nine-thirty p.m. when the hotel's bar tender finished his stint. In his place, the 'cavalry' had been taken up by Dino, Mike 2, Dominic and a volunteer called Chris.I walked over to the bar.

'What'll you have?' asked Dino. 'We're out of vodka, so it'll have to be wine or beer.'

'Nothing, thanks, I'm good. But what is everyone still doing here?' addressing Dino first, but looking along the line at Mike 2 and Dominic.

'Hey, everyone just kinda wanted to stay after the buffet supper and it seemed a shame to kick them out,' Mike 2 opined. 'And Hannah's still here, so we kinda thought if she was still around, it'd be cool to stay open. After all, this is supposed to be a facility for our guests, is it not!'

I could not argue with that and looked around the room to see Hannah ensconced at a table, which had tripled in size during the course of the evening to become 'the court' of Xavier Torres – himself surrounded by his own entourage of a small army of Argentinean filmmakers and a coterie of Spanish TV and print media.

Ric and Shane were also in attendance for this impromptu Cine Latino moment.

I walked over to them to introduce myself to Xavier Torres. As I had no idea what he looked like, I quietly asked Hannah if she could point him out. There was a sharp intake of breath as she did so, for the man she discreetly nodded towards was tall – as he stood up to shake my hand – achingly good-looking and with a toned physique. I was surprised when he greeted me in fluent English, for I had assumed that it would be 'broken' at best, and even more surprised to learn that he spoke fluent French and Spanish, in addition to his native Portuguese.

He graciously apologized for the extra work caused by his last-minute delay in leaving Rio, thanked me for changing his flights and for having 'such a nice car and driver to meet me at LA.' I was captivated, as I had been when I first met Rob, telling Xavier 'it's a great pleasure and if there is anything else at all that you need during your stay, please just call me or the suite.'

He thanked me, saying this was his third visit to the festival and so he knew the format. 'Congratulations in advance for the award you are to receive tomorrow afternoon,' I quickly added, before leaving them to resume discussing the burgeoning new wave of Latin America cinema.

Hardly being able to concentrate, for I found myself continually glancing over to Hannah's table and, in particular, to Xavier Torres, I logged onto Virgin's website to check the flights leaving London the next day. At this point, there was no indication that Daniel Eversleigh's flight would be cancelled or delayed, so I scribbled a quick note for Lizzie to ask her to ensure there would be a top-of-the-range Mercedes S600 model Sedan available to meet Daniel, adding that I wanted either Frank or Johnnie, our best drivers.

As the clock above the long bar chimed midnight, the guests started leaving to make their way either to other parties in town or their hotels; the vodka was long gone and the stocks of wine and beer had run perilously low.

When everyone had left, Dino, Mike 2, Dominic and Chris ran around the room, stacking all the detritus into neat heaps for the hotel cleaners to deal with during the night.

It was now after one o'clock and my phone rang again. Good God, I muttered to myself, who and what now? My spirits soared when I heard Rob's voice.

'Hi honey. Surprise! Guess where I am?

'In Tijuana?'

'Nope, Javier and I thought we'd fly on up to join you all, so he flew into Millionaire. I'm in the bar at the Hilton. You can't still be working, so come join me for a restorative nightcap and I can tell you all about Mexico.'

All I could think of was my wonderfully comfortable bed at the Hilton, for this was the last night I was able to stay in town. From tomorrow, it would be back to zipping down the Freeway at whatever hour in the morning, no matter how exhausted I was. But I also wanted to see Rob.

'Yeah, that sounds a plan. See you in five.'

The Hilton bar was jammed with our filmmaker guests as I looked around for my Bradley Cooper-doppelganger. He was leaning against the grand piano, holding out an enticing Dirty Martini as I approached him.

'Oh, it's so good to see you,' I said, hugging him as if for the last time. 'Where's Javier?

'He's hooking up with some old mate who just happens to be up here at the festival. You'll see him tomorrow.'

'I want to hear all about Mexico, but I've hit a wall. Can you tell me tomorrow?'

‘Sure. Over breakfast in bed, and no arguments. I’ve been following this crazy festival and you need a break.’

‘Yeah, like that’s going to happen.’

The piano player returned. Finishing our drinks, we picked our way through the heaving throng, inching our way to The Tower Guestrooms elevators. I suddenly felt panic-stricken that I would not be good enough in bed for Rob but, as it turned out, I need not have worried. He was tender and very considerate of my extreme exhaustion and, as I melted into his arms, a charge of energy swept through me like a lightening bolt. After the passion finally ebbed and I snuggled up against him, breathing in the aroma of his skin, I focused on switching off my ‘fried’ brain.

I reasoned that tomorrow must surely be a calmer day.

Except, of course, it turned out not to be.

CHAPTER SEVENTEEN

An intoxicant air pervaded the suite as word soon spread about Vere Gough's debut movie which had been screened the previous evening. Ric came flying in, went straight over to the Media desks and into conference with Shane, while Dominic craned his neck to listen in on the red-hot news; it transpired that The Yardley Company had agreed to buy the North American distribution rights to Vere's film for one million dollars.

'Obviously their PR people are doing the main release for the wires now, but Iaine has agreed that we could do one also on behalf of the festival, which was cool of him,' said Ric, as he briefed Shane on the content and tone of their version. 'Ring John Haines at the LA Times and tell him it's being emailed to him in five. Let's see if we can get ours in there first.'

In def-con mode, Shane punched furiously at his keyboard and within a couple of minutes Ric was reading it over his shoulder; a couple of adjustments and it was off to the LA Times, then the local paper and the main entertainment 'bibles' – The Hollywood Reporter, Variety, Screen International and Entertainment Weekly.

'Hell, I know we're doubling up, but get it off to the main TV news desks now. They'll run the story for sure, but let's see if we can't get in there first to flag up the festival,' directed Ric. 'And then email a copy to Duncan, Ed and Harry so that they're in the loop.'

Shane suddenly looked panic-struck as he said, to no-one in particular, 'Oh s***, all the media that are still here will want to do interviews with him today. Which means the ones we've set up for the filmmakers will probably get canned. Which means we lose the festival angle. Oh dear Lord, give me strength to get through the rest of the day.'

Scrolling through the list of interviews scheduled for the day on his iPhone, he yelled across the room to me, 'Which hotel's he staying in?' I could not resist trying to lighten the stress for a second, and raising my eyebrows at him in feigned surprise, nonchalantly said, 'Try where all the A-List have been staying. Where else would he get a private butler!'

Shane grinned, Dominic's smile grew exponentially and I laughed as the PR hysteria mushroomed. 'Have a good day, my friends,' I trilled as I packed my life – walkie-talkie, mobile, laptop, Day File and diary – into my Saks Fifth Avenue tote. 'Mine's going to be just as kooky.'

I drove over to the cinema complex in the older part of the city, and which had the largest auditorium and a rear garden, to check on the arrangements for the early afternoon screening of Xavier Torres' new movie. This would be preceded by a buffet luncheon for the festival Board, the director himself and other key guests – sponsors and dignitaries from the city and the wider entertainment industry.

The hired caterers had already started setting up on the terraces, draping the trestle tables in a beautiful ivory voile and scattering rose, peony and winter jasmine petals over them. The silver plate cutlery and rows of gleaming crystal wine glasses sparkled in the strong sunlight; all this because his film had received a standing ovation when it was shown at Sundance and that he was being presented with a major award that evening.

A semi-seismic ruction greeted me when I got back to the suite. While I was out, Anna's boyfriend Chris – who was helping out as a volunteer in the suite – had had something of a difference of opinion with an older lady, a long-established volunteer who had worked shifts in the suite for a number of years. Nobody seemed quite sure what the mêlée had been about or how it had even started, but Chris had had a meltdown, thrown a true Sicilian-style tantrum and told the lady to leave and never come back.

I liked Chris, for he was a 'do-er' and, most of the time, had heaps of positive energy. I only ever had to ask him to do something once and it was done immediately.

'What's up?' I asked briskly. 'It'd better be good. You can't go around telling volunteers to leave. We need them Chris.'

He looked unrepentant. 'She's an a***. She was telling some guests they couldn't use the Internet, couldn't have a drink and saying they had been in the suite too long. I told her they could have a drink, and proceeded to go and get the drinks for them and that she was not, under any circumstances, to talk to guests in that manner. She had a hissy fit in front of everyone and I told her to grow up or leave, and then told her to forget the first bit and leave anyway. Which she did.'

'Okay, Dino, Mike, Chris, can you walk the room and ask guests if they would like a drink and tell them that we'll be bringing out the lunch buffet early. If they don't want a drink at the moment, ask if they need anything else like Internet access, copies of newspapers or magazines, any help with tips on sightseeing, etc. Just keep talking, or get them their drink, but do anything to distract them, in case they were aware of what has just happened. *Capiche?* I'll call the restaurant and ask them to deliver lunch now.'

They nodded and set about their task as I called the restaurant, while wondering what Rob was up to.

Right on cue, he appeared in the doorway – an achingly hip figure oozing sex appeal and cool in equal measure.

'Hey, can I hang here for a bit?' he asked, gently kissing my ear. 'I thought I might be able to meet some studio execs and pitch my script.'

'Sure, honey. I'll log you in as a freelance writer. But if anyone asks if you've been credentialed, just say yes and direct them to me if there are any issues.'

He soon merged into the sea of distressed-denim jeans, white T-shirts and black leather jackets that qualified as the uniform of choice for young film industry 'blades'. Watching him with a feeling of lust, pride – and bewilderment that I had even managed to hook such a perfect specimen – I saw that he lost no time in tapping Tim Gray, the influential editor-in-chief of Variety, followed expediently by Rory Cohen, the rude NBC executive I had met at the Chairman's Benefit in my first week.

As the restaurant waiters delivered lunch and hastily arranged it on the bar top, a tidal wave of blue, white and black rolled up and, lapping at the bar, gratefully piled their plates with the sushi, sashimi and Tempura prawns. Rob, caught up in the current, popped a couple of pieces of makizushi roll into his mouth, gulped down a Bloody Mary and hurriedly asked, as if something had just happened, 'Sweetheart, can I borrow the pick-up for a few hours?'

'Yeah, I guess Diana won't mind. But I need it back here by six o'clock latest. Where are you off to? Anywhere interesting?'

'Erm, Javier's just phoned, gotta meet him pronto. We'll be back by six. Promise.'

I tossed him the car keys. He leant over the bar, cuppping my face in his hands and pulled me forward for a kiss on each cheek and then on the mouth.

'Be good,' I teased.

'Try not to be!' he laughed, twirling the keys in his hand as he reversed away from the bar.

I arrived at the cinema complex just in time to grab a cup of cinnamon coffee. Hannah had kindly given me a pass to watch the movie: a story about two young men, one of whom would later become a controversial political leader, shaping their lives through a journey traversing South America, and I had read that it had taken Xavier Torres five years to produce – two years of research and three years of filming.

The movie was deserved of its numerous prior plaudits and received another standing ovation; the audience, though, was eager for the in-depth interview with its director, raising their arms in excited anticipation of being chosen to ask him a question.

One gentleman asked, 'How do you see the future of Latin cinema?' to which Xavier replied, 'Twenty years ago, very few films were made in the continent. Nowadays, it is growing at a very fast rate, both in public audience terms and in critical response.'

Another audience member asked, 'Did you feel a connection between either of the two men while directing the film?' to which the answer was a firm 'Absolutely, it was more than a film. It was a rite of passage.'

It was just after three o'clock and I needed to get over to

the other cinema to do my wrangling for Tamara Danzig's Q & A appearance following the first screening of her new movie. Slipping quietly out of the auditorium, I called Dino once I was in the car to check that *entente cordial* had been restored in the suite and, more importantly, that Chris was under control; when he said everything was fine, I continued making my way to the Arlington Theatre's private garage.

A chauffeur-driven Mercedes Sedan with heavily-tinted windows pulled up promptly at three-thirty p.m. and I waited while the chauffeur walked around the back of the car to open the rear passenger-side door.

Stretching out my hand to greet Ms Danzig, I said, rather limply it seemed, 'Hello. It's a pleasure to meet you. I'm Vanessa Vere Houghton, head of VIP guests and I'll be with you while you're here at the theatre. If you'd like to follow me.'

She issued a curt 'hello' and checked what time the chauffeur was picking her up; he looked at me and said he thought it was in an hour. I nodded in confirmation.

Feeling uncomfortable about walking over to the movie theatre in silence, I told her I was an avid fan of the D.C. political life television hit series and that it had achieved cult-status in England. It was probably the wrong thing to say as I realized, too late, that undoubtedly *everyone* said what a fan they were of the show and it must come across that no one rated any of her other myriad films and TV performances. She was polite enough to acknowledge me, albeit with a brief 'thanks' and, as I desperately tried to salvage the situation, recalled her critical success in 'Separation', opining that it was one of the best movies of the early nineties.

Hannah was waiting to greet her in the lobby, by now

full of Bank of America corporate guests all wanting to be photographed with the star. While coffees, champagne truffles and hand-made cookies were being served, Ms Danzig charmingly accommodated their requests for autographs and photographs. My role was now to listen at the door of the cinema itself and get at least a minute's notice of the Q & A ending from the first screening so that we could get Ms Danzig ready to go into the theatre.

As I heard the audience vacating their seats, I signaled a 'three', as in minutes, to Hannah, who nodded. The audience filed out and, when the cinema was empty, I went over to Ms Danzig and escorted her inside, leading her towards the stage where she was joined by the director and Hannah.

As the 'second-sitting' audience made their way to their seats, Hayden, the festival's Theatre Operations Director, made some last-minute adjustments to the stage lighting and mic wires. We were on, or rather Hannah was, as she ascended the stage steps to firstly thank the audience for taking the time to attend the screening before briefly outlining the story and introducing the director and Ms Danzig.

Rather than the usual format of the Q & A coming at the end, it had been reversed this time to accommodate Ms Danzig's schedule, and so the director explained the concept of the movie and why he wanted to make it, and then Tamara Danzig told an enthralled audience why she felt this was the movie to make at this point in her career. Naturally, a lot of the questions re-visited her hit TV show, but she deftly deflected those and gracefully brought the topic back to the movie they were about to watch.

She was there purely to introduce the movie and director and say why she had accepted the part; her role accomplished, the lights went down and the festival logos and credits rolled. I escorted her out of the theatre and back along the pathway leading to the private garage where the chauffeur was waiting. She thanked me, again, briefly, for my assistance and off she went. And that was my wrangling done for the day.

Or so I thought.

I was immersed in paperwork in the suite, having just tried to sort out, with Lizzie, the next day's transport schedule, when my mobile rang. It was about six thirty p.m.

'Hello, is that Vanessa? It's Daniel,' said an English voice. Momentarily caught up in the exponential mess that was our car transport grid, and suddenly realising that Rob had not returned with the pick-up, I did not register for a second or two who it was.

'Hi,' I said slowly, still scanning the car grid.

'It's Daniel,' said the voice. 'Daniel Eversleigh.'

'Oh my God,' I whispered slowly under my breath. I had forgotten that he was arriving at about this time, though mercifully Lizzie had followed my scribbled instruction to the letter from the previous night and, while I was wrangling Ms Danzig, had dispatched a Mercedes S-Class Sedan and driver to pick him up at LAX.

'Hi Daniel,' I quickly said, pretending that I had known – for all three seconds – who it was. 'How are you? How was your flight?' I was not expecting his answer.

'Actually I am not feeling too good. In fact, I feel pretty damn awful.'

This immediately snapped me out of my despondency. 'What do you mean?' I asked, a trace of panic appearing in my voice. 'Are you coming down with something?' There was a brief pause.

'Well, I feel pretty nauseous and dizzy, I've got muscle

pains and I think I'm running a temperature. I've probably just picked up a bug from the cabin air-con, but I feel like s***.'

'No, way too soon to have caught any bug off the plane and, anyway, I think that's unlikely. More likely something you've eaten in the last twenty-four hours. But to be safe, I'm going to get the hotel doctor to come out and see you. I take it you've got medical insurance?' He said he had.

'Good. Why don't you just go and curl up in that blissfully comfortable bed and we'll see what the doctor has to say when he's seen you. I'm hoping he'll be able to come within the hour. I'll call you after I have spoken to him.'

In def-con mode, I punched Charlie Rutherford's speed-dial number; he picked up straight away.

'Hey, Charlie, got a problem. Your new guest, the British actor and director Daniel Eversleigh, arrived today from London and he's just called me to say he's not feeling at all well. In fact, he says he feels like s***. Nauseous, dizzy, running a high temperature. Possibly food poisoning, but could be a bug, who knows. But I think he needs a doctor. Actually, change that. He *does* need a doctor. Can you call the hotel doctor and get him out to see Daniel A.S.A.P. He's in his villa, but he does need to see someone straightaway and I'd be happier if it were the main hotel doctor. Can you sort that Charlie. Please?'

He said he would call and let me know as soon as he had reached the doctor. Within five minutes, he called. 'Dr. Holmes is on his way now. He should be at the hotel in about fifteen minutes.'

A wave of relief swept over me. 'Oh thanks Charlie. Will you ask Dr. Holmes to call me as soon as he's seen Daniel to let me know what the problem is, and what we need to do in terms of medication etc.'

I called the hotel and was immediately put through to Daniel's villa.

'Daniel, Dr. Holmes, the hotel's main doctor, is coming out to see you now. He should be with you in about fifteen minutes. I'll call you back in about forty-five minutes to see what he thinks is wrong, and whether you'll live!'

'At this precise moment, not sure I really want to,' he quipped.

I waited anxiously in the suite. 'What's up?' asked Dominic as he passed by my desk.

'Have you heard of a British actor called Daniel Eversleigh? His directorial debut is the Closing Night movie,' I said, grabbing a glass of Coke off a passing tray.

'Of course. Everyone has. He's well-known in the US.'

'Well, he's just arrived from London, he's in his room and he's not at all well by the sound of things. I've just arranged for the hotel doctor to come out to see him. I hope to God it's nothing serious, but I'm just waiting for a call from Dr. Holmes. Oh, and Rob's disappeared with the pick-up. He's had it all day. God knows where he is and what he's up to.'

Dominic threw me one of his gorgeously sexy smiles and gave me a lingering 'it's-all-going-to-be-OK' hug.

'Let me know if there's anything I can do. I'm just hanging around until the Xavier Torres presentation. Are you going to make that?'

I shrugged my shoulders. 'I really want to go to it, but I'll have to see what Dr. Holmes says.'

After what seemed an eternity but was, in reality, only forty minutes, Dr. Holmes rang.

'Is that Vanessa Vere Houghton?'

'Yes, hello Dr. Holmes. Have you seen Mr. Eversleigh?

What do you think is wrong?'

He confirmed he had examined Mr Eversleigh. 'His pulse rate is rather high, which is concerning me a little. Does he have any heart conditions that you know of?'

Blindsided by this I stuttered, 'Erm, no, not that I am aware of. But then we probably wouldn't know that kind of detail anyway. Do you think its his heart?' Now I *was* worried.

'Well, he has got severe food poisoning and heartburn, that's for sure. It's possible the increased pulse rate is due to that, so I'd like to see him again tomorrow to check. In the meantime, I've prescribed Protonix. I've rung this through to the Pharmacy and you should be able to pick the prescription up in about half-an-hour. He should take two capsules a day for one week and keep him on a mild diet with lots of liquid to hydrate. Soups, salads, that sort of thing, but nothing spicy and no dairy produce until he is fully recovered. I'll call in on him again in the morning.'

Thanking him profusely, I then called Daniel with a much more upbeat voice.

'Hi Daniel, it's Vanessa. Dr. Holmes says you're going to live! But you have got severe food poisoning. I'm going to the Pharmacy to pick up your prescription. I'll bring it into the hotel, probably in about forty-five minutes.'

He thanked me and apologized for being a nuisance.

'Hey, it's no problem. I just wish for your sake you'd arrived feeling merely exhausted.'

I was just about to put the phone down when I suddenly remembered Dr. Holmes' question about a possible heart condition. 'Erm, Daniel, just a quick question. Have you by any remote chance got any heart conditions that you are aware of?'

There was a pregnant pause before he responded in a

slow, measured manner. 'No. Why are you asking that?'

Not wishing to alarm him or make him feel any worse than he was feeling at the moment, I breezily continued, 'Oh, it was just that Dr. Holmes said your pulse rate was rather high. But he did say that it could just be because of the food poisoning. However, he does want to come and check on you in the morning, just to be sure. I hope that's alright with you?'

'Yes, fine.'

'Okay, well I'll drop the prescription off at the hotel so that you will be able to start taking something tonight.'

Scooping up car keys of one of the festival's pool cars, I called over to Dominic. 'It's unlikely I'll make it to the Xavier Torres presentation but, if I can I'll sneak in towards the end.'

'I'll keep a glass of Napa's finest for you,' he declared in mock solemnity.

The sun had just set, bathing the sky and mountains in a warm orange glow as I drove over to the late night Pharmacy; I picked up the prescription and paid for it with my credit card, knowing Daniel would reimburse the festival before he left.

Pulling up at breakneck speed in front of the entrance of The Four Seasons, I tossed the keys to the Valet Parking guys and sprinted through the lobby to the Front Desk.

'Hi, I've got some medication for a guest who arrived today,' I said urgently. 'Can you ring through to Mr Daniel Eversleigh. He's in one of the private villas.'

The Night Manager rang his room and Daniel answered in a moment. 'Good evening Mr Eversleigh. We have Vanessa Vere Houghton at the Front Desk with some medication for you.'

Before he could say anything else, I grabbed the phone.

‘Hi Daniel, it’s Vanessa. I’ve got your medicine. Can I bring it down to you, so that I can see for myself that you *are* still alive!’

He said that as long as I did not mind him being in a bathrobe, looking crumpled and sweaty, and generally not at his best, he would be delighted if I were to bring the medicine over.

I ran through the Rose Garden and along the pathway that led to the private villas at the end of the hotel grounds; upon reaching the villa I knocked, with a degree of trepidation, on his door.

He opened it and beckoned me in. ‘Hi Daniel, it’s great to meet you, albeit in your hotel room. Can’t imagine the rumours that will start flying!’ I laughed.

‘Hope you don’t mind, but I think I’ll stay in bed – it’s closer to the bathroom!’ he smiled weakly.

I followed him through to the master bedroom and, as he slouched back onto the plump pillows, I sat cross-legged at the end of the bed, still clutching the bag of pills that would, hopefully, diminish his woes.

‘Sorry about my appearance. Not the best way to meet me,’ he said deprecatingly.

There was nothing to apologize for. Despite an obviously fevered brow, tousled hair and slightly ashen face, he was the same achingly good-looking guy that he had always been since he hit the movie screens back in the early 1980s; accordingly, he had always been cast as the romantic interest in every movie he had done. It was only of late that he was being cast as, and accepting the role of, the villain of the piece, and he was mastering those parts with equal aplomb.

Daniel duly swallowed the pills Dr Holmes had prescribed and drank a couple of glasses of water, and then considerately poured me a glass of wine from the ice bucket that took up centre stage in the arrangement of freshly-cut flowers, fruits, cheeses, crackers, chocolates and soft drinks on the enormous table in the sitting room.

'How is it?' he asked as I took a sip. 'Will I enjoy it tomorrow?'

I laughed as I replied, 'After the past few days I've had, you think there's going to be any left for you to have tomorrow!'

We chatted for a while, about his flight and what, *exactly*, had he eaten on it?, his drive up here, how he thought his new movie would be received by an American audience – he was a little concerned that they would not 'get' the irony or humour – what he wanted to do while he was here at the festival, "several spa treatments for starters", and his plans once he got to LA afterwards.

Sensing he was getting tired, I unfolded my legs and got up to leave.

'Will you be OK tonight, or do you want me to have a nurse look in on you later on?'

He grinned at me as if this had a double meaning.

'No, no, I mean a *proper* nurse to really come and check you're OK. And Dr. Holmes is coming back in the morning anyway to check on you.'

He smiled. 'I'll be fine thanks Vanessa. I'm just going to go to sleep now and hope to God that I do feel OK tomorrow, otherwise it'll be a hell of a waste of the day.'

Although I knew he had my mobile number, as part of the contacts list he had been emailed in London, I wrote it down again on a piece of paper and left it on the bedside table.

'Just in case you need it. Don't hesitate to call if you do need or want anything. I'm always working until at least midnight or one o'clock, so you won't be interrupting any play time. Don't even know what that is anymore!'

I bade him goodnight and departed.

It was almost ten o'clock by the time I got to the movie theatre. Hoping to catch the end of the presentation to Xavier Torres, I sneaked in through a side door and walked quietly to the back of the auditorium which, luckily, was still in semi-darkness. On the stage, swathed in spotlights, were Xavier Torres, Duncan, Christian and Hannah.

As a leading exponent of Latin American cinema, often referred to as Cine Latino, and with several critically-acclaimed films to his name, he was being awarded – or rather, he had *just* been awarded – the festival's International Filmmaker Award for Directing, Producing and Mentoring. Xavier Torres knew the intrinsic value of this award, for tonight's presentation would be picked up, both in photographic and editorial terms, by not only the LA Times and the four leading entertainment industry magazines ('the bibles'), but also by the news bulletins on all the LA-based main television channels, as well as the key entertainment television shows Entertainment Tonight, The Insider and Access Hollywood. Ric and Shane would see to that.

Holding the award up in the air so that the audience could see the bronze statuette, he said, 'Every single prize given to a Latin American filmmaker is shared by a much larger number of people. Therefore, it is a recognition I gladly accept in my name and the growing Latin American culture.'

The audience gave him an ear-splitting ovation – the second one, for they had applauded his new movie with equal vigour at the afternoon screening – which took a good few minutes to ebb away, allowing me to stealthily pick my way over to where Dominic, Ric and Shane were standing.

Dominic, still clasping the glass of 'Napa's finest' that he had promised he would keep for me, passed it to me as he asked, 'How's our friend from England?'

Taking a large sip first – for I had only had one glass in Daniel's bedroom despite joking that there would not be any left for him tomorrow – I explained that Dr. Holmes had diagnosed severe food poisoning and I had picked up the prescription and taken it over to Daniel.

'Do you know, I met him in his bedroom!' I smiled. 'And he still looks gorgeous, even in a bathrobe with a *very* fevered brow.'

Ric looked at me, his jaw slowly opening. '*In his hotel room?* That's going to be around the festival in no time!' he shrieked. 'Vanessa, I know you are supposed to be looking after these guys and gals, but going to their hotel room. Well that's dedication way beyond the call of duty.'

Thank goodness I liked Ric so much and knew there was not an ounce of malice in his joking.

'Yeah, yeah,' I mocked. 'Come on guys, he is pretty ill and despite his only-too-true reputation as a ladies' man, I think even that was the last thing on his mind this evening.'

Dominic could not resist getting in on the act; grinning from ear to ear, he mischievously purred, 'Vanessa dahling, it may be how it's done in England, to meet talent in their hotel room, but here we tend to err on the side of deference. Hey, it's just not cricket, you know!'

At least I knew they were not being sardonic and that it was merely playful fun, for we had had precious little of that of late.

Filing out of the theatre, Ric and Shane trilled, as they said goodnight, 'And *whose* room will you be in tomorrow?

On a need-to-know basis, of course!'

I headed back to the suite to check if Daniel had called for any further assistance. It was empty apart from the hotel banqueting staff clearing up, Dino checking the hotel grid for the next day's departures, and Lizzie, who was tearing her hair out as two drivers had called in to say they had had enough of the constant LAX runs and would not be working for us any more.

Two drivers down would be quite a problem as it would have a domino effect on not only the next day, but on the remaining four days of the festival. Although we were all exhausted, we had to sort this out tonight – if only to have tomorrow's transport schedule back up to speed while we looked around for two other drivers to replace them.

'Any vodka left in the cupboard, Dino?' I pleaded. 'I'm in dire need of a medicinal Bloody Mary, as I'm sure you two are.'

He said he thought there was; hopping over the bar counter to go to the back room, he re-appeared a few moments later gleefully carrying a new bottle of Ciroc.

'Medicinals coming right up,' he chirped as Lizzie furiously tapped her ballpoint on the desk, muttering under her breath about how unprofessional it was for the two drivers to have quit, and at such a late hour.

'What the bleep did they think they'd be doing, if not the LAX runs? They were told during the initial interview that there would be a lot of LAX runs, and they were asked if it would be a problem. They both said no. So what the bleeping bleep is the matter with them?'

I could not answer that question, except to venture that they were probably feeling like the rest of us – completely and utterly exhausted, on our knees and rapidly losing the will to live. At least we had each other to buoy ourselves up and some variety in the job, but they just had the monotony of a repetitive long drive through a fairly inauspicious landscape and tedious urban mass, often two or three times a day. I could empathize with them.

Bloody Mary's in hand and, to the backdrop of happy, relaxed people outside the suite in the hotel lobby bar, we worked assiduously through the complex transport grid, re-jigging jobs to put less experienced drivers on the ubiquitous LA airport runs and shore up the experienced ones for the Beverly Hills and Bel Air drop offs – of which there were plenty scheduled for tomorrow.

It was just after one-thirty a.m. when the three of us sat back, glasses and minds drained, and declared in unison that it was 'as good as it's going to get tonight.' The morning departures were all covered, as were the early afternoon ones; but there was a question mark over two early evening departures to Bel Air and Beverly Hills.

'Let's call it a day. We can re-visit those two in the morning, when we feel a bit more human,' I said. 'Don't know about you two, but I am beyond exhaustion and I have to get home, although Rob still hasn't brought back the bloody pick-up. As it is, I've got the joys of the Freeway before I even see my ...'

Before I finished the sentence, my mobile buzzed. It was Rob.

'Hi honey, where on earth are you? I need the pick-up to get home and NOW! It's nearly two o'clock and I've already hit about five walls just this evening. What are you doing?'

'Just waiting for a man,' he lilted down the phone.

'Well, I hope you've got more than $26,' I quipped.

'Ah, I didn't know you were such a Bowie aficionado,' said Rob.

‘Oh yeah, huge fan of Bowie and this was his 1970 cover of the Velvet Underground’s 1967 hit Waiting For The Man, written by Lou Reed. Now, if I have passed the pop trivia quiz, can you tell me when you will materialise with my car?’

Still in thrall to the song, Rob nonchalently responded ‘tomorrow’, explaining he was ‘waiting for a friend’, before realising his mistake.

I loved the record and I adored Rob, but utter exhaustion re-visited me and I was now irritated. I wanted my bed, sleep and nothing else.

‘ROB! When will you get here with the Dodge? I need it right NOW.’

‘Twenny mins honey. No later, I promise.’

Pulling out of the hotel car park, I slapped my face to keep awake. I had only had one glass of wine at Daniel’s – the sip from Dominic’s glass did not count, I reasoned with myself – plus one Bloody Mary which had so much ice in it I decided that did not count properly either. I knew I was way too tired to be driving, but there was no other way of getting back to Diana’s house. Taking the short-cut through the north canyon, I soon entered the Freeway and swung out into the fast lane, quickly crossing over the nearside four lanes and put the Dodge into cruise-control. The only other traffic at that time of the night was the truckers in their gigantic ‘train lorries’ and I was relieved that the Freeway was not any busier. I could feel my eyes getting heavier and heavier, so started singing Hotel California to stay awake, the first two lines of the Eagles classic summing up precisely my milieu.

I was not sure how far along the Freeway I had driven before I was suddenly aware of flashing lights and a police siren indicating me to pull over. Checking the rear view mirror again, I indicated and pulled over to the right, coming slowly to a halt on the hard shoulder. The Sheriff pulled right up behind, got out of his patrol car and, with hand on gun, walked towards me. Flashing his torch in my face, he asked if I was alright.

'Yes, I'm fine, thanks. Just rather tired. I'm working at the film festival. Been working all day and most of the night. Actually twenty-hour days for the past week!'

He looked at me again. 'Have you been drinking?' I was suddenly nervous, realizing the sheer exhaustion I felt probably exacerbated the small amount of alcohol I had had that evening.

'Well, I had a glass of white wine about six hours ago, a sip of white wine about four hours ago and a very weak Bloody Mary about two hours ago, but I have eaten as well.'

The Sheriff pulled out a Breathalyser machine and told me to blow into it; after a minute or two, he turned back to me and, as my heart pounded, said, 'OK, you're clean. Where are you headed to?'

A wave of relief swept over me. 'Oh, I'm getting off at Washington,' I said, trying to muster all my energy and not sound so utterly drained.

'And where to after that?'

'Oh, just a block, that's all,' I lied. It was, in fact, another three miles, but he did not have to know that.

'Do you know what happened back there lady and why I stopped you?'

'Erm, no, not really. Did I do something wrong?' I asked, genuinely not sure what had just occurred. His answer stunned me.

'You just drifted across five lanes of Freeway. Guess you must have fallen asleep at the wheel. You were very lucky it was this time of night and there isn't much traffic. But those trucks don't stop for anyone and anyway they can't stop quickly, you know. You had a lucky escape tonight.'

Had I really just drifted across the *entire* Freeway? I did not remember any of it, so I guess I had fallen asleep at the wheel.

'We'll escort you to the exit to make sure you get off the Freeway safely,' I vaguely heard the Sheriff say.

'Thanks, but I'm fine now. I'm wide awake.'

Just as I thought I had dodged a bullet, his walkie-talkie burst into life. 'Hold on lady.'

Walking back to his patrol car and picking up the in-car phone, I could barely make out what was being said, but thought I'd heard the word drugs. Good, nothing to do with me, I thought, as I waited for him to return and let me get home. But he came back with his partner and a dog.

'What's in the back?'

'Nothing as far as I know Sir. I'm literally just coming back from work.'

'Get out and take off the tarpaulin,' he commanded, his manner having changed in a second from one of concern to suspicion.

'Is there something wrong?' I asked again, seemingly the only words I could get out of my mouth, suddenly aware that in my extreme tiredness, I hadn't even noticed the black tarpaulin.

'Just do as we say and take it off.'

Before I could get the tarpaulin off, the dog jumped frantically against the wheel-base, barking furiously as the Sheriff and his partner stepped forward and yanked it back.

Neatly arranged under the tarpaulin were twelve-bottle wine cases, placed five lengthways by three deep, all marked with wines from the Williamette Valley Wineries.

'What's in the boxes lady?' demanded the Sheriff's partner.

'I have absolutely no idea. They're not mine and they weren't here this morning.'

Climbing into the pick-up and unbuckling knives from their belts, they ripped open the top of the boxes to reveal a row of Pinot Noir bottles neatly nestled in styrofoam trays.

'Well, this little lady and her friends have got taste,' said the Sheriff. 'They sure produce a world-class Pinot Noir at Oregon's Williamette Valley. Had some myself 'bout six months back.'

Breathing out slowly for having dodged another bullet, I was about to ask if I could continue my journey when the dog's barking ramped up a gear while pawing at the boxes. Looking at each other, the Sheriff and his partner lifted the top tray of wine out of the three boxes at the back of the truck bed and let out whistles of jubilation as they discovered the true contents – not wine, but one kilogram-size bags of sugar.

They emptied the three boxes and, as the packets of sugar tumbled to the floor, they split open to reveal a transparent bag inside. Brushing away the sugar with his hand, the Sheriff held up the transparent bag and inspected it with his torch, now on full beam.

'Now what do you think this is, lady? It certainly ain't sugar. You don't look like a *narcotrafficante*, so are you just the mule? And if so, who're ya working for?'

I looked in disbelief as the Sheriff and police officer slashed each box open, ripped into the sugar bags and packets and stacked them in piles at one end of the pick-up.

'Sir, I don't work for a dealer. I don't know any and I don't even live here. I'm working at the film festival on a temporary basis and staying with a friend. I have no idea what's in these transparent bags or why they are even here. It must be a mistake. I can only think that someone must have mistaken my pick-up for someone else's in the dark and put the boxes in. I don't even own a tarpaulin, so that's not mine either.'

'Well, lady, you're gonna come to the station with us while we sort this out and see what this white powder is. Don't suppose you have any ideas what this white powder might be?' he asked sarcastically.

'Erm, I'm guessing it might be cocaine?'

'Yeah, you might just be right on that. And there's a helluva lot of it here. Worth a small fortune if it is cocaine. We'll get it tested at the station. I don't need to tell you that you're gonna be in deep trouble unless you talk. Now get in the car with me. Officer Suarez will drive the Dodge to the station.'

Meekly, or was it still exhaustion?, and in hand-cuffs, I followed the Sheriff back to his patrol car and slumped into the front seat. This must be a dream, I thought, I'll wake up soon and be back at the fun factory in a few hours.

'Just so that you know, my name's Sheriff Mitch Jenkins and I'll do the prelim report at the station. If the white stuff does turn out to be cocaine, and I hope to God for your sake it isn't, then you'll be processed by the DEA.'

'DEA? What's that?'

'The Drug Enforcement Administration. We've already called for one of their local lead guys to come up and meet us at the station. But depending on what you say, it may be that they'll want one of their guys from the DEA Intelligence Centre at El Paso to come down.'

It was now three o'clock in the morning and while most normal people were soundly asleep, I was at the Police station being searched, photographed, finger-printed, swabbed, given a criminal number and reams of forms to complete.

The night shift had grown exponentially with the news of this 'exciting' new development. Officer Suarez was issuing instructions to anyone who would listen, while Sheriff Jenkins was handing over to station Captain Ed Gray and Lieutenant Mike Lewis as the DEA agent arrived with his own lab technician and what appeared to look like a mini lab.

After another hour, Captain Gray and the DEA agent, who introduced himself as Special Agent Jonas Reubens, came into the holding room where I nursed a mug of insipid coffee.

'OK Ms Vere-Houghton, the bad news is we've tested the substance and it is indeed cocaine,' said Special Agent Reubens. 'But not just any old cocaine, this is high-purity, premium cocaine. So, who are you working for?'

'The only person I am working for is the Executive Director of the film festival,' I wailed into my insipid cofee. 'I keep telling you all, I don't know anything about this stuff or where it came from or how it got into the back of my pick-up. Why don't you believe me?'

'Well, let me help you a bit more. This stuff, as you call it, is absolutely pure cocaine. The very best you can get on the market. And it doesn't just come from anywhere, it comes from Columbia. There are only two cartels who can handle this quality of 'blow', as it's also called, and they are in Mexico. And there's one in particular I am thinking of, the Sinalopéz Cartel, based in the city of Culiacán in the state of Sinoloa. So, who do you know down there?'

As if struck by lightening and now wide awake, it all suddenly fell into place; Rob's trips to Mexico with his friend Javier Pajares and Javier's great friend Manuel Sinalopéz; the fact that he had never actually told me what he was doing in Mexico, aside from "vacationing" at Manuel's family ranch *near* Culiacán; always flying back from Tijuana in Javier's plane and never driving (to avoid customs?); he and Javier hanging out at the film festival, but me never seeing Javier; and the Bowie song *'Waiting for The Man'* which is all about a white guy waiting to meet his drug dealer.

Was Rob using me and the festival as a cover, and the festival as a source of buyers for him and Javier? I could not believe it, but there were too many coincidences and my expression must have given away that I knew something.

'Ms Vere-Houghton, I cannot stress the trouble you are in right now. Talk to us and give us a name, or some names, and we can protect you,' Captain Ed Gray said, equally wearily. 'If you don't help us, we can't help you. But be sure of one thing. Either way, we will find out who owns this blow and if you don't co-operate, your gonna be looking at something in the region of ten to twenty years in jail, plus a fine of anything between ten to fifty million dollars. That should sure focus your mind a bit more.'

I could not give up Rob without at least calling him to see if he was involved.

'I think I'm allowed a phone call? Can I do that now?'

Refusing the offer of a phone at the station as I knew it would be bugged, I called Rob on my festival cell phone, fingers trembling as I tapped his number.

'Hi honey. Sorry to wake you, I know it's very late, but I'm in trouble. I got pulled over on the Freeway as I fell asleep at the wheel but, unfortunately, the Sheriff and officer found a whole stash of cardboard wine boxes under a black tarpaulin, with packets of sugar in them.

'The sugar packets turned out to have a cache of cocaine hidden in them. I'm at the Police station and a DEA agent has tested the powder. He says it's high-purity grade cocaine from Columbia and it would have come in through Mexico. He mentioned a cartel called Sinalopéz. Manuel's last name is Sinalopéz. He says they're based at Culiacán. Wasn't that where you were staying with him and Javier?

'Honey, do you know anything at all about this? Please, please tell me the truth. The DEA guy says that if I co-operate, they'll protect me, which means they'll protect you. If you are involved, that is.'

I waited nervously for the answer.

'Ah, s***. It's Javier's gig and I was along for the ride. I can't let you take the heat for this, so tell the DEA guy that I'll co-operate, but only on the condition they give me Witness Protection.'

'Jeez, hon, is that really going to be necessary? Is it that serious?'

'C'mon Vanessa, you know what the cartels are capable of. Or perhaps you don't. But with a street value of nearly one-and-a-half million dollars, they're gonna be mighty pissed it's been impounded. And that would be my fault, wouldn't it, so who do you think they'll come after?

'OK hon. Will do. Guess the DEA'll come for you now. So, see you down here!' I quipped, trying to lighten the mood.

My thoughts of a night's sleep in my own bed at Diana's were pushed to one side as I was shown to a cell. Laying down on the metal bed, with only my clothes for padding, I went over what the hell had just happened: two hours ago I was just doing my job at a film festive. Now, at four o'clock in the morning, I was implicated in drug trafficking and had a criminal record which may, or may not, be expunged, and

I was reliant on one person for that.

I must have dozed off as I awoke to hear Rob being brought in. It was five-thirty a.m. and he was taken straight to be processed. I could hear arguing denials and, finally, a confession that he, with a friend, had stowed the boxes in the pick-up. He explained he had only put them there as he believed I would not see them in the darkness, that they would be safe overnight at Diana's house and that I would be bringing the Dodge back to the festival's hospitality suite early the next morning.

He had thought my 'hampster-wheel' work mode meant I would just get straight into the driver's seat the next morning and not even register the tarpaulin; he had never meant to involve me and I certainly was not to be implicated. It was all his fault and nothing whatsoever to do with me. I was an innocent bystander.

'Sign here', I heard Special Agent Reubens growling. 'Here, and here.' And then it went quiet.

I must have drifted off again as the next sound to jolt me was the clanking of the cell door. Captain Ed Gray came in and told me I could leave. It was six o'clock and I had to be at work again in an hour.

'Don't leave town,' he said invidiously. 'You've got off lightly but the DEA and FBI will need you.'

'Where's Rob?' I demanded, indignation now taking over.

'He's fine. We'll take care of him. Don't you worry your pretty little head about that. We see this all the time. The rich kids who think they're above the law and invincible. But if he co-operates with us and gives us what we want, we'll look after him as we said. A deal's a deal.'

Escorting me to the door, he lightened up. 'Hey, I'm sorry if we kinda scared you, but these days the cartels and dealers use the most unlikely people as *narcotrafficantes*. We can't assume that anyone is innocent until we know they're innocent. Do you need a ride home?'

'Not unless you've still impounded my Dodge?'

'Nah, all the stuff, as you call it, is out and in safe custody. The Dodge is again yours. But be more vigilant in future. You were lucky this time that your boyfriend was involved and spoke up for you. Often times, a stranger plants the drugs and then you'd have had a very deep hole to dig yourself out of.'

'When can I see Rob?'

'We'll call you depending on the DEA and FBI's next operational step. But don't try to contact him any time soon. The less you know, the better for you.'

I collected my car keys and tote from Officer Suarez at the Front Desk, signed for them and walked out into the already hot morning air.

Panic, or now instinct, made me look at the back of the Dodge; there was no tarpaulin and no boxes. I drove very, very slowly for the next three miles through the town to Diana's house.

Now I knew that this crazy existence was getting way out of hand.

But worse was still to come.

CHAPTER EIGHTEEN

'You were *w--h--e--r--e?*' screamed Diana, as she scooped the strong Columbian coffee beans that passed as breakfast in her house into the Nespresso machine. 'In the County jail because you had cocaine in the back of my Dodge? Are you f***ing kidding me? And you fell *asleep* at the wheel? For f***'s sake Vanessa, you could've been killed. Those truckers don't stop for anything.'

Machine grinding, she turned back to me and, checking to make sure I was giving her my full attention, continued the tirade. It was only six-thirty a.m. and I had had barely one hour's sleep.

'Is Rob a drug dealer? He seems so normal for someone from La-La-Land. Jeeze, do not get mixed up in cocaine or meth. The cartels are brutal and will have dug a hole in the desert for you and Rob before you know it. This is f***ing serious Vanessa.'

She banged her mug down as the rant changed tack.

'And I've told you before, you're doing way too much. No one at the festival is going to appreciate you trying to be super-woman and they certainly won't thank you for what you've done. I know you don't believe me, but they will forget you once you've gone back to England. That's how this business works.

'You have to be useful to someone and in their face for them to remember you. I know that goes against the grain with you, but this is how it works here. It's a kooky business. Remember what I keep telling you. Don't work hard. Work Smart!'

I gulped my coffee, showered and was already half-way out of the door – though still only half-dressed – when Diana returned from walking her dog.

'Got to rush, I've got to go and pick up breakfast from the restaurant.'

She looked at me as if I were mad. 'Oh for Christ's sake. I'm going back to bed.'

As I drove along the wide palm tree-lined boulevard, with its perfectly manicured lawns and pristine flower beds, I reflected on Diana's statement about "working smart". This usually equated to delegating and the problem, as she was only too aware, was that there was no one to delegate to – Dino, Lizzie, Mike 2 and I were already stretched to breaking point.

As the last of the guests finished their breakfast in the suite, Dino brought three plates of eggs to my desk where Lizzie and I were bent over the drivers grid, assigning ones for the Bel Air and Beverly Hills journeys this evening. One passenger was one of the most influential producers in Hollywood, while the other was the president of one of Tinseltown's leading artist management agencies; both drivers would have to be the best – we could not afford any stupid mistakes such as not knowing the exact address location or taking a longer-than-necessary route.

'We've got to pull Frank and Johnnie in for tonight,' I said to Lizzie. 'So, let's see how we can give them time off in the next few days, bearing in mind we are now coming up to the main departure runs to LAX.'

I had no sooner placated Johnnie and Frank with extra time off, and bribes of movie screening vouchers, when my mobile again rang. It was Daniel Eversleigh.

'Hi, how's the 'English Patient' this morning? Has Dr. Holmes been in again?'

Daniel said he had and that Dr. Holmes confirmed his diagnosis of food poisoning, before adding that he felt considerably better.

'That's great. You had us *really* worried last night.'

Daniel asked where I was and what I was doing.

'I'm in the Hospitality Suite, sorting out a few driver glitches.'

'I think I might come over,' he said. 'Got any decent coffee there?'

'Yes, and I'll pick you up from the hotel in ten minutes.'

He was waiting by the lobby doors when I pulled up. Telling my Valet Parking friends that I was just picking up a guest, they let me park immediately opposite the *porte-cochère*. As I walked into the lobby, I could immediately see that he was over the worst, for he was back to his stunningly handsome self.

'See the drugs are working!' I laughed as he gave me a peck on the cheek in gratitude of my assistance the previous evening. 'I'm afraid you're not travelling in the style you're accustomed to. I'm using a friend's husband's Dodge pick-up while I am here. Hope you don't mind?'

We clambered into the Dodge. 'This reminds me of the old Land Rover I used to have on my farm in Somerset,' he said graciously. 'No, I don't mind this at all, makes a change from the limos.'

We drove to the suite and, as I took him over to the Reception Desk, Dino was scrambling.

'I can't find his Welcome Pack,' he muttered quietly.

'Oh, that's fine. I put it in his hotel room a couple of days ago,' I replied in an equally conspiratorially hushed tone. 'Sorry, forgot to tell you.'

I walked Daniel around the suite, stopping first at the breakfast bar to get an adrenaline fix, before introducing him to Christian and Hannah, who were with a group of Israeli filmmakers – all of whom saying they loved his films – as well as Dino, Lizzie, Mike 2 and, finally, the Media Desk.

'If you want any press assistance at all while you are here, Shane's your man,' I said as Shane, trying to be very cool, casually stood up and held out his hand. 'He's with our PR agency in LA. And this is Dominic, who is actually a filmmaker himself, but has helped out on the Media Desk over the years and likes to keep his hand in.'

Dominic, throwing Daniel one of his mesmerizing smiles as they shook hands, told him he, too, was a great fan of his work.

Pulling up a chair next to my desk, Daniel sat down and surveyed the whole scene. I asked him if he wanted anything to eat, but he said he would wait until lunchtime. What he did want to do was to check that the promotional packs for his movie – selected as the Closing Night film – had arrived and were here in the suite. Walking up and down the tables, he could not see them and asked Dominic, busily putting out the new copies of Variety and Hollywood Reporter, where they were.

Dominic said he had not seen them and questioned whether they had yet arrived as nobody had any knowledge of seeing them.

This changed Daniel's mood and, clearly frustrated, he said he needed to talk to his LA agent. Fearing that the suite would be too noisy for what I presumed would be a delicate call, I suggested to Daniel that I take him back to the office and he could call from there.

As we were leaving, Diana rang. 'I'm coming over to the suite, are you there?'

'Just heading back to the office so that Daniel Eversleigh can have a private conversation with his LA agent. Why don't you meet me there, then you can also meet Daniel.' I knew Diana was a huge fan of his.

'Sounds a plan,' she yelped joyously. 'See you there.'

I had not been to the office for days – it actually felt more like weeks – and had not factored into my thinking the damage caused by the storm at the weekend. I pushed open the front door, breezily introducing Daniel to an open-mouthed Sherri on Reception and led him through to the 'Hollywood Hills', where I stopped in horror; aside from the copious buckets and saucepans, a large section of the ceiling had come down and thick black bin liners were taped over cans of films, boxes of files and telephones. It was too late to back out now.

'Uh-oh, we had a terrible storm at the weekend, the worst in California for twelve years. I'm so sorry that it's such a mess. It really was a nice office before the rain wreaked such havoc.'

Seemingly nonplussed, he grinned and said he did not mind at all, as long as the phones worked. Sitting him down at my desk, I dialled his agent's number just as Christian walked through the door – a look of horror sweeping across his face before he fixed an icy glare on me.

'Hi, is this Lakeside Entertainment?' I asked, as a young girl answered the phone without giving anything away.

'Yes, it is.'

'Is Standon Cantor there please? I have Daniel Eversleigh calling for him.' I waited while she connected me.

'Hey Danno-boy,' came a deep, chocolate-brown voice.

'Mr Cantor, I'll just put Daniel on the line.'

Mouthing the words "he called you Danno-boy!" to Daniel, I passed him the receiver and went to the kitchen to grab some coffee. Christian was hovering by the water cooler.

'What the f*** are you doing bringing talent to the *office*, especially in this condition. Just *what* is he going to think?'

I was in no mood for Christian, nor his snippy remarks, and so turned to face him full on.

'H-e-l-l-o. Planet Earth to Christian. Firstly, he's English and we're not hung up about superficial appearances in the way *you* are. Secondly, and more importantly, he needed to call his agent in relative peace and quiet, and I think even you would agree that the suite is not the place to have a quiet, discreet conversation. OK?'

Without waiting for a response, I grabbed the two large decaffeinated Lattes and walked back to my desk, just as Diana was coming out of Duncan's office.

'Daniel, meet my friend Diana who's handled all the marketing for the festival.'

Diana, clearly star-struck and rooted to the carpet, beamed at Daniel. 'Hello Mr Eversleigh. It's such a pleasure to meet you. I'm a huge fan of your work and seen *all* your movies.'

Daniel looked both pleased and slightly uncomfortable; I quickly pitched in with mock admonishment to Diana. 'Oh Diana, for God's sake stop being so sycophantic. He's English remember, we don't do fawning.'

This obviously appealed to Daniel's sense of humour, for he smiled and leant forward to kiss Diana on the cheek, rendering her speechless; a *rare* moment indeed.

The conversation with Standon Cantor had revealed that the film's promotional items were in transit and should be with us later today, leaving Daniel looking visibly more relaxed. The three of us left Christian, scowling still amid the buckets and saucepans and Sherri still with open jaw, and drove back to the hospitality suite.

As it was almost lunchtime, I suggested to Daniel that if he wanted to see one of the city's coolest, hippest eating places, the three of us should go to Flemings for a burger – at which point he emitted a low, evidently mocking groan. It was only then that he admitted that he had asked the driver to stop at a well-known domestic fast-food chain so that he could have a 'typical American burger'; he had not eaten that much on the flight and was hungry.

'Which burger chain?' I demanded. He told me the name.

'Good God, you stopped to eat *there*,' I screeched in horror. 'Nobody in their right minds eats at one of those places. No wonder you've got food poisoning. Please don't ever go to one of them again. You're asking for trouble.'

The three of us drove off in the Dodge pick-up, much to the amusement of the Valet Parking guys who, naturally, were more accustomed to seeing stars getting into limousines, S-Class Sedans or Maybachs.

Over lunch, in which we indulged in our own bit of star-spotting – a high-octane film producer and similarly high-profile agent, plus a young pop singer who was supposed to be in rehab, but clearly was not bothering with such trifling matters.

'What should I be seeing around here, while I have some time?' asked Daniel.

'Well, there's whale-watching, the mountain cable car, horse-riding along ocean-front trails or hopping aboard an open-top Hummer for a 'back-roads winery tour', suggested Diana.

Surprised at the volley of suggestions, he settled on the cable car, as long as I would drive him there and collect him when he had finished.

'Sure, no problem. Just call me from the top of the mountain when you're done and I can be waiting for you at the bottom.'

After driving back to the suite, so that I could pick up a complimentary pass for the cable car, I drove Daniel to the kiosk at the base of the mountain before again heading back to the suite which was, by now, crowded and buzzing.

Variety magazine, generally regarded as *the* entertainment industry 'bible', was hosting a reception in the early part of the evening at Caravaggio – a supremely swanky restaurant on the outskirts of town – and we needed to take current issues and cases of Ciroc vodka, along with their stunning plastic ice-cubes which emitted a brilliant bluey-purple pulsating light when pressed.

I also had to call the Vice President of Marketing to see if I could get Daniel added to the tightly controlled guest list; this reception at this festival was not unlike the coveted Vanity Fair party at the Oscars. After the Awards Gala, it was the hottest ticket in town and which everyone, but everyone, wanted to be seen at.

Yes, they "would love to have Daniel Eversleigh, of course he *must* come", I was informed by a gushing underling as I simultaneously asked Lizzie if everything was OK for the two Bel Air and Beverly Hills runs.

'Yeah, we're good, it's just that Frank and Johnnie have both been on, having a bitch about having to do them tonight.'

My brow furrowed. 'But they were fine when I spoke to

them this morning. What's the problem?'

Lizzie shrugged her shoulders. 'Oh, you know. They feel they can bitch to me, but not to you.'

I leant across the desk and looked her straight in the eye. 'But they *are* going to do these runs, aren't they? I mean, there's no question of any problems or, God forbid, a no-show?

'There'd better not be any hassles. I'm at the Variety reception, well at the beginning anyway, so I'm leaving this one to you. But there'll be blood on the carpet if it gets screwed up, and neither of us wants to face Duncan while he's having one of his better temper tantrums.'

We laughed as we visualized the virtual carnage that Duncan could wreak. 'Hung, drawn and quartered, you mean!' giggled Lizzie. Our hallucinations were interrupted by my mobile. It was Daniel; he was ready to come down off the mountain.

'Be there in ten,' I said as my mobile went again; but this time it was the DEA.

Daniel was waiting for me at the entrance to the cable car, reading a script.

'Well? Was it worth it?' I shouted through the open window as I pulled up sharply, dust and grit flying everywhere.

'Yes and yes,' he said as he jumped into the passenger seat. 'Yes for the view and yes because it gave me some space to read and think.'

I was intrigued. 'What exactly is it that you have to think about, aside from scripts and whether to take the next role or not?'

He looked at me for a moment before breaking into a

smile. 'Oh, you know. Relationships, life. Why am I being sent all these crap scripts!'

Pulling away with the same momentum as I had arrived, I turned to him, the sunlight catching his still chiseled features.

'Well, I can't help you with the first two, but if the last one is now a problem, then why don't you just keep on directing. The UK reviews of your directorial debut have been very positive.'

He shot me a sideways glance. 'How do you know?'

Smiling at the windscreen, I laughingly said, 'Do you know, we have something called the Internet in our office. And I Googled your movie and read them online. How cool is that!'

He laughed at my gentle teasing. 'OK. Touché.'

'By the way, I've added your name to the Variety party guest list this evening. Do you feel like going to it?'

'Yes. I feel so much better, thanks to Dr. Holmes' drugs! A party sounds the perfect antidote. But before then, I'd like to see a bit of this famous town.'

The sun was now getting lower and a wonderful yellowy-orange glow was blanketing everything as we cruised the boulevards, side streets and winding back lanes on the outskirts of the old part of town – where the old money lived – with its gated compounds, large estates and small ranches. I dropped him back at the hotel so he could change and said I would pick him up in two hours.

The Hilton's bar lounge was already full at five o'clock with cocktail drinkers as I sat down in a quiet corner to await Special Agent Reubens. He had told me on the phone that he was bringing a colleague and two FBI agents; they arrived looking distinctly non-authoritarian in jeans and sweat-shirts, trying to blend in with the crowd, but the ultra-short haircuts gave them away.

Special Agent Reubens expediently dispensed introductions – Agent Darren Fischer from the DEA, Special Agent Nat Parker and Agent Dirk Wynter from the FBI's Federal Justice Center in El Paso – and, after ordering drinks, we got down to business.

'Your boyfriend has been helpful and we think we've got enough to set up a bust,' said FBI Special Agent Nat Parker. 'But the problem is that he's mentioned you to his trafficking friends Javier and Manuel, so we're gonna need you to act out a role in this bust. As you may, or may not, be aware, Manuel's family run the most notorious cartel in Mexico – the Sinalopéz cartel. He thinks you're Rob's girlfriend, so we need your relationship to continue as usual until we do the bust. Are you OK with this?

'Yes, but I can only see Rob or help you guys around my work at the festival. That has to come first. My dating Rob, as you call it, was pretty spasmodic anyway as I never really had time to see him on a normal basis. We only ever had snatched moments or odd hours here and there. I'm amazed it ever progressed.'

'That's fine, we'll keep that routine so Manuel and Javier do not suspect anything.'

Special Agent Reubens cut in. 'OK if I call you Vanessa?' I nodded, as he continued.

'Vanessa, the cocaine in the back of your Dodge came from Medellin in Columbia, hence the very high-purity. We're trying to smash the producers down there and to do this, we need to bust the Mexican cartels who are bulk-transporting it up to Mexico and then smuggling it into the US.

'There are only three cartels in Mexico that are capable of doing this – the Sinalopéz, the Tijuana and the Juárez – and only *one* cartel that the Medellin producers trust. And that's the Sinalopéz cartel, where Manuel Sinalopéz and, in turn, your man Rob, come in.

'The Sinalopéz cartel, with its presence in seventeen Mexican states, is the single largest and most powerful drug trafficking organisation in the Western hemisphere. It's grown during the drug wars due to its non-hierarchical organisation structure. The cartel is more like a confederacy of groups that are connected through blood, marriage and regional relationships. Decisions are made ultimately through 'board-of-directors-type' mechanisms and not by a single leader.'

He sipped his beer before solemnly continuing, 'The US Justice Department considers the Mexican drug cartels to be the greatest organised crime threat to the United States. They already have a presence in most major US cities, including LA, San Diego, Phoenix, Tuscon, Atlanta, Miami, Chicago and New York.'

I sipped my margarita nervously as FBI Special Agent Nat Parker took over.

'The US State Department estimates that ninety percent of cocaine entering the US is produced in Columbia, with the main transit route being Mexico, resulting in the cartels there controlling some seventy percent of the foreign narcotics flow into the US. Analysts estimate the wholesale earnings from imported illicit drugs to be in the region of $45 billion annually. So you can see why we take this so seriously. Basically, we are at war with the cartels.'

Ordering another margarita, I glanced at the two other agents. As if reading my mind, FBI Agent Dirk Wynter chipped in.

'They have elaborate recruitment strategies targeting young adults to join their cartel groups. Rob's friendship with Javier Pajares, coupled with his LA lifestyle, made him a natural target.'

DEA Agent Darren Fischer took up the slack. 'The cartels generally, but the Sinalopéz obsessively, maintain incredibly high levels of security. It's why they've lasted, and thrived, for so long. But they're fighting their own war against the Tijuana cartel over the highly lucrative smuggling route across the border to San Diego.

'The internal drugs war is conducted by *sicarios*, or cartel hitmen. They guard the shipments, the money and protect the cartel's turf from rivals. And they kill to order.'

He paused to check I was paying full attention.

'They are well-armed, with an arsenal of automatic weapons including AK-47s, known affectionately by the traffickers as "goats horns" because of the curved clip for the bullets, M4 carbine assault rifles, FN Five-Seven handguns, which are a popular choice due to its armour-piercing capability, and M203 grenade launchers. Oh, and some cartels have also been known to use improvised explosive devices. So you can see why your friend Rob wants Witness Protection.'

I gulped down the remains of my margarita, my face obviously ashen.

'Have we frightened you enough Vanessa?' asked DEA Special Agent Reubens. 'You need to know just how serious this is for both Rob and you. The Mexican cartels are no longer constrained to being mere intermediaries for Columbian producers. They are now powerful organised-crime syndicates that dominate the drug trade in the US. And the cartels operating today along the south-west border are far more sophisticated and dangerous than any other organised criminal group in US law enforcement history.'

'Oh – kay,' I said slowly, turning to FBI Special Agent Nat Parker. 'So how does this work? The bust, that is?'

'We'll work out the details with Rob and come back to you. But we can't rule out that the Sinalopéz haven't already got *sicarios* in town, even though Manuel is here. So, whatever you do, just act normal, get on with your job, see Rob when we allow it and do not, I repeat, do not give anything away that might alert Manuel or any of his visiting henchmen that something is up.'

'Understood. I need to go now as I have to pick up a director for a reception this evening. I think I'll try and forget we've had this meeting.'

'Vanessa, I cannot impress upon you enough that this will not be fun,' said DEA Special Agent Reubens, as we all stood up. 'The cartels engage in murder, kidnapping, ransom, robbery and extortion of migrants. It will be dangerous for all involved and that includes you. Are you sure you're up for this?'

'Do I have a choice?' I shrugged. 'If it helps Rob and you guys, sure.'

The large ornate wrought-iron gate, set within a beautiful stone wall encircling the whole property, was decorated with a large, tear-shaped wreath of white roses, white peonies, lilies and gardenia, and wrapped in a garland of Eucalyptus and Bay leaves. On either side of the gate, holograms of the film festival and Variety logos were beamed onto the wall, while a smaller up-lighter illuminated the sweeping curve of herringbone-brick steps behind the gate – leading to Caravaggio's main terrace – which was edged in clusters of pillar candles in varying heights.

The terrace, ablaze with tiny white and peach fairy lights, was dotted with spiral stem-ball Bay and Olive trees housed in over-sized alternating zinc titanium and terracotta planters; small wind chimes hung from cast iron torch brackets and, on the linen- and voile-covered tables, hurricane lamps stood festooned with Swarovski crystals and peony petals around their bases.

A waiter appeared suddenly, as if out of nowhere, with a silver salver bearing the tallest champagne flutes I had ever seen.

'Just out of curiosity, do you know which champagne it is?'

Taking his glass from the tray, Daniel frowned at me as the waiter said, without hesitation, 'Oh, I believe its Perrier Jouet, from France. Do you need me to check for you?' Thanking him, I declined his offer.

'Why did you ask him that?' asked Daniel.

'Oh, you know, just wondered whether Variety was doing it properly, as in French, or whether we'd be given sparkling wine from Napa. Actually, the sparkling wines from Napa are generally very good. But I just like to know what I am drinking.'

Scanning the terrace area, but not yet recognizing anyone apart from Ric and Shane who were briefing John Haines from the LA Times, I guided Daniel through to the main bar and restaurant area, adorned with black and white celebrity portraits and film festival banners, where we spotted Duncan talking to Ed and Jacky Florschon. I led Daniel over and introduced him.

'Hi Ed, Duncan, Jacky. Can I introduce Daniel Eversleigh, who just got in yesterday. Daniel, this is Ed Harrison, Chairman of the film festival and Duncan Northcote, the festival's Executive Director.'

Daniel leant forward to shake hands with Ed who, never one to undersell himself or anything associated with him, said, 'Welcome to one of the largest, but the *best*, film festivals in the United States. I trust you had a good flight?'

I knew the real reason Ed was asking this; it was not out of concern for Daniel's comfort, merely that he had approved the cost of a First Class ticket and wanted to ensure he had got every quota of value for his buck.

'Yes, it was fine, thanks,' said Daniel, with typical British under-statement.

Ed looked momentarily askance, before recovering his composure. 'I hope we've also taken care of everything you might need while you are here as our guest. If there is anything we have forgotten, then Vanessa will see to it.'

'The hotel's perfect, the chauffeur is reliable and I'm looking forward to trying out the Spa tomorrow,' said Daniel as he turned to shake Duncan's hand. Jacky leant forward and gave him a kiss on the cheek.

'We like to do things a little differently here,' she laughed. 'A kiss is so much better than a handshake, don't you think?'

'I quite agree,' smiled Daniel, leaning forward to return the gesture as Ric came over to ask me if Daniel would be willing to do a couple of media interviews the next day.

'You'd better ask him. He wasn't feeling brilliant today, but I'm sure he'll be fine tomorrow. Go ahead and ask him if he wants to do them.'

Ric turned to Daniel. 'Hey, good to see you again. Any chance you'd be up for doing an interview tomorrow with John Haines of the LA Times. He's their key entertainment news reporter. We've told him that your new movie is the Closing Night one and that you have just arrived in town. Obviously I've pitched this on behalf of the festival, but it'll be great exposure for you and the movie. The LA Times reaches more than two million readers.'

Daniel, being a good seven inches taller than Ric, looked down intently while Ric was employing his persuasive powers.

'Sure, no problem. What time do they want to do it? Hopefully not at the crack of dawn.'

Thirty minutes later, the party was in full flow and the restaurant manager sensibly had all the tables moved to one side to allow the guests maximum standing room; as many of the ladies were in bandage-tight Hervé Léger dresses, it would have been near-impossible for them to sit down anyway.

A sea of immaculately-groomed, pencil-thin women clad in Armani Privé, Dries Van Noten, Zac Posen, Roberto Cavalli, Marchesa, Atelier Versace and Badgley Mischka – not to mention the ubiquitous Hervé Léger bandage dress – took delicate steps in their Jimmy Choos, Manolo Blahniks and breathtakingly vertiginous Christian Louboutins, while their necks, wrists, ears and fingers were bejeweled by Cartier, Van Cleef & Arpels, Tiffany, Harry Winston, Chopard and Hollywood A-List favourite, Neil Lane.

The men were much the same; tanned, toned and groomed – male exfoliation products flew off the shelves in this town – all shod in either Gucci and Briony loafers or Salvatore Ferragamo brogues, and clad in Michael Kors, Ralph Lauren and Marc Jacobs suits and jackets, accessorized with Rolex Oyster and Tag Heuer watches, Tiffany Paloma's Groove silver cufflinks, and sunglasses perched atop their foreheads by Oliver Peoples and Prada.

To ensure the social x-rays remained so, the silver platters of food being airlifted through the room contained only bite-size portions of pan-seared Sonoma fois gras, Roquefort tartlets, crisp fried oysters, mini-Kobe cheeseburgers, seared Yellow Fin tuna, sautéed Nantucket sea scallops, fried coconut crusted shrimp and Thai ginger crabcake, together with baby artichoke slivers, water chestnuts wrapped in Radicchio and chopped vegetable Martini salad in shot glasses.

The twenty-five bartenders deftly navigated their way through the five-hundred-odd guests, dispensing Jack Daniels, Cosmopolitans, Bellinis, margaritas, wines, beers and shots of Tequila.

Daniel, recognizing a couple of producers and studio executives, went off to talk to them as Jacky cornered me.

'I want him to come and do a piece on my show. Do you think you can persuade him?'

'I'm not his handler Jacky. Why don't you ask him yourself?'

'Oh, it'd be much better coming from you. So, I can expect you both tomorrow morning, say about noon. You can drive him over and come and sit in on the programme if you want.'

'Guess it depends on what time he has to do the LA Times interview, but I'll do my best to get him there. Bye Jacky.'

I circled the eclectic gathering, spotting several well-known TV actors and actresses locked in conversation with people whom I presumed to be either their agents or current series producers, the odd supermodel, entertainment TV chat show hosts and senior executives from Tinseltown's studio behemoths, as well as the 'young blades' who were clearly the vanguard of the independent production companies and the younger voting element of the Academy (of Motion Picture Arts & Sciences).

Some thirty minutes later, I found Daniel in conversation

with his LA agent Standon Cantor and Hollywood über-producer Kyle Yablonski, who had decided to stay on after the Awards Gala and spend a few days at his nearby sumptuous home. They were soon joined by Conrad Young, still staying with Kyle Yablonski before leaving next week to start shooting his new adventure thriller in New Orleans, and Curtis Nickelow, looking even thinner than I thought he did at the Awards Gala, plus Ed, Jacky, Duncan and Hannah.

iPhones and BlackBerrys hummed, glasses clinked and the banter grew exponentially as the evening wore on and the Zeltiq'd females – those who had just undergone the new 'must-have' rapid weight loss treatment, a freezing technique which supposedly dissolves fat cells – slinked down the curved brick staircase to their waiting Mercedes convertibles.

As Daniel was in safe hands with his agent, I decided to call it a night, for it was already after one o'clock – extremely late by LA standards where most people, usually required on set by six-thirty in the morning, are in bed by ten o'clock.

Bidding him goodnight, I briefly told him about Jacky's request and said I would explain it in more detail in the morning when I rang to advise him of the time for the LA Times interview.

I checked he was happy to stay on at the party, which he was, with Hannah quickly interjecting that *she* would drive him back to The Four Seasons and, having bid everyone else in the group goodnight, made my way to the Cloakroom where I liberally doused my face with cold water.

I was not prepared to meet another Police officer on my way home; I would, however, meet several officers the next day – but for a reason we were all totally unprepared for.

CHAPTER NINETEEN

I called Daniel from the suite, Ric having advised that the LA Times interview was scheduled for ten-thirty a.m. ‘Hi Daniel, how are you feeling?’

He sounded a lot better than forty-eight hours earlier, replying in an upbeat manner, ‘I’m fine thanks. In fact, back to normal. Now, didn’t I get roped into doing an LA Times interview last night?’

‘Yes, you did. It’s this morning and Ric says it’s scheduled for ten-thirty. It will be here in the Media Room adjoining the suite. I’ll come over and pick you up in fifteen minutes.’

As I was putting down the phone, Dino swung around in his chair at the main reception desk and called out, ‘Vanessa, it’s for you. I think she said her name was Jacky. Who is she?’

Nodding for him to put it through to my desk, I grinned. ‘Oh, I’ll tell you later.’

Jacky’s voice pulsated down the phone, like a micro-cyclone. ‘Hey Vanessa, how’ya doin? Did’ya enjoy the party last night?’ Without waiting for my answer, she launched forth again, without coming up for air.

‘Great, wasn’t it. I really liked your friend from England, what’s his name, Daniel? In fact, I really want him to come on my show this morning. Did you mention it to him last night? Is he going to do it? There'll be a couple of other guests on as well. I need to know ASAP so that I can work out the running order and format. You know my programme, don't you? And you know where the office is that I broadcast from. Can you let me know? Bye sweetie.'

The micro-cyclone evaporated as quickly as it had formed.

Leaning back in my chair, I took a deep breath. I had listened to Jacky's radio show a couple of times; it was extremely irreverent and whacky, which was part of its appeal, but I was not sure if it would be the right fit for Daniel to promote either his new movie or himself. Deciding to confer with Ric and Shane, I walked over to the Media Desk and asked them what they thought. Shane was quick to offer his opinion.

'OK, so it's only a small, local radio show, with a small audience. And it is very offbeat. But hey, it's still publicity for his movie which, let's face it, is probably going to be a hard sell to American audiences, given the large doses of irony and subtle English humour. And it's only a few blocks down the road. I'd go for it.'

Ric, far more concerned with Daniel doing the LA Times interview, merely opined, 'It will be amusing for him, if nothing else. Now, what time will he be here for the John Haines interview?'

'I am picking him up from the hotel now and we'll be back here by ten-fifteen latest.'

He smiled, put his arm around me and said, 'Thanks honey. See you then.'

Daniel was in the lobby reading the LA Times, along with the past two editions of The Envelope – its weekly entertainment industry supplement and essential reading for anyone remotely interested in the film business – when I arrived.

'Morning. Doing your homework, I see,' I laughed as I went up to the armchair.

He got up, folding the paper as he did so and smiled, saying 'Darling, it's always good to be prepared, and I wanted to see John's writing style. Actually, there's a fascinating article about movie residuals and how the smart money is saying they are about to go through something of a sea change.'

En route to the suite, I told Daniel about Jacky's plea for him to be on her show today. I put forward the pro's and con's and asked him what he thought.

'Do I *really* have to do it?'

'No, of course not. But hey, it's only a few blocks down the road and, if nothing else, it may be highly amusing.'

'Alright. But you'll have to drive me there. In fact, consider yourself still my chauffeur.'

'Fine by me. Her show goes out live at noon so we've got time for the LA Times interview and perhaps even a coffee before we set off for Jacky's bag of tricks.'

By the time we got to the suite, Mike 2 and Dino had diplomatically displayed all the promotional material for Daniel's new film that his agent had sent up from LA. Daniel's face looked as though we had just pulled a rabbit out of the hat as he ran his fingers over the material, mentally checking it was all there.

'I'll call Standon for you and let him know everything has arrived,' I told Daniel as he made his way to the Media Desk for his briefing by Ric and Shane.

As the three of them walked out to the adjacent Media Room, Dominic came over for an update on life.

'Is he always this *friendly*?' he asked, laying on the

sarcasm. 'He was quite snippy with me yesterday just because we couldn't find the damn promo items. It's not my fault his agent hadn't sent them up here in time.'

Pausing for breath and now bored with the subject of Daniel, his mesmerizing smile once again returned as he continued, 'Hey guess what. My movie was shown last night and the audience seemed to like it. It got a resounding applause at the end. How 'bout that?'

Daniel's interview with John Haines lasted a full forty-five minutes – lengthy by LA standards – and it gave Dino and I a chance to finalise the invitations for the Closing Night party at the Hilton for the mainstream guests, plus, for the favoured few, a coveted invitation to a formal dinner and 'after-show party' at Mrs Jackie Blumberg's palatial estate in the old part of the city.

As if by some sixth sense, for we were musing over which VIPs would receive this hallowed invitation, a courier suddenly appeared in front of me and dropped onto my desk a heavy yellow jiffy bag.

'Who's this for and what is it?'

'It's from the Blumberg estate and I guess there'll be a name on the envelope inside. Just sign here.'

Signing as instructed and carefully opening the jiffy bag, I pulled out a white laid envelope, replete with seal and ribbon, bearing the name of the addressee, inscribed in calligraphic lettering, Mr Daniel Eversleigh.

'Shame we shan't be getting one of these,' I murmured to Dino as I placed it carefully in the bottom drawer of my desk. 'Still, we'll have a more relaxed time and a lot more fun at the main Closing Night party.'

Daniel and Ric sauntered back into the suite and over to my desk. 'How did it go?' I asked.

'Well darling, I think it went very well,' said Daniel.

'John Haines seemed a really nice guy, asked all the right questions and certainly knows his stuff. But I guess we'll have to wait and see what the article is like when it appears.'

'And when is that?' I asked, glancing from Daniel to Ric.

'He thinks it'll either be this Saturday in the Calendar section, as they are planning a piece on actors' directorial debuts, but if that doesn't happen then it'll definitely be in next Wednesday, in The Envelope section.'

'Well, talking of envelopes,' I said slowly as I leant down to pull open the bottom drawer. 'I have one for you here.'

Ric leant forward over the desk to try and see what it was before I could give it to Daniel and, realizing it was the holy grail, looked distinctly chuffed with himself.

'Did you have a hand in this?'

'Might have done,' he grinned.

'What is it darling?' asked Daniel as I handed him the envelope.

'You are now elevated to deity status,' I laughed. 'Your movie is premiering in the United States on Closing Night and thus you are summoned to enjoy yourself afterwards with the great and the good of LA and this town.'

I watched his face as he opened the envelope, grimacing at the seal and ribbon. He smiled as he pulled out the stiff laid card, again inscribed in calligraphic lettering.

'Well, I guess I *have* arrived! Have you got one Vanessa?'

'Good Lord no! I am merely a worker bee,' I remonstrated in mock horror as Ric interjected, 'Queen bee darling,' before I continued, '… and worker bees don't get invited to the inner sanctum of the honeycomb. Let's get real here.'

'But of course you should be invited,' said Daniel. 'Who do I talk to about it?'

'No one,' I shot back. 'Actually, not sure I'd really want to go to it anyway. I think I'll have much more fun downing margaritas by the Hilton pool and pushing a few people in.'

Dino turned and grinned at me, for he knew exactly to whom I was referring.

'You might be right,' said Daniel. 'Do I *have* to go to this party? Can't I just come along with you to the main party?'

'Nope, sorry. You are summoned and they'll expect you. You'll have a great time Daniel and there'll be some serious industry players there, so it'll be useful for you, even if you don't enjoy yourself! You know, there are people in this town who'd sell their mothers for tickets to the Blumberg gig. If nothing else, enjoy the house, the estate – and the experience.'

Dino could contain himself no longer. 'Ah, but think of The Lesbian Tossing you'll be missing at the main party!'

Daniel did a double-take. 'Now this sounds so much more fun. How many lesbians are there and where are they being tossed?'

Dino, eager to pursue this ridiculous dialogue, calmly replied as he punched his keyboard, 'Oh just the one that we know of and *it* will no doubt be tossed into the pool, probably by Vanessa, but there is a line of people behind her who will gladly step up to the plate if she doesn't do it.'

Shane had joined us and caught the last part of the conversation. 'Which lesbian? Is it the one I'm thinking of?'

Dino nodded confirmation, for he knew that Shane also had little time for her. 'But guys, you're all forgetting that The Lesbian will more than likely be included in the

Blumberg dinner.'

There was a horrified silence at the thought. 'OK, bizarre conversation over. Daniel darling, we have another interview to get to. Shall we go?'

Grabbing my phone, tote and new Michael Kors sunglasses, I steered him out of the suite and into the wall-to-wall sunshine, where we stood and appreciated the momentary heat on our shoulders while the Valet Parking guy ran to get my car – a look of bemusement on his face when he returned in a Dodge pick-up.

Jacky's studio was relatively easy to find as it was on one of the main roads. Pulling up in a parking bay almost outside the building, I looked at it and then at Daniel.

'OK, ready for this?' I giggled, as I knew instantly that this was going to turn into something of a farce.

'Is this it?' he asked, looking as bemused as the Valet Parking guy at the hotel had done a few minutes earlier.

We pushed open the door to an office suite which had, sadly, seen better days and followed the sound of voices through the Lobby area and into an ante-room which doubled as the studio. I had not realized that it was not a proper studio and a sudden wave of guilt washed over me at dragging Daniel down here to do an interview. Jacky, sitting at the head of what was clearly just an old boardroom table and with a microphone speaker and head set in front of her, jumped up as we tentatively knocked on the door to announce our arrival.

'Come in, come in,' she squealed in delight. 'Mind the wires everywhere, don't trip. Vanessa, come and sit down as well.'

It was difficult not to trip, for they were everywhere; wires led off the individual guests' microphones on the table to reference monitors, wires linked a series of preamplifiers around the room, wires linked the preamps to the main mixing console, and wires fed in from four incoming phone lines.

We picked our way through the electrical detritus and took two seats on the left side of the table and which afforded a view out onto the street. Jacky introduced Daniel to the two other male guests: an up-and-coming white soul musician and a self-help book writer.

Daniel, trying to contain himself, turned to me and, marginally lowering his voice, said, 'It's hardly the BBC, is it darling!'

Jacky, testing her microphone, 'One, two, three. One, two, three,' had not heard Daniel's comment; while I found it highly amusing, it would have offended her.

Satisfied that the table mics were all working and giving us a stern warning of a ten-second countdown to going live, Jacky launched forth.

'Good morning folks and welcome to the Jacky Florschon show on KPSK 92.6 FM. We've got a great line up for you on the programme today, including tips on how to shed those pounds without avoiding chocolate or carbs, how to revitalise your wardrobe without even buying anything new, and how to create the perfect family room for just $250.

'And if that weren't enough, our guests today include a famous English actor now turned director, and whose directorial debut is the Closing Night movie at the film festival; a young white soul musician already tipped for Grammy stardom; and a writer whose new book on how to heal the soul has just made it onto the New York Times best-seller list.

'So, without any further delay, let's rock on.'

Cue show soundtrack while Jacky fumbled with her

sheaf of papers and mouthed to Daniel, 'you'll be first. I'll cue you in.'

After what seemed an inordinately long soundtrack, particularly for a small, local show, and which was followed immediately by a spool of local commercials, Jacky again launched forth.

'Good afternoon everyone. Today we have a very special guest for you. A famous actor all the way from England. He has been beguiling us on the movie screen and on our TV sets for nearly three decades. His charm and good looks have won him numerous parts in some of the biggest movies over the years and, ladies, I'm looking at him right now and I can tell you those good looks are very much still evident today.'

I looked at Jacky. Was she flirting with Daniel? I looked at Daniel. He was looking down at the table and I could not quite work out whether he felt uncomfortable with all the fuss or was just wishing he was anywhere but in this cramped, makeshift studio. But there was no stopping this particular Scud missile.

'He has worked with some of the biggest names in the business, on both sides of the pond, and has delighted audiences with his take on classic British period films and television programmes. His latest project, his first shot at movie directing, opened in England recently and has already garnered great reviews.'

A deliberate pause kept the audience in suspense as to who this amazing person was going to be; still stringing it out, she continued, 'Ladies and gentlemen, it is my great pleasure to have on the show today ... Mr Daniel Eversleigh.'

Build up over, Jacky calmed down and switched to normal interview mode; she was highly professional, asking all the right questions and not at all sycophantic, as I had thought she might be. Daniel, too, was the consummate professional, talking eloquently about his latest movie, his earlier work and why he had chosen to be an actor.

The segment lasted twenty five minutes, longer than I had expected and, when it came to a mutually apparent conclusion, Jacky wrapped it up by saying, 'Daniel, thanks for taking time out of your undoubtedly frantic schedule to be with us this morning. I'm looking forward to seeing the movie tomorrow night. Ladies and gentlemen, Mr Daniel Eversleigh,' as she nodded to the guy in the booth to her left side to fade in music and commercials.

The other guests looked on in awe as Daniel nodded a 'thank you' to Jacky, mouthing, 'I'm sorry, but I have to go. Got another interview in twenty minutes.'

I knew this was code for the fact he wanted to get out as quickly as possible, so we stood up as quietly as we could and then both tripped over the tangle of wires on the floor by our chairs.

'Sorry about that,' I said meekly as I revved from the kerb.

'Oh, that *was* amusing,' he grinned, 'but please don't ask me to do any more like that.'

Deciding that it was time for lunch, it was apposite that I took Daniel somewhere fairly swanky in order to compensate for what he had just been through, and so suggested we went to Le Manoir.

The canopies and parasols at Le Manoir were all out to protect the pencil-thin diners from the searing rays of the mid-day sun, while waiters in overly-starched Nehru-style jackets rushed about their business carrying enormous cut-glass jugs of iced water crammed with wedges of lemon and lime, and garnished with mint. The maître d', patently wondering if Daniel was whom he thought he was – for he studiously eyed him – led us to one of the best tables at the edge of the terrace overlooking the ornamental lake and golf course beyond.

Almost before we had sat down two waiters were upon us, whisking out the stiff linen napkins from the goblet-sized crystal glasses and placing them gently on our laps; they filled the large crystal tumblers with the lavishly-laced water before enquiring if we would like iced tea or a cola to accompany our meal. We decided a bottle of Chablis was the order of the day.

The lengthy and eclectic menu – a fusion of French and American took some studying to make a selection; Daniel opted for the Escargot and Artichoke Hearts to start, followed by Tangerine-seared Sea Scallops with shaved fennel and crispy prosciutto, while I selected the Baby Spinach and Pecan salad, followed by Coriander-crusted Venison Loin.

For dessert, we both opted for the mouth-watering Chardonnay Poached Pear Soft Chocolate Cake with pear ice cream. Choices made, we sat back and once more savoured the heat on our shoulders.

'You know something, I could learn to put up with this,' I joked to Daniel as we dipped the thinly-pared slices of olive and walnut bread into the ramekin of white truffle oil. 'This makes up for the twenty-hour days of the past four or five weeks.'

He peered over his varifocal glasses and looked at me in stunned amazement. 'Twenty-hour days?'

'Yep, everyone's been slammed against the wall,' I shrugged. 'But it has been an amazing experience, albeit utterly exhausting, crazy and, at times, totally surreal.'

I regaled him with snippets of the Awards Gala and my extra-curricular nocturnal encounter with the Sheriff the other night, his eyes widening as I told him that I had apparently careened across five lanes of Freeway, dicing with juggernaut trucks while I was asleep.

'You clever girl!' he laughed. 'But you can't possibly work like this day-in, day-out. No one can. It's complete madness.'

'Well, too late now. And we're almost done. Only another few days to go and then it's take-down and wrap time. And, I hope, a bloody magnificent staff party. I think we all deserve one.'

As we relaxed into our appetizers, our new-found sublimity was rudely interrupted by a screeching woman with a southern accent.

'Oh. My. Lordy. Lord. It's Daniel Eversleigh. You *are* Daniel Eversleigh, aren't you? I've seen all your movies. I just *l-u-r-v-e* those English Empire-type period movies.'

Daniel, looking somewhat aghast, weakly smiled a confirmatory acknowledgement. Before he could say anything, the woman reached into her garish vinyl handbag and whipped out her mobile phone.

'You wait 'til I tell ma good man I'm in a restaurant with Daniel Eversleigh.'

Stabbing at the speed dial button with a horribly long white acrylic talon, masquerading as a finger nail, she screeched into the mouthpiece, oblivious to the fact that she was in an upscale restaurant rather than a tacky burger joint, 'Bud, BUD, you're never gonna believe this. I'm in the same restaurant as Daniel Eversleigh. And I'm standin' right next to him. Do you want to talk to him as well honey?'

Upon hearing this, Daniel shot me a look which simply said, 'Get Me Out of Here. Now.'

Pushing my chair back and signalling for the maître d' to come over, I tapped the woman gently on her shoulder.

While she paused her conversation with Bud, I locked my eyes onto hers and said firmly, 'Would you mind very much. We are actually in the middle of a meeting and having to do it over lunch as there simply isn't any other time. Yes, it is Daniel Eversleigh. And like all the other diners here, he'd like to be able to eat his lunch in peace. Please would you be kind enough to step away and allow him to do that.'

Looking thoroughly offended, as though it were her right to interrupt our lunch and chat to Daniel as if he were her property, she stepped back a few paces, saying into the mouthpiece that she would call him later.

'Well, there ain't no need for that,' she snapped in an aggrieved tone. 'I was only tryin' to be friendly.'

'Well Mr Eversleigh doesn't need anyone being friendly with him just now, thank you. So, if you don't mind, we'd like to continue our meeting without any more interruptions.'

The maître d', having arrived as the fracas was dissipating, firmly ejected the woman from the terrace and returned her to the Brasserie area where she had been eating with a group of friends, before returning to apologize profusely for the interruption.

'It comes with the territory,' said Daniel wearily. 'A nuisance we have to put up with. But we're fine. Thank you for your help.'

Clicking his manicured fingers high above his head, a waiter was upon us bearing a tray with two crystal flutes and a bottle of Roederer Cristal in an ice-bucket.

'Compliments of the house. By way of an apology,' he said, with a slight bow and an exaggerated circling of his hand.

'In that case, bring on the rest of the weirdos,' I laughed as the cork separated from the bottle neck without a sound and the waiter deftly poured the champagne. Equilibrium restored, we sated our appetites with the delicious appetizers and entrées and, finally, the most divine chocolate cake dessert I have ever had.

'Hmmm, that was to die for,' I said, dabbing the napkin at my mouth. 'Chocolate cake and champagne, what more could a girl want, except some sleep! Do you know, that's the first proper food I have had in weeks.'

My phone rang. 'What is it?' asked Daniel, seeing my frown.

'Um, not sure. It was Ed's secretary saying I had to drop everything and come to Ed's office immediately. Apparently, very urgent. No idea what it's about, but I'll drop you back at the suite.'

Duncan met me at the door of Ed's office and ushered me in. Ed was leaning against his desk, knuckles white as he gripped the edge; Harry was pacing up and down, looking ashen; Duncan slumped back into a chair, putting his hand to his head; while Ric stood staring out of the window as if he'd seen a ghost. I went to join him. The three Beverly Hills Police Department officers continued outlining the reason for their visit.

Raine Daysen had been murdered last night as she drove home from a movie premiere after-party. We looked at each other in utter disbelief.

'Oh. My. God. I had only said goodbye to her a couple of days ago,' I whispered to Ric.

'What the f*** happened?' growled Ed, staring at the most senior officer, Deputy Chief Noah Schofield. He told us what they knew at this point.

'She left the party in Hollywood shortly after midnight.

She was stopped at a red light at the intersection of Sunset Boulevard and Whittier Drive which, as you know is a quiet Beverly Hills residential street, though oftentimes used as a cut-through between Wilshire and Sunset. And that's where we believe she was shot.

'Whittier residents at the intersection called 911 and reported hearing gunshots in front of their homes. But one woman who called said she'd looked out of her bedroom window to see a Black Mercedes Coupe crashed into a street-light. She says she went down to help and found Ms Daysen slumped at the wheel, bleeding heavily from chest wounds.

'We got the call around twelve-thirty and radioed for the Beverly Hills Fire Department paramedics. When we arrived at the scene, one block up Whittier from Sunset, we saw Ms Daysen had been shot point blank in the chest, four times. She was barely alive, drifting in and out of consciousness. She was taken to Cedars-Sinai, where doctors fought to revive her, but died at ten minutes after one this morning. Christ knows how she did it, but she somehow made that left turn into Whittier before crashing.'

'God-damn-it. She was the last of the real old-school publicists,' snapped Harry, still pacing. 'She had old-fashioned values. She directed Academy Award campaigns for more than 100 films during her career, and had a work ethic that earned her the respect of her peers.'

'We've no clue as to why the shooting happened,' said Commander Ben Schwarb. 'We're trying to establish a motive. Whether it was just a random car robbery or whether the killer targeted her...'

'Yeah, we're right in the middle of awards season,' growled Ed.

'....and followed her from the after-party to the stop sign on Sunset at Whittier. He then must have walked up to her vehicle, tapped on the window and, as she let it down, shot her point blank. She didn't stand a chance.'

'Any insight you can give us will be appreciated,' continued Deputy Chief Noah Schofield. 'Mr Harrison, Mr Neumann, we'll keep you posted.'

'Just get the son-of-a-bitch who did this,' growled Ed.

Driving back to the suite, I ran over in my mind what I had just heard. I had never known anyone who had been murdered; it was too surreal to be true. At the suite, I was about to tell Dino and Lizzie the news when my phone rang. It was Ed, again. 'Get back to my office. NOW.'

I had no idea I was about to be royally hauled over the carpet.

Ed was incandescent. He paced back and forth between his desk and the floor-to-ceiling double windows in his office, every vein in his forehead throbbing with rage.

'What the f*** do you think you are doing?' he screamed at me. 'I've god-damn spent thousands of dollars on a First Class ticket to fly Daniel Eversleigh over to attend the Closing Night. You have the pick of the best Mercedes, Lincolns Town Cars and limos at your disposal. And yet I am told that you are driving Mr Eversleigh, a director, around in a f***-ing pick-up truck. How dare you. How the f*** dare you. Does your f***-ing brain need re-wiring? You'd better have a f***-ing good explanation for this.'

I sat in stunned silence as the velocity of Ed's wrath swept over me, though I knew the real reason for his anger. 'I'm sorry if it has upset you Ed, but …'

'You'd f***-ing better believe its f***-ing upset me,' he yelled.

'… but when Daniel first called me in the suite, when

he had recovered from his food poisoning, he asked me to go and pick him up from the hotel. There weren't any cars available at that *precise* moment. Lizzie and I *did* check. And I only had the Dodge so, rather than keep him waiting, I went over and picked him up in it.

'I did apologize to him and said that we had a Mercedes Coupe or Sedan available for his use while he was here, plus a driver.

'But he said he liked the pick-up because it reminded him of being on his farm in England. He said he was happy with me to do the driving and that he preferred the pick-up to a high-end vehicle, because it was more relaxed and fun.'

Ed stared at me as if I had just landed from another planet. 'Well lady, I can tell you I am NOT f***-ing *happy* with any of it. He is to be chauffeur-driven in a Mercedes from now on. Do I make myself clear?'

'Yes, of course.'

'As in crystal clear?'

'Yes. Sure. Sorry.'

I repaired to the suite where, jungle drums being as they are, everyone had heard about Raine's murder, but wanted to know why Ed had summoned me back; they knew that was never a good thing.

Dominic rushed over first, followed by Shane, Dino, Mike 2, Lizzie and Alexis from Print Traffic, who was searching for a couple of misplaced reel cans. Ric, by this time, had returned to LA and to his luxurious office suite on Wilshire Boulevard to handle the media calls regarding Raine's murder.

'What's going on?' asked a concerned looking Dominic, studying my downcast face; they all waited anxiously for my answer. As I was about to explain, Daniel sauntered over, ‘What’s the matter darling?’

I repeated, verbatim, what had just happened. Daniel looked livid, but did not say anything; collecting his scripts, he said he had some calls to make, which he would do at the hotel and would catch up with me later.

After several commiserating hugs and, dusting myself down, I returned to the current task in hand, but before I could get on with that, the next irritation rose to the surface. It transpired that several people, mostly the Theatre Operations staff, were gossiping that, because I had met Daniel in his hotel bedroom and he now often called me ‘darling’, we must be having an affair. Dino kindly alerted me to this, while Dominic nodded that yes, stupid as it was, it was doing the rounds.

‘Oh for God’s sake people,’ I wailed. ‘Let me explain. Firstly, yes, I did meet Daniel in his hotel bedroom. But that was because he was extremely ill when he arrived and I had to call out a doctor. If no one believes me, check with the hotel.

‘Secondly, in England it is very commonplace within the thespian community, and particularly in theatre, for everyone to call each other “darling” in the same way many of us do with our own friends. It does not mean we are having affairs with all of them. Thirdly, and for the record, no, I have not slept with him and no, we are not having an affair. OK?’

Dominic was the first to offer succour. ‘Hey, *we* know that. It’s just the other stupid Operations people. But if it gets back to Ed there will be fireworks, particularly after the car situation.’

‘Yeah, I know, but it’s all so stupid. Anyhow, I must get back to work. It’s Gay-La night boys.’

As if any of them had forgotten. Aside from the Awards

Gala and the Opening and Closing Nights, the Gay-La (a pun on Gala) is the biggest and most heavily subscribed-to party in town. All the boys – and a few girls – want to be there, to be seen, to get some action, and to heroically let their hair down and squeeze onto the postage stamp-sized dance floor to boogie like never before. Hosted by the amazing Bella DeBall – a giantess of a drag queen, glammed up to painful levels of glitter and *maquillage* – it is always held in the same venue and never finishes until five or six in the morning.

Hannah joined the group, having heard Daniel was in the suite. She was her usual breezy self.

'Hey, how are the Hollywood Hills today?'

'The Hollywood Hills are fine, thanks.'

'Are you sure?'

I looked quizzically at her. 'Unless you know something I don't?'

'Well, I just heard about Ed's outburst and wondered if you were OK. You know, most people would crumple at that. I know you're stronger, but it still must've stung?'

'Yep, it wasn't too pleasant, but I can handle Ed.'

My phone went again; this time it was Special Agent Jonas Reubens from the DEA.

'Hi Vanessa, it's Special Agent Reubens here. FBI Special Agent Nat Parker and I need to meet you urgently, to discuss strategy for the bust. We can be over at The Wyndham in twenny mins. How's that suit you? We'll need about thirty mins for the meeting and then you can get back to work. We've booked a guest room for privacy. Room 412. See you at the room in twenny...'

The line went dead before I could reply. 'Yeah, OK,' I muttered to myself.

Lizzie was holding court with her coterie of drivers, matching them to the VIP list, when Daniel walked back into the suite and came over to our desks.

'I've just had a word with Ed and I told him that I was very happy being driven around by you in a Dodge pick-up, and that it reminded me of when I had my farm in Somerset.'

I looked at him, my eyes widening, as he carried on, 'And I also told him that I was not happy with the fact that you had been balled out by him just because you were doing your job, albeit in a somewhat unconventional car.'

'Oh my God. He won't have liked that. What did he say?'

'You're right. He didn't like it. But I played the trump card, reminding him that I was the guest and you were just doing your job. I also told him that you had gone beyond the call of duty by getting a doctor out the evening I arrived and had even gone to the Pharmacy late that evening to collect my prescription.'

'Oh, and what did he say to that?'

'Well, he didn't know about it, obviously. But he was pleased that you had been so vigilant and let's just say that he's fine with everything now. He said if I really wanted to ride around town in a beat up old truck, I could…'

'It's not beat up!' I retorted.

'I told him it wasn't and he is relaxed about the whole thing now. But he did say that tomorrow night I am to be in "the right car" for both the arrival at the movie theatre and for going on to the Blumberg party.'

'Sure. We've already got a Mercedes Maybach allocated to you and Johnnie will be driving you again.'

'OK, so we're all sorted. Now, this evening I'd like to

see one of the foreign films that's tipped for an Oscar and I expect to be picked up from the hotel in the Dodge.'

'You got it. See you at six-thirty.'

The hotel guests waiting by the Concierge Desk for their cabs stood with jaws wide open as Daniel, immaculately attired in Gucci loafers, Tommy Hilfiger Madison Chino black trousers, a crisp white linen shirt and a deep grey silk/ linen mix Nehru-style jacket, opened the door to a not-quite-clean-enough pick-up truck and leapt in.

'Hey Daniel, how are you?' asked Diana, who felt she should be Daniel's chauffeur for the evening. 'Good to be back in a regular American vehicle again, huh?'

'Yes, it certainly is. And as I told Ed this afternoon, I rather enjoy riding around in the truck. It's a hell of a lot more normal than being ferried everywhere by limo and a driver.'

I had told Diana about my pasting from Ed and Daniel's subsequent conversation with him.

'Oh. My. God. I wish I'd been a fly on the wall. Nobody, but *nobody ever* questions Ed. He probably didn't know what'd hit him! But what can I say? The guy's a total control freak.'

I thought now was as good a time as any to put "the bust strat", as Special Agents Reubens and Parker called it, into play.

'Daniel, hope you don't mind, but a screenwriter friend of mine, Rob Palmer, and two of his friends are joining us for drinks later at Midnight Rescue. They're an intesting trio and Rob is dying to meet you. Midnight Rescue is a hugely popular joint with the LA crowd, especially producers, agents and development execs, so might also be useful for you. Would you mind?'

Diana frowned at me. 'Is Rob out of ….'

I interjected, winking at her. 'Yeah, the producers demanded a couple of re-writes, but they've finally let him out of the editing suite.'

CHAPTER TWENTY

Midnight Rescue's bar was heaving as Diana and I fought our way to the banquettes at the far end of the lounge, next to the ceiling-height open doors which led onto the terrace fire-pits; groups of young producers and studio execs huddled around the flames, sharing cigarettes, cocaine, Jack Daniels and gossip.

Rob appeared as soon as we had sat down. 'Hey, let's go outside to the fire. Javier and Manuel should be here in about five minutes. Where's Daniel Eversleigh?'

'He's having an early night, in preparation for the Closing Night tomorrow, and then the Blumberg party afterwards, which I don't think he really wants to go to. So, sorry, but you aren't going to meet him tonight. I'll work something out for tomorrow or the day after.'

Out of the corner of my eye I could see DEA agents Jonas Reubens and Darren Fischer, and FBI agents Nat Parker and Dirk Wynter, attempting to camouflage themselves by mingling with lone female drinkers at the bar. They needed to identify Javier Pajares and Manuel Sinalopéz so, at Rob's suggestion, we had hatched this plan in room 412. I caught Special Agent Jonas Reubens' eye and gave the signal – a flick back of my hair – to indicate that everything was on track. Javier and Manuel arrived as

Rob and I were walking towards the terrace and joined us there, followed by Diana with a tray of drinks.

'No idea what you guys want to drink, but we have margaritas, Dirty Martinis, beer and Jack Daniels. Should be something here to everyone's liking,' she trumped.

'Javier, Manuel, you haven't met Vanessa. She's been looking afer all the A-List who came in from LA for the Awards Gala, as well as 200-odd filmmakers from all over the world,' extolled Rob, as if he were pitching me for an audition. 'And she set up the hospitality suite, arranged all the goody bags and flew Olivia Lautner up here in a borrowed Lear jet. Isn't she something?'

'OK, honey, that's enough. You've got the job as my publicist,' I laughed. 'But it's really good to meet you guys at last. I've heard so much about you and I know Rob's had a great time on his trips to Mexico with you.'

Diana coughed loudly. 'Oh, I'm sorry,' I continued. 'I haven't introduced you to Diana Harmsworth, the festival's marketing director and a long-standing friend of mine. I'm staying at her house while I do this crazy gig.'

'Buenas noches,' said Manuel. 'Nice to meet you.'

'Hola,' grinned Javier. '*Gracias por las bebidas,* for the drinks. Next round's on us.'

We fell into an easy conversation about the economy, the best US TV shows, tourism to Mexico and, interestingly, the prevalence of drugs within the LA film industry, with Manuel nonchalantly saying, 'I hear supply cannot keep up with demand. The Tijuana cartel guards that supply route with a passion. And with more than a few *sicarios* and guns!'

'Is that so?' asked Rob, trying to mask a shaky voice. 'I wondered how it came in. All I ever have to do is go Zuma beach and meet my supplier. Dead easy.'

Agents Reubens, Parker, Wynter and Fischer had now brought themselves and their four female companions to the adjacent fire-pit as Rob turned to me, joking, 'Well, if I can't successfully pitch a script within the next two months, perhaps I'll switch careers. Do'ya think I'd make a good trafficker, sweatheart?'

We all laughed, but my heart was in my mouth; I had just glimpsed a semi-automatic pistol in the inside top pocket of Manuel's leather jacket.

'So, Javier, Manuel, are you both coming to the Closing Night party tomorrow? It's at the Hilton, a huge buffet-style affair around the pool, with plenty of food, alcohol, creative people, music and dancing. Be a fun night.'

'Sure, we're planning on being there,' said Manuel, 'but we also have a party on the outskirts of town that we have to be at. Rob's coming too, so I guess you can also.'

I frowned at Rob. 'Oh, I didn't know you had to be somewhere else,' I said in a loud voice, standing up, as if to get more drinks, but so that the agents could hear. 'Where is it and what time?'

The last official day of the festival. How any of us had got through it in one piece I do not know, but here we were at the final furlong.

The PR desk was, by now, thinning out, with only Shane, his assistant and Dominic left to handle the few remaining media interviews today and the red carpet event this evening. The Opening and Closing Night movies always had their own red carpet to ensure that either the director, producer, screenwriter or lead actor was suitable fêted.

Shane ambled over to my desk. 'Hey Vanessa. Who's

Daniel Eversleigh's handler?'

'He doesn't have one.'

'Well, he's on the carpet tonight, so he'll have to have one. If someone hasn't been assigned, then I guess it's going to be you.'

'Oh, OK. I'll do it. Put my name down. What time do you need him?'

'Screening starts at six. Allow fifteen minutes for his intro speech on stage, fifteen for getting into the theatre and to his seat. We've got about twenty media already accredited, mix of print, digital and broadcast, so I guess we'll need him at the start of the carpet at five sharp. OK?'

Harry strode into the room as I was nodding 'yeah' to Shane. A hushed silence ensued.

'I'm offering a $100,000 reward to anyone who provides information to the Beverly Hills Police which leads to the conviction of the killer. Raine Daysen was a long and dear friend to Ed and me, and to the festival. We want her killer caught and behind bars for the rest of their miserable life.'

Charlie Rutherford was hovering in the lobby clutching two goody bags when I arrived to collect Daniel. 'Hey gorgeous, haven't seen you for a while.'

'Are you coming to the Closing Night movie and party?' I asked.

He tilted his head to one side and laughed. 'Stupid question darling girl. Of course I am coming to party. It would be rude not to come and drink the bars dry. Can't make the movie though, but Daniel has promised me a screener. What time do you plan on getting to the Hilton?'

'Erm, guess around nine by the time I've ensured Daniel's driver gets him off to the Blumberg party. I don't think he really wants to go to it, but he's had his summons!'

Daniel appeared, looking resplendent in a Ralph Lauren Park Avenue tuxedo over a pleated white wing-collar shirt, also by Ralph Lauren, complemented by a dove-grey silk cummerbund and bow tie. Charlie kissed me on the cheek as he turned away. 'OK darling, see you later.'

'*V-e-r-y* dashing!' I exclaimed. 'You'll have all the ladies that lunch swooning at the party!'

The Concierge threw back the entrance doors for us, simultaneously clicking his fingers for our driver; a gleaming black Mercedes Maybach purred to a halt as he stepped forward to open the rear passenger door for his star guest.

Feigning surprise, Daniel turned to me, 'What! No truck tonight Vanessa?'

'Oh right. You thought you could roll up to the red carpet in a Dodge pick-up?'

'Well, it would have been different, and given everyone something to Tweet about!'

We climbed into the gleaming $450,000-worth car and set off on the short journey to the cinema; at five o'clock precisely, we were at the main entrance and pulling up at the start of the red carpet. Searchlights rotated, television crews directed their Outside Broadcast cameras towards the car, wire news photographers' cameras flashed, local media reporters and photographers jockeyed for the best positions on the steps leading up to the cinema and on the entrance patio itself – while the paparazzi outgunned them all, shouting 'Daniel, Daniel, this way', as he stepped out of the Maybach and into near-blinding floodlight.

Daniel dutifully walked slowly along the carpet, stopping to be interviewed or photographed when asked or prompted by Shane. We both shadowed him and I could see from the look on his face that he was not enjoying any of this; by the time he got to the end of the carpet he was visibly uncomfortable – a situation not helped by the fact that Diana was waiting for him with her camera and she was damn well not leaving until she had *her* picture.

Duncan and Hannah were waiting for him at the main entrance and, after pats on shoulders and strategically-placed air-kisses, ushered him through the VIP-cordoned area to meet some of the festival Board directors. Spotting Ed, I could not resist going over and assuring him that Daniel *had* arrived in a Maybach. 'It's still outside. Go check if you want to.'

He gave me a withering look, saying, patronizingly, '*Thank* you Vanessa.'

The audience, already seated, was impatient for the proceedings to start. A drum roll heralded the start of the show as Ed – with his customary *élan* – and Duncan ascended the stage to begin their introductions.

'The movie you are about to see is the US premiere of the directorial debut of an actor with whom I am sure you are all familiar. He has been entertaining us in movies and on TV for nearly three decades, he has worked with some of the biggest names in the business on both sides of the Atlantic and has delighted audiences with his take on the classic British period genre.

'His latest project, which recently opened in England, has already garnered great reviews. But I shall let him take to the stage to tell you the storyline and how he came to write and direct it.

'Ladies and Gentlemen, it is our great pleasure that he has been able to take time out of his hectic schedule and be with us tonight. Mr. Daniel Eversleigh.'

A resounding applause greeted Daniel as he skipped up

the steps with that innate air of charm, combined with a slight reserve, that marked him out as the quintessential Englishman.

With the spotlight firmly on him and his star-dust delicately sprinkled around the room, he walked to the microphone in the centre of the stage and proceeded to enthrall the gathering with his repartee.

'Have a good time,' I said to Daniel as the Maybach pulled away from the kerb and joined the line of limousines snaking their way from the cinema out onto the main boulevard and in the direction of the Blumberg estate. 'I'll see you tomorrow.'

Diana roared up in her SUV, shouting urgently through the passenger window, 'Hey, c'mon. It's time to party.'

We drove through the city to the Hilton and, eschewing the line for Valet Parking, parked the SUV in an adjacent hotel's car park as if we were its guests. By the time we had taken the short-cut through the gardens of both hotels and reached the Hilton's floodlit pool – around which the Closing Night party was taking place – the lines for the bar and food stations were already long.

'Bar first, food later,' instructed Diana as we scanned the landscape for the shortest line. The hotel had done a superb job on transforming the pool and surrounding area into a Mardi Gras-themed party. A jazz ensemble greeted guests as they entered through an archway illuminated by theatre-style light bulbs; waiters and waitresses in beaded masks and feather boas roller-skated along the pathways scattering streamers and confetti over guests; huge ice sculptures bedecked each corner of the Olympian-sized pool, while a jazz quartet and a Mariachi band played at each end of the food stations.

Hundreds of tiny yellow, white and pink fairy lights adorned the Jacaranda and Tamarisk trees. Giant Roman-style flame torches lined the pool and the terrace balustrades; large, scented Church pillar candles lined the garden pathways and steps to the hotel's rear entrance, and smaller votive candles perched on the edges of the bar and food stations.

The enormous bars, each one four trestle tables long to accommodate as many thirsty revellers as possible, were draped in Stars and Stripes flags, while the food stations were covered in crisp white linen and scattered with rose and gardenia petals.

Clusters of tall bar-style tables, each seating four persons and layered in soft white, red and blue voiles, were scattered around the pool and on the terraces; the bushes in the immediate gardens were liberally doused in gold and silver glitter stars; the pathways were imprinted with oversized Walk of Fame-style stars with the names of the A-List celebrities who had attended this year's Awards Gala, while the festival logo was hologrammed onto the pool.

I noticed Xavier Torres with several other Argentinean and Brazilian filmmakers, and so went over to say 'hi' and ask if everything was OK. He was his usual charming self, saying he had had a wonderful visit, but was 'looking forward to going home tomorrow'. I confirmed we had a chauffered car to take him to LA in the morning. He thanked me while flashing his stupendously sexy smile that was so utterly mesmerizing.

Hunger setting in, Diana and I joined a food station line where we bumped into Alexis from Print Traffic – still in a state of high anxiety as she now had the unenviable task of ensuring all the reel cans were shipped back to their respective origins – and photographer Annie Highmount, who had been covering the Awards Gala for Getty Images, for whom she freelanced.

'Hi,' I said, giving both of them a hug. 'Haven't seen either of you for a while.'

'No, head down sorting out all the bleeping reels to go back,' Alexis said wearily.

'Same,' said Annie. 'In my case all the Gala pictures that Getty didn't use from the first wiring. I also got called back to LA to do a couple of jobs, including a premiere and after-show party. Just got back yesterday to cover tonight. Your director friend from England is rather good news, isn't he?' she grinned, as Dominic and Shane joined us.

'Oh God, not you as well,' Dominic cried in mock exasperation.

'But he still doesn't beat George, whom I photographed at a party last month,' intoned Annie, as if to hold onto the thought for as long as possible. 'No one beats him in my book.'

Grabbing two tables by the pool and pulling them together, we swapped our empty margarita glasses for Dirty Martinis and ginger-beer vodkas as we all debated what the fuss was *really* about George Clooney.

'I don't get it,' I said. 'Give me Kevin Bacon or Bradley Cooper any day.'

'Well, here he comes!' quipped Diana, as Rob walked towards us, followed by Javier and Manuel, both of whom fervently eyed the landscape.

'Hi guys, come join us,' I commanded, relieving a passing waiter of his entire drinks tray. 'You know Diana, but you haven't met Alexis, who's in charge of getting all the film reels here, and Annie Highmount who works for Getty Images.'

I knew it was not my imagination when I saw Manuel shudder at the mention of Getty Images.

'Do you mind if we work the venue for a while? We need to help Rob pitch his script, don't we Rob?' he said fixing intently on Rob. 'But we'll have a quick margarita now that we're here.'

'Hey, let me get a shot of all of us,' said Annie innocently, as she reached for her camera and began to focus.

'NO!' barked Manuel, swiping at her so hard that the camera went flying into the pool. 'No pictures. Never.'

I looked at Rob, who looked away, unable to meet my eyes, as Annie exploded.

'You stupid arse, what the f*** do you think you're doing. That's $5,000-worth of camera you're gonna be paying for, not to mention compensation for the shots on it I've just lost. That's my work you've just ruined, arsehole. I only wanted a shot of us. What the f*** is the matter with you?'

Spotting a sinister-looking guy in shades, wearing black gloves and carrying an over-sized bag, approaching us – whom I figured must be Manuel's bodyguard – I quickly calmed down Annie and said I was sure that Manuel would pay for the camera, as I stared at him and then Rob for affirmation.

'Sure, I'll pay for it,' growled Manuel. 'C'mon guys, we got stuff to do. See you later Vanessa. And sorry about the camera.'

Rob apologised to Annie, kissed me quickly on the cheek and said he would see us all later.

We had hardly finished eating before the tables were cleared away to make room for dancing. 'This is going to be interesting,' squealed Alexis. 'We're perilously close to the pool and no doubt everyone is now pretty hammered.'

'Let the show begin,' laughed Shane. 'This *will* be interesting.'

As the DJ fired up the turntables and Bill Medley and Jennifer Warnes' voices drifted across the pool in incremental volume, ringing out the first line to the iconic Dirty Dancing theme tune, guests – straights and gays in equal number – leapt up and began their own versions of Dirty Dancing. As the night progressed, a clearly refreshed DJ had fast-tracked his way through forty years of the best soft rock and, by the time the Stones had belted out 'Jumping Jack Flash', followed by Bob Seger's 'Hollywood Nights' and Bruce Springsteen's 'Dancing in the Dark' – both highly apposite songs at this point several guests had salsa'd themselves straight into the pool.

Though past midnight, it was still very warm and the pool was a refreshing respite. So many people were in it that the hotel staff had no option but to acknowledge the fact that it was now a pool party and serve us drinks in the pool albeit, for safety reasons, they demanded that we use acrylic glassware.

As the guests began to thin out, it was easier to see who was around. I was delighted to see that The Lesbian had not been invited to the Blumberg party and a brief moment of *schadenfreude* was provided by Diana discreetly jutting out her foot and tripping The Lesbian into the pool, destroying the unusually coiffed hair and ensuring her mascara ran south like a raging river.

We partied on for another hour – a much needed chance to let our hair down – before calling it a day at around one a.m., just as Rob, Javier and Manuel returned.

'Thank God the pressure will be off tomorrow,' said Alexis.

'OK for some,' I riposted. 'It's going to be full-on in

the suite tomorrow with the airport and LA runs. And we're doing breakfast again, so another bloody six-thirty a.m. start.'

'Well honey, I hate to shatter any illusions of sleep, but we have a party we *have* to go to. Remember?' said Rob, as Manuel cut in. '*Hola. Si,* you both come to my friend's party, Rob *especially*.'

I looked nervously at Rob, then turned to give Diana a hug, holding her tightly for what seemed several minutes.

'Thank you my dearest friend, for everything. For your friendship, your faith in me to do this utterly crazy gig, and your support. And for putting me up and letting me use Sam's Dodge. I love you.'

'Oh for God's sake Vanessa, what's up? You're talking like a crazy person, as if we're not going to see each other again. I'll see you tomorrow in the suite. Careful driving on the Freeway.'

I mawkishly watched her stumble along the path, wondering if, indeed, I would ever see my old friend again. Rob put his arm around my shoulder, whispering, 'C'mon Vanessa, let's get this done. Are you still OK to do it?'

'NO! I'm suddenly feeling s***-scared and have a really bad feeling about this Rob. Can't we just leave now and let the DEA and FBI deal with Manuel and Javier at the party?'

'Nah, we gotta do it. If it helps, I'm f***ing s***-ing myself too. But whatever the outcome Vanessa, I want you to know I really dig you. And if we come through this, I hope you'll stay on for a while, so we can have some normal time together?'

'Yeah, that'd be great. OK, let's get this over and done with.'

Manuel was impatient. 'C'mon man,' he sniped at Rob.

'We gotta go. Change of party venue, bit further away than originally planned. Javier's gone to get the Hummer and the birthday boy's present.'

I tried not to look at Rob, for fear Manuel would sense something was up, but I was panic-struck that the venue had been changed and that the DEA/FBI would be at the location Manuel had originally cited.

'Where's the party, and how far away?' I casually asked Manuel, my heart about to explode. 'I have to be at work at six-thirty, so I hope it's not too far away?'

'My friend's ranch at Rancho Sante Fe', he replied coldly. 'You don't have to come. To be frank, I don't want you there, but Rob said he wouldn't come unless you did. And I want Rob there. We'll get you back in time for work.'

'Does your friend's ranch have a name? Just in case you guys decide to crash and I have to call for a car to bring me back.'

He had not yet suspected anything. 'It's Rancho Los Pinos on El Secreto. It's a secret place, hidden in the hills, so a taxi won't find it anyway,' he laughed scornfully. 'You might as well just stay with us tonight. Rob'll get you back in the morning.'

He had assumed I would not know where Rancho Sante Fe was. As we hastily walked to the car park, I made my apologies about needing the Bathroom. Dashing to the Restrooms, I shot into a cubicle – having first checked under the doors that no-one else was in there – and called DEA Special Agent Jonas Reubens.

'Change of location,' I whispered urgently. 'Party now at a ranch called Los Pinos on El Secreto at Rancho Santa Fe, which is *not* on the outskirts of town! It's a good two-three hours' drive away. What do I do?'

'Stick to the plan. I'm guessing Manuel will have

Javier's plane to fly down. We'll fly down in the FBI jet and set up base nearby. Don't worry Vanessa, we're on board.'

'OK, we're leaving the Hilton now. Please, please be there.'

Re-joining the others in Javier's Hummer, we roared off into the night; my heart thumping so loudly I was convinced the whole city heard it.

What the hell had I signed up to?

CHAPTER TWENTY ONE

We landed at a small airfield just outside Rancho Santa Fe – an exclusive community near San Diego, often billed as one of the world's most desirable and expensive pieces of real estate – at one-forty-five a.m. Awaiting us were two stocky, menacing-looking, men wearing camouflage bullet-proof vests, each with AK47 and M4 carbine assault rifles slung over their shoulders and both carrying Glock semi-automatic handguns.

'Hola amigo,' cried Manuel, jumping out of the plane to hug one of them. *'Grazias por venir a nuestro encuentro.'*

'What's he saying?' I whispered to Rob.

'Thanks for coming to meet us.'

'Quick, quick. We go,' urged Manuel. 'Ramos, the present for our host is following with my men. They should be at the compound in thirty minutes.'

Climbing the hill roads, we eventually came upon a pair of heavy wrought-iron gates, set within a never-ending massive twenty-foot high wall. Punching in the security number, Ramos drove us into the compound. The floodlights – judiciously erected all over the grounds, themselves screened by pine, eucalyptus and calabash trees and so well hidden, as Manuel had said – portrayed a sprawling, sumptuous estate, the centre-piece of which was a magnificent house flanked by two wings.

Opulent did not begin to describe the new venue, it was sumptuous in the extreme; it's only vague nod to a ranch being that it sported a stable complex with six stalls, riding arena and grooms' quarters at one end of the fourteen-acre estate, which featured expanses of manicured lawns, tennis courts, vast waterfalls and an enormous infinity pool. CCTV cameras were everywhere, to record every movement.

Approaching the house, Ramos scrambled his phone and called the host to say Manuel was here with his guests. As we ascended the marble steps up to the imposing, open teak doors, a tall, distinguished-looking figure awaited us in the entrance hall – our host, Pablo.

He flung one arm around Manuel. '*Hola amigo*. How are you and have you brought my birthday present? I hope it's what I want! And who are these?'

'Ah, this is my good friend Javier Pajares, his good friend Rob Palmer from LA, and Rob's girlfriend, Vanessa. She is working at the film festival I told you about, where Rob has also been, trying to sell ... his movie script. And your present, *amigo*, will be here momentarily. It's coming with my trusted commander.'

'*Bienvenida*. Welcome. Come through. Ramos, when Manuel's men arrive, have them put my birthday present in the main tack room, but bring four random packages to the wine cellar. I'll test it there.'

As he led us to where the main party was taking place, Rob hung back, whispering to his upheld wrist, 'Stable block'. I turned to him. 'I'm wired,' he whispered, as Pablo ushered us all into a cavernous room with a twenty-five-feet-high trussed-beam ceiling, solid teak flooring, magnificent open fireplace with marble surround, huge gilt-framed mirrors on the walls, open doors to both wings and double-height folding glass doors out onto the pool patio.

Revellers of all ages and description were either draped over the couches, propping up the walls or caressing the Persian rugs dotting the floor. Among the guests – most of whom were either stoned out of their minds or overly-refreshed by Jack Daniels – were the requisite *sicarios*, themselves having evidently indulged in the party's bowls of 'blow'.

'Margaritas, martinis, champagne or beer, *amigos*?' asked our genial host, who turned out to be Pablo Dieguez Escovedo, one of Mexico's most ruthless drug dealers and money launderers, and a key ally of the Sinalopéz cartel. We dutifully took what we wanted from the waiter's tray, before Pablo produced a long wooden box of pre-rolled joints, grass and cocaine – the latter looking identical to the 'blow' that had been in my Dodge.

'Take some, it is *el mejor,* the best. *El verey mejor,*' said Pablo, as Manuel and Javier placed a line on the back of their hands and snorted, arching their heads back appreciatively. To keep up the pretence, Rob also took a line while I asked for a joint.

'You don't *participar*?, partake?' asked Pablo.

'Couple of times in London, but it doesn't do anything for me, just makes my teeth go numb. And that's a very expensive way of having a numb mouth,' I laughed nervously. 'Maybe later, if there's any left!'

Ramos appeared, beckoning to Pablo and Manuel. 'Come,' said Pablo. 'We go downstairs.'

Following Pablo through the en-suite family room, with its gigantic ninety-two-inch wall-mounted TV, to the east wing, we walked through an equally cavernous kitchen, replete with its own elevator to the underground garage, and down a winding staircase to a wine cellar-cum-dining room.

‘Wow!’, whistled Rob. ‘There must be at least six-hundred bottles here.’

‘Actually, *amigo*, there are eight-hundred and many, many fine wines,’ said Pablo.

Ramos appeared with Manuel’s ‘commander’, a brutish-looking man called Carlos, also equipped with the regulation armoury. They carried a large box and placed random samples of its contents on the table, carefully cutting the transparent bags with glinting knives before dispensing small amounts into four bowls.

I nudged Rob, whispering. ‘Is that the same cocaine? How’d they get it?’

Pablo took four silver spoons out of the table drawer and deftly poured a line at the front of his left hand and snorted loudly as he jutted his head back; he repeated this task, putting the second line at the back of his left hand and the same for his right hand, before relaxing back into the chair.

We all waited. He smiled at Manuel. ‘That, *amigo*, is *excelente*. Is all the 67.5 kilograms (149 pounds) here?

‘*Si. Todo acqui*. All here. And this is only the first consignment.’

‘*Muy bueno*. Very good. Ramos, the payment. Now that business is done, let us enjoy ourselves.’

Rob and I hovered between the main room and the firepits on the pool patio, anxiously awaiting the cavalry while trying not to appear overly nervous. The night was still, almost eerily quiet and, aside from the revellers’ inebriated chatter and Manuel’s *sicarios*’ raucous banter, all that could be heard was the neighing of the horses in the stable complex. Rob’s mobile pinged; a text from DEA Special Agent Reubens simply stated, “in five. Go to point.”

'They're here. Better get out of the way sweetheart. It's gonna kick-off.'

Pretending to re-fill our margaritas, we inched our way through the main room towards the kitchen; the plan had been to go to the garage and wait until it was all over. Just as we had made it to the kitchen, Manuel and Carlos appeared, ominously blocking our way.

'Going somewhere *amigo*?' asked Manuel, threateningly.

'No, we just wanted some water. Vanessa has to be at work in three hours, so we wanted to clear our heads.'

'No, no, come back to the party. Pablo wants to celebrate with us. We take you now.'

The eerie quiet outside was suddenly pierced by the sound of the crack of gunshots. Grabbing our arms, Manuel and Carlos pushed us back towards the main room. More shots rang out as panicked, then angry, voices issued urgent commands, while Pablo's and Manuel's *sicarios* bolted grenade launchers onto the underside of their M4 carbine assault rifles and clipped cartidge magazines to the rifles.

'What the hell is going on?' cried Rob, in method acting perfection.

'We've been f***ing *reventado*! Busted!' screamed Manuel. 'You're coming with us.'

The volley of fire, and counter-fire, increased exponentially as the FBI snipers attached 30-round box magazines to their M4 carbines and unleashed a barrage of firepower with deadly, supersonic bullets as human screams and petrified horses' snorts simultaneously pierced the night air. It came from the stable complex and, through the open doors to the patio, we could see flashes of a green hue from the FBI and DEA agents' helmet-mounted night-vision goggles interspersed with the yellow spark of gun-fire. The colours were making their way towards the house as Pablo screamed at his *sicarios* to 'f***ing finish them.'

Now shaking with terror, I grabbed Rob's shirt. 'We're going to die, aren't we?'

'Only if Pablo suspects me before the agents reach the house. Hey, it'll be alright.'

'Which piece of s*** betrayed me?' an incandescent Pablo screamed. 'I'll cut your f***ing head off here and now.'

The FBI snipers, now near the front of the house, unleashed another volley of bullets – travelling faster than the speed of sound, they hit the doors and windows before we had even heard the 'sonic boom' of the shot – as the *sicarios* reacted with equal ferocity with grenades, assault rifles and Glock handguns.

As the approaching agents fired through the doors and windows, shards of glass, mirrors, crockery and splintered wood rained down on us like a snow-storm. Rob and I dived under a mahogany table behind a huge sofa and, as the crossfire intensified and bloodied bodies dropped to the floor, he tried to shield me with his body.

'We gotta get out of this. We'll crawl to the fireplace and then out by the hall door. C'mon Vanessa, this is no time to freeze.'

Two bullets smacked into the table, a third ricocheted off the wall into Rob, hitting him in the shoulder. I could not hold back the scream, 'Oh God. *Help, help.*' But no-one came as a sound like a swarm of angry bees enveloped us as magazine rounds constantly pounded the room.

I pulled off my shirt and wrapped it tightly around Rob's shoulder and upper arm to try to stem the bleeding; after what seemed an age but, in reality, was only a few minutes, the crossfire suddenly ceased and I heard a triumphant cry.

'We got them!' FBI and DEA Special Agents Nat Parker and Jonas Reubens chorused, as I saw two bodies being dragged along the floor – those of Pablo Dieguez Escovedo and Manuel Sinalopéz.

'They're still alive. Get a medic here NOW! We need to keep them this way!'

'Hey, we're here, under the table,' I screamed. 'Rob's been hit. Help us.'

Two San Diego Police Department helicopters hovered overhead, their floodlights trained on the three emergency ambulences, as medics labelled body bags – which included Javier Pajares – before pushing them into one ambulence, along with numerous *sicario* fatalities; a second took Pablo Dieguez Escovedo and Manuel Sinalopéz, while the third one took Rob and a couple of injured FBI and DEA agents to the ER room at the nearby Scripps La Jolla hospital.

'How did you guys get in?' I asked FBI Special Agent Nat Parker.

'We've long suspected Pablo Dieguez Escovedo as being a key Sinalopéz distributor, but never had hard evidence or realistic intel to grab him. But we've had close surveillance on this property for six months and knew there was a separate, private road into it which came into the stable complex.

'And thanks to Rob, we've now got both the Sinalopéz cartel's key supplier for southern California and one of their most senior enforcers. The Sinalopéz won't be happy with that and there'll be retribution, which is why you can't see Rob until we've got him into Witness Protection.'

'Another question. Was that the cocaine from my Dodge that Manuel had? And how did he get it?'

Special Agent Nat Parker smiled. 'We put it back in the Dodge as soon as you got to the suite the next morning, to make it look like you were never stopped, so that Javier could pick it up as planned. Couldn't risk Manuel thinking we were on to him.'

Police formalities completed, we drove to the waiting FBI jet to take us back. I had to be at work in two hours.

The drivers for the key filmmaker guests came and went, collecting car keys and briefing sheets from Lizzie and myself. I wanted to catch Daniel before he checked-out.

'Hi, how was the Blumberg party and what time are you planning on leaving? I've extended Check-Out for you, in case you wanted to leave after lunch.'

'Thanks, but I need to get to LA fairly quickly, so I'm planning on leaving in about thirty minutes. The party was OK, probably not as much fun as yours, but I met some interesting people.'

'Good. Well I can't let you leave without saying goodbye, so I'll pop over to the hotel in half-an-hour. See you in the lobby.'

Leaving Lizzie and Dino on the carousel of drivers and hotel check-outs, I drove to The Four Seasons; Daniel was already at the Front Desk when I arrived.

'I'll take care of that,' I said, relieving him of his guest bill. 'Are you all set?'

'Yes, got everything. It's been great and thanks for everything you've done. I'm sure going to Pharmacies at night for drugs is not in your job description, but thank you.'

'It's my pleasure and all part of the service. Johnnie is driving you back to LA, though I'm afraid I could only swing a Mercedes S-Class Sedan and not a Maybach. Enjoy the rest of your time on the coast and I'll send you an email when I get back to the UK.'

His brow furrowed. 'Ah, you've forgotten that I have all your London contact details,' I teased. He leant forward and kissed me on the cheek. 'Sure, send me an email, be delighted to help.'

Everyone in the suite was de-mob happy apart from Shane, who had been commanded by Ed to get the 'wrap' press release out on the wire in order to hype this year's record attendance and box office revenue. He sat at the Media Desk furiously thumping his keyboard – ' … the largest ticket generating revenue film festival in the country, with audience figures topping 150,000 and box office revenue of more than $1.55 million.'

He called Duncan. 'Just sent you and Ed the proposed wrap release. Can you let me have your approval soonest, so that I can get it over to Associated Press, the LA Times and the trades within the hour.'

The rest of the day was 'take-down'. In the midst of the mayhem, Anna arrived with large red envelopes and handed them out. I opened mine with a degree of trepidation.

"It's All Over Bar The Shouting" headlined the invitation to the annual post-festival staff party at Duncan's house the following evening. "Dress: Optional. Bottles: No Need. Be there or Be ****-ed", it read.

'You coming Vanessa? Need to know numbers for food,' Anna commanded. 'Oh, and wear a swimsuit under your clothes. The pool tends to get a bit crowded by the end of the evening, if you understand what I mean!'

'Sure I'm coming. But why isn't it tonight?' Anna gave

me a pitying look.

'Remember something called wrap reports? They have to be done by tomorrow latest and so this is a bribe. No wrap, no party. And everyone would be way too hung-over tomorrow to write a decent report if we partied tonight.'

'Hello Hollywood Hills,' trilled Hannah as she negotiated her way past towering stacks of reel cans and vodka boxes lining the route from her office to what had been Guest Services. 'Time for our own impromptu staff party. We're meeting at Midnight Rescue in fifteen. Come along.'

'Sounds a plan. Can Dino and Lizzie come?' I asked. 'And Diana?'

'Sure, the more the better.'

Kicking the last of the beer and wine boxes into the kitchen area, I called Diana. 'Party time. We're meeting at Midnight Rescue in fifteen. See you there.'

The bar was already packed with Happy Hour devotees in full verbal Howitzer-style mode when we arrived. I glanced around to see where the group were; they had amassed at one end of the U-shaped bar, with tequila shots lined up to 'chase down' the Dirty Martinis as our "festival tiaras and tantrums" debriefing began – the highs, the lows, the bitching, general moans, positive suggestions, reports of back-biting, innuendos – the lot!

It was going to be a night of hard partying.

It seemed very strange walking into the office with Diana the next morning. It was *the last* day of work, a day designated purely as Wrap Report Day – a warts-and-all summary of our specific roles, our assigned staff and how improvements could be made for next year. I sat down at my desk and fired up the computer; how incongruous, I thought, that here we were, having just finished one of the biggest and most glamorous film festivals in the USA and we were surrounded by saucepans – for they still had not been cleared away since the torrential rainstorm ten days earlier.

There was a template to follow – primary remit, sponsorship achieved, areas of the role to be done by another department, internal relationships, departmental interaction, final budgets, project deadlines, recommendations for both the specific role and the wider scope of the festival for the next year and, finally, summary.

Each section had ample boxes in which to add comments and recommendations. The final budget sheets – actual spend versus allocated budget for airfares, hotels, cars, celebrity wallpaper and celebrity incidentals – would be the most taxing section to complete, but I knew that, at the end of the day, this would be the *only* page that Ed and Harry would be interested in.

I told Dino and Lizzie to do their report minus the budgets, and that we would amortize them in the afternoon. As I stared at my blank document, I contemplated whether I should be diplomatic – and thereby somewhat sanitized – or, tell it as it really needed to be told. I decided upon the latter.

After four hours, my twelve-page forensically-thorough 'publish and be damned' report was completed. I had fired from the hip, but only because I felt that it was the only way for the person doing the job next year to remain sane. I smiled as I glanced over some of the Summary bullet points – need a secretary/admin assistant, increase department staffing levels, do not bother with celebrity wallpaper, younger volunteers needed who could 'hit the decks running' and internal communication needs to be stepped up.

The one overall bullet-point summary of my role was that, to do everything seamlessly, as opposed to constant defcon mode, it required three people – one for setting up the suite, one for the Awards Gala and one for Ed's cocktail party and goody bags.

'Not that that will happen,' crowed Dino and Lizzie disparagingly, as my phone flashed.

FBI and DEA Special Agents Nat Parker and Jonas Reubens, together with a third, distinguished-looking man, were waiting for me in one of the Wyndham's meeting rooms.

Jonas Reubens greeted me warmly. 'Hi Vanessa, good to see you looking so well, all things considered. This is Assistant State Attorney Mason Quinn, who'll brief us on the next steps.'

Mason Quinn pushed back his chair. 'We'd like to thank you and Rob for assisting us in pulling off a major bust. As you know, we've long suspected Pablo Dieguez Escovedo to be a key distributor for the Sinalopéz and now we have him. And stopped a major supply route.

'If it hadn't been for the twist of fate that you were stopped on your way home from the festival with the Sinalopéz cocaine, then we wouldn't be here now. Pablo and Manuel are looking at ten to fifty years in prison and a $50 million fine. If Rob hadn't turned state witness, he'd be looking at a $10 million fine and a prison term of twenty.'

DEA Special Agent Jonas Reubens cut in. '67.5 kilograms, or 149 pounds. A street value of $1,890,000. And that was just the first consignment. This was a major operation and the department is very grateful to Rob and you, for your support.'

'We've got him into Witness Protection and he's been taken upstate,' confirmed Mason Quinn. 'He has a new identity, a house, car, social security number, the lot. You can see him in about a week, but only under supervision of one of our guys. Understand?'

I looked at FBI Special Agent Nat Parker, who had not yet spoken. 'Vanessa, I can't gloss over this, but you need to be careful while you're in California. The cartels are notorious for revenge on *informantes* and their aides. We'll watch your back 'til you go home, but be alert at all times.'

I took a long, deep breath.

In keeping with the festival's genre of international cinema, Duncan had spent the day transforming his home into a mini 'Casablanca'. A large, traditional-style Kidal tent dominated one end of the pool terrace, replete with low sofas, leather pouffes, hand-woven Moroccan rugs and carved wood screens.

Tall Roman flame-torch candles lined both the driveway to the pool's side gate and highlighted the four corners of the pool, while smaller ones lined the flowerbeds and the Jacuzzi. Jacaranda trees, ablaze with fairy lights, were adorned with glass lanterns; up-lighters dotted the flower beds along the outside walls, and groups of candles provided both lighting for the buffet and bar tables, as well as tethering the voile cloths in the warm evening breeze. Giant Bang & Olufsen speakers flanked the doors to the kitchen, and cotton bar-stool cushions lined the edge of the pool.

The tables, groaning under the weight of a sumptuous buffet and bar, were more than adequately stocked for the invasion of an eclectic group of individuals – all of whom were needing much succour after an exceptionally gruelling eight weeks. An array of terracotta pots filled with bougainvillea, gardenia, winter jasmine and nicotania, completed the tableaux.

'Hey Duncan, this looks great!' I kissed him on the cheek. 'To be honest, I wasn't sure many of us would even make it to the finishing line. This is so much needed, so thank you.'

'It's a pleasure, darlin'. You all deserve it.'

We certainly did. Kicking off shoes, we unwound with heroic quantities of margaritas, wine, martinis, vodka and beers. As the 'intravenous line' of alcohol began to anaesthetize us, inhibitions were shed and I realized why Anna had instructed me to wear a swimming costume. By nine o'clock everyone – Duncan included – had been pushed into the pool; there was nothing else for it except to eat our supper in it, using the four inflatable beds as 'tables', though not terribly successfully.

As the evening wore on, work colleagues who had simply been that became friends, while those already friends forged stronger, lasting relationships. Sitting in the Jacuzzi at the head of the pool with Duncan, JP, Alexis and Hannah, I asked JP to pinch my arm.

'Why?'

'Because I want to know that this isn't a dream, that it all really happened. Because I can't quite believe it has all happened!'

'Oh, it all happened,' he laughed. 'And it will happen all over again next year. The same traumas, the same meltdowns, the same craziness. Never changes.'

'Want to do it again next year darlin?' asked Duncan, in mock disbelief.

'Not sure. I guess it's probably like childbirth. You'd forget the pain in about six months!'

We raised our glasses to the culmination of another artistically- and financially-successful festival – and for getting through it in one piece.

JP, having decided he was the DJ *du nuit*, dexterously flipped a succession of Arrowsmith, Coldplay, Journey, Rolling Stones, Bowie and the Eagles onto the record-decks and cranked up the volume. Alexis led the dancing, swiftly joined by everyone else cramming onto the terrace to rock, roll and party like it was 1999 again.

Duncan, Diana and I remained in the pool, for we were in no hurry to be parted from our Dirty Martinis.

'Have you enjoyed this madness?' asked Duncan, clinking his glass with mine.

'You mean the whole festival or just bits of it?'

'The whole god-damn show darlin!'

'You know, there were days – the three right before the festival started – when I thought I physically couldn't go on. But adrenaline kicks in and you keep going. And you were right about many of the LA publicists, one in particular I could've gladly throttled. But yes, overall, it's been a blast. Certainly an experience I'll never, ever, forget.'

We drained our glasses as Duncan shouted to Christian over the exquisite guitar riffs of *Hotel California* to get us refills.

'Sublime party Duncan,' I mused, snuggling into the Jacuzzi jets. I gazed up at the star-encrusted night sky and reflected on the stars that had been on the ground not so long ago.

The LAPD had called Harry and Ed to advise that they had a suspect, had gone to his apartment in a drab part of town and, upon knocking on his door, the suspect – an African-

American itinerant – had shot himself. They now viewed the Raine Daysen case "closed", for this itinerant had obviously just chanced upon her at a light in Beverly Hills and seized his opportunity.

None of us believed this for one minute – and neither did the wider film community in LA, as we later discovered – for it made no sense; Ed considered that the LAPD had taken the easy option with closing the file on an African-American killer. We would probably never know the truth; we had all lost a good friend – and, for me personally, a kind mentor – and a publicist of great talent.

I had spent a blissful few days at Diana's house – relaxing by the pool, lunching at country clubs and sailing over to Catalina Island – when the call came through. Diana came into the sitting room, where I was semi-comatose on the couch watching Entertainment Tonight, with the phone in her hand, looking worried.

'It's for you, from Scotland. He says he's your aunt's neighbour.'

A shaft of panic seared through me, for I did not have to guess what this call was about.

'Hi, David, it's Vanessa.'

'Vanessa, hello. I'm so sorry to have to call, but Mary has collapsed and the paramedics think the aneurysm has burst. They're with her now and taking her to hospital, but they honestly don't think she'll make it. I'll call you in a couple of hours when I know more.'

Tears tumbling down my cheeks, for I was extremely close to my aunt, I managed a barely audible reply. 'Thanks David. Please call me as soon as you know anything. Anything at all.'

I hung up and told Diana the news. She had only lost her husband to cancer a few years earlier and so knew my despair at not being able to say goodbye and how hopeless I felt.

It seemed an endless wait for David's call.

'I'm so sorry Vanessa. She's gone. They tried resuscitating her at the hospital, but there was nothing they could do. At least now she's out of pain.'

Although numb, a small voice from out of nowhere simply said, 'Thanks for calling,' as I put the phone down, tears streaming down my cheeks. Diana plied me with tissues and Merlot.

'I'm going to have to go back to the UK. The funeral probably won't be for another two weeks as my cousin has to fly over from Australia.'

'Yes, I guess you'll have to. But I'm here for you if you need anything. OK?' She gently wiped the tears from my face and gave me a huge hug.

The rest of the evening was spent in a haze as I called Robert and Juliana to say I would not be able to go back to Scottsdale to stay with them again, and to a few other people to cancel pre-arranged visits post-festival. I finally fell into bed just before midnight; knowing that I would not be able to sleep, Diana had raided her drugs cabinet and force-fed me a couple of Atavin. I slept like a baby.

A warm breeze blew through my hair as I gently steered the Dodge northwards onto the 405 Freeway in the direction of San Francisco.

To keep my spirits up, I sang part of the lyrics of Grammy-nominated American folk-rock singer Shawn Mullins' fabulous hit song 'Lullaby': the lyrics forming a lullaby that tells the girl, as she hangs her head to cry, that, despite what she's been through, everything is going to be alright.

I had to return to the UK to go to my beloved aunt's funeral in Scotland and say goodbye to her and, with that, the last links to both my family and Kenya.

But before I left, I wanted to go up to Sonoma to see one person. Someone whom I felt might just change my life.

Printed in Great Britain
by Amazon